Piers Anthony was born in Oxford in 1934, moved with his family to Spain in 1939 and then to the USA in 1940, after his father was expelled from Spain by the Franco regime. He became a citizen of the US in 1958 and, before devoting himself to full-time writing, worked as a technical writer for a communications company and taught English. He started publishing short stories with *Possible to Rue* for *Fantastic* in 1963, and published in SF magazines for the next decade. He has, however, concentrated more and more on writing novels.

Author of the brilliant, widely acclaimed *Cluster* series, and the superb *Tarot*, he has made a name for himself as a writer of original, inventive stories whose imaginative, mind-twisting style is full of extraordinary, often poetic images and flights of cosmic fancy.

VIRTUAL
MODE

Piers Anthony

HarperCollins*Publishers*

HarperCollins*Publishers*
77–85 Fulham Palace Road
Hammersmith, London W6 8JB

Published by HarperCollins*Publishers* 1991
9 8 7 6 5 4 3 2 1

The Author asserts the moral right to
be identified as the author of this work

A catalogue record for this book
is available from the British Library

ISBN 0–246–13860–2
ISBN 0–246–13887–4 (Pbk)

Set in Palatino

Printed in Great Britain by
HarperCollinsManufacturing Glasgow

CONTENTS

1

COLENE

Colene had a study hall during the last period, and as an Honor student she had a regular hall pass. RHIP, she thought: Rank Hath Its Privileges. She smiled marginally, remembering a cartoon she had seen: two gravestones, one plain, one quite fancy. The plain one was lettered RIP, the fancy one RHIP. She liked the notion. No one challenged her as she got up and walked out of the room and down the hall to the bathroom.

She was in luck: it was empty at the moment. She went into the farthest stall, closed and latched the swinging door, lifted her skirt, took down her panties, and sat on the seat. But she did not actually use the toilet. Instead she held up her left arm, and used her right hand to unwrap the winding around her left wrist. It was a style only a few girls affected: bright red cloth on both wrists, complementing her blue skirt and yellow blouse. It was attractive, of course, and Colene preferred to be esthetic, but it was more than that.

For as the band came loose, her wrist showed, horribly scarred. There were welts all across the inner side, some old and white, others fresh and raw. She gazed at it with mixed awe and loathing. She was artistic and creative as well as smart, but this was none of these things. This was closer to her real nature, ugly and dull and tragic, that had to be hidden from others.

Then she reached down to fetch her compass from her purse. A knife would have been better, but might also have

7

brought suspicion on her. She lifted the point, set it against her wrist, and made a sudden, sharp slice across. 'Oh!' she exclaimed as the pain came. She hated the pain, but it was the only way. Maybe she could get a small, sharp knife, seemingly decorative and harmless, that would cut almost painlessly, and deeper. If she had the nerve. The nerve was not in the cutting, but in the acquisition; if anyone saw her with the blade out, and asked . . .

The scratch was stinging, but only a bit of blood was showing. She clenched her teeth and made another pass, in the same track, harder. This time the surge of pain was rewarded by some real blood. It welled out and flowed slowly across her wrist. It was beautiful, like a rich red river wending across a desolate terrain.

She spread her legs and nudged back on the toilet, so that she had more space in front. She angled her wrist so that the blood could drip directly into the water below. The first drop gathered itself, bunched, and finally let go. It struck the water and spread out, losing its identity as the water diluted it. It was dying.

Dying. There was the thought that counted. Oh to fall like that drop into the water, and dissolve, and dissipate, and be no more. Just to fade away, forgotten.

Drop by drop, coloring the water, turning it slowly pinkish. Like menstrual flow, only more vital. Menstrual flow was associated with life, or potential life. This was associated with death, and that was infinitely more important.

Another drop fell to the water, but this one was not red. It was a tear. That seemed fitting: blood and tears. For a man it would be blood, sweat and tears, but it wasn't feminine to sweat, so just the blood and tears would do. Her life, gone into the water, flushed down the toilet, cleanly. Part of the problem with death was the sheer messiness of it. She didn't like mess. She liked things neat and clean and in order. If only she could find a way –

The bathroom door opened. Instantly Colene snapped out of it. She put her wrist to her mouth, licking off the salty blood. She dropped the compass into her purse. She rebound her wrist with a practiced motion, and tucked in the end so it was tight. Then she slid forward on the toilet and used it as was its custom, taking care to make a splash so that the sound advertised the fact of her urination. There were levels and levels of concealment, and she had learned not to assume that others would get the message she intended. It had to be too obvious to miss. Nothing but pissing going on here, ma'am.

The other girl chose another stall and settled down. She was not suspicious. Still, it was nervous business. If anyone were to catch on, Colene would just die of embarrassment. That was not the way she wanted to die!

She stood, reassembled herself, and flushed the toilet. No blood showed; the drops had fallen cleanly into the water, leaving no giveaway stains. Yet somehow she feared that the traces were there, a guilty ambience, so that the next person who used this toilet would somehow know that a person had flirted with suicide here.

But maybe not. A girl could have changed her tampon, and that was where the blood had come from. Not a pad, because that couldn't be flushed. A tampon would leave no evidence. Some girls used pads so as to maintain the pretense that they were virginal, but most preferred convenience, as did Colene herself. So she was covered.

She went to a sink and washed her hands, carefully. No blood showed on her wrist, thanks in part to the wrapping: red covered red. The inner layer was absorbent, and would take up the blood and help it thicken and clot. She would have to wash out the cloth at home, but she was used to that.

Back in the study hall she brought out her compass and wiped the point on a tissue, just to be sure. Then she brought out her geometry homework, so that no one would wonder about the compass. Geometry was a snap; in fact it was boring, because it was two dimensional. It would have been more of a challenge in three dimensions, or four. If only they had a class in cubic geometry, or multi-dimensional constructions. Or fractals: now there would be one she could truly sink her teeth into. *Class, today we shall take our little pencil and graph paper and define the complete Mandelbrot Set.*

Colene stifled a smile. The Mandelbrot Set was said to be the most complicated object in mathematics. Even mainframe computers could not fathom the whole of it. Yet it was simply an exercise in algebra, plotted on paper. How she would love to explore that beautiful picture! To lose herself in its phenomenal and diminishing convolutions, for ever and ever Amen.

But this was mundane school, where brains were routinely pickled in trivia. No hope here.

As the final bell approached, Julie came to sit beside her. It was Friday, and the teacher in charge knew better than to try to keep things totally quiet in the closing minutes. As long as they didn't make a scene, they were all right.

Julie had long yellow hair, which she liked to swirl about her face and shoulders. It was a nice complement to Colene's similar brown tresses. But in other respects they differed more widely. Julie wore glasses and braces, which made her by definition unattractive; Colene, with neither, was far more popular. That was a barrier between them, and their friendship was only nominal, because it was mutually convenient to walk home from the bus stop together.

Actually, Colene had no friends, by her definition, though many others called her friend. It was as if she had an invisible barrier around herself that kept all others at a certain distance. No one touched her heart, and her heart was lonely. She wished it could be otherwise, but the truth was that no one she knew at school was the type she cared to sincerely like and trust. Maybe she was just an intellectual snob, and she felt slightly guilty for that, but only slightly. If she ever encountered someone with really solid intelligence and integrity, someone she could truly admire for maintaining standards she herself could not, then maybe –

'Did you hear?' Julie inquired in a breathless whisper. 'The Principal canceled the rally tomorrow!'

Colene had planned on skipping the rally anyway, but she acted properly outraged. 'The nerve of the nerd! Why?'

'Too many Bumper Stinkers in the parking lot.'

Colene remembered: there had been a rash of bad-taste stickers, using four letter words and concepts. Principal Brown had laid down the law: no more of them on the school grounds. Evidently some of the stupid high school boys had tried it anyway. The Principal wasn't satisfied to punish the errant boys; he had to punish the whole school too. Actually there was reason for this: those stickers would keep reappearing until there was a climate of rejection among the students, and that would come only if all of them paid the penalty. Colene understood, but it would be traitorous to argue the case.

'What will we do with Brown?' Julie demanded rhetorically. It was a matter of definition: no matter what happened, the Principal was always wrong. That was one of the unifying principles of the student body.

Colene glanced around, saw that the teacher in charge was not paying attention while nearby students were, and launched into one of her clever little stories. She was good at this sort of thing, and she enjoyed it in her fashion.

'Why, we should hold a benefit for him,' she said brightly.

'A benefit?' Julie asked blankly, playing the straight man to Colene's act.

'Yes. When he drives up in his Datsun with the tags saying OBITCH –' She paused, giving them time to put that together: DATSUN OBITCH. An expanding circle of sniggers indicated that the joke had registered. 'Then we should stage a gala fund-raising extravaganza, a dunk-the-idiot benefit, with Principal Brown as the main event. Three balls for a dollar, and whoever scores on the target makes Brown fall on the biggest, loudest, smelliest whoopee cushion ever put out by the Ack-Mee Novelty Company!' She put the back of a hand to her mouth and blew the whoopee noise.

It came out too loud. The teacher glanced quickly over at them, and they all had to stifle their laughter. Then the bell rang, saving them. That reminded Colene of a recording she had once heard at a party she wasn't supposed to attend: a 'crepitation' championship match, in which the contestants broke wind in novel ways, each effort appropriately named, such as the sonorous 'Follow-up Blooper' and cute little 'Freeps', and the end of the round was signaled not by a bell but a flatulent horn. The school buzzer was actually more like that than a church bell.

Julie and Colene got off the bus and walked home. It was a

11

pleasant neighborhood, with neat lawns, trees, and even some overgrown lots that were almost like little jungles. Drainage ditches were forming into the beginning of a stream that wound on out of the city. Colene had explored the recesses of that nascent river many times, on the assumption that there had to be something interesting there, like buried treasure or a vampire's coffin. Maybe even, O Rapturous Joy, a lost horse looking for someone to love it. But all she had ever found were weeds and mud.

'Groan, I have to go in for X-rays tomorrow,' Julie was saying. 'Those damned hard ridges on the pictures always slice up my gums. I don't know why they can't make them softer.'

'Easy to fix,' Colene said brightly. 'Just bring the president of Code-Ack in for X-rays, and have *his* gums and roof-of-mouth cut up by those corners. Make him really have to chew down on them for retakes, and tell him "Don't be a difficult child now; those things don't hurt!" I guarantee: next day those edges would be soft as sponges.'

'Yes!' Julie agreed, heartened. 'If only we could!'

But they both knew that nothing that sensible would ever be done, and that sharp edges would continue to find their helpless victims. That was just the way of it. The people who manufactured things never actually used them themselves.

As they approached Colene's house, her wandering glance spied something in the ditch. It was probably just a pile of cloth, or garbage tossed from a car; there were creeps who routinely did such things. But she felt a chill, and surge of excitement. Suppose it was something else?

She said nothing to Julie. She wanted to check this by herself. Just in case.

They walked on. Julie's house was beyond Colene's house, so Colene turned off. Her parents weren't home at this hour, of course; they both worked. Not that it mattered. She had ways in her imagination to glorify the empty home. She liked to pretend that the drainage ditch behind was a great river that wended its way past the most illustrious regions: The Charles. Her simple residence became a gloomy mansion on the bank of this river, where death was a familiar presence. Thus it was the Charles Mansion, a takeoff on a grim killer in a text on legal cases. Her folks wouldn't have thought that funny, and her schoolmates wouldn't have caught the allusion. That seemed to be typical of her life: she couldn't relate well to either parents or peers. But she was the only one who realized this.

She unlocked the door and entered. She set her books on the table and walked straight on through to the back door. She unlocked that and went out, glancing back over her shoulder to make sure that there was no one to see her. It was fun being secretive, despite the fact that her whole life was pretty much an act, papering over her secret reality. She fancied that she was a princess going out to discover a fallen prince from a far land. What she would find would most likely be garbage, but for thirty seconds she could dream, and that was worth something. Even garbage might be better than tackling her stupid homework early.

She came to the cloth, and froze. It was a man! A grown man, lying face down on the weedy bank. His clothing was strange, but it was definitely a man. Was it a corpse, thrown here by some drug gang? Such things did happen, though not in this neighborhood. Of course the neighborhood wasn't what it represented itself to be, either; a lot was covered up for the sake of appearances.

Thrilling to this morbid adventure, she approached. Death fascinated her, though she hated it. This was as good as watching her blood flow. Would the body be riddled with bullet holes?

She remembered one of her favorite lines, from a song she could not otherwise remember. It was about some great Irish or Scottish battle, and a sore wounded soldier had staggered back from the front line. But he had not given up. 'I'll lay me down and bleed a while, then up to fight again!' he declared. She knew she would have liked him. Maybe this was such a man, who had laid him down to bleed and had forgotten to get up again before overdoing it.

Then it moved. Colene stifled her scream, for all that could do was alert the neighbors and bring a crowd, and her little adventure would be over. Cautiously, she approached.

The man lifted his head, spying her. He moved his right

arm, reaching toward her. He groaned. Then he sank back, evidently too weak to do more.

But if she stepped within reach, he might suddenly come to full life, and grab her ankle, pull her down, and rape her. It could be just a ruse to get her close. After he had his way with her, he might kill her and roll her body under the brush near the trickle of water that was the river. After several days she would be found, covered by flies, and he would be long gone.

It was as good a way to die as any. When it came right down to it, it hardly mattered whether death was pretty or ugly; what counted was that the escape had finally been made. A certain amount of messiness could be tolerated for the sake of the novelty. She stepped deliberately within reach.

But the man did not respond. He just lay there, breathing in shudders. Maybe he was sick with some deathly malady, and she would catch it, and die in horrible agony of a disease unknown to science.

She squatted. 'Who are you?' she asked.

The man reacted to her voice. He lifted his head again, and uttered something alien, and sank down once more.

He really did seem to be too tired to do more. He hadn't even tried to grab her ankle or to look up her skirt. He didn't look diseased, just worn out.

That clothing was definitely strange. His language, too, was unlike anything she had heard before. Could he be a diplomat from some faraway little kingdom who somehow got off at the wrong stop and was hopelessly lost? Unable to speak the local language, perhaps with no local money, he might simply be starving.

Or he might be hideously dangerous in a way she couldn't fathom. As an innocent fourteen year old girl, she definitely ought to get quickly away from him and phone the police. They could handle it, whether he was a diplomat or a criminal. That was the only proper course.

Colene felt the thrill of danger, and knew she was about to do something monumentally stupid.

She leaned close to his ear. 'You must come with me. I will help you. I will help. Help. Do you understand?'

His hand slid across the ground, toward the sound of her voice, the fingers twitching.

Maybe he was dehydrated. The day had been hot, though the night would be cold; that was the way fall was in Oklahoma.

'I'll be right back,' she said.

She straightened up, paused as dizziness took her because of the sudden change of position, then walked quickly back to her house. She went to the messy kitchen and fetched a plastic glass. She filled it with water from the tap, and carried it out.

The man had not moved. She sat down beside his head, set the water down in a snug depression, and reached for him. 'I'm back,' she said. 'I brought you water. Can you drink it?'

He tried to raise his head again. She put her hands on it and lifted; then she scooted on her bottom so that she could set his head in her lap. She held it tilted up, then reached for the glass. It was a stretch, and she had to lean over his head. Her bosom actually touched his hair. He did not seem to notice, but the contact sent new waves of speculation through her. Wasn't this the way the Little Mermaid had rescued the drowning prince? Holding him close, helping him survive – until he recovered and married somebody else, never realizing what he owed to the mermaid. The tragedy of not even knowing!

She got the glass and brought it to his face, which was now propped against her front. 'Water,' she murmured. 'Water. Drink. Water.' She touched his mouth and tilted the glass.

Suddenly he realized what it was. Eagerly he sipped. She tilted further, spilling some, but he managed to drink most of it. She had been right!

'More?' she asked, still holding his head and feeling very maternal. 'More water?'

His hand came up, questing for something. He seemed to have more strength than before, but that wasn't saying much.

She set aside the empty glass and caught his hand with her free one. His fingers were cold. She squeezed them with her warm ones. His squeezed back.

She was thrilled again. Communication!

Then she decided that she had better get away from him

before he recovered too much. She had already taken a phenomenal chance; it was time to stop pushing her luck to the brink. 'More water,' she said firmly, and pulled herself away. She set his head back on the ground, scrambled up, got the glass and hurried back to the house.

When she returned with the next glassful of water, the man was struggling to his hands and knees. He was definitely gaining strength. It would be absolutely crazy to get near him again. Anything could happen.

She brought the glass to him. But he had now recovered to the point where he might walk, and he was trying to get to his feet. He was a good deal larger than she was, and surely stronger, which meant yet again that it was time for her to get away from him. So she dropped the glass and stepped in and helped him stand.

She put her arms around his body and heaved, and he lurched to his feet. They staggered toward her house.

At which point Colene thought things through just a bit further. It didn't matter whether she was being sensible or foolish – as if there were any question! – because once the man got to her house, and her parents came home, the game would be over. They would call the police, and the police would take the man away, and both parents would bawl her out for her stupidity before settling into their usual pursuits for the evening. Her father would head off for his date with his current liaison, and her mother would settle down to serious drinking. Things would be back to normal.

'No!' she gasped. 'Not there – there!' She shoved him away from the house and toward her shed. This was a solid structure, larger than a dollhouse but considerably smaller than a real house, perhaps originally intended for storage, but she had taken it over and made it her own private place. Her parents had learned not to bother her there. It was often enough her main link with sanity. Sometimes she spent the full night there, rather than watching her mother drink. She called it Dogwood Bumshed, because a small dogwood tree grew beside it. It wasn't a great tree, and it wouldn't survive at all if she didn't water it, but it did flower nicely in the spring, its moment of glory.

16

The man moved in that direction, yielding to her shove. She wrenched the door open and he stumbled in. He collapsed on her pile of cushions; his brief strength had been exhausted. Perhaps that was just as well. 'More water,' she told him, and shut the door on him. Now he would not be discovered, by her parents or anyone else.

She fetched the glass, which had fallen and spilled when she helped the man walk. She took it to the house, filled it again, then checked the supplies of food. There was a loaf of bread; she took it whole. That would do for a start.

She brought the things to the shed. The man lay where he had settled, but revived when she entered. Now he was able to drink by himself; he accepted the glass from her.

He did not seem to know what the bread was. She opened the package and took out a slice. He gazed at it blankly. She took a bite of it. Then his face lighted; he finally understood. He took a slice and bit into it with considerably less delicacy than she had. Oh yes, he was hungry!

Standing there, watching him eat, Colene finally had time to reflect on what all this might be leading to. She had rescued a man; now what was she going to do with him? He did not seem to be aggressive, but of course he was weak from hunger and thirst. What would he be like when he had his strength back? She really should report him, now; she had taken much more risk than she should have, and gotten away with it, but there were limits. She knew nothing about him except that he was a man, and that was warning enough.

She returned to the house and fetched two blankets from her closet. She knew already that she was not going to turn him in. He might turn on her and kill her, but that risk intrigued her more than it frightened her. She would see this through to wherever it led, no matter what. If she could only keep anybody else from finding out about him.

Did that mean she was going to try to keep him captive? After all, how could she stop him from simply walking out? She didn't know, but until he did depart, she would take care of him.

The man finished the loaf of bread, and Colene returned to the house to get more food. She couldn't take anything

17

else that would be missed; it would be difficult enough explaining the bread. She found some old cookies, and some leftover casserole in the back of the refrigerator; she could say it was getting moldy so she threw it out. It *was* getting moldy, but she trimmed off the mold and took it anyway. She was an old hand at trimming mold, because her mother constantly forgot things; she knew it wasn't anything to freak out about.

The man was glad to have the additional food. But he remained weak, and she knew she couldn't send him back out into the world. He would just collapse again.

But there was something she had to make clear to him. How could she establish communication, so as to tell him what she needed to? For the fact was that her parents would be getting home soon, and if the man showed himself, the game would be up. He had to remain hidden.

Well, all she could do was try. First maybe they could exchange names. She tapped herself on the breastbone: 'Colene. Colene.' Then she pointed to him.

He looked at her, then tapped himself similarly. 'Colene.'

Oops. She cast about for something else. She picked up a notepad and pencil, and quickly drew two figures, one small and female, the other larger and male. She pointed to herself, then to the female. 'Me. Colene.' Then to the male. 'You.' She paused expectantly.

He took the paper. 'Me. Colene,' he said, pointing to the female. 'You. Darius.'

Well, it was progress. 'Me Colene, girl,' she said, tapping herself again. 'You Darius, man.'

He nodded, pointing to her. 'Me –'

'No, *you*.'

He looked perplexed, but managed to get it. 'You Colene girl. Me Darius man.'

She smiled. 'Yes.' It was a beginning. He did not know her language, but he could learn. She drilled him on Yes and No until she was sure he understood them, and tested him on the picture of the horse on the wall, titled 'For Whom Was That Neigh?' 'Man?' she asked, pointing to it. No. 'Girl?' No. 'Horse?' Yes. He had it straight. Then she gave her message.

18

She opened the door and pointed to the house beyond. 'House. Colene. Yes. House. Darius. No.'

After some back and forth, he seemed to understand. But he seemed uneasy, even uncomfortable.

'What's the matter?' she asked.

Finally he made what might have been taken as an obscene gesture, but he did it in such an apologetic manner that she knew he wasn't trying to insult her. He touched and halfway squeezed his groin.

'The bathroom!' she exclaimed, catching on. 'You have to use the –' But she couldn't bring him to the house for that!

'Wait,' she told him, and dashed back to the house. She dug out a big old rusty pot and brought it to the shed. 'This.' She pantomimed sitting on it. She even made the whoopee noise.

He looked extremely doubtful. 'No, I won't watch you!' she said, knowing he couldn't understand the words, but hoping the sense of it came through. 'I have to go to the house, there.' She pointed to it. 'So my folks won't know anything's up. I'll try to check back on you, when I can. You just stay here.' Then she stepped out, and closed the door on him.

She was just in time: her father's car was pulling into the drive. She hurried to the back door and in. She checked the kitchen to make sure that nothing there would give her away, then went to the front room to pick up her school books. But no, this was Friday, and she never did homework on Friday. She didn't want to arouse suspicion. She had to be perfectly normal. So she turned on the TV too loud and plumped down on the couch.

Her father came in. 'Turn that thing down!' he snapped.

She grabbed the remote control and diminished the volume just enough to accede without quite ceasing to annoy him. He went on to his bedroom.

One down. One to go.

An hour later her father, clean, shaved and neatly dressed, went out again. Colene stared at the TV, pretending not to notice. She didn't care about his date with his mistress, as long as he was discreet. Well, maybe deep-down she did care, but that was worse than pointless: it only cut her up further.

19

There was nothing she could do about it anyway. So it was safer not to care.

Fifteen minutes after that, her mother's car arrived. Colene remained before the TV. Actually her mind was on the man in the shed; she wasn't paying any attention to the program. But she had to play her role, more so today than usual.

Her mother went straight to the kitchen, and Colene heard the first drink being poured. Good; there would be no trouble from that quarter this evening.

She got up, leaving the TV on, and went to the kitchen. 'I'll just take a snack out to the shed, okay?' she said, picking up some candy bars and raisins. She put tap water into a plastic bottle. Her mother, intent on hiding what could not be hidden, offered no objection.

Colene carried her things out. It was strictly live and let live, in her family; none of them wanted the hassle that a challenge to any of them would have brought. If someone insisted on visiting, all three of them shaped up to put on a good act for the required time. What was to be gained by letting the truth be known? A philanderer, an alcoholic, a suicidal child. Family love? It was a laugh. Ha. Ha. Ha. Maybe there had once been love. Now it was merely strained tolerance. Typical American family, for sure!

She knocked on the shed door, just to warn Darius. Then she opened it.

He had used the pot. She could tell by the smell. She should have brought a cover for it. Without a word she walked across, set down the candy bars, picked up the pot, and carried it outside and around to the back of the shed. There was an old rusty spade there with a broken handle. She used that to dig a hole, and she dumped the pot and covered up the stuff. She had had some experience with this sort of thing, and knew that it wasn't worth even wrinkling her nose. It wasn't as bad as cleaning up her mother's vomit, after all.

She found a battered piece of plywood, banged it against the ground to get the dirt and mold off, and set it on the pot. She brought the set back into the shed. She put them down in a corner.

Then at last she faced Darius. 'I can't stay long,' she said.

He nodded as if he understood. He smiled.

She smiled back. Then she picked up the candy and raisins. 'More food for you.'

He insisted this time on sharing it with her, so she ate one bar while he ate the rest. He was much more alert than he had been, which was a relief. He was also halfway handsome under his dirt. There was nothing wrong with him that food and a washcloth wouldn't cure.

Well, that she could handle. She found a tatter of colored cloth she had pretended was the flag of her imaginary kingdom in the Land of Horses and poured some of her cup of water on it. 'Clean,' she told him, and proceeded to rub it across his face. He did not protest; in fact he seemed used to having such a thing done for him. Finally she fetched her comb and combed his hair back. Oh, yes, he was handsome, when allowance was made for his stubble beard. But that kind of beard was considered macho, because of all the undercover criminal-playing cops on TV.

They drilled on vocabulary. Darius was a quick study – a very quick study – and so was she. Soon they had the words for the parts of the body and items of clothing, and were working on other parts of speech. For the first time Colene appreciated basic grammar, now that she was teaching it. It was convenient to say 'noun' or 'verb' in some cases when clarifying the use of a word. When Darius indicated the door and said 'verb' she knew he was zeroing in on things like 'open' and 'close' and 'walk through'.

One bit was fun in its own fashion. She had a little box of wooden matches in the shed, which she used for lighting her canned heat so she could do a tiny bit of cooking. An electric hotplate would have been better, but she didn't have one. This was good enough.

Darius saw the box, and inquired. 'Matches,' she explained. Then she demonstrated by striking one. He gaped as it burst into flame. Then he wanted to try it himself. She let him – and he burned his fingers on it. But he was really intrigued by the phenomenon, like a little child. 'Keep them,' she told him generously. 'I can get more.'

He put the box away in a pocket, smiling. It was as if he had found a charm.

She tried to learn his words for things, but they were melodious and extremely strange, with nuances she was sure she was missing. She was apt at language, but knew that there was nothing like this on this side of the world. So she concentrated for now on teaching him. When he could talk well enough to tell her where he was from, she would look it up and learn a whole lot more about him. Somewhere in the Orient, maybe, though he did not look Oriental.

She realized in the course of this session that she had lost her fear of Darius. He was unusual and mysterious, but not dangerous. He was also fascinating.

It grew dark in the shed, for though there was a line here, Colene had used it only to listen to tapes in the day, and had never brought out a light. Now a light would be disastrous, because it would show that Darius was there.

'I have to go,' she said abruptly. 'Mom will wonder if I stay out here too long. But you stay here, and I'll bring you more food in the morning.'

'Yes,' he said. She hoped that he really did understand. She slipped out the door, not opening it wide, just in case her mother were looking this way, and closed it quickly behind her. Actually there would be nothing visible inside except darkness, now, but it made sense to practice safe management. She returned to the house.

Her mother was pretty much out of it by this time. Good. Colene scrounged in the refrigerator for more to eat, and gobbled it down without bothering to sit. Then she went to her room. There was her bed, neatly made, and her desk where she normally did her homework, and her dresser and mirror, and the guitar she hoped someday to learn to play decently. All very conventional. She kept it that way deliberately, so that no one could garner any secrets about her by analyzing her living space. There was even a set of standard dolls on the dresser, Ken and Barbie. What a visitor would not know was that she had renamed the male: he was really Klaus. Thus the pair was Klaus Barbie. There had been a notorious Nazi criminal by that name. She flossed her teeth, brushed her hair, changed into her pajamas, and lay down on her bed. She stared at the ceiling.

Sleep didn't come. All she could do was think about Darius, out there in the Bumshed, and her heart was beating at a running place. She had to slow it to a walking pace before she could nod off. She knew from experience with bad nights.

After a time she got up, went to the closet, and changed into her silky nightgown. She loved the feel of it against her skin. It was long enough so that she wore nothing under it, which gave her a deliciously wicked feeling. It was a good outfit in which to dream. Very good.

In fact, too good.

Now her heart slowed, but her thoughts turned darker. She remembered the time a few months ago when her beloved grandmother, one of the mainstays of her young life after the default of her parents, had sickened with cancer and then died. It was as if the last leg had been knocked out from under Colene's will to live. Without Grandma, what was the point? She had not exactly told Grandma about the horrors she had experienced, or how her life had been falling apart, but she suspected that Grandma knew. It was better to go where Grandma was, and have her reassurance again. Colene had taken her mother's pills from the cabinet, one sniff of which, as an *Arabian Nights* tale put it with suitable hyperbole, could make an elephant sleep from night to night. She swallowed three, then another, pondered, and finally two more. Six was a good number. Six-six-six was the devil's own number. Sick-sick-sick was what these pills would make her. Sick unto death. Then she lay down in her sexy nightie – the one she was wearing now. She wanted to expire in maidenly style.

The elephant pills did not exactly kill her. They put her into a trancelike state in which she had a vision. In the vision she was exactly as she was, in her naughty nightgown, and gloriously dying; the church bells were warming up for the somber death toll, and there would be mourning until the funeral. How sweet she would look in the casket, a red-red rose on her cold-cold bosom. Other girls would envy her the beauty of that nightgown, knowing that they would not have the nerve to be shown dead in such an outfit.

23

Three figures entered the room, coming through the wall, so it was obvious that they were of the spiritual persuasion. Two were her grandparents, now reunited in the afterlife. Grandma approached. 'Dear, you may not yet die, because there is something you have yet to do with your life. We love you and will always be with you.'

Then the third figure, the stranger, approached. He was clothed in a dark robe and wore a cowl over his head, and his face was shaded by mist. Who he was she dared not guess, but there was an inherent glow about him that bespoke his authority. 'Colene,' he said, his voice full of compassion and knowledge. 'You have to go on. You will not be able to quit. Your life will get better.'

Buoyed by that message, she had roused herself from the vision, stumbled to the bathroom, poked her finger down her throat, and gagged out the remaining contents of her stomach. 'Just call me bulimic,' she had gasped with gallant gallows humor as her heaves expired. She had changed her mind about dying. For a while.

No one had known. Her mother hadn't even missed the six pills.

Had she done the right thing? Colene could not be sure. Yet now, with the appearance of Darius, it seemed that there was indeed something for her to do with her life. Maybe her vision was coming true.

After more time she got up again, slipped her feet into her slippers, turned out the light, and cracked open the door. She made her way through the house. If her mother asked, she was just going for another snack. But her mother didn't notice her passage.

Colene got the spare house key, stepped quickly out the back door, and locked herself out. That way her mother would assume that she had locked them in for the night, and would not check her room. Colene would use the key to let herself in again later.

It was chill outside, and she shivered as she made her way across the dark back yard to the shed. Her heart was pounding, but not because of the temperature. She was embarking on another suicidally foolish risk.

She knocked on the door, then opened it. She couldn't see anything inside, but knew he was there.

Indeed he was, hunched under the blankets. They really weren't enough, considering his weakened state. He needed more warmth.

'I should have brought another blanket,' she murmured. 'But I would have had to take it from my own bed, and that would be chancy. I'll see what I can do.'

She sat down beside him, and pulled at the blankets, rearranging them. Then she lay down, full length beside him, and drew the blankets over them both. 'It's warmer, this way,' she explained.

He rolled over to face her, and she stiffened with fear. 'Please don't rape me,' she whispered. 'I really don't like it.' Yet she had come out here in her provocative nightgown. He couldn't see it, of course, but he could feel it. She had gotten under the blankets with him, in the dark. No jury would convict him.

'Rape?' he asked, not knowing the word.

Now she had to define it! How could she do that? If she managed to get the concept across, without the use of her pad and pencil, it would have to be by touch, and he might think she was asking for it. But she had used the word, and she had to explain it.

She pondered, her heart beating so wildly she almost thought her mother in the house could hear it, let alone Darius. Then she found his right hand under the blanket. She brought it across his body and up to touch her head. 'Yes,' she said. Then she took it down to touch her right breast through the nightgown, as she lay on her back. 'Maybe.' Finally she put it against her thigh. 'No.'

He considered that, while she lay breathing rapidly, her body stiff. Then he reached across her, not to embrace her, but to find her left arm. He brought it across her body and up to his head. Her fingers touched his mouth. 'Yes,' he said. Then he took it down to his clothed crotch. 'No.'

He understood! 'That's right,' she said, squeezing his fingers with hers. 'I'm here to warm you, and that's about it.'

'Thank you.' He brought her hand to his lips again, and kissed it.

Colene experienced a wild thrill. She knew she should just lie where she was, having made her point. But it was her nature to risk disaster. Suicide was merely the most extreme extension of a syndrome that permeated her existence. Whatever she did, she had to push the limit, courting trouble. This was folly, but it was her way. Had she been a man, she would have been a daredevil cyclist, hurdling lines of cars soaked in gasoline, daring the flames to get her. But she was only a teenage girl, so had to settle for lesser dares.

She rolled over toward him, scooted up a bit, found his head, and lifted hers to kiss him on the mouth. Then she lay against him, her body touching his full length. Of course he was clothed, but she wasn't; all she had was the flimsy nightgown. With her wickedly bare torso within it, her breasts nudging him with each breath she took.

He put his right arm around her and drew her close. His hand did not wander. She put her left arm around him. They were embraced.

She had intended only to remain for half an hour or so, but this was such dangerous delight that she couldn't bring herself to break it off. Slowly her heart eased its horrendous pace, and she relaxed.

She woke, and realized that she had been asleep for some time, nestled against Darius. He was warm and she was warm. As far as she knew, he had not touched her even in the 'maybe' region. She was almost disappointed. She fell back into sleep.

She became aware of the creeping light. 'Ohmigod!' she squeaked. 'Morning!'

She scrambled out from under the blanket, startling Darius awake. 'My parents!' she said. 'I have to get back to my room, so they don't know where I was!'

He nodded, seeming to understand. She found her slippers, slipped out the door and almost flew, wraith-like, across the yard to the door.

The door was locked. 'The key!' she breathed in anguish. She turned about and flew back to the shed.

A hand reached out. It held her key.

'Thanks!' She snatched it and ran back. The door seemed

26

to make a thunderous noise as it unlocked and opened. She went in, then turned to lock it again. She put the key away.

Then she forced herself to walk slowly through the house to her room. No one was up. She was unobserved.

She entered her room, went to the bed, and threw herself into it. She had made it!

Now she remembered how Darius had given her the key. He knew what it was for and where it was. He could have kept it from her. He could have raped her. He could have taken the contact of his hand on her breast last night as a pretext to go wild. It wasn't the kind of breast found in macho male magazines, but it didn't exactly require padding for a formal gown, either. She had given him every opportunity.

He was either a decent man or he just wasn't interested.

She cursed herself for her total, absolute, unmitigated folly – and knew she would try to find out exactly which it was. Decency or disinterest. If it killed her. And it just might. Which was perhaps the point.

2

DARIUS

Darius woke as the maiden jumped out of bed in the wan light of dawn. For a moment he was disoriented, but it quickly came back: she was Colene, and she had come back to spend a chaste night with him, warming him with her company. He appreciated that very much.

She hurried out. She did not speak his language, unsurprisingly, but had taught him some of hers. She had made it plain that she shared her domicile with her parents, who would not understand Darius' presence here. That too was understandable. Certainly he did not want her to be distressed before he could get to know her well enough.

He felt something cold against his ankle. It was her key. She would need that to enter her locked house. He picked it up and moved to the door.

In a moment she appeared, shivering in her pretty nightdress, her breath fogging in the chill morning air. He saw her small high breasts heaving enticingly. He extended the key. She took it and ran back the way she had come. He shut the door.

Colene. She was young, but by the same token fresh and pretty. She had courage, too, and intelligence. She seemed eminently suitable. But would she want to do it? It was too soon to tell.

He had time to find out. Unless there was trouble before he did. If there was trouble, he would have to –

Then he remembered that aspect. He couldn't! He had lost the signal key!

What was he to do? Without that key he couldn't return. He would be locked in this reality, and he had already discovered that he was not equipped to survive here.

Well, did it really make a difference?

It was pointless, but the knowledge of his likely demise here caused him to set a higher value on his life than hitherto. With renewed interest, he reviewed the events of the last few days.

The post of Cyng of Hlahtar was an enviable one, but it had its desperate drawback. A castle was provided, fully staffed and supplied. The Cyng's magic was virtually limitless. As long as he performed.

It was impossible to endure alone for long; every Cyng soon was depleted. The only practical way to survive was to marry a strong, abundantly happy woman, and draw on her resources until she was depleted, and then cast her aside in favor of a new one. Because the post was prominent and the perquisites excellent, many women were willing to endure this, and it was feasible to maintain a chain of marriages indefinitely. But Darius, new to the post, had rebelled after divorcing his second wife. She was not a bad person, and they got along well, but she was depleted. He did not want to marry a series of women for their life forces, daring to love none. He wanted to marry one for love, and to remain with her for the full tenure.

The wiser heads had nodded. It was often thus with newlings; they just had to learn from experience. Once a Cyng came to proper terms with the inevitable, he generally settled down and performed adequately.

Darius went to the Cyng of Pwer. 'What are my options?' he inquired.

'If you will not heed the wisdom of experience, you must learn in your own fashion,' the old man said. 'You may marry for love, but you can not keep her long. She will die if you do not let her go in time. I think you will find it better to marry for other than love.'

'The Modes,' Darius said. 'What are my options there?'

'The Modes are dangerous,' the man reminded him. 'Of every ten folk who risk them, three do not return. Of those who do return, half do not achieve their desire. This leaves about one in three who are successful. I do not recommend this course.'

'You would have me suck the joy from endless innocent women instead?'

The Pwer shook his head. 'No one forces them. They do it to escape poverty, nonentity or pointlessness. It is a good bargain for them. They do not die, and they recover slowly after you turn them loose. It is a feasible system.'

'Not as I see it!' Darius retorted. 'I see love and marriage as ennobling.'

'You are young.'

'Tell me more about the Modes. What can I expect?'

'You can expect the unexpected. Do you understand the theory of it?'

'I understand only that when I appealed to the Cyng of Mngemnt, to provide me some better way, he sent me to you for the Modes. I never heard of them before.'

'Then I will tell you in capsule what we know of them. As you surely do know, I handle the broadcasting of the magic power that enables all other magic to operate. That power must have a source. The first Cyng of Pwer found the source in the Modes. We have a number of what he termed Chips which enable us to relate to the realms beyond our own, and one of these has limitless raw power. He constructed mechanisms to harness this power and convert it to a form we can use. It is my special ability to channel it, and to keep the mechanisms operative. The Chips still relate to what seems to be an infinite number of other Modes. But we explore these others at our considerable risk. We conjecture that they are alternate realities, and that each Chip attunes to the spot where it would be in that other Mode. In many modes that spot is empty, without even earth, water or air, and whoever goes there immediately dies. In other modes there is something there, but not what we like. We have brought back the bodies of those we have sent through, and they have been burned or dehydrated or mauled, as by some monster. But in some Modes there are worlds like ours,

30

only different. By that I mean they may have a comfortable environment, and people, but those people have drastically different customs from ours. In fact, it seems that even the fundamental laws of magic differ in them, so that much of what is truth here is falsity there.'

He looked hard at Darius. 'We have located a region of fairly safe Modes. But even there, the risk is as I described. Also, there seems to be imprecision in the tuning of the Chip; no person seems to go to the same other Mode that any other person has been to. Thus we can not get to know any one of them well, and it is always a serious gamble. I suggest to you that it is unwise in the extreme for you to take this gamble, because not only do you risk your own life, you risk the welfare of our society, which truly needs your ability as Cyng of Hlahtar.'

'Another can assume the post,' Darius said.

'But not one as talented as you. That is why it came to you, after the retirement of the prior Cyng of Hlahtar. You can be the best, and if we lose you, we will have only the next best, and that will hurt us all to some degree.'

He spoke truth. Darius felt guilt. But it was not enough to sway him from his purpose. 'What I may gain must be worth the risk,' he said.

'Exactly what do you hope to gain?' Pwer asked sharply.

'A woman who will not be depleted by close association with me. A woman I can love and not lose. A woman I can marry and never divorce.'

'There is no such woman.'

'Not in this reality,' Darius agreed. 'But elsewhere, where other fundamental rules obtain, there may be women of another nature, who can not be depleted. If I can find one of them, and bring her back here –' He broke off, alarmed. '*Can* I bring her back?'

'Oh, yes. If you are in contact with her when you signal for the return, she will come with you. Your problem will be finding her – and if you do, convincing her to come with you. There are several problems in that connection.'

'This has been done before?'

'Yes. Not by a Cyng of Hlahtar, but by others. They have

31

brought back people or things. Some women have brought back babies or odd animals. But if you want to marry and love her, you must explain to her what this entails; you must not abduct her, for then she will hate you and be no true wife to you.'

'Well, of course I wouldn't abduct her!' Darius exclaimed. 'If I were inclined to treat women in that manner, I would be better off simply marrying a chain of wives here and casting them aside!'

'Precisely.'

'If that is the only problem, then certainly I will –'

'No. There is worse. We have ascertained through sometimes bitter experience that not all people or things can be taken. It seems that any person who plays a significant role in his or her or its Mode –'

'Its?'

'Some Mode-folk are sexless, and some are mechanical.'

Darius shuddered. 'Go on.'

'No person of significance can be taken. Apparently there is a certain stability; a Mode will not let go of what it needs to make it what it is. This has a peculiar effect.'

'Go on,' Darius said, experiencing a chill.

'In general, only those folk who are destined to have minimal impact on their realities can be taken. It may be that their Modes know that these folk are soon to be lost anyway, and do not try to hold them.'

'Do you mean they are about to be accidentally killed?'

'Not necessarily. They may have some terminal malady. You could bring such a one here, but she would soon die anyway. Or possibly she merely is of little account, so will live but will have no significant impact. You might find that she has similarly little effect here.'

Darius was still struggling with another aspect of this. 'You said their Modes know, and hold those they want. The Modes are conscious? The Modes are like people?'

'We don't think so. It seems more like a stone that does not readily give up any of its substance. But if part of it has been cracked, a chip may be flaked off with less effort. So you will have to find a loose flake.'

32

Darius pondered this. A diseased woman? It would be better to take one who was about to be killed. But what kind would that be? A criminal? He did not want to marry that kind either. The prospects were dimming.

'I anticipate your next question,' Pwer said.

That was good, because Darius didn't know what to ask next. 'Yes.'

'How do you locate such a woman?' the man said. 'The answer is that we can help you there. There are settings on the Chips. Not many, but enough. We can put you through to a reality that is livable, with human beings much like us, and where one is suitable. We can make that one female. We can not guarantee that she is not already married, but of course if she dies that will not matter. We can not guarantee her age or health or personality. But we can put you close to her. Not completely close, for our command of this alien device is imperfect, but in her Mode and in her vicinity. Then you can inspect her, and bring her back here with you if that seems appropriate. Which brings up your final question.'

'Yes,' Darius agreed, as before.

'How do you return? And the answer is that you will have a signal device, an aspect of the Chip. When you activate that, I will receive the signal, and will revert you and whatever you hold to this reality. If you do not signal within a month, I will assume you are not going to. Because you are dead or unable to signal. Without that signal we can not bring you back, because the Chip is unable to fix on you.'

So now Darius had all the information, and was not reassured. He understood perfectly how three of ten could fail to return, and three or four others would not attain their desire. But at least some did succeed. That left him hope.

'Suppose I go, and return without a woman,' he said. 'Could I then go again, and perhaps that time find one?'

Pwer stared at him. 'Go again? Few have been interested in that! Each time a person goes, he has about one chance in three of not returning. If you went twice, you would double your chance of that.'

'But I would also double my chance of finding what I need,' Darius pointed out.

'Perhaps. But you could not return to the same other Mode. There are too many of them, and our way is imprecise. Some few have tried to go again to the same one, but none we know of has succeeded.'

None we know of. Because some did not return. 'Could that mean that they liked it there, and stayed voluntarily?'

Pwer shrugged. 'It could. But it does seem doubtful. It seems more likely that they found a wholly new situation, and could not survive it. Those who did return the second time reported that their experience was just as difficult as the first time.'

'I want to do it,' Darius said. 'If I lose once, I may try again. If I lose twice, I may decide to do it the conventional way, and marry the chain of women.'

Pwer sighed. 'We are a free society. Your position and your need entitle you to take this foolish risk if you choose. Return tomorrow, and I will have the Chip prepared.'

'My thanks to you,' Darius said gratefully.

Darius got up, for he needed to urinate. The maiden had brought a pot and indicated that he should use it for such purpose. Her method of communication in this respect had been quaint: she had made a vulgar poop noise. He was not easy about this matter, but realized that it was best to oblige her desires. Surely she had reason to keep him out of sight; his limited experience here had suggested the merit of her case. So he remained confined, and did what was necessary. He used the pot and covered it.

He was hungry again, and hoped she would bring more of her strange food. He knew that she could not act with complete freedom, because she was young and had to maintain the semblance of her normal life-style. She seemed to be resourceful, and she was certainly healthy. How could it be that she would either have minimal impact in her Mode, or soon die?

He thought of the night just past. He had expected to be alone. Evidently she had sneaked out to join him for a while, then stayed longer than intended. He was grateful for that; he had been cold, and her warm little body had been a great comfort.

More than that. It was clear that she knew the effect such a body could have on a man, and she had addressed the matter forthrightly, considering their lack of a common vocabulary. She had set his hand on her head, breast and hip, identifying what was a permissible touch and what was not. Then she had slept against him, trusting him. He liked that.

Of course he had not touched even that part of her where the proscription was vague. It was not that her breasts were inadequate; they were extremely nice, being neither insignificant nor ponderous. They had the filling perkiness of youth. It was that he could tell by her nervousness and tightness that she was afraid. She had offered him somewhat, hoping that he would be satisfied with that, but even that much was not her desire.

Why, then, had she come at all? Because he was cold, and she wanted to warm him. She was generous despite her fear. He liked that too; in fact he was quite impressed.

But that was not quite all. She had come dressed in only the sheerest of garments, no protection against the cold. No protection against any inclination he might have had. She had made sure he knew it, by causing his hand to touch it. Her pulsing breast might as well have been bare. Was it to tease him? No, for she had not labeled that breast 'No.'

Why had she placed herself at what she surely believed was serious risk, when she could have avoided it by wearing more substantial clothing?

Perhaps she had come out on a whim, and not thought to dress more appropriately. She had intended to sleep in her warm house, but stepped out to check on him; then, finding him cold, she had warmed him. Yes, that would explain it. She was young, and therefore somewhat foolish, not thinking things through. If he remained here another night, and if she came again, she would be better clothed.

She was obviously the one he had come for, and he liked her very well. He had maintained a mental blank in lieu of a picture of the kind of woman he sought, but Colene was far superior to whatever he might have envisioned. As soon as he knew enough of her language to make his mission clear, he would ask her whether she would like to return with him to his reality and be his wife. He would of course have to make clear the nature of the relationship, which was no ordinary marriage. She would have to understand that if she turned out to be unable to withstand depletion, he would have to divorce her despite still loving her. He could appreciate how that might annoy her.

Then the brutal realization struck him. How could he even risk taking this sweet maiden to be depleted? She was evidently no special type who would be immune to the effect. And even if that were not the case, how could he bring her back – when he could not return himself? *He had lost the key!*

Dispirited, he returned to the blankets and buried himself under them. The cold was not merely of the body, now.

He returned to his review of recent events. What else was there to do?

So Darius went to the alien Mode, armed with the signal chiplet and a pack with supplies of food and water, because he had no certainty of finding either quickly in the other reality.

The actual process was simple enough, from his perspective. Just a matter of standing in the circle that marked the focal point of the Chip. Pwer did something – and Darius found himself standing at the edge of a level place, surrounded by what were evidently domiciles. But what oddities they were! Each had many crystalline windows, and peaked roofs, and bits of vegetation around. The level place sent out squared-off offshoots which reached right to the edges of the structures, and sometimes right into them, as if feeding on them.

He stepped out onto the level region. It was completely hard, as if fashioned of stone. But it was not stone, and not packed dirt. He squatted, touching it with his finger. Less hard than stone, actually, but still impressive.

There was the blaring of a horn. Darius looked up and saw some kind of creature charging him. It was not a dragon, for the smoke puffed from its tail, and it seemed to have no mouth. But it was definitely aggressive.

He scrambled erect and stepped back. The creature charged

on by him. There was the sound of a human shout. A human arm projected from the side of the creature and made a gesture with one lifted finger. Apparently there was a person inside who remained alive.

Uncertain how to respond, Darius emulated the gesture. He signaled the creature with one finger.

The creature squealed as it turned and slewed back toward him. Darius retreated farther. It halted, and mouths on its sides abruptly opened. Human men emerged, in unfamiliar apparel. They converged on Darius, shouting incomprehensibly. They looked angry.

He tried to withdraw, as he did not want trouble, but the men attacked him. He was so surprised at this uncivilized behavior that he invoked an elementary pacification spell – and it had no effect.

Then he knew: this was one of the realities in which magic was not operative. At least not the type he knew. He was defenseless.

He tried to explain that he sought no quarrel, but his words seemed only to enrage the young men further. They struck at him with their fists, knocked him down, and kicked him. One of them grabbed at his pack and wrenched it away. Then they sent him rolling down the incline toward what might have been a stream.

His head collided glancingly with a rock. His consciousness faded.

After a period, the maiden came again, bearing food. This time she was somewhat better prepared: she had a box and a jug and a bowl and a curious spoon. She opened the box and poured some bits of something into the bowl, then opened the jug and poured something he recognized – milk – into the bowl with it. She gave him the bowl and spoon, and made gestures as of using the spoon to eat the peculiar mixture.

He tried it. He dipped out both milk and food-bits and put the spoon in his mouth. The bits were crunchy, and the milk not sufficient to slake his thirst, but of course this was only one spoonful.

Colene smiled. Evidently this was the proper way to do it.

She was now attired in a completely different outfit: a heavy shirt, solid cloth shoes, and some kind of tight blue trousers. No woman in his reality would allow herself to be seen in such clothing, for it was disturbingly similar to nakedness from the waist down. The muscles of her posterior flexed visibly as she walked, and there was no looseness at all in the region of her groin. The contrast between her decorous upper section and indecorous nether section was startling.

She sat on the floor to watch him eat, folding her legs so that her feet were crossed and her thighs were wide apart. He tried to avoid looking at this embarrassing display, but he could not do so without turning his face completely to the side. The worst of it was that the maiden seemed to be completely oblivious to her erotic display. Her manner suggested that her concern was only with his consumption of the milk-and-bits concoction.

He tried to be similarly oblivious, but her spread crotch was directly in the line of sight of his bowl and spoon, and his gaze could not help but center on it. There was no doubt: she wore no diaper beneath those alarming trousers. He was getting a reaction. He felt a flush coming to his face.

'Trouble?' she inquired, becoming aware of his distress. 'Food bad?'

How could he explain, without similarly embarrassing her? But she insisted on knowing. Finally he set down bowl and spoon, put his two hands on her projecting knees, and pushed them together.

For a moment she was confused, then startled. Then she burst out laughing. She laughed so hard that she fell over backwards, drawing her legs up against her body and kicking her feet from the knees. This was no improvement; not only was her indecorous region in view, it was flexing. His face was now burning.

Finally she exhausted her mirth. Then she kneeled beside him, kissed him on the cheek, and gave him another lesson in clothing and culture. 'Blue jeans,' she said, touching the tights. 'Okay. No show bad.'

Maybe so, by her definition, but the suggestion was nevertheless overpowering.

She pointed to his crotch. 'You. Sit. Same.'

That was true, but he was a man. Also, his clothing was considerably looser in that region, revealing no private contours.

Colene was unconvinced. 'Oh, Darius – you me laugh.'

True, he had made her laugh – and he had experienced no depletion. But he realized that was because magic was not operative in this reality. Here, it seemed, the transfer of emotion did not cost the source. Indeed, he had not even been trying to make her laugh; she had done it on her own.

That gave him something to think about. Was it possible that she was a self-generating joy person? If so, she was perfect! But he could not presume too much; her ready laughter might merely be because her level was high, and could be as readily depleted as that of any other person.

At least he had learned something: in this reality, the mere fact of physical material covering a region was considered sufficient discretion. Her entire genital region had been exposed in outline, but because there was opaque material between her flesh and his vision, she had no concern. That explained her action of the night, too: her breast had been quite tangible to his touch, soft and warm, yet because there had been a thin barrier of material, she considered it no exposure. Apparently she believed that he could have no sexual excitement if he saw or touched the outline, rather than the direct flesh. Perhaps that was the way of men here, being unmoved by views that would have maddened men of his own reality. He would school himself to react accordingly, difficult as it would be.

Now he was glad he had been cautious during the night! Had a woman of his own reality come to him in the manner Colene had, lightly garbed, sharing his bed, and placing his hand on parts of her body, it could only have been because she wished very much to fornicate with him. Her Yes and No would have been merely indications of the approach he was to make: first kissing, then fondling, and finally copulation if she did not change her mind. It would have indicated phenomenal trust in him, for men were not known for diffidence once embarked on the exploration of female flesh. He had assumed that her actions were not identical in significance to those of women of his own reality, and made no attempt at all to pursue a sexual experience. This, as it had turned out, had been the correct course.

But how would it have been, if he had not been greatly depleted from exposure, thirst and hunger? At that time, the thing he needed most had been warmth. She had brought him that, and it had enabled him to sleep in comfort and to recover more of his well being. A sexual effort might have been beyond his means. So he had taken her warmth, and nothing else, gambling that her ways differed from those of women in his own reality. Had he been robust, he surely would have interpreted her actions as an invitation. In that he would have been gravely mistaken, as he now understood, after seeing her way with clothing.

He had, he knew, been lucky.

'You. Think.' She tapped her head as she spoke, watching him.

'Yes. I. Think.' He tapped his own head. That was a new word, but clear in this context.

'Think. What?'

'What' was a general query term he had learned to use. When he pointed to an object and said 'What?' she would name the object. Now she was inquiring what he was thinking.

How could he tell her? It was complicated, and he lacked the vocabulary, and perhaps the information would affront her. 'No,' he said, smiling to show that this was intended as a positive negation rather than bad feeling.

'Yes,' she said insistently. He was beginning to realize that she did not respond well to 'No' when she wanted something. 'Tell. Me.'

He was obliged to try. He cast about for some way, and saw a small inert figure in the corner, in the likeness of a very young girl. There was something common to both realities! Like all who were serious about magic, she had effigies.

Serious about magic? But there was no magic here, as far as he had been able to ascertain! He had been making another potentially dangerous assumption.

'Try,' he agreed. He pointed to the effigy. 'What?'

Colene looked. 'Doll,' she said, picking it up. She cradled it as if it were a baby. 'Play.'

Play? Was that what they called sympathetic magic? No, probably it meant something quite different. He would have to be extremely careful about that term, until he was sure of its nature. 'Doll. Me.'

She gave him the effigy. He held it with his left hand, and extended his right hand. 'Doll. Me.'

Colene considered momentarily, then went to the corner. There, in a box, was another figure. This one was male. Good.

She gave him the second doll. He held up the male. 'Me.' Then the female. 'You.'

She nodded. She was paying close attention.

He put the male down and covered it with a corner of a blanket. Then he brought the female, as if she were walking. She came to lie beside the male.

'Last Night,' Colene said.

'Night,' he agreed; that seemed to be the time of darkness. But he made sure. He waved his hand, indicating their surroundings. 'What?'

'Day. Light.'

'Night – Light,' he said, pairing the opposites.

'No. Night. Day. Dark. Light. Night–Dark. Day–Light.'

After a moment they got it straight. This was Day, and the time of sleeping was Night.

He indicated the dolls. 'Day. No. Night. Yes.'

She nodded again. 'You. Me. Night.' There was no doubt of her interest.

Now he needed to convey the concept of his home reality. That might be impossible. 'You. Me. Things. Here.' He gestured, trying to show themselves and their surroundings. 'Day. Night. Day. Night. There.' He tried to indicate something far away.

Colene said something, seeming to understand. He hoped that was the case. 'Here.' He touched the two dolls. He moved the arm of the male to touch the female's head section. 'Yes.' Then her chest region. 'Maybe.' Finally her leg. 'No.' After that he put them close together without motion.

Colene nodded. 'Us. Last Night.'

Us. Evidently the two of them. 'Yes.' Then he made the

faraway gesture. 'There.' He moved the dolls to another place. Then he repeated the action between them. But this time the male doll did not sleep. Instead it became more active, covering the female.

She still seemed to understand, but was not concerned. 'You. Me. Here,' she said firmly. 'No. There.'

Clear enough. She understood that in his Mode, she could not expect to be left alone at night. But in her Mode, the local customs prevailed.

Days passed. Each night Colene came to share her warmth with him, though she brought another blanket that sufficed against the cold. He held her and did no more, though his strength was returning and he did desire her. She was young, he reminded himself, probably not more than five years into nubility, but enticing.

They continued to talk, and he learned enough of her language so that in due course they could cover more sophisticated topics. Now he could tell her where he had come from, and what his mission had been – and what had happened. Their dialogue was extended and fraught with misunderstandings and missing terms, but in essence it was this:

'So you came all the way here from your fantasy world to marry me?' she asked. 'Only you got mugged and lost your ticket home?'

'This is too simple,' he protested. 'I came here to discover whether you were right to marry. But this is uncertain. Now it does not matter, since I can not return.'

'And am I?'

She cut so quickly to her aspects that he often had to pause to follow them. 'Are you right to marry? I am not sure, but I am hopeful.'

'What would make you sure?'

'That is complicated to tell. But there is no need, since I will die here.'

'Why will you die?'

'Because I cannot endure without magic. I have no way here to support myself, and soon you will tire of bringing me food.

42

Already I feel the depletion of my separation from my reality. When it becomes too great, I will seek as easy a death as I can manage.'

'You hurt, and you will die?'

'Yes. I am not like you. But I thank you for the great comfort you have given me.'

She looked at him intently. 'You are not joking, are you?'

'The King of Laughter does not joke.' This was hardly a precise translation of his role in his own Mode, but it was what she best related to.

'If you were going back, would you take me with you?'

'If I could return, I would want to do that. But only if I knew that it was right, and that you wished to. Marriage to Hlahtar is no easy matter.'

'Even though I am only fourteen?'

Darius was startled. 'I thought you were older! Unless our years differ.'

'I don't think they do. Everything you have told me suggests that your world is the same as mine, except for the way you live. So does it matter?'

'In my reality it does not. Every person does what he chooses, if he can do it well enough. If you truly understood the requirements of the marriage, it would be honored.'

'Like having sex with you?'

'No, marriage is not necessary for that. It is a more important commitment.'

'Because of the mergence of life forces?'

'Yes.'

She shook her head. 'You know I don't believe you.'

'Yes. I think you would believe only if you could be in my reality. What you have done for me has been most generous, since you can gain nothing in return.'

'Do you really live in a castle with many servants, and do magic?'

'My servants usually do the magic for me. My ability is joy, not conjuring.'

'Tell me again about what you do.'

'Colene, I will not be doing it any more, because –'

'Tell me!'

43

He did not understand her intensity. 'I bring joy to the multitudes. I make them laugh.'

'Then you are a comedian.'

'No. I do not tell funny stories or do funny things. I infuse joy directly, so that they can laugh at what merits it.'

'That's what I don't understand! How can you – I mean, that's not the way it works!'

'How does it work here?'

'Each person's pleasure and pain come from inside him. If he sees or hears something funny, he laughs and feels good. If he sees something bad, he is unhappy. If something hurts his body, he feels pain, but the pain is from his nervous system, not the other thing. If he loves or hates, the emotion is all in himself. He can't receive it like an electric current from anyone else.'

'Physically that is true for us too. But emotionally we can transfer. It is my post to transfer joy to others.'

'But if you can do that, that doesn't mean you lose it yourself!'

'Indeed it does! It is my emotional substance being shared.'

'But then you would be miserable after making one person happy.'

'No. I have a special qualification for the post. I can magnify my joy as I transfer, making a thousand people happy, while I suffer only a little depletion. Most people can exchange only on an even basis, as you say, but some can multiply, and I can multiply better than any other. That is why I am Cyng.'

'Then what's your problem?'

'There are many thousands who need joy. So many that I cannot serve them all without eventually being depleted. But I can not stop, because then everyone would become unhappy.'

'What does a wife have to do with it?'

'My wife shares her joy with me. I can then share it with others, multiplied. Were she able to share on an even basis, that would double my ability to serve. But normally women are found who can multiply somewhat themselves, so that I may receive what two or three others might provide. That can enable me to carry on for a year or more, before we are both depleted.'

44

'What happens then?'

'I must divorce her before she dies, so that she can recover. Then I must marry another, so that I can continue my work.'

'How could you do that to one you loved?'

Darius spread his hands. 'I can not. That is why I elected to search in other realities.'

'So you could find me, and take me back, and deplete me, and cast me aside after a year?'

'Oh, no, Colene! I am looking for a woman who can multiply the way I do, so that I can love her and never cast her aside. There are none in my reality.'

'And you think I might be one like that?'

'I hope you are. The Chip oriented on women who might be like that. But the Chip is fallible. It may be that it is a misreading.'

'How can you tell?'

'There is no sure way except to bring you back with me.'

'And if I am not right?'

'Then I could not marry you. You would be provided for; I could make you one of my servants.'

'One of your servants!'

'The Chip can not focus on precisely the same reality twice. You could not return to your own realm. But you could have a good life with me. Just not as my wife.'

'Thanks a lot!'

She was evidently angry. 'I do not understand.'

'That's for sure!' She lurched to her feet and charged out of the shed.

But later she returned, with more food. 'I am sorry I blew up at you, Darius,' she said. 'I know your culture is way different from mine, and you didn't think you were insulting me.'

'That is true. I am sorry I insulted you. Please tell me in what manner I did that, so that I can avoid doing it again.'

'With us, a wife is different from a servant. A wife you love; a servant you maybe don't care much about. If you see me as a potential servant –'

Darius was stricken. 'No! It is this way in my land too! It is that at least I could be with you, if I couldn't marry you.'

She stepped close to him. 'How do you really feel about me, Darius?'

'It is my hope that you are suitable, and that you will be willing too –'

'Forget suitability! What about *me*?'

'I *can't* forget suitability, because marriage to me would kill you if –'

'But you can't go back, so that doesn't matter! All there is is you and me. So how do you feel?'

That made him pause. She was right; he could not go back. All he could do was remain here until he died. 'I can not marry you here either, because –'

'Nobody asked you to!' she flared. '*Will* you answer the question!'

He looked at her with an altered appreciation. He had been so girt about by the problems of his isolation and his dependence on her for food and information that he had not allowed himself to think of her as a feeling creature.

She was small, the top of her head reaching just above his shoulder. Her hair was brown, with slight curving, just touching her shoulders. Her face, framed by it, was rounded, except for a slightly pointed chin. Her eyes were large and round and brown. She wore a dress, perhaps in deference to his problem with the blue jeans, and she never sat in that particular position when wearing it. But now she was standing, nicely proportioned, small of chin, breast, waist and hip but well balanced and extremely feminine.

But appearance was only one aspect of a person. Colene had shown great patience, teaching him her language, and good judgment in the food and clothing she had brought for him, and had been responsible about things like emptying the privy-pot. She had wanted him kept out of sight, and though it made him a virtual prisoner here, he felt she was correct in her judgment about this. She had made it as comfortable for him as was feasible. Her personality was nice; she laughed often, and was direct in her dealings with him. She was generous, going to the trouble and discomfort of sharing her warmth with him at night despite the risk of discovery.

Yet still he could not answer, for there was more than all of this in the question. Feelings were bidirectional things, and if hers were not there, his could not be either. There was one more thing he had to know.

'May I handle you?' he inquired.

'You want to have sex with me?' Now she was guarded.

'I must give that a qualified answer. I do find you desirable, but that is not my intent at the moment.'

'You may handle me,' she said, understanding that this was not a casual thing. He had to do this in order to determine the answer to her question. How he felt about her depended in considerable part how she felt about him.

He put his arms around her back, drawing her in close. Her body yielded to him, and she lifted her face. He knew that magic did not work here, but perhaps just a bit of his peculiar power could be invoked. His power to relate to the emotions of others: to receive and return their joy. Perhaps, with the closest and most evocative contact, he could know.

He kissed her: just a touching of his lips to hers.

3

KEY

She knew it had not been long, externally, but internally it was as if she had stepped across realities, or Modes as Darius put it. Then she was sobbing against his shoulder, and it wasn't disappointment but relief: now she knew how he really felt about her – and he knew how she felt about him. She had not really believed in electricity between people, or in instant knowing. Not until now.

Soon enough she pulled herself together. She had learned to make quick recoveries. She drew him down, and they sat side by side, leaning against the back wall of the shed, her right fingers interlaced with his left fingers.

'So it's love,' she said matter-of-factly. She had to tackle it this way, as if it were something she had observed from afar, that didn't concern her, because that was the only way she could handle it at the moment. 'We have to talk.'

'We have talked,' he said.

'Not this way. You can't marry me here, because I'm underage and you'll die soon anyway. But you can –'

'No. Your love suffices.'

She laughed. She did that often with him, and now she knew why. 'I wouldn't tell, Darius. I'm good at keeping secrets, honest. You've been a real gentleman, and I like that a lot. But that's not it. You can tell me exactly how to get to your reality.'

'But even if I could return, and take you there, there would be no certainty –'

'I know. If we went there, and you couldn't marry me, I'd be your servant. The forms don't matter. Now I know how you feel. I want to go with you, Darius. Just tell me how.'

He seemed surprised. He thought this kind of discussion was useless. He might be right, but she had a notion. 'I must have the key. That, in my hand, becomes the signal. Then Pwer will revert me to my reality, together with what I hold.'

'So if you are holding me, I'm there too.'

'Yes.'

'How do you activate the key? Is there a button on it?'

'No. My mind does it. I touch it to my forehead and make my desire.'

'You make a wish!' she exclaimed. 'That makes sense!'

'Yes. No one else can activate it. It is attuned to me. It amplifies my wish to return, and that signal crosses the realities, and the Chip responds. I need it, and it needs me. Separate, we both are useless.'

She squeezed his fingers reassuringly. 'So if you could recover that key –'

'I could return. But it is lost.'

'But if I found it for you –'

His fingers stiffened against hers. 'If you could do that –'

'I can't promise, Darius, but I'll try.'

'You give me hope! If I had that key, I would take you with me.'

'That's the idea, you know.'

His face turned to her. 'But you don't believe.'

'I believe you love.'

'That is enough, I think.' They leaned together and kissed. Again she felt the magic tingle of passion, intimacy and commitment. All that she lacked in her own poor life she had found in Darius. She *knew*.

She spent the afternoon stocking supplies. She had some money of her own, and she used it to buy groceries at the only store within walking distance that was open on Sunday. She piled them into the shed. 'These are canned goods,' she explained. 'You open them with this can opener. They may not taste good, cold, but they'll feed you.'

'But why are you doing this?' he asked.

She faced him seriously. 'This is Sunday. Tomorrow I go back to school. I think I know how to find your key. But getting it may be tricky. If I don't come back, I don't want you to starve. Stay here as long as you can, and when you can't, well, you'll just have to go out. But I'll try to get back here okay. This is just in case.'

'Just in case what?' he demanded, alarmed.

She shook her head. 'Darius, it's been beautiful here with you. You have made me believe in human decency again. But out there's the real world. It's not all that nice. Please don't ask me to tell you any more.'

'If I ask, you will tell?'

'Yes. But please don't.'

'Then I ask you only to be careful.'

'Thank you.' She kissed him. She liked doing that. Not only did it make her feel good, it made her feel good about it. He was a good man, and he welcomed her kisses, and he asked no more than that. It was love fulfilled. For now. Until she had the chance to prove her love, in a way he might not understand if he knew.

Monday, school-day, Colene headed out to the bus with her books. Her attendance the past two weeks had been spotty; she had pleaded illness, then sneaked out to be with Darius. But she had done her homework, because she didn't want to bring any unnecessary suspicion on herself. She had done it with Darius, teaching him words and explaining things as she went along, and it had actually been pleasant.

The thing about Darius was this: he might be crazy, or he might be lying, making up a story about a magic land so he wouldn't have to say where he really was from. But she liked his story, and the meticulous detail of it, and she liked him, with his archaic ways and respect for her body. It was fun having a man to herself. Since she had found him, she had not sliced her wrists. Her skin was healing over; she could probably take off her wrist wraps now, and the scars would not be fresh enough to attract attention.

In fact, all the time she had known him, she had been very like a normal girl. She had laughed, meaning it, liking his confusions, liking his company, liking him. When at last he had kissed her, she had become a normal woman. A woman in love.

Love. At first she had held it at arm's length, uncertain what to do with this weird emotion. Was it real, or just something she imagined? She had heard that girls her age only thought they could love, and were actually in love with the idea of love. Maybe that was true for some. Maybe for most. But not for her. What she felt swept all other considerations aside. It was like a magic fire, burning away all her prior supports, making ashes of other interests. Now there was only Darius. Everything she did was with his welfare in mind. Even what she would do today.

'Tell Biff I want to deal,' she said to a boy she knew had a connection.

He was startled. 'You?'

'Not his way. But if he has what I want, I'll deal.'

She went to classes, and she shone. That extra homework time was paying off. Normally she skimped on schoolwork, and was bright enough to get by with high grades anyway; now she was prepared with research done for the joy of doing it with Darius, who was unfailingly interested in all the things of her world. What had been dull became interesting with him, and by the time she got it all explained to him, she knew it better than she had thought possible. But her performance was incidental; it was only to reassure everyone that Bright Little Colene had everything to live for, and nothing on her mind except classwork.

At lunch she was about to sit down with her tray when she saw a young man of about eighteen standing in the doorway to the rear exit. That was Biff. He was theoretically a student, but somehow he never attended classes. Students carefully ignored him unless they wanted something illegal. Then they dealt, making what deals they could. If the school administration knew about it, it pretended ignorance, knowing that Biff could quickly be replaced by something worse.

She set her tray on a table, picked up the half-pint carton of milk, opened it, and walked to that door. Biff faded back out of sight. She came to stand between the doorway and the large

51

trash container, drinking her milk. She faced back toward the main chamber.

'Yeah?' It was Biff's voice from the other side of the doorway.

'I want something.'

'What?'

'It's a sort of gray metal button, like a slug, only thicker and brighter. It was on a bum who got rolled two weeks ago. He wore funny clothes. He gave some punks the finger, and they pounded him.'

'What's it to you?'

'It's a memento. I heard it's a luck charm.'

'I don't mess with luck charms.'

'I want it bad. This one, no other.'

'How bad?'

'I'll game for it.'

He laughed, harshly. 'You want it, you bring money.'

'I have no money. Make another offer.'

'Stand out where I can see you.'

She finished her milk, dumped the balled carton into the container, and stepped into the center of the doorway. She was wearing a light white sweater and black skirt, both too tight. She inhaled, turning. She hated this part, but it was all she had to bargain with. Biff could get girls, but they were either his type, which was no novelty, or under duress, which was no fun. What he wanted was a high class young one who would pretend she liked it. Colene had acted high class for years, and she knew how to pretend.

'Okay. One week.'

Now she laughed. 'I'm a clean girl! One night.'

'You ain't clean! Four guys had you.'

'Not lately. I'll put four guys in jail, they come near me again. I never ate or sniffed. I'm clean.'

'But you drank.'

'Never again!'

'No jail, if you deal. None of that.' He meant no charges against him.

'None of that,' she agreed. 'Two nights.'

'You don't want it bad enough.'

'You don't even have it.' Then, signaling the approach of someone dumping a tray in the trash, 'Pause.'

When the person moved on, she said 'Resume.' Part of the deal, when anyone talked with Biff, was to keep it quiet.

'I can get it.'

Her heart leaped. 'You know of it? It has to be only that one.'

'They couldn't fence a slug. No value. I can get it. Tomorrow.'

'I said I'd game. I win, what I want. You win, what you want.'

'That slug against one week, smiling.' Not only would she have to do anything he wanted, short of drugs – there were reasons to keep a clean girl clean – she would have to take his side if they were caught, swearing she was his girlfriend and that there had been no coertion. She gagged at the notion, but had to accept. There was a screwball honor in this sort of dealing, enforced by those who had no conscience, just business sense.

'Yes.'

'What game?'

'I'll decide.'

'Before my friends.'

'Before your friends. But I deal only with you.'

'For sure! Tomorrow, after school. Come to my car.'

'Only if you have what I want.'

'I'll have it.'

She walked away. The preliminary deal had been struck. He would bring the key and she would bring her body. The outcome of the game was uncertain, but if she had to, she would game again for the key after paying off the first game. The important thing was that he knew what it was and would get it. Darius could have it back.

This was the part Darius might not understand. He had odd notions about honor and chastity. If she had to give her body to a lout like Biff to win back the key – well, she had a ploy she hoped would avoid that.

In the afternoon she was in a daze. She went through classes mechanically. She would get the key – but would that really

53

solve anything? For she simply did not believe in that alternate universe of his. If she gave him the key, what could he do except prove that it didn't work? Then his fantasy would be exposed, and a major part of his appeal for her would be diminished. As long as he lacked that key, he was the King of Laughter from an alien reality. With it, he might be only a deluded refugee from some mental hospital.

Why was she risking so much, for such likely disappointment?

Maybe she had been fooling herself. She remained as suicidal as ever. She had merely found a new way to flirt with death. Because if she lost the game, and Biff had his way with her for a week, she might as well die. Maybe the key was just a pretext. Maybe her love for Darius was just a pretext.

No!

The teacher paused. 'A problem, Colene?'

Her pain had shown on her face. 'I'm better, Miss Grumman, honest! Maybe I ate too fast.'

The teacher let it pass. Colene suppressed her thoughts and paid better attention in class. It was a fair deal.

But on the way home that question resumed. She hardly responded to Julie's chatter. Was she making a mistake? Was she about to torpedo her dream? For even if the illusion didn't end for Darius, it would for her.

Back home, she hurried to the shed. 'Oh, Colene, I am so glad to see you!' Darius exclaimed, embracing her. 'I feared I would not.'

'I have made a deal to recover your key,' she said. 'Tomorrow.'

He stared at her. 'You really can recover it?'

'The punks who mugged you couldn't fence it. They thought it was just a fancy slug. I can get it.'

'You can buy it?' He had had trouble with the concept of money, but understood it reasonably well now.

'I asked you not to ask.'

He was silent. She kissed him, and it was good.

But that night she broached the matter herself. She had discovered that an aspect of love was an extreme reluctance to deceive the object of that love. That was awkward, but there was nothing for it but to play it through. 'Darius, there are two ways to do this. I am going to gamble, and if I win, I will have the key for you. If I lose, I will have to be away from you for a week, at night, anyway. I – you said you desire me. I think maybe tonight –'

'No. I want to marry you, unsullied according to your code.'

'But I –' She could not continue. How could she tell him she might be bound for a week of disgusting sex with a criminal lout, pretending she liked it, when she had told Darius no? He thought she was pure. 'All the same, I think –'

'No.'

If she won the game, and got the key without having to pay, and he used it and it didn't work, then the dream would be gone and it would be foolish to have sex with him. If she lost, she would have no pretense of being the kind of girl he wanted. Now was the only time.

'Darius, I told you no, before, but now I tell you yes. Please –'

'No. I will not have you sully yourself by your code for me. I will marry you in honor.'

She had never expected this. It wasn't that she was eager for sex; that was far from the case. It was fraught with liabilities the sex-ed teachers hardly imagined. But if she had it with anyone, she wanted it to be him. If she had to have it with someone else, she wanted it first with Darius. But he, with his incomplete understanding of the situation, would not hear of it. If she told him the full truth, he would probably forbid her to recover the key that way.

They were, in their fashion, having a lover's quarrel. It was not nearly as delightful as she had thought such a thing would be.

She thought of trying to seduce him, of sleeping naked with him. But she realized that this would only demean her in his eyes, and she didn't want that.

How she wished she could believe in his reality!

Tuesday after school, modestly garbed, she sought Biff's car in the parking lot. Students she knew were runners stood casually here and there, making sure there were no authorities. That protected her as well as him, because both wanted to deal in private.

'You have it?'

He lifted a gray disk that exactly fitted the description Darius had given.

'May I see it?'

He handed it to her. She turned it over. There, in tiny etching, was the coding Darius had described. She had not told anyone of this. It was genuine.

She handed it back. 'This is it.'

'In,' he said. 'Down.'

She walked around the car and got in. She ducked down so that she was not visible from outside. He drove cautiously out, and around the block, checking for pursuit. Satisfied there was none, he drove to his club house across town.

'Up,' he said, and she sat normally in the front seat. 'How come a clean chic like you wants a damn slug so much?'

She was prepared. 'There's a man. He said I could have what I wanted if I got it for him. He doesn't really want it; he just thought I couldn't get it. So I'm getting it.'

Biff did not seem to believe her, but was satisfied that she did want it. Few people in his business cared to give their real reasons.

They arrived at the club house. They entered. Inside were four men. She had expected disreputable types, but these were clean-cut. They were also older, in their thirties and forties. No juvenile thugs, these; they were the real thing.

'Before we deal,' Biff said. 'This never happened. No one was here.'

'Yes. You too. No one talks. You win, no one knows how I paid. Not like those four rapists.'

Biff nodded. 'No one talks. It's private.' There was, as she had reflected before, a certain honor in such transactions. No one wanted the police to get wind of either drug operations or juvenile sex. The police wouldn't get rid of either, they would only complicate things for all parties.

'And no welshing,' she said. 'I win, you give me the slug and take me back near where I live. No rape.'

Biff smiled. 'If you win to the satisfaction of my friends, no problem. I settle my deals.'

'You win, you have me smiling for a week,' she said, making sure they were agreed. 'Nights only; I can't skip more school. No drugs, no bondage, no hurting. No marking.'

'Kid, I like you,' Biff said. 'Agreed. Now what's your game?'

Colene nerved herself. Then she began removing her clothes. 'You, me, naked. Endurance. The one who fills most cups without falling wins.'

Biff smiled. 'Naked endurance? Chick, I know you ain't thinking what I'm thinking!'

'For sure,' she agreed, removing her shoes and socks. 'Naked to prove there's no cheating. No hidden tubes or things. We stand separate. Each has a bucket, or whatever. Several cups, maybe. No one touches either of us. We get no help.'

'We got buckets,' Biff said. He gestured, and one of the men left the room, returning in a moment with two plastic buckets. He set one before each of them.

Colene continued to strip. She had her shirt off, and removed her bra. She was doing something she had dreamed of: a strip tease before strange men who were honor-bound not to touch her or to tell. She could see that all of them were now fascinated, and not just because of her increasing nudity; they wondered just what she was up to.

'I can do that,' Biff said. He removed his own shirt.

Colene started on her lower half, pulling down her skirt. 'Knives. Good ones. Sharp and clean.'

'I got a blade,' Biff said. A handle appeared in his hand, and from it suddenly snapped a wicked narrow four inch blade. It was obvious that he knew how to use it.

'I need one too,' Colene said. She turned to one of the spectators. 'May I borrow yours?'

The man was surely a killer, but he looked startled. Then he reached into his jacket and brought out an old fashioned barber's shaving knife. He unfolded it. The blade was a good inch longer than Biff's, but it wasn't the same kind of weapon. It was a slicer, not a stabber. The kind used to slit throats. She felt a chill, now realizing the nature of his business. He was an enforcer, a contract man. He extended it to her, holding it by the blade.

Colene smiled most sweetly, though there was a layer of the ice of fear coating her heart. 'Thank you sir,' she said, taking the handle. 'I will return it to you soon.'

Now they were twice as curious as before. 'Kid, I got to tell you, if you figure to knife-fight Biff –' the owner of the razor started.

'Not exactly,' Colene said. Holding the razor carefully so as not to cut herself, she tucked her fingers into her panties and slid them down. Now she was all the way naked, and the eyes of all five men were locked onto her body. What a fantasy she was playing out, for real! She turned in place, all the way around, so that they could see everything. She was really pleased that they liked it; this did wonders for her self esteem, in its macabre fashion.

Biff had meanwhile stripped to his jock, but here he hesitated. She knew why: her little show was giving him an erection, and he didn't want to bare it unless sex really was part of the game.

'You can wear that,' she told him. 'I'm satisfied there's nothing in there.'

Biff scowled, but one of the men chuckled.

'All right, what's your game?' Biff demanded.

Then she dropped her bombshell. 'Just this: who can bleed the most before falling. You know, like a knockout, count to ten, you're out. The one left standing wins.'

'Bleed?' Biff asked, dismayed.

'I'll cut my arm, you cut yours. We bleed into our buckets. The men measure the blood. If I faint at two pints and you're still standing, and you've bled two and a half pints, you win.'

'That's no game!' Biff protested.

'It's *my* game,' she said evenly. 'It's as good a game as knife-fighting, only we bleed ourselves. Isn't it fair?' She looked at the other men.

They looked at each other. Then the one who had lent her the razor shrugged. 'It's fair, Biff,' he said. 'We knew she wasn't coming here to play posies. She said endurance. She didn't say what kind.'

Biff swallowed. He was now in the position of put up or shut up. 'Okay. You start.'

He thought she was bluffing. He didn't know she was suicidal. 'Gladly.' She extended her left arm over her bucket, lifted the razor, and made one fast pass across her forearm. No bluffing here!

The edge was, by no coincidence, razor sharp. It cut much deeper than she had expected, almost painless in the first seconds. Blood welled out immediately, flowed across her arm, and dripped into the bucket. There was so much of it that it threatened to spill onto the floor. She had to lower her hand, so that the blood flowed down and off her fingers. Now the pain was coming, but it really wasn't bad. It was masked by excitement. She had done it! With aplomb, even. She had never cut herself like this before! What a sight it was!

She looked up. Biff was standing there, staring. So were the others.

'What's the matter?' she inquired sweetly. 'Never seen blood before?'

This time two of them chuckled.

She addressed Biff. 'You're a lot bigger than I am,' she said. 'You must have twice as much blood in you as I have in me. You can beat me easy, if you care to.'

'She's right,' the razor man said.

Still Biff stood, not moving.

'But you have to play the game,' Colene said. 'It's not fair to let me bleed myself out if you don't even start.'

The men nodded. 'Do it, Biff,' one said.

'But what good's a bled-out chic to me?' Biff demanded somewhat plaintively. 'Me weakened, and her unconscious –'

'There's no time limit on the payoff,' Colene said. 'I thought you'd want it right away, but you can take a rain check. Make it six months from now. I'll be there. You know where I live.' She looked down again at the blood dripping from her hand, so bright and beautiful. She felt dizzy, and knew it wasn't from the blood loss; it was exhilaration.

Still Biff hesitated.

'Biff, she's got you,' the razor man said. 'Cut or yield.'

Biff considered a moment more. At last he smiled. 'Okay, kid, you beat me. You win.'

'Thank you,' she said. But she didn't move.

'Here's your slug,' he said, handing it to her. She took it with her knife-hand, carefully.

'Thank you,' she repeated. She had the victory, if she didn't lose her nerve now and do something monumentally stupid. So she did nothing. That seemed safest.

Biff took his clothes and walked from the room. One of the other men fetched some bandage material. Trust them to have such supplies; they probably had to doctor their own bullet wounds. 'You won, kid; we won't touch you. But you gotta let us help you before you bleed to death.'

'Thank you,' she said a third time, smiling.

They did a competent job of closing and bandaging her wound, and helped her get dressed. Not one tried to handle her body even 'accidentally', but they seemed to like handing her the panties, bra and skirt. It was as if each wanted to have a personal part in what had turned out to be a most unusual game. 'I'll take you home, if that's okay with you,' the razor man said. 'I don't think Biff feels like it.'

'Just remember, no −'

'Kid, you *won*. No one touches you. Not now, not ever. Not until you say so. We're − you know what we are. But you got our respect. Just keep your mouth shut, and it's done.'

'Thank you,' she said once again. 'You may take me home.' She completed her dressing, donning her shoes.

The razor man extended his elbow. Startled by this bit of chivalry, Colene put her hand on it, and walked with him out of the building.

He drove her home. 'Kid, you're as gutsy as I've ever seen,' he said. 'If you're ever in bad trouble, ask for Slick. We'll make a deal.'

'Thank you.' It seemed to be the only thing she was able to say, now. She was riding on a high like none before. She had played her scene flawlessly, every part of it, and it had worked exactly as she had hoped. What a dream come true! It wasn't just that she had won the key, it was that she had made one of her weird fantasies come true, and gotten away with it.

She had *liked* stripping before those tough men, having them admire her body. Rape she did not like at all, but this had been showmanship. See, no Touch. There was all the difference in the world.

He drew to a stop a block from her home. 'You can walk from here. I'll watch, then go.'

'Thank you.' She slid out.

'You got a nice little body,' he said as she closed the door. 'Damn nice. Keep it clean, kid. Don't mess with our kind if you don't have to.'

'Thank you,' she said yet again, experiencing another thrill of pleasure. Then she walked away, knowing he was watching that body in motion. His name was Slick, as in slick-as-a-razor. She would remember.

Things were normal at home: Dad was out and Mom was drunk. Colene fixed herself a generous meal and bundled it up and took it out to the shed. If she was spending more time there now than she used to, nobody noticed. As long as she kept her grades up and stayed out of trouble, nobody cared. There had been a time when that bothered her.

She knocked, then entered. Darius had been snoozing; there really wasn't much for him to do, as he had not made much progress learning to read her books.

She brought out the key and held it up.

He seemed almost afraid to touch it. But when he turned it over and saw the coding, he knew.

'Colene, I didn't think you could do it!' he said, hugging her. 'But you have! You have recovered the key! We can go to my reality!'

Now she was descending from her euphoria. She had not actually lost that much blood, but she had taken a phenomenal risk, and knew it. It had been her luck that Biff had been squeamish about letting his own blood, and that his criminal friends had had a sense of honor about a game played by their rules. In the letting of her own blood she had shown guts, not quite literally, and they had respected that. She knew that some killers had very conservative family lives and were kind to children. But some were otherwise. She had gambled that not only could she beat Biff, but that his friends would side with her. She had won, but she wouldn't care to try it again.

Now she faced another gamble: that Darius wasn't crazy or a con-man. Because either that key would work or it wouldn't. And she knew it wouldn't. Which meant that the lovely bubble would burst, and things would be back as they had been before.

She set down her bundle of food. 'I think we'd better talk,' she said. She spread out the makings, and they began to eat.

'Yes, of course.' His actual speech was much more limited, but she liked to think of it as educated and courtly, and her fancy filled in the nuances. 'I realize that it is a daunting decision, to leave your family and your entire Mode, without any guarantee that –'

''Snot that, Darius. I want to go. I love what you have described. I have nothing much to hold me here. And if you can't marry me, but all the rest is real, well, I'll be your lover instead. You've been up-front about that aspect. But there's a problem.'

'You don't believe me,' he said.

'I wish I could! But I just don't.'

'When I take you there, you will believe. I will take you there now, if you wish. With the key –'

'Here's the thing: suppose you take that key, and hold it to your head, and make your wish – and nothing happens? What then?'

'Colene, it will work. The same Chip that sent me here will bring me back. But as I said, you do not need to believe, because this is not a matter of faith. I will take you there, and then we shall discover whether you can multiply your joy, and – oh, I want so much to marry you!'

'You have faith, but I don't, and these things don't necessarily work unless you believe in them.'

He smiled. 'If it doesn't work, I will be amazed!'

'If it doesn't work,' she said doggedly, 'you will be crazy.' There: she had said it.

He glanced more intently at her. 'You believe I am not sane?'

How she hated this. 'Darius, I think I love you, but I'm

a realist. I think you are deluded. I think you have a dream that's a wonderful thing, and you've spent years perfecting it, but somehow you got out of the institution and I found you, and now it's my dream too, but I know that's all it is. When you try to use that key, the dream will be over. Because I'm not crazy, and I'm not going to be. So what do we do, after you try that thing and nothing happens?'

'You do not wish to try it, and discover the truth of it directly?'

'Discovering the truth directly can be a whole lot of trouble,' she said, pushing down memories that were trying to rise, like bodies buried in muck. 'I'd rather know what I'm getting into first.'

'What would persuade you to try it?'

'If there were some way it could be believed. I mean, I don't believe in ghosts either, but if one came in here and said "Boo!" to me, I'd sure check it out and maybe change my mind. Same thing for a flying saucer, a UFO.' Here it took some time for her to get the concept across, and they finally settled on Ship Containing Alien Creatures. 'But if one landed beside my house, I'd consider it. Can you show me anything to make me believe you?'

'I fear I can not. But perhaps I can clarify the rationale.'

'How about this: if you try it, and it works, we're both there and we see about getting married or whatever. If you try it and it doesn't work, you turn yourself in for mental treatment.'

He laughed. 'If they provide food and shelter, I will not mind if they think I am deluded! If I can not return, my life will not be long in any event.'

'Because if they cure you, I'll still marry you,' she said. And there was another crazy thing she was doing! Seriously talking of marriage to a man she believed to be crazy! But crazy or not, he was a lot better for her than death.

'Let me clarify the rationale,' he said. 'Because then I can use the key, and it will be done. There are an infinite number of Modes, in which different people live and different fundamental laws obtain. The Chips enable us to establish contact with the others. In mine, magic –'

'Like computer chips,' she said.

'You know of the Chips?'

'A chip is a sort of section of a computer that enables it to do what it does,' she said. 'To address a lot of memory, for example. The fancier the chip, the more sophisticated the computer. Take the 86 series, for example.'

'There are eighty-six of these "computers"?'

She laughed. 'No, silly, that's what they're called! The 8086, 80286, 80386 and so on. There was an 80186 but I think it was the same as the 8086. Anyway, they may seem similar, but the amount of RAM they can manage is –'

'Ram? A male sheep?'

She laughed so hard she let herself fall over backwards, which was fun. She tended to be happy when she was with him, which was an exhilarating experience. Then she remembered that she wasn't in her blue jeans now; she didn't want to freak him out. Not right at this moment, anyway; better to save it for when she needed it. He had endearingly quaint notions of propriety. She drew herself up and forced herself into sobriety. 'No, RAM stands for Random Access Memory. Memory you can change about, any which way you want. So you can do a lot with it. But that's irrelevant. The point is that when you said you had chips to make contact with other realities, well, I thought of the way our computer chips make contact with a lot of memory, among other things. It's just an analogy.'

'Perhaps,' he said seriously. 'But it sounds so much like an aspect of what I was discussing that I think I had better learn more of it. Exactly what is a computer, and how does the chip relate to it? The chip is an integral part?'

'You really don't know?'

'I really don't know, Colene, and it may be important.'

'Okay. We use computers in school for homework papers and math problems and things. Oh, we still use books, but the computers make it easier. We can set up our problems and push a few buttons, and it's much faster. We can write papers on the screen, and edit them, and print them out when they're all done.'

'Where do you get these devices?'

'We make them. There are companies in California and Japan and all over. Where do you get your chips?'

'They are ancient relics apparently deriving from some other Mode. We do not know their origin, only their power, and we understand only a little of that.'

'Gee – mysterious ancient otherworld science! I like it!'

'You like everything. You are wonderful.'

She felt a warm thrill. When she was with him, that was the way she felt. If she could be with him forever, would she become normal? It was an intriguing notion.

But there was business to handle. She had to go into some detail about exactly what problems and papers were, and how they were done with computers. Then they got down to the essence:

'So the 186 chip addressed one megabyte RAM,' she said. 'One million bytes. Maybe 165,000 words if you used up all the space in writing a novel: one pretty solid book. But the software only addressed about two thirds of that, six hundred and forty kilobytes. Then the 286 chip addressed sixteen megabytes RAM, but the software was still limited to six forty K. So what was the point? They had to develop a new operating system to catch up with the hardware. The way I see it, the 186 was like a line: it did a lot, but was sort of limited. The 286 was like a square, adding a whole dimension to computing. Then the 386 was like a cube, because it addressed four thousand megabytes RAM and could do stuff the other chips only dreamed of. So it's the 86 series, with the numbers telling how many dimensions: one, two or three. And then four, for the 486, and so on. But each one is based on just that key chip.'

'Dimensions,' Darius said. 'How many points does it take to establish a dimension?'

'Huh? We were talking about computers!'

'We were talking about an analogy. Chips, computers and dimensions. In my reality, when we deal with a line, it requires two points to establish the orientation of that line. Is it the same here?'

'Oh, sure. You can measure a line with two points, marking it off.'

'And three points for a plane? Defining it in space?'

'You mean like balancing a tray on three fingers? Sure.'

'And four points for a three dimensional object.'

'Sure, I'm with you. Length, width, thickness and time, 'cause if it doesn't exist for some time, it's not there at all. What's your point?'

'Five points for a four dimensional Mode,' he continued. 'To fix it in space and time. The Cyng of Pwer mentioned that. The infinite number of Modes are each fixed in their own places, like planes in a cube, and one of these is mine and another is yours.'

'Oh, you mean like – like mica. That rock that you can just peel apart?'

'Mica,' he agreed, after she had clarified the nature of the stone for him. 'Each layer infinitely thin, but a universe to those who are of it. The Chip enabled me to cross vertically, from my layer to yours. Because it addresses many megabytes. But my finding you was essentially random, because there are only a few parameters we could specify, and infinity to choose from.'

'Gee, I wonder if it could set up a Virtual Mode?' she said musingly.

'What is that?'

'Well, I told you how each new chip addressed a whole lot more memory. But that's not the half of it. The 386 can extend that way beyond by making it seem that there's a lot more memory. There's not, really, but you can use it same as if it's real. Fake memory, I call it.'

'Pretend memory? But surely that would be a fantasy!'

'No. Like when you have the disk drive, and it's too small for what you want to do, but you have a whole lot of memory, so you make up a virtual drive out of memory, and it acts just like a real disk. Or the other way around, making memory out of extra storage on your hard disk. When you turn off the computer, it's gone, but as long as you're running it, it works. Virtual memory is real, it just isn't quite what it seems. The 386 can make your memory act like sixty-four million megabytes, which is a lot. And it can set up a Virtual Mode, too.'

'Tell me of Modes.'

Colene had been privately convinced that he was crazy, but he now seemed more like an ignorant but smart person.

66

Like someone who was from another reality. She began to doubt, and to believe, as she talked. 'I don't remember all the computer modes; it's been a while since I had that class. I think there's Native Mode, that's sort of whatever the 386 chip would do if left to itself. Then there's Real Mode, used to run the regular AT software; it's limited, just sort of choking down the chip's potential to make it seem like a simpler one.'

'Like one slice of mica,' he said.

'Yes. And Protected Mode, used for the Operating System Two multitasking. That's like a three dimensional chunk of mica. And Virtual Mode, that will take the chip as far as it will go; it can be set up any which way, and however it's set up, it acts just as if it's real.'

'With that we could institute a reality that included you with your science, and me with my magic, yet we would be together, neither giving up anything.'

'So it wouldn't have to be one or the other!' she agreed. 'I'd like that, Darius! Then I could just walk across to you, and if I couldn't marry you, I'd just walk back to here.'

'A reality that consisted of a slanting place across the block of mica, permanently linking us,' he agreed. 'Unfortunately, that is not what brought me here. I am a mere intruder into your reality, with no permanence. When I take you with me, you will be an intruder into my reality.'

She shrugged. 'So I guess there's no way you can show me your reality, without my actually going there and not being able to return.' A journey into madness?

'I see I have not convinced you.'

'Right. That computer analogy is nice, but I never fooled myself that I can step into the picture on the screen. My reality is a lot uglier.'

'Ugly? But you are beautiful and cheerful!'

She sighed. 'Something you better know about me, Darius, before you marry me. I'm not happy. I'm suicidal.'

He was astonished. 'You seek to destroy yourself? I can not believe —'

'Believe it!' She began unwinding the bandage on her arm. 'I slice my wrists and watch the blood. Some day I'll get up the courage to go all the way, and then I'll be free.' She showed the inner padding, soaked in blood. 'See this? This is how I got your key back for you. I challenged the punk who had it to a bleeding contest. He thought I was bluffing, but I wasn't. Freaked him out. So I won. If I had lost, I'd either be dead or as good as dead, paying off my bet.'

'You are depressed!' he exclaimed, horrified.

'You bet! I think the only time I've been happy this year is when I've been with you. So I guess I'm crazy too. It's been fun dreaming of being in your world with its magic, and loving you, and I guess I do love you, but I don't believe you. It's my misfortune to be too firmly grounded in reality, and I don't mean your kind.'

'Oh, Colene, this is terrible!' he cried.

'Why?'

'Because it means I can't marry you.'

'Well, if you get treatment and get cured –'

'Not so. If I take you to my reality, where joy can be transferred, you would have no joy to give me. You have the opposite. That makes it impossible.'

'You're changing your mind?' she asked. Her feelings were horribly mixed. She wanted to love him and have him love her, but she knew that marriage between them had always been an impossible dream. Now that he had his key, and his fantasy would soon be dashed, it was time to end it. But how she wished this sweet interlude could have been forever!

'Colene, I love you, and I want nothing more than to bring you home and marry you! But that would destroy us both! I was willing to take you as long as there was a reasonable chance of it being right, but now I know there is not. I blinded my mind to one of the major possibilities for your availability, and that was my folly. My mission has failed. The kindest thing I can do for you is to leave you behind.'

So he knew the key wouldn't work, and was calling it off. That did make sense. It also meant he didn't have to make the deal, and go to a mental hospital when he failed to go where he thought he was going. He was defaulting, just as Biff had. Getting set up to walk out of her life when his bubble of illusion was popped.

She felt the tears starting down her cheeks. 'I guess you're right. I guess you'd better use your key now. You know where I am, if you ever change your mind.' For now she did not have to disparage the fantasy; she could let him depart in his own way. It hurt terribly, but it was for the best.

'If there were any way —'

'If there were any way,' she agreed.

He came to her and kissed her, and it was excruciatingly sweet. It was like an old movie, with them parting at the train station, knowing they might never see each other again. Maybe that analogy wasn't so far off.

'I can't even leave you anything, to repay you for your great kindness to me,' he said. 'It has been for nothing.'

'For nothing,' she agreed. 'But I really liked being with you, Darius. I'm sorry I can't believe in you. If I did, I'd go with you, even if you had to marry someone else.'

'I would not care to do that to you.' He lifted the key to his forehead. 'Farewell, Colene.'

'Goodbye, Darius.'

He closed his eyes, seeming to concentrate.

Then he disappeared.

Colene blinked her tears out of the way. She stepped forward and swept her hand through the space where he had stood. There was nothing except the faint smell of him; he had not been able to wash up well, here.

The door was closed. He had not walked out. He had just — gone. Exactly as he had said he would.

Now she knew that she should have believed. She should have gone with him to his magic reality. Her disbelief had cost her everything.

4

VIRTUAL MODE

Darius looked around him. The familiar landscape of his home reality was newly unfamiliar, after his acclimation to the alternate reality. He gazed at it with a new appreciation.

He stood on a dais, the one addressed by the Chip. One hop distant – or about twenty meters, in Colene's system – was the larger dais of the Cyng of Pwer. Between was the serrate wilderness: a land surface so jagged that it was not possible to walk on it. Only by pounding a temporary path through the crystals could it be made passable by foot, and that was pointless, because in days the crystals would regenerate, and their new, smaller spikes would be sharper than the old ones had been. Also, who would want to damage such prettiness? The original crystals were all the natural colors and some generated ones, shifting iridescently in the changing light of the sun.

He glanced up. There were good cloud formations, pink above green and yellow. A heavy purple cloud was slowly descending, and below it the trees on their common dais were extending their black leaves, ready to draw nourishment. The light of the sun was refracting through a colorless cloud, its beams reradiating out to be intercepted by other clouds, each of which took its color from the color of the light it received.

It was good to be home!

A figure appeared on the main dais. The man spied Darius.

He made a gesture, and a bridge appeared, spanning the ragged gap between them.

Darius stepped onto the bridge, and felt his weight diminishing. It was what Colene would have called a virtual bridge: it acted like a real one, but it was mock. He was able to use it because his weight was being reduced almost to nothing. Pwer had simply invoked a miniature bridge with a figurine, and was marching the latter across the former. Darius had allowed him to make the figurine because it was essential to the process of traveling to another reality. Otherwise the magic would not have had effect.

He completed his crossing and stood before the Cyng of Pwer. 'You return alone,' the man said.

'I found her,' Darius said. 'I love her. But I misjudged her. She was depressive.'

Pwer was startled. 'How could you make an error like that?'

'There is no transfer in her reality. I judged by appearances, not direct mental contact, and she laughed much. But it was because she liked me. Her contacts with me were limited, and her joy was limited to her time with me. Her underlying nature was suicidal.'

'Your power did not work there?'

'Not at all. I thought it did when I kissed her and felt love, and she felt love, but it seems we were each generating our own in the company of the other. I was entirely dependent on verbal language. Much of my time was spent learning it, so that we could communicate. It was in that period of close association that we came to love each other.'

'You should have brought her.'

'I could not marry her! It would have killed her.'

'And what will she do, alone?'

That made Darius pause. 'She – she could kill herself.'

'Could? You fool! She surely will!'

'We can't know that! Maybe her experience with me will change her outlook, and she will become less suicidal.'

'Unlikely, since she is slated to die anyway.'

'What?'

'Don't you remember? Only those who are destined to have

little effect on their realities can be removed from them. That is why the Chip oriented on her.'

'I know. Yet in her case, it seemed to me –' Darius shook his head. 'I blinded myself.'

'The Chip was set to orient only on those whose impact is minimal. Some may have more impact by dying than by living. But in most cases, an early death best accounts for it. This may usually be by accident or disease, but it is evident that your young woman will soon kill herself.'

'I left her there, to do what she would, alone!' Darius cried, stricken. 'I lost track entirely. I forgot the larger picture.'

'Whereas here she could have been with you, and at least died happy.'

'But she did not believe. She fetched me the key, but thought it was my fantasy. She did not want to commit to one she thought crazy.'

'She surely believes now.'

'Surely now,' Darius agreed, crushed. 'I should have insisted – but when I knew I could not marry her –'

'Cyngs of Hlahtar do not remain functional indefinitely. You might have married her when you gave up the post.'

'I was a fool,' Darius said.

'Will you now settle to the normal course?'

Darius thought of marrying a woman he did not love, instead of Colene. 'I can not.'

'Or try the Chip again?'

He thought of searching for another woman of a suitable nature to love and marry. 'I can not.'

'Then it appears we have a problem.'

'There must be another way!' Darius exclaimed. 'I must go to her again! She would come with me, now that she believes.'

'There is a way. But it is fraught with complication and danger.'

Darius grasped at it. 'What way?'

'Before, we set up the simplest connection between realities, as it were a line. It is possible to set up a more complicated connection, if more than one point is established, as it were a plane. The line could be flung out and recalled only once, but the plane would be more durable.'

'A Virtual Mode!' Darius breathed.

'A what?'

'A temporary Mode that crosses other Modes, like a block of mica sliced crosswise. It would be possible to walk from one part to another, from this Mode to her Mode.'

'I had not pictured it that way, but it is true. However you picture it, it may be the way to do what you desire. However, the complications –'

Darius was abruptly certain. 'Describe them.'

'Because it would entail some time away from this Mode, you can not go without finding another Cyng of Hlahtar to serve in your stead, at least temporarily. One as competent as you.'

'There is none!'

'Not among those who have not yet served.'

Now Darius understood his reference. 'A retired Hlahtar? But none of them would serve again!'

'Not unless the inducement were considerable.'

'What possible inducement could there be? They have wealth and power and respect already; they need nothing. None would wish to suffer the agonies of depletion and wife discarding again.'

'You might inquire.'

'And if I can get one to serve, you will set up the Virtual Mode?'

'After this warning: no person who has gone this route has returned. We do not know whether each has found what he sought and been satisfied, or has died. We know nothing, except that we shall wait with no expectation for your return.'

That was why another Hlahtar had to serve in his stead.

Darius was at the moment poorly acclimated to his native Mode, having been so long unable to do any magic, but he did not wait. He did not know how long Colene would linger before letting the rest of her blood drain away.

He walked into the forest and found several twigs and bits of vine. He bound these together into a crude man-figure. Then he pulled out five hairs from his head and tucked them into the two legs, two arms, and one head of the figurine. Now he had made an icon of himself. It was crude, but it should do.

He touched his tongue to it, anointing it with his saliva. Now it was twice tuned to him, to his solid and his liquid. All it required was his air.

He breathed on it. 'You are the icon of the Cyng of Hlahtar,' he murmured, activating it and tuning it in. Then he set it on the ground and marked a circle around it. He also marked several irregular shapes, and a wavy line. 'You are here, among these trees, and near this river.' He marked a square a short distance away, with several points beside it. 'The Castle of Hlahtar is there, beside the mountains.' Then he jumped the figure from the circle to the edge of the square.

The world around him wrenched. He caught his balance, almost falling. Yes, he was clumsy after the layoff! But he was here before his castle, having conjured himself here by the use of sympathetic magic. It was good to be able to travel normally again!

He lifted the icon to his mouth. 'You are inert,' he breathed on it. It wouldn't do to carry an active personal icon around with him, its feedback from his motions interfering with his activities! He put it in his pocket – and realized that he was not in his normal attire, but in the odd clothing of Colene's Mode. It was a good thing he had decided to come home before visiting the former Hlahtars!

A maid spied him and shrieked. 'A strange man-form!' she cried.

'No, a familiar one, in strange attire,' he called. 'You know me, Ella!'

She shrieked again. 'It's the Cyng!' She ran out to come to him, her breasts bobbing, and flung herself into his arms. 'Did you find a wife?'

'Not exactly.'

'Oh, too bad! Then you must settle for me in your bed a while longer.'

'That is no chore,' he said, patting her shapely derriere.

Indeed, it was late, and he needed to rest. He would have to wait until tomorrow to visit the retired Cyngs.

* * *

That night, after celebrating his return with a minor feast, he came to his bed. Ella was there, moving over so he could have the spot she had warmed for him. She had always been thoughtful in such little ways, and often forgetful in big ways. She was cheerful, buxom and pretty, but not phenomenally smart, and she had not the slightest ability to multiply joy. Therefore she would never be other than a servant and in due course a servant's wife. She could be very pleasant as a nocturnal companion.

But tonight he found himself unmoved. 'Please, do not expect more of me than sleep,' he said.

'You are annoyed with me?' she asked, hurt.

'No, Ella, merely indisposed.'

'Why?' This was not a proper question, but part of her delight was her social naivete.

'I have another woman on my mind.'

'Who?'

'The one I wished to marry. But I could not.'

'Oh. Why not?'

'Because she is depressive.'

'But you could have her in bed as a servant, same as me.'

'Somehow I forgot that. I wanted to marry her.'

'Well, you could, if you weren't Cyng.'

It was a foolish statement, readily dismissed. But somehow it struck home. *If he were not Cyng of Hlahtar.*

But he could not just step down. He was the only one who could serve the post with the necessary expertise. Except for the former Cyngs, who would not resume the post any longer than absolutely necessary. If he could step down, without having completed his term, he would be no better than a servant himself, and Colene might not have liked that. No, the only way was to complete his term and retire; then he could have the blessing of marriage for love and permanence.

But if he could use the Virtual Mode to find Colene, and bring her back, and keep her here in servant status until he retired, then he could marry her, and their love would never have been sacrificed. Colene had said she would be willing to endure something of the kind; he just hadn't quite listened.

It was feasible. He just had to get her back.

'Thank you, Ella,' he said, and kissed her.

'Oooo,' she exclaimed, thrilled to have pleased him. She clasped him to her, and didn't mind that all he did was fall asleep.

In the morning he used one of his established icons to travel to the castle of the Cyng of Hlahtar who had preceded him. This was Kublai, a huge red-bearded man. The man's dais was extremely high, so that the trees on it could feed from the higher level, before other plants depleted the nutrients. As a result, the trees were impressive, their trunks brilliant green and their foliage extensive.

Darius stood at the edge of the dais, in the region reserved for visitors. 'I am Darius,' he said. 'Cyng of Hlahtar, come for a dealing.' Again he remembered Colene, who had spoken of dealing for the Mode key. She had done so much for him, considering her unbelief – and he had done nothing for her.

Kublai appeared. 'Welcome, Darius! Come into my house!'

With that invitation, Darius stepped out of the visitors' area and walked the path to the castle. Had he tried to do it uninvited, he would have invoked the dais defenses, which could be of any nature. He would not have attempted to breach courtesy even if prepared for the defenses; a man's castle was his home.

Kublai's young and pretty wife served them condensed cloudfruit while they talked. Her name was Koren. She was evidently happy; there had been no depletion of her joy. That was the delight of retirement. Gazing at her, Darius knew his mission here was lost; Kublai would not give up his love-marriage to resume the post.

'News has spread of your concern,' Kublai said. 'Not widely, but I believe I know how you feel.'

'Surely you do!' Darius agreed. 'I have divorced my second wife, and she was a good woman, and loyal. I could have loved her, but never dared.'

'I divorced ten,' Kublai said. 'Each one was painful. Some I did love. But it was a great relief when you came of age and displaced me.'

'I did not truly appreciate the onus, until I saw my first wife depleted,' Darius said. 'We had known it would happen from the start, and there was no blame, no rancor. But her joy was gone, and I think even now she can not take pleasure in the good life she has as a retired wife.'

'She will recover her joy in time,' Kublai said. 'She may remarry a normal man, and have offspring. Several of mine did.'

'But the flower of her youth will be gone in depression.'

'It is an unkind price,' Kublai agreed.

'I think this is hopeless, but I must ask,' Darius said. 'I can not allow any person to take my place who can not perform as well as I would. Only former Cyngs of Hlahtar can do that.'

'Tell me of the need that brings you to this pass.'

Darius described his visit to the other Mode, and his encounter with Colene. 'I hoped she would be a multiplier,' he said. 'The Chip was tuned to such. But she was depressive. She would have multiplied a negative balance.'

'But you love her,' Kublai said.

'I love her. I thought it was just my expectation, and would fade when I realized that I was mistaken about her. But I hadn't realized that she was doomed to die. Here, at least, perhaps she could live. If not, at least we could try for some happiness before it happened. Pwer says he can institute a Virtual Mode that will enable me to seek her. Perhaps I can bring her here, and if it is suicide she contemplates, she may postpone it while we love. But –'

'But you need a substitute for the post.'

'That is the case. So I come to inquire whether there is anything I can offer you that would incline you to do this for me, and I fear there is not.'

Kublai nodded. 'I am in a position to know exactly how much you are asking of me. Not only would I have to resume the burden of Hlahtar, I would have to divorce my lovely love-wife Koren and marry another for other than love. That is not a thing I would do lightly.'

'You would risk much, while I would have no guarantee of accomplishing my mission.'

'You would have no guarantee of surviving yourself!' Kublai

said. 'I well might be stuck with a full term, until some other prospect matured. That might be a decade!'

'And even if I succeed, and find her, and bring her back here safely, I will not be able to marry her – unless there is someone else to assume the post,' Darius said. 'So I can not even promise that your loss would be my gain; probably I would gain less than you lost, even with full success.'

'You are candid.'

'I am desperate. I made a terrible mistake. I will do whatever I must to ameliorate it to the extent I can. Is there a price that will tempt you?'

Kublai was silent. He gazed at Koren. She had of course overheard their conversation, and now stood with tears flowing down her cheeks.

Suddenly Darius understood the significance of those tears. *There was a price!*

'There is a price,' Kublai agreed gravely.

'Tell me.' He did not want to evince unseemly eagerness, but that was what he felt. At the same time he felt guilty, seeing the dawning misery of Kublai's wife. This was the classic Hlahtar trade-off: joy for many at the expense of a few. But in this case it was joy for one at the expense of one: not a suitable ratio.

Kublai glanced at Koren. 'Come here, my love; this is not the disaster you envision; I am not about to cast you aside. This is something it is best that you also know.'

She went to him and cast herself into his arms, burying her face in his shoulder. He looked at Darius over her shoulder, holding her, stroking her lustrous black hair as he talked.

'When I was young, I encountered a woman. She called herself Prima. I was attracted to her not for her beauty or personality, for she was not remarkable in these respects, but for her ability to multiply. Her power was on a par with my own –'

'With yours?' Darius asked, startled. 'But no woman –'

Kublai smiled. 'In general, women are not as capable as men in this respect, so that while a man may multiply by a factor of a thousand, a woman may do it by a factor of three. But there is no absolute limitation. It may be that women would be as capable as men, were this encouraged in our culture. Certainly Prima was in this respect. She was fiercely independent and assertive, which of course did not endear her to others. She wanted to be the Cyng of Hlahtar, but of course this was not allowed. When I appeared, she asked me why I should assume the post simply because I was male, my talent being no greater than hers. I had not before considered the matter, but I was persuaded by her, and agreed that it was not right. Indeed, I came to love her, and she loved me, for we were one in our ability.

'We went to the council of Cyngs and asked that she be allowed to assume the post. I agreed to marry her and support her in that post, for my talent feeding into hers would make us the most effective and enduring Hlahtar our Mode has known. But they would not allow a woman to be dominant.

'Then we asked whether we could assume the post as co-equals, taking turns being the lead, one supporting the other. But they would not allow this either. They would allow only my own assumption of the post. I could marry her, but she would be only my wife, supporting me. She would never be Cyng herself.

'Neither of us was willing to do that, at this point. We discussed the matter at length, and finally she decided to explore the realms of the Chips. So the Cyng of Pwer set up what you have termed a Virtual Mode, and she went there to seek some suitable situation. Perhaps there was a realm in which women were equal to men, and she could assume the post there without quarrel, and they would appreciate what she was able to do for them.

'So Prima departed, and I became Hlahtar. We agreed that if she did not find her situation, and returned, she would marry me and accept secondary status. I hoped privately that this would be the case, for I could ask no better support than hers. But she had to do it of her own will.' Kublai paused.

'And she never returned,' Darius said.

'She never returned,' Kublai agreed. 'I married ten wives in succession, depleting each, and retired when you appeared. Now I have love, and it is sweet.' He patted Koren's shoulder. 'But always I have wondered what became of Prima. Did she find her situation, or did she die, or is she still searching? My curiosity has become overwhelming. But I lack the incentive to explore the alternate realms myself, now that I have a good life here. So I would ask two things of you: first, that you seek Prima, or news of her, so that I may finally know the truth. If you should find her, and she is ready to return, bring her back. If you did that, I would be happy to maintain the post indefinitely, for with her support it would represent no burden.'

'If you enabled me to search for my love, and bring her back, I would be glad to search also for yours, and bring her back too,' Darius said. 'Once I know the way, any who are with me can come along.'

'But you will cast me aside!' Kublai's wife protested, her voice buried in his shoulder.

'No, my love,' he said reassuringly. 'I would have to divorce you and keep you as my love companion, but that would be little other than a matter of legality. You would remain my love, as you are now. What I felt for Prima has faded in twenty years, and certainly she is no longer young, and never was she winsome. It would be a business relationship, based on my respect for her talent, and the enormous power that talent would provide me. You would remain my love, and you would not be depleted.'

'I still would rather be your wife,' she said.

'The chances are that Darius will return without her,' Kublai said. 'Then he will resume the post, and I will remarry you. I think this is a fair gamble.'

'But you mentioned two things you would ask of me,' Darius said. The second was likely to be the crusher.

'The second is both larger and perhaps easier,' Kublai said. 'I have developed a curiosity not only about Prima's situation, but about the alternate realms themselves. I wish to know the nature of ultimate reality. I would ask you to explore these alternate realms, seeking to understand them, and to formulate and test an explanation for the way things are. Who made the Chips and left them here? Who made it possible for Modes to be crossed? Why? I would like, before I die, to have that explanation.'

'But my mind may not be good enough to compass such

knowledge,' Darius protested. 'I hardly understand the one other Mode I have seen, and I did not understand the nature of the young woman I came to love there.'

'Yet you would make the effort, and tell me all you learn. It might be considerable, and certainly it would be far more than I know now – discovered at no risk to me.'

'But no one has returned!' Darius pointed out. 'I may be unable to honor any part of such an agreement.'

'That is why I ask for two favors: the news on Prima, and the nature of the Modes. If I win, I win all that I have wanted to know. If I lose, I am Cyng until another suitable prospect appears. I am experienced; it is not the worst of fates. In fact, I find myself bored with retirement. Oh, not with you, my dear,' he added quickly as his wife lifted her head. 'You are my perpetual delight! But the rest of it – there is only so much ease and luxury a man can tolerate. I think I am ready to resume useful activity – and keep my love with me.'

She settled back, mollified.

'I can only agree,' Darius said. 'If you will take my place, I will seek what you wish.'

In this manner it was agreed. Darius and Kublai had merged their hopes, and it would be done.

It took time to set up the Virtual Mode and to arrange for the temporary resumption of the post by Kublai. Darius had to do a tour, for the need was growing. The public had to be served.

But he lacked a wife. He did not want to marry for just one tour, but it would not be wise to deplete himself immediately before embarking on the treacherous journey that was the Virtual Mode. What was he to do?

Kublai came up with the answer. 'Borrow Koren.'

'What?'

'My wife Koren. She has it in her pretty head that she wants to remain married to me, even as I resume the post. This is foolish.'

'Of course it is! But –'

'I need to persuade her to step down, and to allow me to marry a woman suitable for that office. But I do not wish to hurt or offend her. However, if she went with you on the tour,

81

she would quickly learn the cost, and I think that would be more persuasive than anything I could say.'

'Surely it would!' Darius agreed. 'But the intimacy of the borrowing –'

'I would rather have you do it, than do it to her myself. I prefer to convince her without instituting that barrier between us.'

'But she is your wife!' Darius said, at a loss.

'Who has never felt my power. Let her feel yours. By the time the tour is done, she will have had enough.'

The man did know what he was suggesting. Reluctantly, Darius agreed.

So it was that Koren came to his castle as ad-hoc wife. She made it quite plain that there was no private aspect to the relationship. She was here because Kublai had asked her to be, and she was certain that her mind would be changed not one iota by this experience. She expected to prove herself to her husband.

'I understand your reticence,' Darius said. 'I will honor your privacy in all things, but when the time of multiplication comes, I shall have to embrace you closely and publicly. You will find it a unique experience.'

'I doubt it,' she said coldly. 'If you touch me anywhere else, I will slap you.'

Yes, she did not understand. She would learn a great deal in the next day.

Sexual energy was part of what enabled multiplication, and it was customary for the Cyng to indulge in it with his wife the night before a tour. This was out of the question with Koren, but he did need to do it with someone. If only Colene had returned with him! If only he had understood all of what was at stake, and had insisted that she come here!

So that night he used a device that he feared would shame him if he thought about it: he closed his eyes and visualized Ella as Colene. Then he was most passionate with her. She was quite pleased.

In the morning they set out on the tour. Darius, Koren, a comedian, a props man and the castle's regular conjurer

82

stepped onto a large disk, and the conjurer lifted a small disk containing a hair from each of them and activated it. They moved upward as the miniature disk did, floating from the castle court until they were high above the dais. Then the conjurer moved the little disk south toward the Model of a castle, and the big disk zoomed in that direction.

It was routine, but Darius' awareness of the other Mode remained, and he continued to appreciate how novel this would seem to Colene. She had told him that her people had huge flying machines, but she didn't believe in magic, so this flying disk would surprise her. Also, the landscape below was beautiful. The rugged crevices of the land formed patterns of ridges, their crystals scintillating, so that it was possible to see circles, triangles, squares, pentagons and hexagons forming and dissipating as they moved across. Some crystals sent up beams of reflected light that formed three-dimensional figures, the green beams intersecting the red beams and yellow beams, the whole being bathed by diffused light from other crystals. It might be impossible to walk across such terrain, but it was lovely to float across.

The sky, too, was a continuing pleasure. They floated around, above and below the colored clouds, swerving as necessary, and these too were beautiful. Some had patterns on their surfaces, projected from the crystals, and the patterns changed as the perspective did. Yes, Colene would love this, and he would do his best to bring her here and show it to her. If only he had thought it properly through before, and brought her with him despite her nature and her doubt!

Then they came into sight of a village dais, much larger than those for the castles or solitary trees. Here there were thousands of villagers, and around it were the lesser platforms where gardens flourished. At such enclaves the fundamental supplies of the realm were grown and made. A potato, for example, did not just appear when conjured; it was grown and saved, and so was ready for conjuration at need. The children of Cyngs sometimes believed that food came into existence when summoned, but the children of peasants well understood the labors of production.

At locations like these the animals were also raised: cows

to produce milk, chickens to produce eggs, and so on. There were grazing dais, and sections where the crystals of the nether terrain were less prominent, so that vegetation could grow and creatures could forage. But people had to watch over these animals, and keep them safe from predators. There were also artisans of many types: woodworkers, metalworkers, stoneworkers, clothworkers and on. All laboring patiently for their sustenance. No, nothing was free; at every stage there had to be the hands of dedicated men and women. Without such workers, the fine society of mankind would not be possible.

These were the folk who needed joy, for their lives did not provide great amounts of it naturally. Each Cyng was granted a good life, but each Cyng repaid it with the unique service which was the speciality of his post. Thus the society was interactive, but the lives of Cyngs were better than most.

Their disk landed. Immediately the group stepped off and proceeded to the setting up. Soon there was a little stage, and the villagers were seated around it in concentric circular rows. The whole village assembled; every member of it was eager for joy.

The comedian took a prop and went into his act. He pranced, he twirled, he made grotesque faces. The villagers watched passively. They were not much entertained. This was exactly according to expectation; had they reacted positively, it would have been an indication that their need was not sufficient to warrant this presentation.

Then Darius stepped to the center of the stage. There was a hush of expectation. He turned and gestured to Koren.

The woman came up on the stage. No one introduced her; the villagers were allowed to assume that she was his wife. The wives of Cyngs of Hlahtar changed often, so her newness here did not excite suspicion. She was young, she was beautiful, and she came when called: that was evidence enough.

Koren came to stand immediately before Darius. She was in a glossy black dress that matched her hair, so that it was hard to tell where one left off and the other began. The upper portion flared so as to conceal the shape of her bosom, and the nether portion spread out similarly to hide her legs, in the

84

decorous manner, but it was not possible to completely mask her beauty.

Darius embraced her. He drew her in very close, so that the full length of her body was tight against his own. She was stiff, not liking this, thinking that he was being too familiar. She averted her face, and kept her arms immobile at her sides. But only with close contact could he exert his power efficiently; the effect diminished with distance, causing needless waste.

Then he drew from her. Her vitality came into his body, measure by measure in its measureless fashion, strengthening him while depleting her. It was not a large transfer, but it was significant.

She stood without moving, evidently uncertain what she was experiencing. Then she tried to struggle, but her determination was weak, being the first thing tapped. Her head snapped around; her eyes came to stare into his with the wonder and horror of a captive animal. She would have felt better giving a quantity of the blood of her body. She sank into herself, her vitality waning. She was helpless. Left to her own devices at this moment, she would soon lie down and die, having no further joy of life. She was depleted.

Darius let her go, and turned. He was flush with Koren's joy, taken from her. Then he fed it out to the multitude. It magnified enormously as it extended from him and bathed every seated peasant. Every man, woman and child received almost as much joy as Koren had lost.

Koren herself received a similar amount, for she was now among the recipients. But her joy was less than it had been, by that small margin, for the multiplying was like the level of water: it might spread to many, but would never exceed the level of its source. She had lost most of her joy, and had most of that loss restored, but that remaining level was lower. Only time would make up that small loss, and she would lose more before she could get that time.

The comedian stepped out again, capering, and now the peasants laughed. Their joy had been lifted to a height not recently experienced. Now they were well satisfied with their lot, and ready to enjoy the festivities.

Darius waved to them, and they cheered him lustily. Then

85

he took Koren by the hand and led her to the traveling disk. She came without resistance, shaken by her recent experience. Her level of joy was now the same as that of the peasants, but to her it seemed inadequate. She had known better; they had not. She had also suffered the shock of sudden depletion, as they had not; their depletion was gradual, as they went about their dull business. She had perspective.

The party gathered on the disk, and the conjurer lifted it, using his small icon-disk. The power for this came from the Cyng of Pwer, who drew it from the Modes and sent it out to be used as needed. The magic was used only to control it; the power itself was physical, like the things grown and made by the peasants.

They floated to the next village, where they repeated the process. This time Koren was not stiff but was afraid when he embraced her, and familiarity did not seem to make her more comfortable with the process. She looked less beautiful than before, even when most of her joy had been restored. Something new and awful had been introduced to her experience. She was coming to understand why her husband believed that love and marriage were incompatible, with a Cyng of Hlahtar.

They served ten villages on this tour, catching up on those that most needed joy. In a few days there would be another tour, to other villages. The process was continuous, for by the time every village had been served, the first village needed to be served again. The break Darius had taken had allowed many villages to get behind, and a faster schedule would be necessary to restore them.

At last they floated home. Now Darius spoke to Koren. 'This is what your husband seeks to spare you. You have lost only about a tenth of your joy this day, but before you can recover that, there will be another tour, and another. In two years, perhaps less, you will be depleted to the extent that it is no longer safe to draw from you, and you will have to be set aside for a fresher woman. Of course I hope to return long before that time, and resume the post. But your love will be better if you become his love-servant instead, for that period.'

She stared back at him with hopeless hate. Yes, now she

understood. How much better for her to hate Darius, than to hate her husband!

His thoughts turned to Colene. She, too, did not understand. She thought love could conquer all. She had been angry when he saw the impossibility of marrying her. Had the transfer of joy been possible in her Mode, he could have demonstrated; then she would have known. As Koren now knew.

The Chip was ready. It would institute the Virtual Mode. 'Now you must understand the deviousness of this process,' the Cyng of Pwer said. 'It seems that we are sending out several lines of force, and that those lines will anchor in several other Modes, and fix in place the Virtual Mode. One anchor is here, and another should be at the site of the girl you encountered – but only if she catches on to it. If she does not, some other person may do so, fixing the Mode, but your girl will not be in that Mode.'

'Colene may not be there?' Darius asked, appalled.

'We can send the line past her, but we can not make her take it. You can judge better than I how likely she is to take it.'

'She has to take it!' But there was a troubling doubt there.

'And if she does take it, that anchors only two points. Three more are required, because –'

'Because it takes five points to fix a four dimensional Mode,' Darius said.

'Ah, I see you understand! But we have no control at all over those remaining three. They can be anywhere, and the Virtual Mode may be strange indeed.'

'At least they will all be human.'

Pwer frowned. 'Not necessarily. I have made the setting sapience rather than humanity. Humanity can include anything from our level to complete primitives. With sapience, at least there will in all cases be minds to which you can relate. We hope they will be human.'

Darius hoped so too! 'I am ready,' he said. He had a new pack of supplies, and this time he had something he had not thought to take before: a weapon. It was a primitive sword, which did not require any spell for its effect. It had a sharp point and a sharp edge. He was not proficient in its use, but was satisfied that it would be effective against either animals or unarmed attackers, such as the young men who had attacked him without provocation in Colene's Mode. He also had primitive tools for cutting wood, breaking stone or making fire. In fact he had the little box of 'matches' Colene had given him. One thing he had learned: not to depend on magic in that realm!

'I hope to return soon,' he said. 'But if I do not, I thank you for enabling me to make this quest.'

'This time I can not bring you back by orienting on a signal key,' Pwer reminded him grimly. 'You must return by yourself. If you do not return soon, you will gradually lose contact, until finally you will be unable. Do not leave any of your things behind; only you can carry them across the boundaries of the Modes. The Virtual Mode will remain anchored until you come here and touch the anchor-place and will it to let go. The Mode exists on its own; we are merely catching an aspect of it and fixing it in place for a time.'

'Fix it now,' Darius said, stepping into the marked circle. Pwer was full of cautions, but not all of what he said was believable.

The Cyng of Pwer nodded. He lifted his hand, invoking the necessary spell.

Something changed.

5

SEQIRO

Colene remained in a daze. *He had been right!* Darius really *was* from a far Kingdom of Laughter where magic worked. She had not believed, and so had thrown away her chance for happiness.

Yet he had changed his mind, too. He had thought she was full of joy, and had recoiled when she told him the truth. He had wanted only one thing from her, and that had been not her body but her happiness. She had been happy with him; without him she was the same old suicidal shell.

Now she was paging through her Journal, which she kept under lock and key here in Dogwood Bumshed, trying to distract her mind from her present distress by contemplating her past distress. She called it a Journal and not a diary, because 'diary' sounded like 'diarrhea' and she was not about to put her sanitary thoughts in an unsanitary place like that. She made her entries in the form of letters to her friend Maresy, who was actually an imaginary horse. Colene had never had a horse, but always wanted one, not just to ride, but to be her understanding companion. People were not necessarily fit to understand, but Maresy had more than human fathoming. Maresy was a most unusual animal.

TO: Maresy Doats
North Forty Pasture
Summerland, OK, 73500

Dear Maresy,
My friend Eney Locke did the craziest thing last night! She was at this party, and she wandered out on a balcony and gazed down into the concrete alley one floor down, thinking her usual dark thoughts. A boy came out, someone she knew mostly casually, a decent type. He said 'Oh, are you looking for the way out?' and she said 'Yes, but it's not far enough.' Then she realized that she had spoken aloud, and he realized that she was neither lost nor joking. He was appalled. 'Eney – you mean you're –?' he asked. And she, faced with this excellent chance to confess her secret and perhaps have some sympathy, blew it. 'I was joking!' she snapped, and pushed on past him, back into the party where everyone was drunk and happy.

The key to this was that Colene spelled backward was Eneloc, broken in two with letters added for camouflage: Eney Locke. She was talking about herself, but not directly, in case someone should get at her Journal before she had a chance to destroy it. She had the need to talk to someone, a desperate need, but obviously her parents were out, and she couldn't afford to trust anyone she knew at school. Once she had made the mistake of trusting a friend at camp. Never again! But Maresy was the epitome of equine discretion, partly because she could not speak in any human language. That did not mean that Maresy could not communicate, just that it required special comprehension to know what was on her mind. A horse could say a lot just in the orientation of her ears.

Actually, the address was fake. Maresy lived only in her mind. So she had made up a place for the horse to live, and used her own zip code rounded off to the nearest even hundred. As far as she knew, there was no such number, which was fine. She was never actually going to mail any of those letters. For one thing, Maresy didn't live where she seemed; that OK in her address stood for Okay. She was always Okay.

There were boxes in the margins of the Journal. They weren't

90

exactly code; it was just that she drew them when she was disturbed, and the more disturbed she was, the more numerous and elaborate those little boxes became. She didn't need to read the actual entries to know how she had felt when making them; the boxes told. Sometimes there were only one or two plain cubes; sometimes there was an elaborate network of boxes that completely surrounded the text. Sometimes they resembled stalls for Maresy, though the truth was that Maresy was a free horse, unbridled, unsaddled, and unstalled. Maresy was as free as Colene was bound.

She turned to the last entry she had made. It was the day before she had found Darius in the ditch. It was a box done in the shape of an optical illusion, with three projections that weren't actually there when traced back to their sources; one was really the space between the other two. Variations on the figure were common; many people were intrigued by it. She thought the original was like a tuning fork, but it didn't matter. The point was, this was her. She looked just exactly like a girl, but when the lines were traced, there was nothing; she was a girl-shaped space between others, and if the others went away, she would cease to appear to exist. She had really been twisted up, then. The day before her adventure had begun.

But from the moment she spied Darius, she had neither written to Maresy nor scratched her wrists. Not till she freaked out Biff with a wholesale slash. No boxes, either. Her inner life had changed completely.

Now she was back in her own reality, as it were. She started to draw a box, and watched it take form as if of its own volition. It looked like a cross between a prison cell and an execution platform.

'Oh, Maresy, I need you now!' she breathed. 'What am I to do? I didn't trust the man I loved, and now I am alone.'

But that wasn't quite true. She had trusted Darius; she just hadn't believed him. She had been willing to sleep practically naked in his arms, but not to stand with him when he tried to go home. Maybe he had seen that, and made it easier for her by pretending she was unsuitable for him.

Pretending? Why should he pretend? He hadn't pretended about anything else. He had told her where he came from though he knew she didn't believe him. He had made her cover her crotch, because blue jeans didn't do the job to his satisfaction. He had learned enough of her language to talk with her, and had shown how well he understood what she told him. He had been his own man throughout, despite the indignities of being confined to the shed and having to use the pot. He had embraced her nightly without even trying to take any advantage of her. In fact, he had refused sex with her when she offered it. Pretend? He had never pretended! He had said she was unsuitable because that was exactly what she was. She was fourteen years old and suicidal. How could she ever have thought he would want to marry her?

Because he had told her he did. He had always told her the truth, and now she knew that even the least believable part of it had been valid. So he had been willing to marry her, until he learned that she was depressive. He had to have joy, to take and magnify and spread about. That was her most awful liability. She could make others laugh by her cutting humor, but if they had been able to read her inner nature, they would have been appalled. Darius would have read it, in his realm. So he had done what he had to do, and had been kind to her, he thought, letting her go.

'Oh Darius!' she cried, grief-smitten. 'I would have been satisfied to go with you, as your servant or your slave, just to be near you. If only I had believed! Now I have gotten what I deserved. I hope you find a woman you can marry.' But that last was insincere. Colene had wanted to be his wife. Deep-down, she didn't want him to be satisfied with any other woman. Oh, she wanted him to be happy, but not as happy as he might have been with her. And to know it.

She closed her Journal and locked it away. She knew what she had to do. There was a good knife in the kitchen, maybe not as sharp as Slick's razor, but it would do the job. No more fooling around with compass points.

She went to the house. But her mother was in the kitchen and she couldn't get the knife. Anyway, she hadn't figured out the right place to do it. She didn't want to splash blood all over Bumshed, for it didn't deserve to be soiled that way. It wouldn't be safe in her room in the house; her parents hardly ever went there, except those few times when she especially didn't want them to. They had some kind of parental radar that made them home in at the exact worst times. Outside wasn't good; someone would be sure to see her. So she would have to figure out a place first; then she could take the knife there and do it quickly.

There was nothing to do except wrap up her homework, so that no one would be suspicious. She would go to school as usual Monday, and keep her eye out for a suitable place. She would certainly find it, and then she would act.

Monday she found herself in the bathroom, contemplating her scarred wrist. But she didn't touch it. She had been playing with suicide, before; this time she would do it right. That meant the right place and the right knife. She had seen how easy it was with the sharp razor; she could bleed herself out quickly by slashing both arms similarly. Once she decided on the place that was right. Where she could do it cleanly, and not be discovered until long after she was dead. She had to guarantee that she would not wake up in a hospital, to the shame of failure. Boys had it easy; they used guns, which were easy, quick and sure. But she didn't know a thing about guns; they frightened her. It had to be by a knife, so the blood could flow gently and prettily.

No place seemed right. Finally, Tuesday night, she did something foolish: she sneaked out to Bumshed in her nightie. She made a mound of books and a pillow, pretending it was Darius, and lay next to him in the darkness. 'Take me now,' she breathed to the quiet form, spreading her legs and breathing heavily. 'Do anything you want to do.' Of course he did not, but that did not interfere with the fancy; Darius would not have done it anyway.

By morning she had come to three conclusions. First, she wasn't fooling herself; she knew there was no man there. So this was pointless. Second, it was too darned cold out here alone, and lonely too. Third, *this* was the place she had been looking for. Here where she had known him, and brief happiness. She could make it sanitary by having plenty of basins to catch the blood, and she could empty them out as long as she was able. She could make a small hole beside Dogwood and pour it carefully in and cover it up; not only would it be practically untraceable, it would fertilize the tree. She liked the idea of her decorative little tree being nourished by her blood. When she was unable to take out the basin, there might not be enough blood left in her to overflow, so it would be all right. They would find her pale cold body, and a neat brimming basin of blood. That would be nice.

She went to school again Wednesday, concentrating on being absolutely normal. She did not give any of her things away to friends, because that was a recognized tipoff for suicidal intention. She did not mope. She laughed and paid attention in class. As far as she knew, no one had a clue to her plan.

That evening she fetched her favorite belongings and arranged them in a circle in Bumshed. Her ancient Teddy bear, Raggedy Ann doll, her book on odd mating customs of the world, one on exotic computer viruses (for 'safe' computing), her guitar, the picture of Maresy grazing, and the artificial carnation she had worn to the Prom last year. The dance itself had not been great, her date had been gawky, she had been gawky too, being thirteen, but it had become her first significant dance, and now would be her last, so this symbol of it deserved respect. Maybe she would float it in the final basin of blood, her last deliberate act. A white flower on a red background, the opposite of a red rose on a white gown.

Then she fetched the knife.

But as she set up for it, she realized that she had forgotten the most critical thing: the basin. It was too late to fetch it; she would be risking the curiosity of her parents. Dad happened to be home this night, so naturally the two were arguing: 'What's the matter, dear – your paramour have a snit?' 'What do you care, you tipsy lady?' That sort of thing. As it progressed, the language would get less polite, and finally they would come to physical contact and have sex on the floor. They fought verbally, not physically, but the sex was in lieu of hitting, and could get pretty violent. Her mother got bonus points for bitchiness if she made him cheat on his mistress. That made him angry, but the woman was sexiest when bitchiest, and he

94

couldn't resist. Colene hated that scene, but also was morbidly fascinated by it. Maybe if she had taunted Darius as impotent, the way her mother did her father, he would have gotten mad and put it to her hard. That tempted her now, in retrospect, but also repelled her. She did not like anything even hinting of rape. Yet at least she would have *had* him! Maybe then she would have felt obliged to believe him, and would have gone with him to his fabulous land of laughter. So what if she was a stranger there, unable to marry him? It couldn't be worse than what she faced here.

So she had no basin, and was not about to go back to the house for it. What else would serve? She was definitely not going to spill her precious clean blood on the floor!

Her eye fell on the privy pot. Oh, ugh! Yet what else was there? And it had the remnants of *his* substance. That was about as close as any part of her could get to any part of him, now. So it would have to do. What an image for a romantic song: Blood and Feces. A sure hit with the anti-establishment crowd.

She brought the pot and removed the cover. The stink smote her nose. Quickly she covered it again. Maybe she could put a clothespin on her nose, if she had a clothespin. Anything else? She leaned on the board over the pot, and set the knife down on it while she considered.

She concluded that it didn't really matter. She would get used to the smell soon enough. So she sat cross-legged, in her nightie without panties, in a position that would have freaked Darius all the way out to the moon, dear man, drew the pot in to her, nestled it inside her crossed ankles, held her breath, lifted the knife, removed the cover board, leaned over, and paused.

Should she do the left arm first, or the right one? She was right handed, so maybe she should do the right one first, so if her left handed slash was clumsy she could do it again, and again until she had a proper blood flow into the pot. Then she could transfer the knife and do the left one with one excellent slice. Then she could grasp the far rim of the pot, keeping her arms locked in place, and watch the twin blood flows. It would be glorious!

So why was she hesitating? She was sure there was a reason. There always was.

She explored her motives, and found the relevant one. 'Oh, Darius, I don't want to die away from you!' she said. 'I'd so much rather die *with* you!'

She pondered some more, then decided to sleep on it. She could slice herself as well in the morning as at night. Maybe she would have a chance to sneak into the house and get a better basin, after her parents had sex-sotted themselves out and turned in. It was worth a try.

She lay down, shivering in the cold. She wrapped the blankets around and around her, and curled up into an almost fetal ball. She knew she would not sleep, but at least she wouldn't freeze.

She woke shivering, after an interminably restless night. The floor was hard, the air was chill, and the blankets seemed to have holes that exactly matched the path of the draft coming in under the door.

But it was her troubled thoughts that caused the greatest disruption of sleep. She was reviewing her life, trying to total up the credits and the debits, to justify her decision to end it. In snatches of dreams she talked to Maresy:

'Dear Maresy, today I decided to end it. Well actually I decided several days ago, but today was the day to do it. Only I didn't want to use a filthy potty for my blood.'

'You lost your nerve,' Maresy replied.

'No! I just want to do it right!'

'You really don't want to die. You never did.'

'That so, smarty? Then what do I really want to do?'

'You want to love and be loved.'

Maresy was right. She always was. She knew Colene better than Colene knew herself, because she was more objective. Death was merely the most convenient escape from a life without love. That was why she had not been suicidal in the time she had known Darius. She had had love.

Now she had lost that love. Oh, she still had it, in a sense: she definitely still loved him. But he was gone, and he had explained how he couldn't come back, because it had been a random setting. So even if he loved her – and she thought he did – it was no good. They were apart forever.

'Why do you think he loves you?' Maresy asked.

'Because he told me he did.'

'But men lie about that.'

'To get sex from women,' she agreed. 'But he never had sex with me, even when I offered it. So he wasn't saying it for sex. Oh, yes, he did want something from me! He wanted my joy. And I would have given him that, if I had had any to give. So he loved me, but couldn't marry me without destroying me, and he wouldn't do that. I believe him. I believe him. I believe him.'

'So you do love, and you are loved,' Maresy said. 'So why do you want to die?'

That made her ponder for some time. She did have love; why wasn't it enough? 'Because it's apart,' she said at last. 'I want to love and be loved and have it close – like hugging close. Like kissing close. Like sex close. I want to be part of him, and have him be part of me, forever and ever. I want eternal romance.'

'You have foolish juvenile notions. It isn't that way.'

'How do you know?' Colene shot back.

'I know from what you've read. The half-life of romantic love is one and a half years.'

'What do you mean, half-life of love?'

'Remember your physics? Radioactive materials keep losing their radiation, getting less dangerous but never entirely finishing. So you can't say how long they last. But you can say how long it takes for their level of radioactivity to drop to half of what it was. That's their half-life, which may be a fraction of a second, or millions of years. So when it comes to the declining excitement of love, the half-life is eighteen months, on average.'

'I don't believe that! True love is forever!'

'Look at your parents.'

Accurate counterthrust! Where was the romance in her parents' marriage? As far as she knew, there had never been any. There had just been absence and alcohol and occasional bouts of hostile sex. Yet there must once have been love, or else why had they married?

So apply the half-life law. Suppose they had fallen in love, and in six months gotten married. She had been born the following year. Presto: their love had halved by the time she appeared on the scene, and halved again in the next year and a half. How many times had it halved by now? Take her age, fourteen, and add that first year and a half before her birth: fifteen and a half years since their first love. Enough for ten halvings. Plus maybe a quartering, or whatever. So if their love had started at a hundred per cent, it had gone to fifty per cent, then twenty five per cent, then – brother! How low had it sunk by this time?

Her thoughts fuzzed out, but her agile brain kept mulling it over, and in due course she concluded that it was just under one per cent. So what she was seeing now was only a hundredth of what they had started with. So now it was just a shared house, some ugly sex, and a messed-up daughter. Their love-child, as it were. More like a tough-love-child.

'You desire that with Darius?' Maresy inquired alertly.

'It wouldn't be that way with Darius!' she protested. But uncertainty was closing in, like dark fog at dusk. If she could be with Darius, and go to his wonderful Kingdom of Laughter, and everything was just perfect, would the romance be down to one per cent in fifteen years? Would she be an alcoholic and he be having affairs with other women? Would they have a suicidal daughter?

Maresy faded out, for Colene was now absolutely, totally wide awake. Now she knew: it was time to end it. There was no hope for romance, even if it were possible for her to join Darius. So she had lost nothing, really; there had never been anything to make her life worth continuing.

The dirty pot would do. It wasn't as if her life were clean. She was the offspring of a garbage marriage, and faced more garbage if she tried to grow up and get married herself. The whole thing was pointless.

She sat with the pot, uncovered it, bared her arms, and picked up the knife. Now was the time. Two swift, deep slices, then hang on. 'I'll lay me down and bleed a while,' she murmured. 'Then ne'er up again.'

Yet somehow she didn't make the first cut. She shivered

from the cold and the anticipation, and her arms were goosepimply, but she just sat there not doing it. She couldn't quite take that final step. She knew she had been playing at suicide, before; she couldn't bleed to death from the scratch of a compass point. She could have done it from the slash of Slick's razor, but that had been in company; she had known they wouldn't actually let her die. But now it was real, and she just couldn't.

'What a hypocrite I am!' she exclaimed. 'I know what to do, and I'm too cowardly to do it!'

The knife dropped from her hand. She sat there and sobbed. She had come to the final test of her life, and flunked it.

Yet she could not quite give up the death, either. She sat there, congealing with cold, breathing the miasma of the pot. Everything was hopeless! Maybe she would die of the cold, or at least catch pneumonia and expire. Or would that be cheating?

Colene! Wait for me!

She snapped out of her drift. Time had passed, maybe a little, maybe a lot. She must have nodded off, and dreamed.

Yet something had changed. She felt a certain imperative, or potential, or something.

Take hold!

It was Darius! It was no dream. Maybe she was crazy, but she was ready to go for it. If it was to be a one per cent romance fifteen years down the line, so be it, but it was a hundred per cent now, and now was what counted. She would give him everything immediately, before the joy of it could fade.

She reached out with her mind and took hold. She felt something settle into place. That was all.

But she knew reality had changed. It was a Virtual Mode: a ramp spanning the realities from his to hers. Darius was coming for her! If he was crazy, she would be crazy too. Gloriously crazy in love!

What now, of the futility of romance? She didn't care; she was going for it. Because while she was orienting on love, she wasn't orienting on death.

She got up and looked around. Nothing had changed, physically. But this was here, in her reality. It would be different in Darius' reality.

But how was she to get from here to there? Well, if this was a true Virtual Mode, all she had to do was walk there. She would be at one end, he at the other. It should be easy enough to cross the ramp and join him.

Why wait for him to come for her? She had wanted to depart this life. Now she could do it – without killing herself. She would meet him half way.

Still, it might be a fair distance. She should travel prepared. She wasn't sure how far it might seem in miles. If there were an infinite number of realities, was that an infinite number of miles? No, it had to be fewer than that. But she should use her bicycle, just in case.

She gathered up her scattered things, such as the canned food she had bought for Darius to eat. He had used some, but she had continued to bring in more as she scrounged it. Now she would eat it herself, if she had to. She also dressed and packed a change of clothing, though what she had here in Bumshed wasn't exactly clean.

Her bike was leaning against the wall of the shed, under the overhang. It wasn't in top condition, but it was functional. She hadn't ridden it much in the past year, because a bike was really kid stuff, and a teenager was not a kid. But a bicycle was the most efficient mode of transport known to man; a person on a bike used less energy than any walking animal or any traveling machine. So she would be a kid again to travel – so that she could be a woman when she got there.

Hastily assembled, she walked the bike out to the road. It wasn't nearly as late as it had seemed in the shed; actually her watch said eight o'clock. Things were hardly stirring outside. She could get cleanly away before her parents caught on.

That made her pause. How would they react to her disappearance? For she knew she wasn't coming back.

She walked back to the shed. There she dug out a pad of paper and a pencil. DEAR FOLKS: DON'T WORRY; I AM FINE. I JUST HAVE SOMEWHERE TO GO. COLENE

She tore off the sheet and set it on top of the board covering

100

the pot. Eventually someone would look in here, and then the note would be seen. That should be enough. They might put out an alert for her, but she was going where their alert could not reach. As she understood it, the ramp intersected her reality only at this spot; everything else was in other realities, no matter how similar to hers it seemed.

She walked her bike back out to the street, got on it, and started pedaling. Immediately her sense of 'whereto' went wrong. This wasn't the way.

She looped the bike and went the other way. Now it was better. It felt like going uphill, only it wasn't physical and it wasn't hard. It was like orienting on a distant light.

Actually the light was a little to the side; the street wasn't going in quite the right direction. But neither were the intersecting streets. She had to turn and go down one, then turn again.

Then she reached a region where there weren't cross streets, and had to keep going straight. Gradually her awareness of the proper direction faded. This was no good; it seemed that she had to stay pretty close to the center of the ramp, or she lost it.

Finally there was an intersection, and she turned and rode at right angles. Before long she felt it: the attuning. Good; that meant that she didn't have to stay on it all the time; she could detour and pick it up later. She might have to do S shaped figures, crossing and recrossing the ramp, but it did give her more freedom.

But was she getting anywhere? Everything looked ordinary, not magical. She had now biked more than a mile. That wasn't far, but how far would it be before something changed? She just didn't know.

Well, she would give it a real try regardless. After all, she was skipping school, and that would get her in trouble if they caught her. She had to get far enough to be sure they couldn't.

She came to a red light, and stopped. She knew that the rules of the road applied to cyclists the same as cars, and she obeyed them scrupulously. To do otherwise was dangerous. It was ironic that people who wanted to live were suicidally careless about such rules, while she who was suicidal was careful. But she knew how close death was. She didn't want her blood splatted across the busy highway; she wanted it handled neatly.

She saw a car going through the intersection. It was a limousine. At the wheel was a seedy looking man; in back was a well manicured dog, sitting up high as if the car belonged to it. That made her smile.

Then the light changed to blue, and she pedaled across. She was entering a parklike section, with trees growing fairly near the pavement. She liked that. She didn't remember any park, here; in fact she didn't remember this neighborhood at all, now that she actually looked at something other than the road in front of her, but that was all right, since she wouldn't be back.

Blue?

She skewed to a stop. Then she turned and stared back, expecting to correct the glitch in her memory.

No, the green light was blue.

She resumed travel. She had never seen a blue GO light before, but that didn't mean they didn't exist. Maybe it was a faulty lens, or maybe somebody had sprayed blue paint on it.

But all the lights thereafter were blue too. Soon the red lenses turned to orange. The color scheme was definitely different!

Move over, human!

Startled, Colene veered off the road. A car zoomed by, with another dog sitting up in the rear. It was as if the dog had yelled at her!

But the yell had been in her mind.

Colene stopped under a tree near another intersection and pondered. Blue traffic lights. Dogs being chauffeured. Telepathy. Was she imagining things, or was reality changing?

A car slowed and stopped near her. The black and white head of a Dalmatian dog poked out of the rear window. *Are you lost, human girl?*

'No, thank you,' she said before she could think. 'Just resting.'

Best get on to your obedience school, the thought came. Then the dog's head withdrew, the window closed, and the car nudged back onto the road and accelerated.

There was no doubt now! Telepathic dogs! 'I don't think we're in Oklahoma any more, Tonto,' she murmured, taking brief pleasure in mixing her references.

Heartened but also nervous, she resumed travel. If this was a region where dogs governed people, it wasn't what she was looking for. Evidently Darius lived somewhere beyond this. She had somehow thought the ramp would proceed straight from her place to his, but of course that wasn't necessarily so. There could be any number of different realities between, and one with telepathic dogs was evidently among them.

The dog had stopped to check on her, as a person might when seeing a lost puppy. The dogs were evidently in charge here, using human beings as drivers. And people were sent to obedience schools? She had better move on through!

But it was good to have this assurance that the Virtual Mode was in place. She had wanted to die, then had loved Darius, then had lost him and wanted to die again, and now was on her way to find him again. Girl meets man, girl loses man, girl regains man: standard story, happy ending. And if she ran afoul of that one per cent factor, fifteen years down the line, well, at least she'd have the pleasure of wearing out the romance the hard way: by loving him to pieces.

The surface of the road changed. Now it was rougher, and the cars had wheels that were more like caterpillar treads. And the animals riding in them were no longer dogs, but cats – big ones.

She paused at another intersection, waiting for the traffic to clear. Almost all of the vehicles were traveling at right angles to her route, which was maybe just as well. She had heard a couple coming up behind her, but they seemed to have turned off before reaching her.

A car came toward her, slowing. A tiger bounded out. *You will make a fine meal, tender girl!*

Terrified, Colene pedaled desperately, bumping her bike over the road-ground. The tiger leaped – and disappeared before reaching her.

What had happened? Had someone vaporized it? No, there

had seemed to be no violence, other than that being practiced by the tiger. It had just phased out.

She had ridden into another reality, where the tiger wasn't after her! It looked much the same, but was different. Her ramp evidently made the terrain of the realities merge smoothly, so she could travel along it, but the inhabitants were not continuous in the same way. That was probably just as well; otherwise there might have been an endless chain of Colenes setting out on their bicycles, all heading for the same set of Dariuses. One of each was enough!

Now she knew two more things: there was direct danger to herself in these realities, and she could get out of it by moving quickly forward. But the farther she moved, the stranger things were becoming. She could get into trouble before she knew it, and be stuck. If that tiger had caught her –

She delved into her pack and brought out the kitchen knife. Now it was not to cut her arms, but to protect her! But she doubted she would be very effective against a telepathic tiger. Surely worse lay ahead.

She realized now why so few cars had been traveling her way. She was going in the 'steep' climb through realities, and the cars were remaining in their own realities, so never reached her. But the streets going at right angles were all in whatever reality she was passing at the moment, like long rungs on a ladder.

Should she turn back? She would be safer in more familiar territory. But that would not get her to Darius. So she would have to go on, and hope she found him before she got into an inextricable predicament, as Principal Brown would put it. Or an inedible picklement, as the kids would translate it.

She rode forward. But this just wasn't cycling terrain. It was more work to ride than to walk. So with regret she walked her bike, hoping to find a better road in another reality.

Suddenly a huge bear was in front of her. It wore a woodsman's hat and held an axe. *A wild human!* it thought. *Exterminate it!*

Colene wanted to run forward into the next reality, but the bear blocked the way. She would have to retreat, and hope it would go away soon. She stepped back, and the bear vanished.

But suppose it didn't go away? Suppose it brought in its henchbears and waited for her return? She could be caught before she could move! Suddenly her life, so worthless a few hours ago, was excruciatingly precious.

She couldn't wait here long, anyway; before long something similar to a bear or a cat would come along the road, and nab her. Maybe she could hide in the forest to the side, but there were two problems with that. One was that she didn't know what monsters were in there, or what bugs. The other was that she didn't want to drift any farther than she had to from the direct ramp, because she might not be able to find it again. Then she would really be in trouble, lost in shifting realities!

Even if she managed to handle those problems, what about night? When that came, and she got tired, and had to sleep, she would be vulnerable. She had to get somewhere safe before night – and how could she find such a place, in these strange worlds? How could she trust even the safest-looking place?

I'm in trouble! she thought, fearing that she was vastly understating the case. She really should have waited for Darius to come for her!

But was he any better equipped to handle these realities? His realm was magic, not telepathy, not animal dominance. He had almost died in her reality, because he couldn't cope without magic. She feared he wouldn't do any better than she, and might do worse – which would mean that he would not survive the journey. So maybe she had better meet him half way, or three quarters of the way, to be sure they both were alive to love when they met.

Are you from afar?

There was another thought, faint but clear. Was it a tiger or a bear? It felt friendly, but that could be deceptive. Should she answer?

Why not? She was in trouble anyway. Maybe this represented some kind of help.

Yes! she thought as hard as she could.

Are you in distress?

Yes.

Are you human?

Yes. I am Colene, a human girl.

Come to me. I need a companion.

So did she! But if this was a tiger trying to lure her in, she would be a fool to go.

Also a fool to pass up a potential friend. *Who are you?*

I am Seqiro. Please come quickly; this mental contact across realities represents a strain.

Across realities? That didn't sound like a tiger! She would risk it. *How can I find you?*

I am on your path. I have felt your approach. Come to my reality, and follow my mind to my stall.

But there was the bear lurking for her. She considered briefly, then walked several feet to the side, faced forward again, and started running.

Her strategy worked. She saw a bear to the side, but by the time it turned to spot her, she was beyond its plane and the way was clear.

She forged on, trusting to blind luck to keep her out of serious trouble. The road deteriorated further, becoming a beaten path. But maybe this was ridable. She got on her bike, set her gears to the lowest ratio, and pedaled hard. Yes, she was moving well.

Here! You are passing my reality!

Oops! She turned and rode back, until the thought agreed that she was on the right plane. Then she turned to the side and followed it, walking the bike over forest floor.

Follow my thought, Seqiro sent. His signal was much stronger now. *There is some danger for you, but my thought will avoid it.*

She hoped so. She followed his thought out of the forest and to a rustic village. There were many oddly dressed people, and horses, dogs, and cats, each going about his business. She did her best to look as if she were one of them, going about her business, but wasn't sure she wasn't ludicrously obvious as a foreigner. At least this didn't look like a bear or tiger camp.

In the course of this travel, she wandered across the reality lines several times, but his mental contact remained. Sometimes she stepped across the boundary deliberately, to avoid being spotted, then back in farther along. She was getting better at using the Virtual Mode.

Seqiro led her through a back alley that passed several stalls where horses were stabled. He had used the term stall; evidently he had meant it literally. But what kind of man would live in a stall? A stable hand?

The presence of horses reminded her of her imaginary friend Maresy. Colene had always liked horses, not in the sense of riding them but in the sense of just liking them. She knew they were not considered very intelligent as animals went; cows did twice as well on maze tests. But there was a basic niceness about horses that other animals lacked. Oh there were those who swore by cats because they were cuddly and purring and quiet, but cats were actually pretty selfish creatures who made friends only with those who fed them well. Some folk swore by dogs, supposedly man's best friend, but there were thousands of dog bites every year, suggesting how thin that veneer of friendship was. There were pet birds, locked in cages or in houses; hardly any of them would remain if given a chance to fly into the wild. But horses – there was just something *about* horses. Oh, some could be mean and some could be lazy, of course. But, taken as a whole, they were better than people. That was why she wrote to Maresy Doats in her Journal. Maresy was a whole lot more serious than her name suggested.

But of course a family living in a suburb, scraping along in the middle class two-incomes-one-child mode, could not even think of having a horse. This had never been an issue; Colene had seen from the outset that it was impossible. Even had it been possible, she would have hesitated to bring a horse into such a situation, because at any moment her mother could lose her job – when her alcoholism began manifesting at her job – or her father could lose his, when he had a fight with a mistress and she made a scene that embarrassed his company. Even without one of those events, there was no love in the family, not even that one per cent romance. The family was a bomb waiting to be detonated. A horse wouldn't like associating with that. So Maresy would always be a mere dream.

Still, it was nice passing through this region, for a reason irrelevant to what she was actually doing. By the look of it, this was an ordinary primitive hamlet where horses were the main animals, instead of a reality in which telepathy was practiced. She wouldn't mind living here, near the stalls, and maybe sneaking treats to the horses when their masters weren't looking. That was the nature of girls and horses.

But she certainly hoped that her telepathic friend really was a friend, because she was getting physically tired and needed a safe place to rest. If it turned out to be another bear or tiger –

Finally she stopped at a particular stall. There was a large brown stallion in it, gazing out.

Where next, Seqiro? she thought.

Duck down and enter my stall, the thought came back. *We must explore motives.*

Enter the stall? Colene stared at the horse with dawning wonder. Could it be?

There had been telepathic dogs, cats and bears. Why not a horse? *You?*

Slowly, the horse nodded.

Something very like instant love blossomed in her heart. A tiger or bear she would not have trusted, but a horse! Of course!

She ducked down under the heavy gate that closed the stall, and came up inside. She stood next to Seqiro. He was about eighteen hands tall at the shoulder, or about six feet in human terms. Almost a foot higher than the top of her head. He smelled wonderfully horsy.

It was all so suddenly ecstatic. A mind-reading horse! What more could any girl ask?

May I pat you? she thought.

Yes.

She reached up and patted his massive neck on the left side. His mane fell to the right side, so didn't get in the way. His hide was sleek and warm. What a beautiful creature!

May I hug you?

Yes.

She reached up with both arms and clasped his neck as well as she could. She put her face against his hide and just sort of breathed his ambience. He was just such a totally magnificent animal!

May I adore you?

Yes.

She felt her emotion surging into overload.

May I cry on you?

Yes.

She stood there and wept, her tears squeezing down between her face and his hide. It was a great relief.

Finally she lifted her face. *I like horses*, she thought belatedly.

I like girls.

That seemed to cover the situation.

6

PRIMA

The world seemed unchanged. He stood on the dais, within the marked circle beside the castle. But the Cyng of Pwer was gone.

He stepped out of the circle, in the direction that seemed proper. A plume-bird took wing, startled. Darius was startled too; that bird had appeared from nowhere.

No, not nowhere. Darius was the one who had stepped into its reality. The geography might be so similar as to be identical, and the animal life too – but men and creatures did not follow the same schedules here as in his own reality. So a bird had been roosting here. He had better move on before the local Cyng of Pwer spied him and asked what he was doing here. He didn't know how many others there might be like him, in these very similar Modes.

He walked on toward the rim of the disk. He hesitated, then brought out his personal icon. He squatted and drew the crude likeness of the dais of the Castle of Hlahtar. He activated the icon and jumped it to that likeness.

He made it, but it was a gut-wrenching experience. Evidently his sympathetic magic was not well attuned to this Mode.

He gazed at the castle. It looked the same, but now he doubted that it had the same personnel. If it did, could he meet himself? That promised only complication! So he decided not to approach it; he would get well away from anything similar to what he knew. In fact, he should get away from the dais region, too, because if his magic stopped working, he would be stranded on a dais.

He knew where there was a lowland region that was almost level. It was almost uninhabited, too; an assortment of wild animals roamed there, and that was about all. His sword should protect him from any predators, if he remained alert.

He stepped his icon there, and immediately arrived, his gut further wrenched. But now he had another problem: he did not know where to go. Pwer had told him that there should be a feel to the right direction, and he had felt it at first. Now he did not. He had gone off the path.

But he should be able to pick it up again. He turned slowly around, concentrating, and felt a faint tingle in one direction. That should be the way to go.

He stepped in that direction. Nothing seemed to change. He continued, and saw an animal: a big reptile, one of the dragons that roamed this region. Some of them could do enough magic to blow fire, but they were no threat to a man who could do magic to douse fire, or simply conjure the creatures elsewhere.

He continued walking, and the feeling of rightness grew stronger. Good enough; he could reach the proper path without having to struggle with the impassable terrain in the vicinity of the daises.

Could he conjure himself along the path across Modes? A moment's thought made him decide not to try. Probably he had done that when he conjured himself before, which was why he had the gut wrenches. The Modes were close together; Pwer had indicated that about three paces should take him from one to another. He had conjured himself many leagues, so must have crossed hundreds of Modes. In so doing, he had almost lost the path. As he progressed on the path, his magic would fade, so it was best not to depend on it.

Were it otherwise, he might have conjured himself all the way to Colene's Mode, and fetched her back immediately. But he knew he could do no magic there. He needed to forge a path by foot, so he could bring her back the same way.

He continued until he reached the strongest sense of the

path. As he did, the terrain changed around him. The plain became a ragged slope, but not as rough as in his home Mode. He could manage.

He had been traveling, as it were, slantwise across Modes. Now he crossed them directly, following the path, and Pwer was right: about three paces took him across. He could tell because though the terrain did not change much if at all, the vegetation changed somewhat and the animal life could shift abruptly, as the first plume-bird had shown.

He passed a pair of ridges between which nestled a small clear lake. He approached it cautiously, alert for danger, because such water was apt to be a drinking hole for animals. Indeed, odd creatures did appear and disappear as he crossed Modes, while the lake remained constant. This brought home to him the fact that though for him each Mode was only three paces wide, he saw the whole of it while he was in it. The lake was in each Mode, so appeared constant, but every three paces it was actually a different lake he saw. He was not approaching the lake he saw, but the lake that would be in the Mode he would stand in when he got there.

He did get there, and there were no animals. There were fish in the water, however, so it was probably clean. He lay down and drank deeply, then filled his water bag. Water was precious!

He stepped into the next Mode. There was a wrenching in his stomach and a lightening of his water bag. What had happened?

He stepped back. There were two wet places on the ground beside the lake, where water had evidently been recently spilled. And his bag was low, and he was thirsty.

Then he remembered Pwer's warning: he could not assimilate the stuff of other Modes. Not rapidly. He could not carry anything with him across Modes except what was of his own Mode or the Mode of one of the other anchors. He could eat or drink the substance of another Mode, but it would not remain with him when he departed it, unless he gave it time to be assimilated by his body. It seemed that it was the isolation of the molecules amidst many more of his own molecules that caused them to become detached from their Mode and to join his. This could happen fairly rapidly with water, and more slowly with food.

He drank again, more moderately, and waited an hour. Then he resumed his journey, and the water did not disappear from his stomach. It had already done that, to be distributed elsewhere in his body, and was captive.

Suppose he ran out of water? Then he would have to remain in a single Mode long enough to drink a lot of it, urinate it out, and filter it through sand to make it pure. That pure water would be of his system, and could travel with him in his bag. It was not the most pleasant mechanism, but necessary. Food was harder; he would not have time to excrete it and grow new plants from it, so he carried what he needed with him. He could mix it with water, expanding its mass, and it would last a good length of time.

He moved on, and now the lake was left behind him, as constant as before, while plants and animals flickered in and out of sight with each change of Modes. The animals he understood, but why the variation in plants? Probably because the animals grazed on them, so changes in animal life meant changes in plant life. Since adjacent Modes tended to be similar, if he saw a dramatic shift in plant life, he would have to be extremely cautious about the animal life, even if he didn't see it. Because it was probably nearby and the next Mode might put him abruptly face to face with it.

The glimpses he got of animals were not reassuring. There seemed to be an increasing number of dragons, and they were getting larger. They seemed to be squeezing other animals out, almost as if –

Suddenly he was caught in a net. He struggled to get free of it, but it hauled him into the air and held him. It was an animal trap, triggered by touching. He hadn't seen it because it had not existed until he stepped into its Mode, moving swiftly.

He drew his sword and started cutting the threads of it. Who could have set up this trap, and why? The second question was readily answered: it was to snare wildlife alive, probably for domestication or later slaughter. The setters of the snare had not figured on a Mode traveler passing through.

He completed his cuts, sheathed the sword, and let himself down through the hole he had made. He landed on the ground – and discovered himself facing a dragon. A big one. A maneater.

The creature had evidently come up while Darius was cutting himself free. He decided to risk a conjuration, because this one was big enough to eat him. He activated his icon and moved it back away.

There was a bit of wrenching in the gut, but his body did not move. He had passed beyond the range of magic already.

Well, he could escape the monster simply by stepping into the next Mode; that was what he should have done first. He started to move – and the dragon leaped.

Darius found himself on his back, with the dragon's snoot at his face. The monster could bite off his head in a moment!

Then a monkey appeared. The creature had another net, a smaller one. It put this net over Darius' head, then yanked it up as the dragon backed off. Darius had to sit up, then stand, with the net covering him from head to knees. The monkeys were in charge of this Mode?

The monkey held a cord connected to the net and walked to the side. When Darius tried to step toward the next Mode, the dragon growled and breathed down the back of his neck. That monster could snap him up in an instant; dragons had hunting reflexes. He had to walk exactly where the monkey indicated.

The path veered to the side, but the monkey guided him in a straight though not level line up a bank and into a forest of giant ferns. The dragon followed closely. The way was marked by dabs of colour on the ferns or ground.

They knew! They knew he was crossing Modes, and they were keeping him in this one!

He figured it out as he was required to scramble across the irregular terrain, hewing to the line that was this Mode's intersection with his route. They had set out nets to snare wild creatures, but also to catch Mode travelers. They could recognize the latter by their odd clothing or alien nature. Then they brought the captives in, confining them to the narrow channel. As long as they were alert, they could do it.

And what did they do with their special captives? He was surely about to find out! He doubted he was the first one; the marked special path showed that. It wasn't regularly used. Probably there were many such, so that they could bring in captives from whatever nets they were found in. With ordinary captures, they used the ordinary paths. So this was't a common occurrence, but neither was it unknown.

In due course they traveled down a sloping field and to a collection of artificial structures. They weren't exactly houses, but they weren't exactly anything else. They had sloping upper surfaces, and walls made of bars.

Most of them were empty, but some did contain creatures. It was hard to see well, because one structure tended to obscure his view of another, but there seemed to be a wide variety of animals and birds. One animal had eight legs and long antennae, but also a cowlike udder, which suggested that it was a mammal, not a huge insect. One bird had four wings, translucent and extended like those of a dragonfly, but it also had a beak and feathers.

This divergence of animal creatures intrigued him despite his present peril. As far as he knew, the animals of Colene's Mode were similar to those of his own, so he had assumed that they differed no more than did the people. He had evidently been mistaken, because he was only part of the way between their two Modes, and had seen no people and a wide divergence of animals.

Certainly it smelled of animals! The odor thickened as they approached the structures, becoming stifling. But he had no way to escape it. He did his best to tune it out. After all, it had not smelled nice in Colene's shed, because of the presence of the fecal pot, but that had not bothered him or apparently her when they were together.

Colene: how he hoped he would reach her! Whether he lived or died was less important to him than whether he was reunited with her. If only he had brought her with him! But he had been put off by the realization of her youth and her depressive nature, and had blundered terribly.

He was brought along his straight line until it intersected one of the structures. Now he saw that the thing was fairly large. Indeed, large enough for him to step inside. The monkey put him in, took his pack, sword, and all his clothing, and carried them out to the dragon. The bars slammed down, sealing him in. This was a cage!

Dragon and monkey departed. Darius looked around. He was now naked, but the air was warm and he wasn't in physical discomfort. There was straw or the equivalent on the floor, and a pot whose function he recognized from recent experience. That was all.

He checked the bars of his cage. They were set close enough together so that he could not get past them, and were firmly anchored in the floor. They seemed to be of wood or something similarly hard, perhaps cut from the stems of the big ferns. The floor under the hay was of the same substance, seamless. So was the roof. Whatever it was, it was too strong for him to bend or break. His sword might have chopped through it, but they had been smart enough to deprive him of that, as well as his food.

He tried to peer beyond his cage, but all he could see was other cages, all empty. Evidently recent trapping in this particular slice of the Mode had not been good.

But *he* had been caught! What was he to do? If he didn't get out of here soon, not being able to complete his mission might be the least of his problems. The monkeys could be building the fires for a roast.

He sat on the straw. If he got any chance, he would dive out of the cage and into the next Mode. Better to be naked and free, than risk recapture by trying to recover his clothes. But he doubted that he would get the chance.

At least now he had a notion why so few ever returned from the Modes! It wasn't that they got lost, but that they were caught and dispatched. It had not occurred to him that there could be predators among the Modes, but it was all too clear in retrospect.

There was a stir beyond the cages. He peered out, and saw a figure approaching, followed by a dragon. It was a human being!

Indeed, it turned out to be a woman. She seemed to be about forty and not unhandsome, but there were deep lines of sadness or weariness on her face. She wore what might once have been a good conventional shirt, its buttons crossing from left shoulder to right hip in the style for the unmarried, but its color had long since faded to gray and it had been patched many times. Her skirt was evidently homemade from native material, puffing out from her hips and extending to the calves; her original one must have worn out. Her feet were in sandals, and were filthy, the toenails growing down and around in a manner that might be practical in a wilderness for protection against abrasions, but was detestable aesthetically. Her hair was long and somewhat unkempt, as if maintaining appearance were pointless here. Surely that was true!

She carried his clothing, which was in a tangle. She came to stand outside his cell, staring at him. Darius would have been uneasy about this at the best of times; he was even less at ease now.

'Ung,' she said, and passed the wad of clothing through the bars. She set his pack on the ground beside her. 'Ung, ung!' She made motions as of dressing.

Human but not of his culture, obviously. Darius said nothing, because it seemed pointless. He untangled his clothing and quickly put it on.

'Ung,' she said. 'Ung pretend ung you ung ung don't ung understand.'

It was his turn to stare. Words came through clearly amidst the nonsense syllables. There was no doubt: she spoke his language, and wanted to conceal that fact from the captors. That probably meant she was on his side!

'Ung?' he asked, scratching his head.

The woman turned to the dragon and said something. The dragon exhaled steamy breath and settled down for a snooze.

'Play dumb,' the women said. 'Look blank. I am testing you for responses to see whether we can learn to communicate. The dragon doesn't understand the words, but he is watching you. If you give me away, we both are dead.'

Darius shook his head in feigned bafflement. 'Ung?'

'You are from my Mode, or close to it,' she said. 'I can tell by your clothing and supplies. Look to my right if you mean yes, and to my left to indicate no. Make no other responses, except obvious ones.' She twitched her right and left hands as she spoke, clarifying the signals. 'Do you understand?'

'Ung?' he said, looking to her right.

'That is agreement. Now indicate disagreement.'

He did not move his body, but he glanced to her left.

'Good.' She stood straight and made a grand gesture of pointing to herself. 'Me Prima.'

Darius had to grab onto the bars for support. Prima! The would-be female Cyng of Hlahtar he had promised to look for! Just like this he had found her!

Actually it made sense. She would have been trapped the same way he had been, and probably many others. She must have proved useful to her captors, so they had kept her alive.

'Me Prima,' she repeated, touching herself again.

This time he responded more appropriately. 'Me Darius,' he said, touching himself. Establishing names was elementary; he had done it with Colene. But he realized that it was important not to let the captors know that he was from the same Mode as she, and that he knew of her.

'Listen closely. The dragons govern this Mode. They have hunted most other species to extinction and are desperate for new creatures to prey upon, because that is their nature. They know about the Modes, but can not travel between them. They are hoping to capture a Mode traveler who can give them the secret. Failing that, they will do what they can to restock this Mode with prey. We must work together to escape. If we do not, they will breed you to me to produce prey they hope will be more of a challenge to hunt. Will you cooperate with me?'

Darius looked firmly to the right.

'They will not let you have your sword. They will let you have your food. Magic is not operative here. Do you have anything that might be used as a weapon that is not obvious as such?'

Darius had to think about that. Then he got a bright notion. He glanced right.

She squatted and began drawing things out from his pack. 'Identify the things in your language,' she told him. 'I have to appear to be making progress. Let your eyes tell me what your weapon is.'

118

She held up a package of beans. 'Beans,' he said.

'Beans,' she repeated, and set the package down. She brought out a loaf of bread.

'Bread.' He remembered how he had been confused by what had turned out to be white (not brown) sliced (not whole) bread in Colene's Mode.

'Bread,' she repeated. So it went, item after item. Then, near the bottom, there was a tiny box with slivers of wood inside.

'Matches,' he said, looking to the right. This was the box he had gotten from Colene and brought back with him. Matches were much like magic, but were actually science, and they fascinated him.

'Matches,' she repeated, this time truly unfamiliar with the term. 'What are they?'

'Ung,' he said, holding out his hand. The watching dragon made a warning puff of steam.

She handed him one match.

Darius held it by the business end and poked into his mouth with the bare wood end. He was using it to pick his teeth!

Both the woman and the dragon looked disgusted. Evidently they had anticipated something more significant.

He reached, signaling for another. The woman gave him one more match. He stuck this in the other side of his mouth.

'This is a weapon?' she asked as she rummaged in his pack for what remained.

He glanced again to the right. Then he put the matches in a pocket.

After the woman completed the pack inventory, Darius risked telling her. 'Ung. Kublai. Ung ung.'

Now she was the one who reeled. Oh yes she knew that name! She had loved Kublai, twenty years ago.

She recovered. 'When can you use your weapon?' she asked. 'At any time?'

He looked to the right.

'Can it kill dragons?'

He looked left.

'Better in privacy?'

He looked right.

'I will come to you at night, to feed you. I can not open the

119

cage; only a dragon can do that. But they will put me in with you if I ask, because they are aware that breeding is not instantaneous with strangers. Can you use your weapon then?'

He looked right.

She verified some words, holding up things they had identified from the pack. Then she departed. The dragon glanced at him, then settled back to sleep.

Darius lay on the straw and closed his own eyes. He had a lot to assimilate!

Dusk came, and then darkness. Prima came, carrying not only his pack with its food, but a bottle of water. She said something to the dragon, and the barred gate swung open. She stepped inside, and the gate closed. How it worked Darius couldn't fathom, except that it was under the control of the dragon. If magic didn't work here, there must be some other type of force. The dragons must have used it to establish dominance in their Mode, just as humans had used magic to achieve power in his own Mode.

'Now you must eat and drink,' she told him, making broad gestures of food-to-mouth so that the dragon could see that she was doing her job. 'And after that, if I am to remain here with you, I must make obvious attempts to seduce you, so that the dragon will know that we are potentially breedable. I realize that this will be distasteful to you because I am too old and unattractive, but our lives are at stake, so I ask you to behave in a manner the dragon will find reasonable.'

'Ung,' he said, taking bread from her. He certainly was hungry!

'As I interpret it, all you need to do to escape this Mode is to step into the next, which is just beyond this cage. If I am in direct contact with you at that time, I should be able to accompany you. This is because it is my home Mode too; were it not, I would be unable to join you regardless of our contact. We shall have to maintain contact continuously thereafter, because I fear I will slip away when we lose it, and be lost in infinity.'

'Ung,' he said around his mouthful. He saw how this could

get complicated, but if the alternative was to be trapped here, it was necessary.

'I believe that once I emerge at the anchor site, I will be secure,' she continued. 'So I will ask you to conduct me there. I realize that this will delay whatever mission you are on, but perhaps I can provide you with information that will facilitate your mission, and in this manner make up for it. I think, for example, I can enable you to avoid similar capture in the future.'

He looked to her right, indicating his interest. It had become obvious that he had entered the Virtual Mode woefully unprepared.

'Now how do you propose to use your weapon?' she inquired. 'I confess to being baffled how those two toothpicks can hurt anything.'

'They make fire,' he murmured. 'I will burn the straw, and burn through the wooden bars. It will also distract the dragons.'

'Fire!' she repeated, surprised. 'But a pyro spell won't work here.'

'This is not magic.' He spoke into his bread, so that the dragon could not see him or hear him. He hoped. 'All I'm concerned about is how long it will take to burn through the bars. If the fire is too big, I'll be burned too; if too small, the dragons will put it out too soon.'

'Correct. Here is a better way: start the fire and feign sleep. I will scream to be released. When the gate opens, you must launch yourself out, and sweep me with you across the boundary.'

Darius was impressed. That did seem to be a better way to do it. Risky, of course, but probably less so than his imperfect notion. 'Then let's do it,' he murmured. 'Say when.'

'Finish eating. Eliminate. Settle down to sleep. I will join you, but you will not yet be responsive. I will tell you when to make the fire.'

He glanced significantly to her right. Then he proceeded to stuff himself, for if their escape was effective, it might be some time before they had another chance to eat. She ate some with him, evidently trying to spark his interest in her.

121

His experience with Colene assisted him with the next stage. He did have to defecate. Prima turned her back, and he did it on the pot. The dragon seemed to be snoozing, but he knew better than to trust that.

He formed a bed of straw and lay down on it. Prima brought some more straw and joined him. Now he smelled her body odor over that of the environment. She must not have washed in years! But probably that was not her fault; the captors seemed to have little concern for the hygiene of their captives.

She made as if to take off his clothing, and he demurred with a curt gesture even the dragon could not mistake. Then she removed her worn shirt, showing her haltered bosom. It was a good one, considering her age. She took his hand and brought it to her halter, and he drew his hand back, but with less force than before. Thus the dragon could see that she was making some progress.

However, he was evidently tired, and dropped into his feigned sleep without being seduced. Prima dug in his pack and brought out his blanket-pac, unfolding it and spreading it over him. He had feared that its magic would be inoperative here, so that its thinness would offer no protection against the cooling night, but it remained effective. Then she rested quietly beside him, seeming a bit frustrated but patient.

He had almost fallen asleep for real when she murmured 'Now.'

He had the two matches in his hand. He brought one slowly out, his arm motion screened by his body and hers, and struck it against the hard wood under the straw. First it sputtered, then it caught. He moved it under more straw, setting fire to it. He nudged the straw away from him so that he would not be burned. He was in luck; there was a slight breeze, and it not only fanned the nascent flame, it moved it away from him.

Prima waited until the fire was well established. Then she screamed. It was a truly piercing sound; it was all he could do to maintain his pretense of sleep. Would the dragon believe that the scream hadn't jolted him awake?

Prima ran for the other end, shouting in what seemed to be the dragon language and pointing back at the fire. The dragon's head snapped up, the big eyes blinked, and the gate swung open to let her out.

Darius scrambled up and caught the strap of his pack as he launched himself after her. The gate began to swing closed, but Prima wasn't clear of it, and it couldn't complete the motion. Then he came through, sweeping his free arm around her waist, and rammed on to the side.

The dragon had been caught by surprise, and had made the mistake they had hoped for, but now its hunter reflexes came into play. It leaped forward, intercepting the two of them and shoving them back and down with its nose. But Darius clambered over its nose, lifting Prima with him, and they tumbled to the other side. The dragon turned to snap at them, its jaws opening – and they rolled into the next Mode. It looked the same as the other, but there was no fire and no dragon. Only the light of the moon and stars. It was as if those two things had ceased to exist. Actually they had never existed, in this Mode.

'Don't let go of me!' Prima gasped.

He had been about to. Instead he tightened his grip around her waist. 'Are you sure we have to maintain contact, if we're not actually crossing Modes?'

'No, but it's a strong likelihood. I've been trapped for twenty years; I don't want to be trapped for the next twenty.'

'But I have pulled you into my Virtual Mode,' he argued. 'You should stay on it now.'

'We must talk,' she said. 'Until then, do not let go of me. Let's get away from here; there are surely other dragons, because this is an adjacent Mode, almost identical to the one we left.'

Sure enough, he saw the outline of a dragon approaching. It looked just like the one they had escaped, but it was beyond several cages. They needed to get away from this entire set of Modes.

Arms around one another's waists, like lovers, they walked into the next Mode. The dragon vanished. They continued to walk, until the cages shrank and finally disappeared. The landscape looked the same, in the dim moonlight, but there was now no sign of artificial structures.

'We had better tie ourselves together,' he said as they paused. 'Otherwise we could lose contact by accident, if we are surprised.' He set down the pack, wondering how to put it on without letting go of her.

'There's no cord in your pack, and I have none,' she said.

'Maybe I can tear off a sleeve of my shirt, and use that,' he suggested. Why hadn't he thought to carry a good length of cord? Its advantage was obvious.

'You may need that to protect your arm from the sun.' She considered a moment. 'I have something. Put your arms around my waist.'

He did so. She turned within his grasp, so that she faced away from him. Then she leaned forward, reached behind her, up inside her shirt, and untied her halter. The front of it, loosened, dropped down against his hands. She reached inside the front and hauled it out, leaving him with her breasts on his hands. He was too startled to react. This woman was of his Mode? 'This.'

They linked arms, his left to her right, hands clasping forearms, the halter bound around the wrists in the middle. It wasn't ideal, and if they fell they could wrench their arms, but they were unlikely to let go by accident.

'As I recall, it requires more than a day to walk to your anchor, and this is night,' she said. 'It will be better to find a secure place to sleep.'

'That may be a problem. I have lost my sword, and have only one match left. A high place may be subject to predator birds, and a low place to predator reptiles. I saw each kind during my journey out.'

'Yes. We had better make weapons. I would also like to bathe.'

That was a relief! Her odor had been bad in the cage; now it was overwhelming. The folk of his Mode were normally scrupulous about cleanliness; he was glad to learn that she remained true to form.

'I passed a mountain lake not far back.'

'Were there trees nearby?'

'Yes. Not any variety I know.'

'Let's go there first. Then perhaps we can hide in a tree, after we talk.'

She seemed to have a better notion how to proceed than he did, so he agreed. He realized that this was good experience; what he was learning now should help him rescue Colene.

They moved on to the lake, proceeding carefully and quietly in the darkness. When they reached it they stripped, but remained linked. More correctly, they remained linked and tried to strip. Their shirts could not pass their linked arms. So they walked into the chill water and washed in tandem, he standing in front with his left arm reaching back, she with her right arm reaching forward. She held his shirt and other clothing while he washed. Then he held the bundle of their clothing while she stepped forward and washed. He felt distinctly awkward putting his hands on her shirt, halter, skirt and diaper, but it was necessary. This reminded him that Colene had not used diapers; she had had almost sheer panties that barely sufficed for concealment. But she normally wore trousers, so that her undergarment could never be seen by accident. The purpose of diapers, of course, was to cushion the secret region from gaze and touch, making it unfeasible to see the shape of it. Now, he was seeing everything, in a manner normally reserved only for one about to undertake sexual contact. But this was a very special situation.

Unable to do much else, he stared mostly into darkness while she washed. After she got the caked grime loose, she rinsed her hair, and though it remained tangled, it assumed better color. It was not proper of him, but linked as he was to her, it was difficult for him not to glimpse her body in the moonlight. He saw that she was lean rather than plump, but her posterior was well rounded and her breasts were of adequate mass. Kublai had said she was not a pretty woman – no, he had said she was not remarkable in appearance or personality, which wasn't quite the same – and that was true. But she had evidently had the stamina to survive twenty years of captivity and retain her ability to speak her native language, and to act promptly to escape when the opportunity presented itself. That spoke well for her personality, and in the appropriate apparel her body would be attractive enough. Perhaps he had been comparing her to a young beauty, such as Colene, which was unfair.

In moments they were both shivering. They came out and shook themselves. Their clothing was dry, but they wanted to keep it that way. 'We must hug for warmth until we dry,' she said.

He was constrained to agree. They embraced face to face, their linked arms somewhat awkward to the side. He was too cold to be sexually stimulated; he was just glad for her warmth.

When they were dry enough, they put their dirty clothes back on. They scrounged for some sticks, but not for a fire; these were makeshift weapons. Then they sought a suitable tree with branches both big enough and high enough to enable them to settle comfortably above the ground. That should protect them from nocturnal ground animals, and the foliage might shield them from great birds.

It was awkward climbing with their arms linked, and awkward getting comfortably settled. Finally they sat facing each other, with their backs braced against the large forking branches of the tree, his feet wedged against knots to the side of the opposite branch, her legs lifted and spread so that her knees embraced his waist while she sat partly on his thighs. His inadequate blanket covered their shoulders.

'I could wish that I were younger,' she murmured, 'for this position would surely drive you mad.'

He remembered how Colene's naivete about the spread of her clothed legs had nearly done so. 'You are not old enough to avoid that risk. Fortunately it is too dark to see.'

'I thank you for that courtesy. However, you have seen my body. Please answer with candor: do I retain sexual appeal?'

'Yes, but –'

'I mean, allowing for my age, of course.'

'That was not the nature of my qualification. I am a man of honor.'

'I thank you again, Darius. You are very much a man of my culture.'

He tried to tilt his head back, so as to rest it against the branch behind him, but that was awkward. 'Please do not misunderstand. I think I must put my head forward, on your shoulder, to sleep.'

'Understood. We shall embrace as necessary to be comfortable.' She put her head on his left shoulder, and he put his on her left shoulder. They linked their free arms to complete the solidity of the position. Thus braced, it would be possible to sleep safely, and their closeness helped shield them from the cold. It was far from ideal, in several respects, but feasible.

'We shall sleep soon, but now we must talk,' Prima said, as if they had not been doing so all along. 'You have been most patient and accommodating. Please, if you will, tell me of your mission here. You surely have most pressing reason to risk the Modes.'

'I made a spot trip to a far Mode, searching for a woman I could both love and marry,' he said. 'I am the current Cyng of Hlahtar. I think you know the problem.'

'Indeed I do! I think you know mine, too.'

'Yes. Kublai wanted most sincerely to learn of your fate. He agreed to take my place if I would search for you as I went.'

She was silent for a moment. Then she asked: 'What is Kublai's present feeling for me?'

'I think it is not love. He has had to marry many times, and discard all his wives, until he retired. Now he has married for love, at last. But he loved you once, and remains sorry it could not be worked out. I think he holds his emotion in abeyance, expecting either to learn nothing of you, or of your death. Now of course, while he takes my place, he has had to divorce his love-wife and make her his love-mistress. She is not pleased with that.'

'I know the feeling.'

'Yes, of course.' Not only had she not been able to marry for love, she had not been able to assume the post for which she was plainly qualified.

'If I return, would he marry me?'

'But the Cyngs of Hlahtar don't marry for love!'

She merely lifted her head and looked at him in the darkness.

Embarrassed, he gave her the answer. 'Yes, I believe he

would. Your power would make no other wife necessary. But I understood that this was not a role you sought.'

'It was not. But I had time to think, in twenty years, and I realized that such a marriage was a better use for me than what I had with the dragons.'

'What did they make you do?'

'Very little. They were saving me for the chance arrival of another of my kind. Then I was either to discover his secret of Mode travel, or to breed with him.'

'But there is no secret!' he protested. 'The Chip must be set from the anchor point.'

'So I tried to tell them. They were not sure they could believe me. So I helped feed the captives, until their Modes expired and they could be freed.'

'Freed?'

'There is no sport in hunting a caged creature. But one that has fled the cages and gone out into the wilds can be a pleasant challenge. I was smart enough never to do that, so I survived.'

'I am glad you did. I think I would not have escaped without your help.'

'I did it for myself as much as for you. But now we must ascertain where we stand.'

'I thought we had done that.'

'No. What do you suppose the chances of your encountering me were?'

'Obviously good enough!'

She shook her head. Her hair moved against his own. 'That is not the case. There are an infinite number of Modes. How did we meet in one?'

'I was crossing Modes, until I was trapped in the same way you were. Thus there was no chance involved.'

'Not so. Infinity is broader than that. There are not only an infinite number of types of Modes, there are an infinite number of each type. An infinite number of Cyngs setting out in search of love. An infinite number of dragons trapping travelers. How is it that you encountered me, when there are an infinite number of variations of you and an infinite number of variations of me?'

128

That had not occurred to him. 'Perhaps it was a fortunate chance.'

'I think not.'

'What are you saying?'

'I am saying that we did not meet.'

He lifted his head, startled. 'This is humor?'

'No. I shall explain. We are from different Modes.'

'But we speak the same language! We have the same conventions! And I know of you, and you know of Kublai! Our Modes match!'

'No. Our Modes are very similar, but they surely do not match. That is why I must remain bound to you until I reach your anchor. Were I identical, I would not need such contact; once you drew me onto your Virtual Mode, I would remain on it, being of the substance of your universe. Were I too far removed, I would not be able to cross with you at all. But I am in between: close enough to cross with your help.'

'But perhaps you *are* identical,' he said.

'No. When I came close to you, and touched you, I did not step on to your Virtual Mode, though I could feel its ambience. I was one of the infinite number of near misses. So you see, there is no great coincidence in our meeting. There are infinitely more mismatches than perfect matches.'

'But then why do you want to return with me?'

'Because your Mode is also infinitely better than the alternative. At least once I am through your anchor point I will be able to remain, for your Mode will surround me far more solidly than does the Virtual Mode. A man very like the one I loved will be there. I hope he will marry me.'

'But surely you would not deceive him!'

'Surely not! I will tell him the truth, and offer him my body and my power for his disposal, as long as he wishes either.'

Darius nodded. 'I think he will accept. But he will be concerned about the fate of his original Prima.'

'She may well be traveling back to the Mode of another Darius, to marry another Kublai.' Her chest heaved with silent laughter. 'We are interchangeable.'

He did not laugh. 'But when I return, he will vacate the post, and need no Cyng wife.'

129

Her face lifted again and turned to his. 'If you return with your love, would you marry me then? I can do for you what I can do for him, and I would be discreet about your love mistress.'

Darius was startled. A power of multiplication rivaling his own! 'Why yes, I believe I would! You understand the nature of the marriage.'

'I certainly do. Consider us affianced, in that unlikely event.'

Darius sank into thought, his mind racing. He had visited the other Mode in search of exactly a woman such as this: one who could expand his power so greatly as to make it no burden, without being depleted herself. He had found her. She was not young and lovely and sweet; she was old and smart and cynical. She was not his love. She was Kublai's lost love. What a strange solution!

'You were correct,' he remarked. 'There was something to talk about.'

'Yes. There is more, but I felt it necessary to clarify our relationship as I believe it is, so as not to deceive you.'

'More?'

'I have had twenty years to ponder the nature of the Modes,' she reminded him.

'Kublai will be most interested in what you have to say.' He might be interested himself, but right now he was tired, and wanted to sleep.

'Delicately put. Let me mention just one other question, whose answer I believe I know.'

'One other thing,' he agreed.

'We are in a provocative position, physically. If this causes you to desire –'

'No. No offense.'

'That is the answer I anticipated, and prefer. We are of different generations, and thrown together only by the chance of our Mode involvement. Now we must share warmth and sleep.'

Darius was glad to agree. He relaxed, adjusting his head on her shoulder, cushioned from her shoulder bone by her shirt and hair and the thin blanket, and closed his eyes. She relaxed similarly against him, and drew him in closer for that warmth.

Her bosom touched his chest, and he became conscious of her breasts as she breathed.

His imagination shaped her body into that of Colene. He did desire a woman, and Colene was that woman. But the two of them had been hedged by imperfect understandings, and it had not been right. Were they traveling the Virtual Mode, together like this, then – well, if it had been Colene who had made that offer, this time, he would have accepted.

'You are thinking of your loved one,' Prima murmured.

'We are sharing minds?' he asked, surprised.

'Some. Bear in mind that I have similar power to multiply as you do; that is a kind of emotional interaction. It is stifled now because I am isolated from your Mode and your special Chip connection, but our minds will interact increasingly as we associate and are in close contact.'

'Surely true,' he agreed. His power had been stifled in the alternate Modes, but she derived from his own Mode, or one very similar. He had no experience with such interaction, because he had never before encountered a woman of her level of power.

'But mainly I felt the tenderness of your touching, and knew it was not for me.'

She was embarrassingly perceptive. 'It is true.'

'If I marry Kublai, I will try to pretend he still loves me. I hope that at least he desires me.'

'He has a young and beautiful and attentive wife,' he said. 'She is Koren. I impressed on her the need to be unmarried from the Cyng of Hlahtar, and she hates me. She will hate you, if you evoke his desire.'

Her body stiffened, then relaxed. 'True. I thank you for that reminder. I have no right.'

Evidently she had been quite lonely, trapped in the dragon's Mode. She had loved Kublai, and perhaps still loved him, having had neither satisfaction nor any other man to dream of. She could represent disaster for Kublai's love life. Yet she had a power that would be invaluable to any Cyng of Hlahtar, himself included.

'If I may make a suggestion –'

'By all means.'

'Marry Kublai, but take a lover. Make it obvious. Then it will be seen that the marriage is purely convenience.'

'That is good advice,' she said sadly. Then she was silent, and they drifted to sleep.

In the morning they were both quite stiff and uncomfortable. It occurred to him that this was indeed a provocative position, but that even had it been Colene here, it would have become relatively unexciting in this situation.

They unkinked their legs, and Prima got her skirt decorously down so that her diapers no longer showed, which was a relief. They worked their way down to the ground and stretched and exercised, jumping together to get warm.

'I must undertake natural functions,' she said. 'But we can not untie our arms.'

'What exactly would happen if we did?' he asked. 'I mean, if we are careful to remain right here in this Mode – or if I stepped across, I could return for you.'

'It might be all right,' she said. 'But my fear is that because I am now a creature of the dragon's Mode, and have no alternate Mode anchored in that, I would fall through the Modes and return there. That is a risk I prefer not to take.'

'Fall through? But if you do not walk across the borders –'

'If you will humor me while I relieve myself, I will explain in more detail.'

'As you wish.' He was sure she had good reason.

He stood facing away while she squatted to do her business and bury it in the dirt. Then she faced away for his turn. This was another firm reminder that there was little actual romance in being bound to a woman; instead the details he would have preferred to ignore were made uncomfortably evident.

Then they made a meal from his supplies, and she explained while they waited for the water they had drunk to be assimilated. 'You understand that a traveler's tenure is limited on the Chip Mode, because he gradually loses contact. If he does not return fairly soon, he never will.'

'Yes. I call it the Virtual Mode, because it is analogous to a state of functioning by that name in the Mode where I met my love. It is presumed that a traveler has been killed or lost or

132

trapped as you were. Now that I have learned what happened to you, I consider this presumption confirmed.'

'Virtual Mode,' she repeated musingly. 'As if it is something not quite real, yet seems real. A useful concept.' She paused, evidently assimilating the notion. 'However, the presumption of the reason a traveler through the Modes does not return is not confirmed. He may indeed be killed, lost or trapped, but the mechanism is more basic than that. You are aware how you must eat and drink cautiously in foreign Modes, because you can not immediately assimilate the food.'

'Yes. I was warned, but forgot. I drank at this lake, and lost the water from my stomach. I had to do it again, and wait.'

'Precisely. Your body isolates the foreign molecules and separates them from their Mode; they must join yours. But the corollary is more dangerous: the more foreign matter you incorporate in your body, the less remains of your original substance. Eventually your body is more foreign than native, and you are unable to remain on the Virtual Mode. Then you are trapped, regardless of the rest of your situation. This happened to me.'

'But the dragons caged you!'

'Yes. They caged me and fed me, and in due course I became too much of their Mode, and could not escape. I had little choice: had I refused to eat, I would have died of starvation. They knew that. They would have done that with you. They allowed me to feed you your own food because they wished me to ingratiate myself with you. They knew that in time your food would be exhausted, and the process of assimilation into their Mode would accelerate. The very process of breathing was already beginning that.'

'Breathing!' he exclaimed.

'When you breathe, you exchange molecules of your substance with those of the air. The longer you breathe, the greater amount of foreign matter you incorporate.'

'I never thought of that! Of course you are right.'

'I have had a long time to ponder the aspects of my failure,' she said with a wan smile. 'It is not surprising that some of my realizations are new to you. I would have told you this had we remained trapped, and the dragons would have noted your reaction and seen that I was impressing you.'

'And if you succeeded in winning my confidence, you might learn from me how to cross the Modes,' he said. 'I see their logic. But you succeeded too well.'

'That was my desire. I think now that I could have addressed you directly without trying to mask it with nonsense syllables; the dragons are not highly vocal and do not really understand the versatility of it. But I was determined not to squander my only chance for escape.'

'So your body is mostly of the dragon Mode,' he said. 'But I am aware of no actual attraction of a Mode. I do not find myself sliding back to my anchor Mode when I relax. Why should it pull you back?'

'It may not,' she admitted. 'But it could work in this way: if I became separated from you, I would be unable to cross Modes toward your anchor. But I might be able to cross them toward the dragon realm, because it is as it were downhill for my present substance. Since the Virtual Mode intersects only a narrow segment of each Mode, I would inevitably stumble across and be moved back. Certainly I would not reach your anchor. My fear is that even a brief separation would prevent you from finding me, for you would not know in which Mode to search, or where within it.'

'Needle in a haystack,' he agreed.

'I do not follow your reference.'

'It is a saying I learned from Colene. They use fine needles for stitchwork, as I understand it, and should such a needle fall into a pile of hay, it would be exceedingly difficult to find.'

'That is apt. So I prefer to take no risk, being sensitized by my long captivity. I shall do my best to repay this inconvenience for you. For example, I may be able to show you how to cross Modes more safely, so that you run no further risk of being trapped.'

'That would be a great help!'

'When we reach your anchor, and I am safe there, I will fetch you mirrors. It should be easy to make a structure to hold a set of them, one reflecting to the other. When the forward mirror is poked across the border of Modes, its light could be reflected through a closed tube to the backward mirror. I think you could then see in the backward mirror the image from the forward one, not overwhelmed by the images of the Mode in which you stood.'

Darius was intrigued by the concept. 'If light can be reflected across the border, why can't we just look across?'

'I think we could, if we were not attuned to the Mode in which we stand. We need to isolate our sight from that, just as we need to isolate our flesh from it if we wish to depart it. Perhaps I am mistaken. It is a concept I played with, and I would like to discover whether it works.'

'I will certainly try it!' he said. 'If it protects me from walking into a net, this delay will have been worth it.' Then he reconsidered. 'I do not mean to imply that it is not worthwhile to rescue you.'

She laughed. 'I understand perfectly!'

She surely did. She was older than he, and not beautiful (though not ugly), but she had a good mind to go with her excellent power. He was adjusting to the notion of marrying her, when he returned with Colene. That would indeed give him love and advantage in his post, though not in the same woman. It would make his foray onto the Virtual Mode a success.

Having assimilated the water, they moved on across the Modes. Darius was now conscious of a resistance in his body, as if the foreign molecules were dragging behind. But it was so slight as perhaps to be his imagination. After all, Prima, who had twenty years' accumulation of foreign substance in her body, was having no apparent difficulty crossing. Unless it was the resistance of her substance, in contact with his, which caused the drag.

He expected their return to be slower than his original journey, but it was faster. His familiarity with the route and her eagerness to reach the anchor made for excellent progress. They did encounter a large predator at one point, but a quick dodge back across the Mode border solved that. Prima also insisted on leading the way, so that she rather than he would catch the brunt of danger. She seemed almost fearless in her cooperation.

When they reached the point at which he had diverged from the direct route, he explained, and she agreed as to the wisdom of that course. They retraced his route across the plain. When he judged they were close to his Mode, he conjured them to the dais of the Cyng of Pwer.

Then sudden doubt assailed him. 'How can I be sure it's *my* anchor?' he asked. 'If there are an infinite number of Darius's entering an infinite number of Virtual Modes –'

'Each should relate to his own anchor,' she said. 'Your Virtual Mode slants across Modes at such an angle that three paces separate them. When you take the final three paces, you should be at the correct anchor. My case differs; I lost my Mode, so have no such orientation and must depend on yours.'

'I hope you are right,' he said.

'And if it is a different anchor, but so similar that it accepts you, and no one can tell the difference, does it matter?'

'Of course it matters! Those awaiting my return would wait in vain, for I would be in the wrong Mode!'

'But that wrong Mode would stand in the same need of your return as your own, and your return would be as beneficial to it.'

He did not feel equipped to answer that. He just hoped it was the right one.

They reached the anchor and stepped onto the marked circle.

7

UNDERSTANDING

But why were you calling me? Colene inquired after recovering control of herself.

I need help to escape, Seqiro replied. *I felt the invitation of the Virtual Mode, and accepted it. But I must step out of my stall to utilize it, and can not without breaking it down.*

I can open it for you, she said. *The latch looks simple enough.*

The horse twitched an ear. *For your human fingers, yes. For my hoof, no.*

She stepped toward it. *I will do it now.*

He brought his nose about to intercept her. *Not yet. I will need feed and some supplies before I travel, for grazing has disadvantages on the Virtual Mode.*

But I thought horses liked to graze!

We do. But the food of other realities is difficult to assimilate, and best avoided until the journey is complete.

She was surprised. *What's wrong with it?*

When you cross realities, what you have recently eaten remains behind, for it is not of your reality.

She had packed supplies because she had been uncertain what she would find along the way. Now she was very glad she had done so!

I'm going to find my lost love, Darius, she thought. *Where are you going?*

With you.

But you may not like it in his reality!

I will like it with you.

He wasn't just saying it, he was thinking it, and the sincerity of his thought was not to be doubted. *Oh, Seqiro, you are so much more than I ever dreamed of!*

I know. I felt you coming from afar, and hoped you were human. It is a strain to think across realities, but with the Virtual Mode it is possible, and I had to find you and bring you to me.

This was sudden, but right. Colene knew her life had changed, in a way she had never expected. She had loved Darius quickly; she loved Seqiro instantly, but in a different way. Instant love was supposed to be foolish, as it was based on infatuation rather than knowledge, but with direct mind contact, that rule was irrelevant.

Soon she learned his situation, because he made a comprehensive explanatory mental picture: this was a reality in which the horses governed, just as the dogs, cats and bears governed some of the realities she had passed. They did it by telepathy, imposing their will on human beings. To an outside observer, this was much like a human reality, but here the humans acted at the behest of the horses, feeding them, exercising them and guarding them.

But Seqiro had too much of a mind for leisure. He wanted to explore new frontiers and gain new understandings. He also tended to be generous to his handlers. This had made other horses look bad, and finally they had acted by removing his handlers, effectively confining him to his stall. He was being pressured to change his ways. He had resisted – and then felt the questing of the Virtual Mode.

There had been such questings before, but he had not cared to risk them. Now he had to, for it was his only likely escape, physically and mentally. It was no coincidence that this connection had come; only those in great need established Virtual Modes, and only those in similar need attuned to them. They were like calls across the realities: I NEED YOUR HELP. SHARE MY ADVENTURE. But such adventure could be extremely strange. Thus only specially receptive minds felt the questings, and only the most strongly motivated folk accepted them.

But there was serious risk entailed, for though he knew he could escape via the Virtual Mode, he did not know who had instituted it, or for what purpose. He did know that other animals had mental powers, and that many of these were predator species. If this happened to be a tiger mode, he would have difficulty relating and would probably perish. If, on the other hoof, it was a compatible species, he might do very well, and gain intellectual satisfaction.

When he had tuned in to her approach, he had perceived what seemed to be a human personality. Could it be a human mode? That possibility had not occurred to him before, but of course any species could institute a Virtual Mode if it knew how. He had never noted any telepathic power in the human kind, but it was certainly possible that it existed in variants of that species in distant realities. Certainly a human animal could be compatible; human animals were a horse's best friend, here.

Then it turned out that the approaching human was only potentially telepathic. This was very promising, because such a human would need a horse for mental contacts, just as a horse needed a human for physical chores. Would the human be amenable to such cooperation? It was female, and females tended to like horses for themselves, apart from their power; that was another positive sign.

By the time Colene reached his stall, he had the answer. The sheer chance of the Virtual Mode had brought him the ideal companion. Their two realities might be different in most cultural and practical respects, but they aligned in what counted most for this purpose: the affinity of horses and girls. It was a bond that needed no further justification.

Yes, Colene agreed.

Now you must get my things, for I can not do it, and bring them to me, so I can travel with you.

But I am limited to a ten-foot swath, she protested. *If I step out of it, I will leave this reality and lose you.*

Not once you pass through the anchor, as you did when you entered my stall. Now you are in my reality, until you approach it from the other side.

She found that hard to believe, but it turned out to be true: she could now leave the stall and cross the aisle without losing track of him. She was now in his reality, all the way.

139

They got it organized: she would hide her bicycle in his stall, then fetch his feed and supplies, then open his gate and they would depart his anchor, as he called it, and resume progress toward her destination. Seqiro had no destination for himself; he merely wished to be free to explore and learn, without suffering undue hardship.

He made a mental picture for her, how she should dress and deport herself so as to pass unnoticed among the local attendants. Any human folk she should ignore, but she would have to respond to any equine queries. She should indicate that she was on private business for her steed, and move on.

The uniform was simple: a loincloth, cape and sandals. There was a supply shed near the stall; she went and changed, under his mental guidance. She removed her own clothing, then put on the loincloth. It circled her waist once, looped into two ends in front, and one end passed down between her legs and up and over in back. It rather resembled the cloth worn by the American Indians, being supremely simple and functional. When she had that properly wrapped, she donned the cloak, which was a circle with a hole in the center; it came down to about her waist. Then sandals, each one fashioned of two slabs of wood linked by cord, for heel and toe, and a loop of cord for the ankle. Again: about as simple and functional as clothing could be. Obviously the human folk of this reality did not rate fancy outfits.

Then she donned the hat. This was what identified her status and affiliation. It was like a beanie with a hanging tassel, and the manner the tassel fell indicated her degree of autonomy. Some humans had more responsibility than others, and could act without constant direction from their horses.

Now she walked to the granary for the feed. She passed other humans, who were similarly garbed. They ignored her. She knew they would not have, had she appeared publicly in her own clothing. Had Seqiro not been guiding her as she first came onto these premises, she would have run afoul of others.

The granary was stocked with bags of grain. *Take two, if you can carry them*, Seqiro thought. *Each represents approximately one day's feed, and I will need eight.*

She picked up two, putting their straps over her shoulders. She walked back with them and set them in Seqiro's stall. She made another trip, bringing two more. She was surprised how easy it was; others seemed not to see her at all. She could take the whole granary, load by load, and no one would care. She tossed her head, feeling carefree for the moment; this was fun in its way. Her cap almost fell off, and she had to jam it back.

Then someone did notice. It was a young man. He glanced passingly at her, did a doubletake, and approached her. He stared at her hat.

Seqiro – something's wrong, she thought, hoping he was tuning in. She could not broadcast her thoughts; it only seemed like it. He was able to think to her alone, so that others of his kind did not know he was breaking confinement, but he might not do that continuously now that she knew what she was doing.

I am here.

She pictured the situation, hoping she didn't have to put it into words, because that would take too much time.

Give me your eyes.

Eyes? could he see through her eyes? She relaxed, trying to let her mind go blank. She hoped that was enough.

Her eyes moved on their own. They cast about, then focused on the man. *He is looking at your tassel. It must have changed position.*

Oops! I did that without thinking.

He is sexually interested. Your tassel must be in the position of urgent invitation.

She had done that when she so blithely tossed her head? Sexual invitation? *I didn't know it could say that!*

There is no spoken language among humans of this reality. Signs of several types suffice. We allow humans to choose their own times and partners for procreation, provided they are proper workers. You signaled him that you find him desirable and wish to conceive by him.

What disastrous luck! *I don't want sex with him! How can I get out of it?*

That will be difficult without causing a commotion. Human males are unsubtle creatures.

141

What else was new! *I don't care how! Just do it!*

Seqiro considered, while the man attempted to embrace her. Her two bags of grain got accidentally-on-purpose in the way. But that dodge would not last long. He was starting to untie his loincloth. *Hurry!* she thought.

Smile and make a fist. Move it slowly down, then open your hand.

She did as bid. The man watched intently, then did the same. Then he got out of her way.

She walked on toward the stall. *What did I tell him?*

That you would meet him here at sundown with your loin-cloth off.

But I don't want to do that!

We shall be gone by then.

Oh. *But I didn't mean to lie to him either! That's not right.* Actually there were qualifications; sometimes a lie was necessary. It depended on the situation.

I will mind-touch another female and suggest to her that one who finds her desirable will be there at that time.

So she would go to meet the man. That might do it. Obviously he had no great prior relationship with Colene! *But I thought you couldn't telepath to other humans.*

I can do so. But my own servitors have been confined, and it is bad form to mind touch others. However, a subtle touch of the mind of a female not otherwise occupied should pass unnoticed. It is any effort to gain freedom for myself that the authorities are guarding against.

But I'm helping you do that!

He made a mental suggestion of unconcern. *You are not of this reality. They do not know of you.*

And that made all the difference for them both! She needed help, he needed help, and they both needed to have nobody else know what they were doing. *I guess it's all right. I hope she gives him a good time. I never meant to be a tease.*

When he sees her without her loincloth, he will not care about any other matter. This is the nature of humans.

These were primitive humans, she realized, stultified by having no real power over their own affairs, no pun. But perhaps not much different from those of her reality. She knew boys who would grab any girl they could, and girls who would tease unmercifully. She had done her share, when she got that key for Darius. In fact she had done more than her share of teasing when she had come to sleep with him in her bottomless nightie and told him no sex.

Straighten your tassel.

She paused to do it. She didn't need any more hot encounters!

She finished hauling the grain and got to work on the other things. There were small tools, and bags of water, and a kind of harness so that he could carry the things on either side of his body. She followed his mental guidance and got the harness put on correctly and the things set in it, working with far greater facility than she ever could have by figuring everything out for herself. This mental contact was like riding the bicycle: it tripled efficiency in a fun way.

She went for other things, and brought them back and put them in their loops in the harness. The horses were mental creatures, here, but obviously they could handle physical work too. It was probably easier than making the relatively puny humans do it. The humans were for minor chores.

She loaded her bicycle on top of his other things, because he thought she would be unable to use it in this vicinity. She was amazed at how much of a load he could bear, but he was unconcerned.

But as she was fetching one of the last items, a block of salt, there was a different mind touch. *What are you doing?*

That wasn't Seqiro! Which meant it was another horse. Which meant trouble. What was she to do? She shouldn't answer, but if she didn't there might be trouble too.

She kept her mind quiet. As far as she knew, a thought had to be conscious to be read. The ordinary mind was such a jumble of this and that and reactions and temporary concerns that it was hopeless as far as any outside perception went. But when she made something conscious, she formulated it, and that was what Seqiro read. So if she formulated no response, the other horse should find her mind a muddy slate. She hoped.

Identify yourself, the thought came imperiously.

Could she risk a thought directed to Seqiro? She doubted it, because she wasn't sending, he was reading, and the other horse could do the same. Maybe Seqiro was able to read the other thought, so already knew. In that case he probably couldn't send to her, because the other horse would pick it up. The other horses might not even know it was Seqiro she was working for; that was why they had to inquire. So she maintained her mental silence, or at least her mental mud. In fact, she should stop thinking of his name, in case they picked that up. It was best if they thought she was just a simple human intruder stealing things.

Pain lanced through her. It felt like what she thought a heart attack would be, hurting from shoulder to gut. The other horse was whipping her with its mind!

The block of salt fell from her twitching hands. She staggered and almost fell. These horses did have ways to enforce their demands!

Identify!

Instead she focused on her legs, and broke into as much of a run as she could manage. She had to get to Seqiro's stall before that creature knocked her unconscious or worse. The boss-horses must have caught on that something was happening, and were investigating.

Now she heard rapid human footsteps. They were summoning the minions! She had to reach Seqiro before the others intercepted her.

But as she rounded a corner, she saw that she had not made it. Three young men were between her and Seqiro's stall. How was she to get past them, even if the other horse didn't blast her mind?

A notion percolated up through her mud-mind, and she put it into effect before a horse could read it. *Humans! They are catching me!* she thought loudly. That should satisfy the horse that he didn't need to stun her; the situation was in hand. One threat sidetracked, maybe.

Meanwhile she reversed her course and broke into a run, away from the men. It was also away from Seqiro's stall, but that was part of the point: if they didn't know about Seqiro, this would keep the secret. Maybe she would be able to lead them astray, then duck back to the stall unobserved.

She whipped around the corner she had just rounded from the other direction. There was a supply nook here; she knew because she had recently fetched things from it. She swung herself into it, ducked down, and held her breath.

The men rounded the corner and pounded down the aisle. They ran right by the nook. It had worked! She had given them the slip by acting fast – by stopping here immediately after turning the corner, when they expected her to keep running. They couldn't read minds; they depended on the horses for that, and meanwhile the horses thought the humans had the situation in hand. She was slipping through a crack.

She resumed breathing, cautiously. She listened, and heard only the receding footsteps. Good enough.

She stepped out of the nook, and walked around the corner. The way was clear. She approached Seqiro's stall. She knew that at any moment things would heat up again, so she wasted no time. She reached into the supply shed near his stall and fetched her clothing and pack.

She came to stand before his stall. Was it safe to think a clear thought yet? She doubted it. Better just to get on with the escape without further mind talk.

She reached for the bar which only human hands could remove, not hoofs. It came up, releasing the gate.

The grain and supplies would have to be enough; she couldn't chance going back for the salt. She got her pack on her back, stuffing her original clothing into it; there was no time to change now, either. She pointed to the aisle before the stall, indicating her eagerness to go before anyone returned. She hoped Seqiro agreed.

Then she heard something. She looked back.

There were two more men, barring the way. They held pitchforks in a manner that made them look exactly like weapons.

Now we know whom you serve, the hostile thought came. *We gave you the chance to show us.*

Go, Seqiro! she thought desperately. She realized that their mental silence had been for nothing; the boss-horses had out-tricked them. *Before they can attack you!*

Seqiro started to move out. The men moved to bar his way,

the tines of the pitchforks orienting on his head. They were the servants of horses, but not of Seqiro.

Colene ran out ahead. 'Get away! Get away!' she cried, hoping to startle them into retreat just long enough to let Seqiro out of the stall.

Instead one man dropped his fork and grabbed her, while the other continued to hold his tines at Seqiro's eye level. They were under expert control, all right. They had neither startled nor panicked.

She struggled, but all she did was get her cape jammed up against her neck; the man was strong. So she tried another tactic: she twisted some more, deliberately causing her cape to ride up farther, exposing her breasts. 'See how nice I am,' she said. 'Watch me, not the horse.'

The man holding her looked down, interested. He evidently did not understand her words, but he could see her body well enough. The other one was looking too, now, his fork dropping low. Colene both loved and hated herself for doing this; it was akin to the way she made others laugh while she thought of the blood flowing from her wrists. She delighted in the power of her body to make men stare, while knowing that she was cheapening herself in the process.

Then, suddenly, the second man forgot her and turned back to Seqiro. The other horse had taken control of his mind! The horses got no sexual thrill from seeing her torso. The fork lifted again. But the man holding her did not let go. Instead he started to drag her back, away from the horse.

Go, Seqiro! she thought again. At least he would get free.

Then the man with the fork doubled over, the weapon clattering to the floor. The one holding her dropped similarly. *Go, Colene!* Seqiro thought back at her.

She realized that Seqiro had used his own power of stunning on the men, now that there was no point in further mind silence. She caught her balance and ran for the stall. She had to go into it, and then out of it on the Virtual Mode. Like passing the other way through a tunnel to another valley.

But before she got there, the other horse stunned her too. It was like a hammer blow to the head; she felt her consciousness fleeting. Just as the other horse had not been able to protect its minions from Seqiro's blows, Seqiro could not protect her from the blow of the other horse.

But it wasn't quite complete. The other horse was farther away, so some force was lost. She fought to hang on to what she could before it overwhelmed her. If she could make it through before losing consciousness –

She found herself falling into the stall. She had made it! But now that she was down, she could not get up. Her body would not respond. She could only lie here, at the anchor but not through it. So close, so far!

Go, Seqiro! she thought again.

Something brushed her face. It was the end of his tail. She grabbed onto it and clung with what she hoped was a death grip.

She felt herself being dragged forward, out of the stall. She was unable to fight any more.

She found herself face down in the aisle. *Rise, Colene*, Seqiro's thought came urgently. *Get on me.*

She lifted her head. Only a few seconds had passed, she thought, but the men were gone. What had happened?

Up! Up!

She responded sluggishly to his thought. She dragged herself to her hands and knees, then caught hold of part of Seqiro's harness and hauled herself up that.

A horse appeared down the aisle. It looked surprised.

Hold on. Seqiro stepped forward, dragging her with him. In a few steps the other horse disappeared.

At last she caught on to what was happening. They were crossing realities! Seqiro had dragged her from the anchor into another reality on the Virtual Mode, leaving the men and horses of his own reality behind. Perhaps that change had eased the pressure on her mind, allowing her to recover a bit. But the adjacent reality was very similar, with more telepathic horses, who would surely interfere if they realized what was happening, so they had stepped into a third one.

Buoyed by that realization, she clung to the harness and made her legs move. She started to walk beside Seqiro. The motion helped restore circulation and clear her mind.

They turned and walked down the aisle, then turned again at the corner and resumed crossing realities. The stalls began to change appearance. They were on their way!

Colene's head cleared. Apparently the other horse's stun-thought had done no physical damage.

They left the village, or maybe the village just faded away in the new realities. They were now in open countryside, with some trails going who-knew-where. It was nice. She realized that the details of her own anchor reality must have been constantly changing similarly, when she started out. She had been focusing only on the road ahead, and had been embroiled in her own confused thoughts, so had paid almost no attention to her surroundings. Also, it had been morning, in the suburbs, with little traffic, so she had not seen cars popping in and out of existence at first. From the first ten feet, she had been in a far weirder environment than she had realized!

'Say, maybe we can find a salt block out here, to replace the one I dropped,' Colene said brightly.

That will not be effective, Seqiro replied. She realized that she had spoken rather than thought, but it seemed to make no difference: he tuned in to her focused thoughts, and she had to focus them to talk. In fact, that was easier.

'Why not? Salt is salt, isn't it? It won't hurt you just because it's from another reality?'

It will not hurt me. But we can not carry such a block across realities.

'Now wait a minute! You explained about not being able to eat anything in other realities, but you're carrying a whole big load of supplies across realities right now, just as I am.'

These are from our anchor realities. You may carry substance from your own reality with you, or from my reality, and I may carry from either reality, but not from the intervening realities.

'Are you sure? These realities seem pretty solid to me.'

It is easy to demonstrate. Pick up an object.

Colene stooped to pick up a pretty stone. She had always liked stones, and not just the pretty ones; she knew that each stone was a fragment of something that had once been much larger, and had formed by dint of terrific pressures or unimaginably long time or both. How was it described in class?

Metamorphic, which meant being squished; sedimentary, which meant settling in the bottom of the sea; and igneous, which meant being squeezed out like toothpaste around a volcano. But that was really one of the other two kinds, because it had to have started somewhere else before getting cooked under the mountain. So each stone had its history, and every stone was interesting in its own way. She wished she could collect them all. This particular one looked like mica, which was about as appropriate as it could be.

Carry it across realities.

They stepped forward. The scenery barely changed, but the stone vanished.

Startled, Colene looked back. There was the stone on the ground, where she had picked it up. But she knew that what she saw was not the stone she had picked up; it was the one of this reality. She could not see across realities, as she had discovered when the bear appeared before her. If she stepped back, she would then see the rock she had picked up.

So she stepped back. The rock was on the ground, but not where it had been. It was in the path where she had dropped it. Except that she *hadn't* dropped it.

'So I crossed, but it didn't,' she said, turning back to face Seqiro.

That is correct. We are on the Virtual Mode, and we can transport only substance from our own realities, because the Mode is tied in to them. Other realities have only partial effect on us, and we on them.

Colene stared. She was receiving his thoughts, but he was not there! The countryside was empty.

Then she caught on. She stepped toward him, and as she crossed into the next reality he reappeared.

She went to him and hugged him again. 'Point made, Seqiro,' she said. 'I guess I just hadn't thought it through. I hadn't tried to pick up anything, or eat anything – brother! I guess food would vanish the same way, wouldn't it!'

Yes, it should. My understanding is that it may be possible to retain the substance of intervening realities if it is digested, but that there is danger in doing that.

'Let's not risk it! Oh, I'm glad I met you! I would have been in trouble pretty soon, just from ignorance.'

It is no shame to be ignorant, when you lack a source of information.

They resumed their walk, angling toward the route she had been following before she detoured to meet the horse. 'How is it that you know all this, when you haven't done this before?'

I learned it from reading the minds of other Virtual Mode travelers.

'But other horses don't seem to read minds across realities. How can you?'

It is quite limited. I could read your mind because we share this particular Virtual Mode. I can read the minds of other creatures only when we intersect their particular realities. The other horses of my reality can not perceive the Virtual Mode, because only I am its anchor in my reality.

'Just as only I am the anchor in my reality,' she said. 'And Darius is the anchor in his reality. Only it's the place too, isn't it? Because otherwise when we left our realities, the anchors would fade away.'

Correct. The anchor place becomes inoperative when the anchor person departs; only when the two are together can the connection be invoked or abolished.

'Abolished? You mean it won't last?'

It will remain until you return and renounce it, just as you accepted it at the start. Or until the Chip that is the source of the full Virtual Mode is changed.

'That would be at Darius' end.' She considered as they entered a forest and climbed a slope. When the way became difficult, she explored ahead a little to find a better passage for Seqiro's bulk, because he weighed about a ton, literally, and could not squeeze through places she could, especially with his load making his body wider. 'You read the minds of folk on other Virtual Modes before this one, though you were not part of those Modes?'

This seems to be my special ability. I have always sought to explore the unknown, and when I became aware of a trace mental current I could not identify, I sought it avidly. Perhaps others of my kind could do the same, but they have had no interest. In time I was able to fathom enough of the occasional Virtual Modes to understand their nature. I learned that I could join one, if I wished, if I exerted my will at the time it was being formed. I decided that I would do so, when the time was right – and this was that time.

'I'm glad you did,' she said sincerely.

I am glad it was you who was on it.

She turned and hugged him again. 'I hope you don't mind all this physical contact, Seqiro. I – I guess I have this need, and you're so wonderful –'

I have not before been loved by a human girl. I feel your emotion, and I revel in it.

'I revel too,' she said. 'I never knew I'd meet you, and I never want to lose you.'

I see no immediate need for us to separate. We shall find Darius, and then I will remain with you if you desire. There is no conflict between me and your human contacts.

'No conflict,' she agreed. 'But suppose it is dull for you, in Darius' reality? You want to learn new things, and magic might not be to your taste.'

Then I can embark on another Virtual Mode.

'But then we would have to separate, because I'll want to stay with Darius forever and ever!' she protested.

Unless he too wished to explore farther on a Virtual Mode.

She hadn't thought of that. 'Well, first we have to get there. From what I've seen so far, that's not necessarily a cinch.'

True. We are entering the region of telepathic carnivores. I can feel their thoughts as we progress.

'Oh! Can they hurt you?'

That depends on their size. I would prefer not to get bitten or scratched.

'And you can't read their minds until you're in their reality,' she said. 'So a tiger could pounce on you by surprise. But not if I go ahead.'

So it can pounce on you? We had better go together.

'Maybe I can get a weapon to fend off – oops, but I can't carry it across realities!'

My hoof knife may serve.

She dug out the knife. It was a solid, ugly thing. 'I don't

know. Most of my experience with knives has been cutting myself, not others. I don't know whether I could use it effectively against a tiger or bear.'

With my direction you could.

'You mean you could tell me in my mind? But still I might miss, or drop it, or something. Girls really aren't much for physical combat.'

Allow me to demonstrate. Pretend that tree is a tiger.

Colene took the knife and stepped to the side, toward the tree, remaining in the same reality. 'Okay, it's a tiger. Suddenly I see it, and it sees me, and it gets ready to spring and I panic and –'

She ducked down, then straightened like an uncoiling spring. Her hand snapped violently forward. The knife plunged into a knot on the trunk of the tree.

Colene fell back, letting go of the knife, shaking her hand, for it had taken a jolt. The knife remained in the tree. She had thrust with more speed and force than she had known she possessed. 'What –?'

I guided your body. We are experienced in controlling humans.

'And that tiger has the knife through his snoot!' she exclaimed, amazed. 'I didn't hurt the tree much, but that tiger would have had one hell of a surprise!'

I believe the knife will be an effective weapon for you.

That was the understatement of the day! Colene went to the tree and tugged at the knife. It wouldn't come. She pushed up and pulled down on it, trying to wiggle it free, but the wood clung to it. Then Seqiro sent a thought, and she wrenched and twisted with special force and skill, and it came out. She had physical ability beyond what she had thought were her limits. Seqiro seemed to bypass her restraints and draw on her full potential.

Holding the knife, she proceeded with more confidence. Actually the chances of encountering a bear or tiger right up close by surprise were small; her episode with the bear might have been the only one that would happen.

You thought of cutting yourself, Seqiro thought. *I do not understand this.*

She laughed self-consciously. 'I'm suicidal. It's a secret, but

152

I think I'll have no secrets from you. I think about death a lot, and blood. Or I did, before I met Darius. Before I got on the Virtual Mode.'

I still do not understand. Why should you wish to die? You are a comely and intelligent young woman.

'Well, that gets complicated, and maybe I don't know the whole answer myself. I don't think you'd like me as well if you saw what's down inside me.'

I read a wellspring of pain. This does not surprise me. You would not have undertaken the Virtual Mode if you had been satisfied with your situation. Think through your pain while we travel. Perhaps I will be able to help.

She laughed bitterly. 'Only if you could make me forget!'

This I could do.

Startled, she realized that it was probably true. He could read her mind, and could make her body perform in a way it never had before. Why not block off a bad memory?

'Okay, Seqiro. But stop me if you get disgusted, because I don't want to make you hate me. When I told Darius how I was suicidal, he –' The pain of that misunderstanding and separation cut her off. At least Darius had changed his mind, and set up the Virtual Mode so they could be together again. She knew there were still problems, because he had to marry a woman with a whole lot of joy, but if she could just be with him, things would work out somehow.

She turned her mind back to the times of special pain. There were several, and she didn't know what related most directly to what or how they tied in with how she felt later. Maybe they really didn't mean much; maybe she had reacted the wrong way, or maybe they shouldn't have bothered her. *Would* they have bothered her, if her folks' marriage hadn't become a shell, forcing her to seek elsewhere for emotional support – which she hadn't found? Maybe the whole business was too dull to review, and she should have forgotten it long ago. Maybe worse had happened to others and they had shrugged it off, and Colene was peculiar to have failed to have done that.

'I don't know. Maybe this is a bad idea. I would feel foolish just speaking some of this stuff, and –'

Then feel it. I am attuning to you and learning to read your nuances. I can read your memories, if you allow me.

He could do that? He could reach deep into her and see her most secret things, if she did not resist? That was scary! Yet she remembered lying with Darius, telling him he could touch her breasts but not her genital region, and he had done neither. Then later she had offered it all to him, and he had not taken it. She had respected him for that, yet also been annoyed. It might have been better if he had been unable to control himself. That would have given the control to her, odd as that seemed considering that he would be having his will of her. He had not, and so she had not had her will of him, which wasn't quite the same.

Spreading her legs for Darius. Spreading her mind for Seqiro. What was the difference? One was a secret of the body, the other a secret of the mind. Of the two, the mind was more private. Yet it was something she wanted to do, wanton as it might reveal her to be. She wanted to tell *someone*, just as she had wanted to show her body to someone. To lay the guilt bare, just because it was there.

'Okay.'

She laid open her mind. It traveled back two years.

She was twelve years old, and visiting Catholic relatives in Panama, in the Canal Zone. One parent was Catholic, so maybe that made her one too, but she wasn't sure whether it did or whether she wanted it to. She went to Mass on Sunday, undecided and really not caring a whole lot. She just loved visiting here, where everything was so much nicer than back at home. If church was part of it, well, it was worth it.

And it did make her feel very close to God. God loved the sparrow as He loved His Son. Surely He loved this whole region, and that was why it was so nice. The American enclave was beautiful, very like paradise, with lovely gardens and ultimate contemporary luxury. After a distance it faded to the natural landscape, which was not manicured but which remained interesting in its tropicality. Every palm tree was a novelty, to one raised in Oklahoma.

She walked to the nearby native village, curious how the

Panamanians lived. Was it the same as the Americans, or different in some intriguing way? They must be very happy, living in a place like this.

Nothing in her life had prepared her for what she saw in that village. The houses were huts with thatched roofs and dirt floors. The people were filthy, their clothing odd. Naked children of both sexes ran wildly in the streets. Young mothers held soiled babies to their bare breasts, nursing them in public. There were sores on the children's legs, scabbed over, with flies clinging to the crust. Insects gathered around their mouths, and no one even bothered to brush them away. It was horrible.

She rushed back to the enclave, back to the church. 'A priest, a priest!' she cried. A priest came to her; perhaps this was confession.

Tearfully, she expressed her feelings of shock and grievance. Suddenly she had seen the real world, right next to paradise. It wasn't better than what she had known, it was worse! It had been hidden from her. Hurt and outraged, she wept bitterly. She felt betrayed. She blamed the church, she blamed the priest, she blamed herself, and she blamed God. Everything was wrong, and she wanted this wrong to be corrected.

The good father was patient. When she wound down, he spoke softly and kindly to her. 'My child, you have seen reality, and it is as uncomfortable for you as it is for all of us. You now have a decision to make. Whatever you have or will get in the future, you may give equally to each poor Panamanian. It is possible to give each one a good meal for one day. Then you will be just as poor as they are. You are allowed to do this, but you are not required to give up your birthright.'

It was her first real lesson in logic, and a giant one. She had thought herself a fast learner, but now she saw how slowly she was learning about reality. Even then, she did not appreciate how much more she had to learn.

She remained shaken when she returned home to the States. She had not been satisfied with her life, and was less satisfied now that the crevices in her parents' marriage had opened into significant faults. Yet she had material things and good health, which was much more than what she had observed in the villagers. What good would it have been to have a unified family, if she had to run naked and hungry in the streets, the flies eating at her open sores? She had too much, and she felt guilty for being dissatisfied.

She went again to a priest. He advised her to donate some of her spare time to work at a charitable institution. She did so, helping out as a junior candy-striper, bringing mail, newspapers, drinks and phone messages to the patients. She had a pretty little uniform and the patients liked her. She was, some said, a breath of fresh air in hell.

For these were not people in for pleasant recuperation following hangnail surgery. This was the accident ward, and some patients were bandaged all over, in casts, or with amputated limbs. Some could not move at all, yet their minds were whole. She read to them from the newspapers, and they appreciated it. She was doing good; she was giving back to the world some of what she owed it.

She was moved to the Sunday morning shift. The wee hours: midnight to six AM. This wasn't properly candy-striper business, it was more like Gray Lady business, but few cared to take those hours, and she volunteered. The doctors knew she was underage, but she was a good worker and mature for her age of just thirteen, so they did not make an issue of it. The nurses needed the help, and it wasn't as if she was alone. So when patients were restless, the nurses did not force sleeping pills on them, they had Colene come in and read the paper. As often as not, that did put them to sleep, and it was always appreciated.

One man was recovering from abdominal surgery. He had fallen on a spike and punctured his gut; they had had to cut out the affected intestine and sew the ends together. He had lost a lot of blood, and they didn't have enough of his type. Infection had set in. But he was tiding through, though too weak as yet to lift his arms. When the nurses were busy at the far end of the ward, he spoke to Colene: 'Not that dull stuff. There's a novel under my mattress. Read me that.'

She felt under the mattress and found it. A visitor must have left it for him, or read it to him during the day. There was a marker in it. She opened it at the marker and started reading.

It was an erotic novel. Colene was fascinated. She had never read anything like this, and knew she wasn't supposed to. The four letter words were there, and not as expletives. The man didn't know how young she was, probably. She did not let on. Instead she read the text as it was, about steamy hot women who approached virile men with indecent offers, and amply fulfilled those offers. Colene learned more about raw sex in one hour (with pauses; she had the wit to switch to the newspaper when a nurse came within hearing range) than in all her prior life. She learned exactly what men did with women behind closed doors, squeeze by squeeze and inch by inch. She was doing the man a favor, but he had done her a much greater one, inadvertently: he had completed her education in a forbidden subject. She was grateful.

A week later, wee Sunday morning, she read to him again. The marker was well forward of the place she had left it, but that didn't matter; plot was the least of this story. This time she read about man, woman, and animal, and it was a further education. It was as if God were rewarding her for her good work by sneaking in this secret information she so valued.

The third week the man was gone; he had recovered enough to be moved to another ward, along with his book. A new patient was in the bed: a perfect young man with a bandaged head. He had shot himself, trying to commit suicide. This, too, fascinated her. She offered to read for him, but the nurse told her not to bother. 'He's in a coma. He'll die soon. He's a vegetable. We are waiting for him to die.'

'But he's so handsome!' Colene protested, as if that counted for anything in this ward.

The nurse laughed. She was old, with decades of grim experience; she had seen death hundreds of times, and was callused. She lifted one of the man's legs and let it drop with a thud onto the bed. 'Look, he is as good as dead. He can't feel, see, or hear. Don't waste your time.' She went on about her business.

But Colene lingered, unwilling to believe that such perfection of body could simply die. Why had he shot himself? What reason could someone this handsome have to want to die? It was a mystery that lured her moth-like to a candle flame.

She bent over him. 'Don't die, elegant man,' she whispered. 'God loves you – and I love you too. You are too beautiful to die!'

Suddenly his eyes opened, focusing on her. Colene was startled and frightened, for it was the first motion he had made on his own. She ran from the room and told the nurse. 'He's conscious! He looked at me!'

The nurse returned with her. She checked the man's pulse and eyes. There was no reaction. 'You are mistaken,' she said gruffly. 'There is no change in him.'

Colene couldn't believe it. She *knew* the man had looked at her. She went to the bed and took the patient's hand. 'Please open your eyes,' she pleaded.

His eyes opened. But when he saw the nurse, his eyes closed. Tears trickled down his cheeks.

The nurse was staring. In all her decades of experience, it seemed she had never before seen this happen.

Next week the man remained, undead. It seemed he had not moved a limb or an eyelash in the intervening time. But when Colene took his hand and spoke to him, his eyes opened, and his mouth tried to smile.

He began to recover after that. Week by week he improved, most dramatically when Colene was present, until he was well enough to be taken home. He could not speak or walk without help, but perhaps that would come.

Two weeks later came the news: the beautiful man had gotten his hands on another gun. This time his shot had been all the way true, and he was dead.

What had she accomplished, by interfering with the natural course? She had thought she was doing so much good; instead she had hastened the man's death. She should never have done it. She should have had the humility to know that she could not change another person's destined course.

Suicide. What was its attraction?

She continued with the wee hours Sunday shift, but the heart was gone from it. What was right and what was wrong? She had no sure answers.

Then there was an emergency. A bus had been involved in an accident, and there were horrendous injuries. The

158

call went out: all available personnel report to assist in the emergency room.

Colene went down. In the throes of it, no one challenged her. She carried bandages and ran errands for the harried doctors. There were so many bodies to deal with all at once, they were doing triage.

A teenager not much older than Colene herself was hauled in on a stretcher, his legs crushed. Colene passed the bandages as the doctor tried to stanch the flow of blood; as he said, succinctly, the legs would have to wait, because they would do the kid no good if he bled to death. A woman was almost unmarked on the body, but she had been struck across the face and her eyes gouged out. Colene held her hand while the doctor gave her a shot to abate her screaming. A man was sitting, waiting his turn, coughing up blood, helpless, bewildered and in despair. Colene went to him and put her arm around his shoulders. 'The doctor will be with you in a moment,' she whispered in his ear. He turned his face to her, started to smile, and slumped. Now at last the doctor came, performing a hasty check. 'He's dead.' And he was; they could not revive him.

Now a nurse recognized Colene. 'Child, you don't belong here!' she exclaimed, horrified.

'Yes I do,' Colene said. But she left, knowing the nurse would not report her if she got out before anyone else caught on. Most of the injured had been classified by this time, anyway.

But it was enough. She asked to be relieved of her job, saying the night hours were interfering with her sleep and her homework. The hospital administration, covertly aware of what had happened, gave her a fancy Certificate of Merit and let her go. It was their secret. Colene was learning about secrets, learning well.

Now Colene's interest in death, a sometime thing before, became dominant. The last man had smiled as he died. Death had been a relief. The way those people had been suffering, death would have been a relief for all of them. What right did she, an undistinguished girl, have to be healthy and happy?

But she told no one of her experiences, and indeed she wasn't sure what significance they had. Was death the proper

159

destiny of man? If not, what was? Until she knew the answer, she hid her feelings and acted normal.

She started dating. Her mother thought she was too young, at mid thirteen, but her mother didn't want to quarrel about it. A quarrel could lead to a discussion of her mother's drinking habit. Secrets – Colene was learning how to borrow against their power, how to finesse them, to get her way. So she went to the movies with a boy she hardly cared for, and let him kiss her, while in her mind ran the scenes from the dirty novel of twining bare bodies. What would it be like, actually?

An older boy asked her out. He had a car, but he didn't drive her to the movie. He said it would be more fun at the party his friends were having. There would be great entertainment. Colene didn't care about the movie either, so she didn't object.

There were three other boys there at an apartment, and no other girls. They were drinking. They gave her a drink, and she tried it, curious. This, too, was new experience. Soon she was pleasantly dizzy. She had another drink, and another, reveling in the feeling.

Then she was in the bedroom with her date, and he had his trousers off. Suddenly the descriptions in the dirty novel registered, and she knew what he was after. She started to protest, but he pushed her down on the bed and got her dress up and her panties off and rammed into her with a whole lot less art than the novel had described. By the time she realized that it was rape, it was done, and he was getting off.

Rape? Even tipsy as she was, she realized that no one would believe her. So she played it cool, and pretended she had liked it. That way maybe she would get home safely.

But the other boys came in, and she had either to continue the pretense or make a scene, and if she made the scene she feared she would not only get raped, she would get beaten up and maybe killed. That wasn't the way she wanted to die! So she smiled and said it was all right, and one by one they pressed her down and jammed in, and it was so slick and messy now that it didn't hurt the way the first time had.

She did make it home safely, and her mother was so drunk she couldn't smell the liquor on Colene or see her condition.

Colene went to the bathroom and washed and washed, but she couldn't get the awful feel of those men out of her. The novel had been wrong; it was no fun for the woman.

She never told, and neither did the boys. Not where it counted. They knew the trouble they would be in if news got to the authorities, considering her age. So the secret was kept, to a degree. But Colene stopped dating. Her reputation in certain circles was shot. Her mother, ignorant and relieved, did not question that decision.

Time showed that she was neither pregnant nor infected with VD. She had gotten away with it, such as it was. But she was saddled with a deep, abiding disgust. The worst of it was that she couldn't really condemn the men; they were what they were, opportunists. It was herself she condemned, for being such a fool. She had indeed asked for it, by her naiveté. How could she have read all about it in the dirty novel, and not caught on that to such men a girl was nothing more than a walking vagina waiting to be unwrapped and plunged? Fool! Fool!

Why was life such a grubby mess? She hated every aspect of this, but still didn't know what to do about it. There seemed to be no justice, only opportunity and coping. Opportunity for the men and coping for the women.

After that her double life had come upon her. She was bright and cheery in public, suicidal in private.

Did you share your feeling with anyone?

She had forgotten that Seqiro was tuning in. Well, not really; she had gone through it all for his benefit, buoyed somewhat in the fashion of her nude display before criminals at the time of the bleeding contest. In that she had in a devious manner made up for her disastrous date: instead of getting raped by four men and having to pretend to like it, she had tempted them and beaten them in sheer nerve, and they had had to pretend to like it. They weren't the same men and it wasn't the same situation, but it aligned in her perception. This wasn't the same situation either, but it also aligned: instead of baring her fascinating body (it had to be fascinating, or there was no point) she was baring her fascinating mind, and there was a dubious glory in it, a thrill of release, almost of expiation.

161

No, this was not parallel to the physical business, she realized as she reviewed it. It was parallel to mental business. She *had* shared her feeling with a friend, once before. And that had been another bad mistake.

It was this past summer, at camp. Naturally her folks got her out of the house when they could, not because they disliked her but because they were more concerned with their own problems than with hers. Camp wasn't bad, actually. There was swimming and hiking and dancing and woodwork and nature. She liked all the events, yet her depression remained. It was as if she were a mere shell going through the motions. What was real was the blood on her wrist.

But her roommate Mitzi spied the scars. Things could be hidden from parents, teachers, friends, psychologists, and the man on the street, but roommates were deadly. Rather than try to bluff through, which was a bad risk, she was frank, telling how she secretly wanted to die but didn't quite have the courage to do it. So she flirted with it, and the flowing blood relieved something in her, a little, and one day she would get up the nerve to go all the way and truly be dead.

Mitzi expressed sympathy and promised to keep her secret. She watched out for Colene after that, as if afraid she would keep her head under water too long or eat poison instead of dessert or throw herself off the precipice instead of admiring the view from it. It was fun for a while, having this constant attention. But soon it became annoying, and then oppressive. For one thing, the roommate was alert at night too, and the toilet wasn't sufficiently private. Colene just couldn't cut herself, and was getting restive.

She tried to distance herself a bit, to go on events without the roommate, so she could get the necessary privacy to do what she hated to do. Otherwise she was afraid she really *would* hurl herself over a cliff, having been unable to alleviate her need in a lesser and more controlled manner. The problem with the cliff was that she knew she would be unable to change her mind in mid air, and that the job might not be complete; she might survive, broken and ashamed. But mainly it would be messy. Instead of lying pale and beautiful in her coffin, she would be bruised and battered, with her nose broken and teeth stoved in. That was no way to die.

It came to arguments, not about anything in particular, but about what wasn't said: Colene's need to do her own thing, even if that was self destructive. First they were private, then they spilled over into public. Finally, in the last week of camp, the roommate blew up: 'I'm sorry I ever tried to stop you from killing yourself!' she cried.

There was an abrupt silence in the mess hall. Then, studiously, the other kids resumed eating and talking, not looking at Colene. Colene got up and dumped the rest of her meal in the trash and left. She went to her room and bared her arm, but couldn't do it; she was too humiliated and angry to focus even on this.

That night the roommate came, but they did not speak to each other. Camp life went on as usual. But something had changed. Colene realized that people were speaking to her, about nothing in particular and everything in the ellipses – and they weren't speaking to Mitzi.

A girl approached her, seemingly by coincidence. The girl was younger and seemed perky. But she showed Colene her arm, and it was scarred where the sleeve normally covered it. 'I thought I was the only one,' she murmured, and moved on.

A boy approached at another time. He was handsome, and Colene liked his look, but had had no personal interaction with him. 'I, ah, she shouldn't have done that,' he said. 'I didn't know. I didn't ask you before, but now, ah, maybe there isn't much time. The last-night dance, will you, ah –?'

'Because you're sorry for me?' Colene asked, witheringly.

'Ah, yeah, I guess. I guess I'd be mad too, if –'

'Okay.'

'What?'

'I will go to the dance with you.'

He seemed stunned. 'Ah, okay, then.'

They did go. He gave her a small corsage of wild flowers he had made himself. Her held her very close as they danced, and suddenly she realized something. She halted on the floor. 'Was that the truth?'

He knew what she meant. 'Ah, no. I lied. I just didn't have the nerve to tell you I liked you. Are you mad?'

'Furious,' she said, and pulled his head down and kissed him firmly on the mouth.

There was applause from the other couples and those along the sidelines. A counselor forged her way to them. 'Go to your rooms,' she said severely. 'You know that's not permitted.'

'See, I got you in trouble already,' Colene told him as they separated.

'Yeah. Thanks,' he replied, looking stunned again.

Mitzi was there in the room. Colene looked at her, surprised.

'No one asked me,' the girl said. 'No one would dance with me.' She was near tears.

She was not suicidal, but she was suffering worse than Colene was, now. 'Maybe I can fix that,' Colene said.

'No! I don't deserve anything from you. I'm sorry I – I said what I did. I knew it was wrong the moment I – Colene, I'm *sorry*!' She buried her face in her handkerchief.

'I know. But I guess you did me a favor.'

The head counselor arrived. 'Colene, whatever possessed you to let him kiss you like that?' she demanded. 'You know I shall have to report both of you to your families as well as apply demerits for discipline.'

'You kissed him?' the roommate asked, astonished.

The counselor glanced at her, startled. 'Why aren't you at the dance?'

Colene spoke before Mitzi could answer. 'We had a quarrel. I got back at her. I got her date to take me instead, at the last minute, so she was frozen out. He didn't kiss me; *I* kissed *him*. Ask anyone; they all saw it, except the chaperon, who only looked when she heard the applause. So I fixed them both good.'

The counselor stared at the roommate. 'Is this true?'

'Why do you think she's been crying?' Colene demanded.

The counselor was at a loss for only a moment. Then she acted in the decisive fashion of her kind. 'Colene, I am appalled at you. I will deal with you later.' She turned to Mitzi. 'You come with me. You *will* attend the dance with your date.'

164

In moments they were gone. Colene lay on her bunk bed, gazing at the ceiling. She was proud of herself. She knew her date would play along. Not only would it get him out of trouble with the counselors, it would make him a celebrity for the night. Two girls had fought to date him!

Next day the buses came and the kids went home. They were from all over the country and had no contact with each other apart from the camp. The counselors were busy keeping things moving, and there wasn't much chance for any talking. But every time a camper caught Colene's eye, he or she smiled and made a little gesture of a finger across the throat. It was a temporary camp convention, signifying credit for getting punished for doing something daring or decent. It had special meaning in Colene's case. They all knew, and all were pleased. Naturally no one told the counselors. Secrets – secrets were the stuff of life.

That was it. When Colene's mother received the discipline report, she was perplexed. 'What did you do?'

'I kissed a boy in public.'

Her father burst out laughing. 'About time!'

Colene wondered what he would have said if he had known about the rape. Her world was such a schizoid place, where a gang rape went unnoticed while an innocent kiss got a girl in trouble. For all that, the last week of camp, betrayal and all, had been a high point in her life.

Why did she want to die, anyway? Now she felt far more positive. It was because of Darius, she knew: even the hope of him made her want to live, for she had to live to love, and she did love. Even the notion of sex, which had pretty much turned her off, now turned her on. With *him* it would be beautiful, she knew.

But it was also Seqiro. She had loved horses from afar. Now she loved one from up close. Very close. Right-inside-her-mind close. She could tell him her secrets, and he would not betray them. That made her feel much better about living.

'Seqiro!' she exclaimed. 'Are you helping me? I mean, messing with my mind, making me forget the pain or whatever?'

I could do this, but have not, because I see that it was that pain

165

that caused you to embark on the Virtual Mode. Without it you might give up your quest.

'You mean you're selfish, Seqiro? You want my company?'

That is true. He sent a non-specific companion thought of agreement that was so complete it had to be believed.

She was thrilled in much the way she had been when she learned that the boy at camp had really wanted to dance with her. It meant he was not just putting up with her. 'Don't worry. I want to get together with Darius, and I want to stay with you. I'm glad you didn't mess with my mind. That means I really *am* feeling better. Just going through those memories with you makes me feel better.'

What is your desire of life?

Colene thought for a moment, and then it poured out of her. 'I like to consider myself apart from the whole earth. There is no dignity left. I would like to be able to float away with my books and music and my guitar. It just seems to me that there are few people left with any integrity, and two of them happen to be my favorite writer and my favorite musician. I do too much thinking for my own good. I compose poetry in my head, but it won't come out right on paper. It's depressing. I dream too much, also. I have so many ambitions, and I am crushed when I realize how very few will ever be achieved. I want to be an author, a musician, a veterinarian, a researcher working with dolphins and other marine life, a friend of those I admire. I want to be someone who would die for her cause. I want to be creative. I want to be a starving artist. I want always to be traveling, never in one place for long. I want to be defending everyone's rights, especially animals and women. I want to be free, inspiring, compassionate. I want to be everything. I want to live under a night sky with someone I love intensely, and never have to move. To sit and gaze at the heavens with someone. I want never to be tied down or held back as I am now. Above all, I want to be free. I want it to be nighttime forever.'

I share your feeling. But what you have thought is not all. His thought was sympathetic.

She laughed. 'No, that's not all! It's not even consistent. I want never to have to stay in one place and never to have to move. I want total freedom and total irresponsibility and total dedication. I want everything and nothing, all at the same time. I know it doesn't make any sense, but this isn't sense, this is desire. So does it make any sense to you, or would it, if you were a girl?

I am a stallion, neither human nor female, and I have similar desires. You express them better than I could formulate them.

She felt another surge of the continuing thrill of being with him, of telling him her secret heart and being understood. She was talking, but her mind was carrying harmonics that made her whole feeling come across, so much greater than mere words could ever convey. His mind was sending back background washes and waves of understanding and support, so she knew he meant it. Telepathy: it was like being in a hot tub together, their bodies dissolved away and their minds sharing the essence.

'Do you have religion, Seqiro?'

There was a quick exploration of the concept she lifted to the surface. *No.*

'Maybe that's better. I don't know whether I have religion either. I feel that it's better for me to take my own decisions about religion than to have my beliefs dictated to me. I hate people who go to church just so they can feel better about doing other things that they know are bad. I think I believe more in nature than in God. I can see nature, and feel and be a part of it. God is more of a closed case. I like to feel a little different from other people and have a different view of things. That's part of the reason I'm not too wild about school. Everyone is expected to be the same. It leaves no room for freedom of thought. If you're not like everyone else, you stand out and are not tolerated. I want to break away from this everybody-must-be-the-same type of society. Routine is awful. To do the same thing every day, every week, is torture. I hope, someday, to do something that allows for a lot of freedom and creativity. To live in a small house with natural wooden floors that creak beneath my feet. My home will be on the coast where it stays dark for a long time. I will go outside at night and be inspired by the storm clouds over the ocean. There will be a rocky cliff that I can sit on while I think.'

Yes.

Colene opened her eyes. 'So you see, I dream wonderful things, but in the back of my mind I have always known that I will just end up in some stupid job and live like everyone else. I couldn't even speak of my dreams before, because people would just laugh. They think the dull world is all there is.'

Now you know about the other realities, and are on the Virtual Mode. Your life will after all be different.

'That's right! Say, Seqiro, if everything else doesn't work out, let's you and me just keep traveling à la Mode!'

We do not know how far we shall have to travel as it is, or what dangers we shall face. The day is late; we had better seek sanctuary for the night.

'Yes, that's right. I didn't realize how tired I've gotten, with all this walking.' Which made her realize that it had never occurred to her to ride the horse. Seqiro just wasn't that kind of horse.

They came into a series of realities in which there were thickly forested mountains. Colene knew that there was nothing like this within a day's walking distance of Oklahoma, which meant that the geography changed in nearby realities as well as the creatures and the underlying rules of nature.

'You were right, Seqiro,' she said. 'I can't ride my bike here! But if we come to a region where it's flat or paved, I'll be able to.'

I shall be interested to see how this device operates. I have seen nothing like it before.

They found a clear stream. 'That sure looks nice!' she exclaimed. 'I'd like to have a deep drink and wash up, but if the water won't stay with me –'

There is no problem about washing, for you do not need to have the water stay. As for drinking – perhaps it should be done, as we can remain the night in this reality and assimilate the water. We are sweating, so may excrete some of the alien water in the normal course, without being bound to its reality.

Colene, suddenly desperately thirsty, focused on one thing. 'You mean it's all right to use this water?'

Provided we remain here for some time.

'That's good enough for me!' She threw herself down and

drank deeply. All that water on top of all that exertion made her feel giddy, but it was worth it.

Seqiro drank more cautiously. Then they both washed. Colene got out of her loincloth and cape and splashed naked, screaming with pained pleasure at the shock of the cold water. Then she took a sponge they had packed and sponged off the horse's hide where the bags of supplies weren't in the way. Seqiro did not let her remove his burdens; wary of possible danger, he preferred to keep everything on him, so as to be able to step quickly into another reality without leaving important things behind. Colene had to admit that made sense. She was able to clean him pretty well by pushing away one bag at a time and sponging under it. His hide was steaming hot, but the chill water helped cool him.

It is a delight to have this attention from you without coercion.

'You don't get washed off at home?'

Our humans act only under our imperative. We direct them in all things, and punish them when they do not perform.

'Where I live, girls do these things for horses because they love horses.'

It would seem that the activities are similar, but the motives dissimilar.

'It would seem,' she agreed.

Colene bent twigs and scuffed the forest floor to mark the borders of the other realities on either side, so they would not cross unawares. They had a channel ten feet wide and endlessly long to remain in. It was hard to believe, because the forest and stream were uninterrupted, but she had now had enough experience to treat the boundary with extreme respect.

I have quested through this vicinity of this reality, and found no hostile or dangerous creatures, Seqiro thought. *There may be danger in the adjacent realities, but we need not be concerned about those until we resume our travel.*

'That's nice,' Colene said, relieved. 'Are you going to lie down to sleep?'

That is not necessary. I can rest and sleep on my feet.

'The reason I asked is if you lie down, I can lie down with you, and be warm.'

That is true. As it is safe, I shall lie.

So it was that they lay down in their narrow channel beside the stream. Colene took a heavy blanket from Seqiro's supplies and spread it over him, then settled down against his side, between two bags of feed. It was really quite comfortable, all things considered. She slept, feeling about as happy as she could remember since losing Darius.

8

PROVOS

Darius resumed his quest alone, having delivered Prima to his anchor Mode. His feelings were mixed. He was not glad for the delay occasioned by this encounter, yet it had enabled him to satisfy about three quarters of his commitment to Kublai: he had found Prima, and she had a lot of information about the nature of the Modes that Kublai would find most interesting. He was now about two days behind wherever he would have been, but it was possible that he would have been captive or dead by now if it had not been for her. Probably he was ahead, overall. For one thing, he was now the first in a long time to enter a Virtual Mode and return.

Prima had fashioned for him the mirror tube she had promised. It did seem to work. He experimented by setting a package of food on the ground, stepping across the boundary, looking back to see nothing, then poking the tube cautiously across. He did see the package in the mirror, when it wasn't visible directly. So it seemed that the way the tube excluded the light of the Mode in which he stood did enable it to carry the light of the Mode beyond. Or perhaps it was just that the device was fashioned of the substance of his anchor Mode, so was able to transmit the light along the Virtual Mode.

But it was not feasible to stop to check every Mode boundary as he went. He would take ten times as long to get anywhere if he did that. So he would have to use it judiciously, when there seemed to be danger. Such as in the region of the dominant dragons.

He moved much faster this time, using magic to take himself as far along the route as it would. Magic seemed to have no difficulty taking him across Modes, in the region of the Virtual Mode where magic was operative. Beyond that he walked rapidly, with the confidence of his prior experience in two directions.

Soon he reached the lake. He had learned a lot here, from Prima. Now he became more cautious. He needed to get safely past the region of the dragons. But he didn't depend on the tube alone. He had another sword, and also a heavy pair of shears which could cut through cord. For this he had more confidence in the shears than the sword, because they would be faster. He also had a fair coil of cord of his own, strong enough to sustain several times his weight without breaking. Experience counted.

He came to the geographic region of the dragons, which on the Virtual Mode was the same as the Mode of the dragons. This time he intended to keep the two separate! He paused to use his mirror tube before crossing each boundary. He could even see his footprints in the soft dirt, in places. To a creature watching, he would seem to appear, walk three paces, and disappear, leaving the prints.

Now he was almost at the place where he had been netted; he recognized the tree ahead from which the net had been suspended. There was no net visible, of course, because it didn't exist in this Mode. But the dragons, or their monkey servitors, had surely restored the damaged one, ready to trap the next unwary Mode traveler.

He moved to the side, then slowly poked his forward mirror across. He turned it, so that the image in the near mirror swept across the region.

There was the net, cunningly set so that a creature who plowed into it would cause it to close and rise, completing the trap. There was no dragon in sight, but he knew how quickly one could come when a trap was sprung.

He pondered a moment. Suppose he threw something across into the net, then crossed behind the dragon when it approached the net? No, he could not move anything from one Mode to another except his own belongings, which he had no intention of risking. It would be better to avoid the issue. He knew how dangerous those dragons were, because they understood about the Modes.

He surveyed the section carefully, turning the mirror around. There seemed to be nothing to the side of the net. Yet how could the dragons be so sure of catching something at that particular place?

He became aware of an itching on one leg. He looked down. He was standing in a bed of nettles. Their spikes seemed to be actually clinging to his trousers and seeking to stab through. That was why: the path he had been following was the only place clear of the nettles. Animals in several Modes must have found the best place through, and it made sense for him too. He had followed it before without even being conscious of the nettles.

He looked beyond. The nettles extended as far as he could see. The mystery of the net's placement was becoming less. There really was no other way through.

He could step cautiously, and cut the anchor line, disabling the trap, and go on quickly. But adjacent Modes tended to be similar. There could be another net in the following Mode, or a pit, or something worse. He did not like this region at all.

He decided to avoid the whole thing. He retreated through the Modes until he found a way through the nettles, then proceeded down the slope toward what had been the dragon's camp in its own Mode. He came to the field, then turned and proceeded across Modes again. There had been no trap in this vicinity, so it was probably a safe crossing. Still, he slowed and tested each Mode as he came to that vicinity.

When he passed the one showing the cages in the valley, he was relieved. There were several Modes with cages; then they faded and the countryside resumed.

He considered whether to find a way back to his original path, which proceeded most directly through Modes toward wherever he was going. But there could be other traps along it, so he continued through the field, and then through the forest, until the slope changed and the hill became a plain. Only then did he return to his direct path, slowly.

Time had passed, and nightfall was approaching. He had come a long way, and his legs were tired, but he was surprised at how fast the day had passed. He had not even paused for lunch, and was only now getting hungry. Was it possible that the length of the day changed along with other things, in other Modes? Yes, that did seem possible. Too bad he did not have a time piece of the type Colene had. It was a little device she wore on her left wrist, which helped to cover the scars there. Tiny pointers moved in it, indicating the hour of the day. Superfluous in Darius' Mode, of course, where things happened when they happened. But now that time might be changing, such a device might have enabled him to verify just how much difference there was.

Colene. She kept returning to his thoughts. On one level he recognized this quest as foolish, because he had already found his answer. He could go home and marry Prima and have an excellent career as Cyng of Hlahtar. She was older than he, but that was irrelevant; Hlahtar's wife was neither for love nor offspring, but for a ready source of joy to spread. Prima was the best possible source. But he was intent on Colene, who offered him none of that. All she offered him was private love.

Well, that was what he wanted. He would fetch Colene, then see about Prima. It might be foolish, but it was what he wanted. At least he knew that Kublai had a good situation during his absence.

He came to a lake at dusk, or perhaps the shore of a sea. There was no such body of water within walking distance in his Mode, but he had long since recognized that though geography changed gradually, it also changed significantly, and it resembled that of his home only in the immediate vicinity of his anchor. Were he to become trapped in the Mode in which he stood at this moment, and walk back through it the way he would come until he reached the spot where his anchor was supposed to be, he would probably find a completely different geography. The Modes changed vertically as well as horizontally, as if each sliver of mica had a different pattern that matched that of its neighbor slivers only when they were

174

close. It was possible that when he had made the first foray into Colene's Mode, it had been to the same geographic spot in her Mode as the one he had left in his.

He searched out a tree whose larger branches spread from one Mode to another. That was ideal. Prima had shown him that a tree was a good place to spend the night, removed from nocturnal creatures of the ground. But attack could come, and the best way to deal with it was to avoid it – by stepping into the next Mode. If he could do so without leaving the tree, so much the better.

He drank from the lake, washed, and ate from his pack. He realized that this must be a lake, because the water was not salty. But he could not see across it. Then he drew out his light blanket, climbed into the tree, braced himself, wrapped himself, and settled down for sleep. He thought of Prima, who had slept in his embrace, sharing warmth. At the time he had wished it could have been Colene, but now he realized that Prima herself had been good company. She had been intelligent and practical and not finicky about niceties, an easy person to travel with despite the awkwardness of their arms being constantly bound together. She was not at all the kind of woman he had been looking for, consciously, but very much the kind he actually needed. Colene, in contrast, was young and pretty and devoted, matching his desire, but quite unsuitable for marriage to the Cyng of Hlahtar. So said his logic. So much for logic. He wanted Colene.

As he was nodding off, something occurred to him that woke him up again. If Colene was at the same spot on the globe as he, one Mode directly over the other, so that his first foray with the Chip had plunged him straight up or down – how could he reach her by traveling on the slant? He was walking horizontally, stepping down into each new infinitely-thin Mode in the course of three paces. It wasn't a physically vertical thing, or the slopes of hills would have put him into new Modes at a great rate. But he was definitely moving across the terrain. By the time he reached Colene's Mode, he should be far from the spot on the globe he had started at, and therefore far from her. How would he be able to find her?

175

No, he had to be near her when he reached her Mode, because she had an anchor there. So that should be no problem. But how was it possible to travel horizontally and arrive vertically?

Then he remembered another part of the explanation the Cyng of Pwer had given, whose significance had bypassed him at the time. The Virtual Mode was like a plane cutting through the Modes at an angle, but it was not infinite. It was really a plane segment bounded by the five anchors. Like a pentagon, or roughly circular in outline. He could be walking around the edge of it. When he got half way around, there would be Colene.

The image helped reassure him, but it did not do the whole job. This Virtual Mode was really not a simple thing, and some of its incidental aspects, such as the business of drinking the water of foreign Modes along the way, were tricky. His image might be all wrong.

At any rate, he slept.

In the morning Darius resumed his travel. He traveled around the lake. At one point he encountered a family of otter-like animals who spooked at his appearance and swam rapidly away. At another he came across a small dragon or large lizard, similarly shy. But he became wary, because where there were small dragons there could also be large ones.

Beyond the lake was a settled region. At first it was just a planted field, but as he passed by it, successive Modes brought it to more intense cultivation and a road appeared. This looked human, but his wariness increased. Human beings would not necessarily be friendly. In fact he felt far more at ease among the animals of the wilderness, for very few of them represented any danger to him, and those few could be fairly readily avoided. But human beings were potentially worse than the dragons. Certainly he would not walk into the center of a village and announce himself!

He walked clear of the fields and found a forested section. The trees were unlike those he knew, being yellow of trunk and blue of leaf, but a tree of any color remained reassuring and protective. This was no jungle, and there was little undergrowth, but it did provide some privacy for his passage.

Then he spied a woman. She was standing in the center of a glade as if expecting him. She wore a small hat with two very long projections like the antennae of insects, a gray woolen sweater, an ankle-length brown knit dress, and high black boots laced up the front. She had what was evidently a traveling bag beside her. She was old, perhaps sixty. What was on her mind?

He approached her cautiously, following the sideways channel of this Mode. He could have stepped into the next Mode and avoided the contact, but she had seen him and he preferred to be polite as long as it was safe to be so. 'A greeting,' he said, speaking in his own language.

She said something indecipherable. Her language was not only different, it was weirdly different; he could not tell whether she had uttered a greeting, curse or gibberish. She picked up her bag. It had straps, and he realized that it was actually a kind of backpack, which she now donned. She was certainly prepared!

He tried again in Colene's language. 'Hi.'

She smiled and put her hand on his arm. She stepped forward, drawing him along with her.

She was evidently harmless, and of course she could not go any distance with him. Having tried to communicate, and failed, he decided simply to walk along with her, and step through to the next Mode when he reached the boundary. He would fade from her sight and touch, and she would think she had had a supernatural experience. An unkind trick to play on her, perhaps, but kinder than rejecting her gesture outright. It was evident that she expected to go somewhere with him.

They walked back to the point where he had been when he had first seen her, then turned to resume his original route. They stepped through the invisible boundary together.

Darius did a doubletake. *She was still there!* Still walking beside him, her hand on his arm.

But Prima had been able to cross Modes with him, as long as she touched him. He had understood that this was because she was of his Mode, or very close to it, despite not being an anchor person. This woman was not close at all. Had his notion been wrong? Could a person of another Mode cross simply by maintaining contact with an anchor person on the Virtual Mode? So it seemed to be.

But that would mean that she would be stranded in a Mode that was foreign to her. It would be wrong to leave her like that.

He turned and stepped back into the woman's Mode, bringing her along with him. 'I must go where you can not,' he told her firmly, withdrawing his arm from her hand. 'I am sorry. I am unable to explain, but I must leave you here.' He stepped across, alone.

He looked back. The woman was gone, of course; she did not exist in this Mode. The glade remained, and there was a small creature in a tree that he thought had not been there in the other glade. It must have watched him appear, disappear, and reappear, with an understandable perplexity.

Then the woman reappeared. She had stepped through after him.

Darius just stared. She had done it on her own! No physical contact! But that was impossible, unless –

Then he realized what the answer had to be. She was an anchor person! There were five of them, and he did not know the identity of three. It had not occurred to him that he would meet any of them, but if he truly was walking around the edge of a figurative plate, he would indeed encounter other anchor folk.

Somehow he had not expected an old woman, despite expecting nothing. What was he to do with her? He couldn't take her with him!

She took his arm again and urged him forward. She did want to go with him, and seemed to know the situation. It was hard for him to say no, because he couldn't speak her language and couldn't stop her from following him. That did not make the situation any less awkward.

He sighed inwardly and resumed walking. What was to be, was to be.

'Yes,' she said.

He was startled again. He stopped in place. 'You speak my language?'

'No.'

'But you are speaking it now! You –'

She uttered a mellifluous stream of unintelligibility. Evidently she knew only a few of his words.

'How did you learn "yes" and "no"?'

'Yes, future,' she said. 'No, past.'

Now he understood the words, but could not fathom the meaning. She might not mean the same thing by those words that he did. But in case she did, it could mean that she expected to travel with him from now on, and had not done so in the past.

They resumed walking. The forest disappeared, but the cultivated fields were gone; they had gone beyond the group of Modes in which these folk operated.

'Provos,' she said.

He glanced at her. She removed her hand from his arm and tapped herself above her slight bosom.

Oh. He tapped himself. 'Darius,' he said.

They stepped into another Mode. Abruptly her hand tightened on his arm. 'No!' she said, trying to hold him back.

He stopped. 'What's the matter?'

She merely shook her head, unable to clarify the matter.

He looked around. There was nothing threatening in view. 'I have somewhere to go,' he said. He started to step forward again.

'No!' She hauled him back again.

Could there be something in the next Mode that she knew about and he could not see? He brought out his mirror tube and extended it forward. But as he started to take a cautious step, she stopped him a third time.

He almost lost his balance. The end of the tube dipped to touch the ground.

A pointed stake shot up from the ground, right beside the end of the tube. The end of the stake was discolored.

'A poison trap!' Darius exclaimed. 'If I had stepped there, it would have stabbed my leg!' Or worse.

He put away the tube, found a stick, and poked beside the

stake. In a moment another stake shot up, and then another. There was a row of them slanting across this Mode segment.

'I think you just saved my health or life,' he told Provos, shaken. 'How did you know?'

But she now seemed to be ignoring the situation, as if it were of no further concern.

He walked to the side, beyond the stakes, and poked some more. There was no further reaction from the ground, and Provos did not balk him. The danger seemed to be limited to that one segment.

All the same, he used the tube to check the next Mode carefully before crossing. This escape had been quite too narrow!

Nothing was in view. They crossed, cautiously. He fetched a stick in this Mode and poked ahead. There was nothing. The stakes seemed to be an artifact of a single Mode, in much the way the net of the dragons had been.

They continued until the afternoon grew late. Darius didn't know how to ask Provos about camping arrangements, so he simply went ahead and trusted her to protest if she chose.

And protest she did, after he had located a suitable tree to use for the night. At first he thought it was because she was prudish about climbing or sharing warmth, but it seemed that she was becoming increasingly nervous about this whole region. He saw no reason for it, but after the experience with the stakes he took it seriously.

He offered to make the same camp in the Mode they had just crossed. To that she agreed. She opened her bag and produced what seemed to be homemade bread and a sweet spread, which she shared with him. He wasn't sure whether he could eat it, because of the problem retaining foreign food when crossing Modes, but realized that if it had traveled with her through all the prior Modes, it was safely on the Virtual Mode and should remain with them. The substance of her Mode was as real for him as the substance of his own or of Colene's. That was the thing about the anchors; they really were firm.

'Thank you,' he said. She did not acknowledge.

They performed their separate natural functions in different nooks of the Mode, then mounted the tree and shared his blanket. Provos seemed to be entirely at ease with the closeness, which surprised him. He was considerably more at ease than he would have been before the experience with Prima.

Prima. Provos. There was a certain similarity of names. Did it mean anything? He decided that it didn't. It was a minor coincidence until proven otherwise.

In the morning they got down and unkinked their bodies. Provos was old but spry; she must have had camping experience. Indeed she produced a set of stones which struck a spark that started a fire, and they were able to have a hot meal of some kind of tasty tubers she brought from her bag. She was certainly doing her part.

Then they doused the fire, got organized, and stepped back across the boundary.

Darius stared. There were foot prints where there had been none before; something had come here in the night. Huge claws had dug into the ground, as if a giant bird had landed here. The bark of the tree they would have slept in was torn away in patches.

'Something came here and smelled our traces,' he said, awed. 'It scratched the ground where we stood, and scratched at the tree where I had started to set up for the night. By the marks, it was huge and predatory: a dragon or carnivorous bird. I think we would have been dead.'

But Provos seemed unconcerned, hardly noticing the marks. She was just interested in going on.

He refused to settle for that. 'What is it with you?' he demanded. 'Twice you may have saved my life, yet you act as if it is nothing.' He pointed to the marks, making her look. 'How did you know?'

'Yes, future,' she said. 'No, past.'

'You said that before, but I don't know what it means!'

She tried to explain. 'I yes future. You yes past. I no past. You no future.'

He tried to make sense of this, in the context of what he had seen. She was yes future and no past. He was no future and yes past. He had no future and she did? He couldn't accept that!

And that couldn't be it, because the corollary would be that she had no past while he did. The only thing that made remote sense was that he could not foresee the future, while she –

She could see the future? She had precognition? That did seem to be the case! And the barrier of language prevented her from telling him exactly what it was that she saw, so she was able to warn him only by crude gestures. But that could not be the whole of it. What did she mean about no past? She could not see the past?

He walked on with her, his mind laboring. How was it possible for her not to know the past? She would have no memory! She would be completely unconcerned with yesterday.

Which was exactly the attitude she showed. Concern for the future, none for the past. It seemed unbelievable, but she *was* from an alien Mode, and its ordinariness in the physical aspect might mask a truly amazing difference in the mental aspect.

He reviewed specifics as they went. She had balked at one place, and there had been a deadly trap there. She had surely not been there before; she was as new to the Virtual Mode as he, and had been waiting for someone to come along it, so she would not have to go alone. She had probably been waiting for days, and acted the moment she saw him. Why had she not been afraid of the stranger? Because she had foreseen his arrival! She might not be concerned about what was past, but she knew she would be traveling with him, so she had made sure to be there at the right time.

Yet she had not seemed to foresee the poisoned stakes, exactly. She had just been very nervous. It was the same with the monster of the night. She had not been concerned about that immediately; only after camping preparations were well along had she insisted on leaving the area. It didn't seem to be straight anticipation of future events.

She had likened her situation to his. 'I yes future, you yes past.' He did not foresee the past, he remembered it, and the farther in the past it was, the foggier his memory tended to become, unless it was something important. Could she *remember* the future? 'I no past, you no future.' She could not remember the past, though she might have a notion of it by judging from the present. If she was here with him, and remembered what they would be doing in the future, she could safely assume that they had met in the past and had some kind of understanding. Just as he could assume that he would be traveling with her for a while.

But that monster of the night – that was not a threat to be forgotten quickly! Why had it taken her a while to catch on to it?

Because it happened in a foreign Mode! He could not remember the past of Modes he had not been in; she could not remember the future of Modes she would not be in. But if he stayed in a Mode for a while, and got some experience in it, he could remember that much of it. She must have become acclimatized to it, gradually, and then realized that something terrible was about to happen there. So she had warned him. When they moved into the adjacent Mode that feeling did not come on her, so she relaxed.

It did seem to make sense. But if so, there would always be some problems. How could they relate, if she remembered only what they would be doing, and he remembered only what they had been doing?

He saw Provos nodding as if she had just come to understand something. Yet there was nothing unusual about the landscape of the Modes they were passing through, and they had not spoken.

But maybe they were about to speak, and she was remembering that! He was concerned with the problem of relating to a woman who could not remember their dialogue after it happened – but could remember it coming.

So maybe there was a way. 'Provos,' he said – and realized that she had started turning to him before he spoke. Yes, she was remembering that he was about to say something to her! 'Night, monster,' he said, making clawing motions with a hand.

She looked concerned. 'Monster,' she repeated.

'You saved me,' he said. He took her hand, put it on his own arm, and acted as if he were being pulled back. 'Escaped monster.'

'Monster no?' she asked.

183

'Monster yes,' he said. He repeated the gesture. 'Then monster no. You warned me.'

'Day monster no,' she said.

Which should mean that no monster was in their immediate future. Except that her perception might be limited to the Mode they were now in. So there could be a monster in the next one. If something threatened in the next step, she might pick it up, as she had with the stakes; but if it threatened in several hours, she might take a while to attune to it.

Did that make sense? Suppose something awful had happened several hours ago in one Mode; would he forget about it in the last half hour before they left that Mode? He didn't think so. Also, if she remembered something bad that was about to happen, and told him, and he changed it, then it wouldn't happen. So how could she remember it? It seemed like paradox.

But maybe not. If something she remembered didn't happen, her memory should change to what *would* happen. But it might be foggy, because of the change. So it could be a while before it clarified for her. The future was not a simple reversal of the past; it was mutable, so her memories could be changed or confused at times. The more distant something was, the longer it might take her to orient on it. Thus a danger in the next step she could catch immediately, but one several hours away would not clarify until she had more experience with the Mode in which it was to occur. Not just because it took her time to attune, but because the more time passed, the more chances there were for it to be changed, fogging her memory. She had to get closer to the event to be sure of it.

At any rate, he hoped he had a workable system. He had just informed her of what had recently happened, and she had informed him of what was about to happen. She had remembered what he was going to tell her, so knew something of the prior adventures despite not being able to remember them directly. She had remembered his telling her. Tomorrow he would tell her again, so she could always have a notion what had been going on. Meanwhile she had told him that nothing bad was about to happen, and he would remember that. When she told him that there would be danger, he would be suitably warned by his memory of her words. It seem like a feasible way to relate. If he had it straight. His mind tended to stretch out of shape as he reviewed the matter.

But if he were correct about the way the new Modes cut off her awareness of the future, she would not do him much good while they were actually traveling. Only when they camped for a time. But that was when they most needed warning of danger, so they could sleep.

His thoughts mostly settled, he resumed his awareness of the terrain. They were out of the forest and were climbing a gentle slope overgrown with waist-high plants whose leaves were pale blue. They made a faint jingling noise as the progress of the two human beings pushed them aside. At irregular intervals there were outcroppings of the underlying rock, which was red. It was a pretty enough scene.

They crested the hill and started down the other side. The plants shifted from blue to purple, and the outcrops to pink, as the Modes shifted. The sky was turning deep green.

Suddenly the two of them were falling. Darius felt a moment of panic. Then his feet struck steeply sloping pink sand. He tried to stand, but could not, so he tried to sit, and it made little difference; he continued sliding down. Provos was beside him, doing her best to maintain a decorous attitude despite being out of control. They were rapidly descending into a huge pit.

Another drop, and another rescue by a steep slope. Then they landed in a pile of pink sand. They climbed out of it and surveyed their situation.

This was evidently an artificial excavation of enormous scope. On three sides it rose so steeply that climbing it was out of the question; they had been fortunate that it had even slowed their fall. The fourth side was flat: a terrace, narrowing into a level road leading out between the towering pink sides.

So why hadn't Provos warned him of this? Because they had stepped into it in a new Mode. Because it was artificial, there was no natural warning, nothing they could see ahead. This ground had once been whole, and now it was hollow, and they had stepped from the ground of

185

one Mode into the emptiness of the next. He had known that she could not anticipate such a thing, yet had somehow depended on it, thinking their periodic descriptions of past and future events would suffice. Only when they remained for a time in a single Mode would that system work well.

Who had dug this monstrous hole? Probably some civilization similar to the one Colene shared. She had told him how they mined deep in the ground, sometimes leaving just such pits as this. So maybe he was getting close to her Mode. That was encouraging.

But not identical, because this was not her village with its paved streets and angular houses. So it was best to get on by this pit before those who dug it arrived. Trying to go back was hopeless; they couldn't even stand on that slope, and could never climb to the top.

Provos evidently agreed. They dusted themselves off and started walking across the level base.

Suddenly there was a giant thing bearing down on them. It resembled one of the traveling machines Colene had described, but was much larger and fiercer.

Both of them stepped hastily back across the boundary. The machine vanished. It least it was easy to avoid, with the Modes.

Darius got out his mirror tube and poked it across the boundary. The machine had passed beyond them, and was now stopping beside another machine, one with a giant set of jaws on the end of a long neck.

They stepped across again. Now he saw that the jawed machine was gouging great mouthfuls of orange sand from the base of the pit, and spitting them into the back of the traveling machine. So that was how the pit was made. The machines must have been working at it for a long time, evidently wanting the pretty sand.

They crossed another boundary. The sand brightened a trace, now possessing more of a yellow component. The pit seemed larger, and there were several dark blue machines eating at the edge of it. All the machines of this section of the Virtual Mode were hungry for this sand!

It seemed that all they needed to do was keep walking across the pit until they reached the far side. Then –

Then what? The far side looked as forbidding as the near side. They would not be able to climb out of it either.

They would have to walk down the road, which surely led out. It was not going in the direction Darius wanted, but once they were free of the pit they could recover their course.

Darius turned to follow the road, and Provos went with him. Now they were remaining longer in one Mode, because the road slanted slowly across it.

A green machine came charging out of the pit. They stepped hastily into the next Mode, and the vehicle vanished. But there was a gray machine coming from the opposite direction. If they ducked back, they could get run over by the first. So they ran on across and jumped into the next Mode before the gray machine reached them.

Here there were yellow machines. These were smaller, though still formidable, and looked like huge insects with antennae. The antennae rotated, seeming to orient on the two living folk. Then two machines started toward them.

They ran on across, to the edge of the road where the next boundary would take them away. But something alarming happened.

They bounced off the boundary.

Darius stared at Provos. She seemed as dismayed as he. This had never happened before.

The machines were closing in on them. As one, they turned and ran back the way they had come, barely crossing the prior boundary before the machines arrived.

Another gray machine was coming. This one slowed, seeming to see them. It too had antennae.

'I don't like this,' Darius muttered. 'These things are aware of us!'

Provos agreed. But it wasn't safe to cross this Mode in front of the machine; it was too big and fast. They had to duck back into the Mode they had just left.

The two yellow machines were waiting. As soon as the two living folk reappeared in this Mode, the machines resumed motion, closing in.

Provos was becoming increasingly agitated. Darius knew that meant that she was starting to tune into future trouble here. They had to get away!

Their best chance seemed to be to cross rapidly through the Mode of the gray machines, so as to be out of this squeeze. He grabbed Provos' arm and pointed. But she demurred. She pointed down this Mode, at right angles.

If she was tuning in, she knew what she was doing. He nodded agreement, and they ran in that direction.

The yellow machines accelerated, quickly overtaking them. But they ran straight ahead, while the road curved, and the mechanical devices couldn't follow well. There was a ditch which was treacherous for wheels on frames to navigate. They had to swerve aside, and the two living folk got clear.

But other machines were now approaching from the opposite direction. One of them had large wheels that could handle the terrain.

Provos ran on, though she was now breathing hard and holding her side. She was an old woman, and evidently not in condition for such activity. But she must remember something to make this effort worthwhile.

Darius drew close to her, matched her steps, and put his right arm around her mid section. He drew her in close and lifted, taking some of her weight off her feet. This might have seemed unduly familiar, but she would remember that he had done this without familiar intent.

So it seemed. She put her left arm around him and leaned into him. Now they ran as one, with his legs assuming much of the burden. He was used to walking and running, and could handle this for a short distance.

A building came into sight. It was large, with several metal lacework towers rising from its top. It crossed their path, and they were headed straight for it.

But if the machines were chasing them now, what would happen when they reached that building? Surely there were many more machines in there!

The machines cut them off. Now Provos urged him to the left, across the boundary. The yellow machines vanished.

The ground was now flat, without the ditches that limited

the machines, and the gray machines were lurking. They were clustered in the vicinity the two living folk had left, but quickly reoriented and renewed the pursuit.

Provos kept running. As the gray machines caught up, she drew the two of them back to the Mode of the yellow machines.

They were now beyond the machines that had cut them off, and close to the building. This was not the kind of structure that creatures of flesh lived in; it was formed of a metal lattice, with spaced supports. He could see through the gaps into its center, where machines and parts of machines seemed to be clustered. Perhaps this was where the machines were bred, birthed and trained.

Provos drew free of him, squatted, and picked up a handful of orange sand. She stuffed it in whatever pockets she possessed. Darius, bemused, did the same. He had to trust her memory of the immediate future, as she had to trust his memory of the past. Then she put her hands on the edges of the lattice, and started climbing. Darius did the same, moving to her right to climb, though the point of this exercise baffled him. The machines would only trap them on the building.

Indeed, yellow machines were moving inside the building, on a platform that was rising by itself. The machines would reach the top before the people did.

Darius tried to find better climbing by moving to his right, but his shoulder banged into the impenetrable wall that was the next Mode. He didn't know what to make of that; surely the machines had not found a way to block it off to travelers!

Provos lost a handhold on her left and hung for a moment in doubt. He quickly steadied her with his left arm. Then she gestured with her left hand, and he saw it pass right through the metal of the wall. No wonder she had missed her hold! The building did not exist in the next Mode, though they could see it clearly from this one. On the ground it didn't matter if they strayed across a boundary, but here it could be fatal.

This minor misadventure had cost them time, and the platform with the machines was passing them. They would surely be made captive or worse when they reached the roof.

Provos held on firmly with one hand, and with the other

dug into a pocket. She brought out some sand and hurled it at the side of the platform, where toothed wheels turned. So Darius did the same. Was this a form of magic, a ritual throwing of sand? If so, it was useless, for this was obviously a nonmagical Mode. But he reminded himself again that she could remember the future, so should know what she was doing to make it memorable. He heaved another handful of sand into the works.

There was an unkind sound. The platform shuddered and slowed. Sparks flew out.

Now it was making sense. The gears did not like sand.

They climbed on to the top of the building, and walked across the metal roof. They remained carefully in their three-paces-wide channel, because the Mode on one side was an impenetrable wall, and on the other was a drop-off. It was a big building, and a fall from it would be devastating.

Provos went to the tower that was in their channel. But it was near the boundary. In fact, half of it was across the boundary; they had to pass it to the right, lest they fall.

But she did not try to pass it. Instead she started climbing it, though she was evidently tired. Her backpack surely weighed her down, with all the running and climbing. Yet the tower went nowhere except up. What was her urgency?

'This thing is only half anchored!' he warned. 'It will fall over with your weight!' But then he realized that this was not the case. The tower was quite firmly anchored, in this Mode. The fact that they could not touch its other side did not mean that it lacked that support. They could climb it, until it narrowed into nothing. Then what?

The yellow machines were getting their platform unjammed. Soon they would be here.

Darius shrugged and started up the tower after her. He hoped she was remembering something that he was unable to foresee, because otherwise they were doomed.

They climbed high on the narrowing tower. Now there was scarcely room for them, even in tandem, because of the half that didn't exist for them. A stiffening breeze tugged at them, making Darius even less comfortable about the height. What could possibly be the point of this?

190

Meanwhile the machines reached the roof and clustered around the base of the tower. It seemed that they could not climb it, but surely they had ways to get at those who did. Probably the only thing that had saved the two living folk so far had been the machines' desire to capture them alive. Maybe the machines, like the dragons, were interested in learning how to cross Modes, and thought that firm persuasion would elicit the secret from the travelers.

Provos stopped. He looked up and saw that she was struggling to get something from her pack. But she was now so tired that she couldn't twist around without being in danger of falling.

'I'll do it!' he said. 'What do you want?'

She made a gesture of throwing.

'Sand,' he said. He dug into a pocket and threw some sand down on the machines.

She shook her head no.

'Throw something else? But all we have is our supplies, and we need those.'

She nodded yes.

Darius gazed down at the machines. Now they were bringing something with a portable platform. They would be getting up here soon.

He sighed. He drew out a package of bread. He opened it and tore off one chunk with his teeth. He wanted to eat it, but this mouthful was for another purpose. What a waste! He threw it in the direction the woman had indicated.

The chunk flew out and down. It bounced against the invisible wall of the next Mode.

Provos signaled for him to throw again, higher.

He tore off another chunk, and threw it in a higher arc.

It disappeared.

'Yes!' Provos cried.

It took Darius a moment to realize the significance of what had happened. That last chunk had passed above the blank wall and entered the next Mode!

The woman made another gesture of throwing.

He worked it out. They had been unable to enter that Mode because there was no deep pit there. They could not step into solid rock. But if they got above the level of the ground, they could jump onto it!

Provided they knew the exact level. Too low, and they would strike the barrier and drop way down. Too high, and they would make it, but hurt themselves landing.

He ripped off more bread and began throwing in earnest. He found the level, about a body length below him. But it was also a body length away from him. How could they reach it?

The rope! If they could tie it to the tower above, they might be able to swing across on it. He could push Provos so that she would go far enough, and then she could let go on the other Mode.

He reached over his shoulder and plunged his hand into his pack. He found the rope and brought it out. It was fine thin cord, light but strong, with plenty of length. But how was he to tie it to the tower above them? There really wasn't room for him to climb up past Provos, and if he did, it would take time, and the machines' capture-platform was now in place and rising toward them. There wasn't enough time!

He gazed up. At the top, the tower had a crosspiece with hooked ends. That should be ideal to tie the rope to, had he the time and position to do it.

Provos looked down. She extended one hand. She wanted the rope?

He passed up one end. She worked the rope around her upper body and through part of the tower, tying herself to it. Then she leaned back, freeing both hands while her body was held by the rope. She formed a double loop in the cord, with an intricate knot. She fished a solid little package out of her pack and tightened the loops around it. Then she untied herself and passed the end of the rope down to him.

Darius realized that she had effectively weighted the end of the rope. Now he knew what to do. He held on firmly to the tower with his left hand, leaned out, and hurled the end straight up as hard as he could. He let the cord play out, holding tightly on to the other end.

It sailed up beyond the crosspiece, and down again, missing. He borrowed from Provos' technique, tying himself to the tower so as to free both hands. Then he hauled up the rope, leaned way out, and threw it with a more looping motion. This time his aim was good, but not his power; it passed just under the crosspiece.

He tried a third time, and a fourth, while the machine platform slowly came up at him. The fourth time did it: the rope passed over and swung down beyond. The weighted end came down and he caught it. He drew on the two ends, working the rope out to the edge of the crosspiece, where it was caught by the hook. Now they were ready to swing, and none too soon, because the machine platform was uncomfortably close.

Provos took the rope again. She removed the package and returned it to her pack. Then she formed a harness with the two ends, and put her legs through it. She certainly knew how to do things with that rope! In a moment she was dangling free of the tower, seated in the harness.

Darius climbed up, glad to get his feet farther away from the machines. He gave her a push to start her swinging. She swung out toward the invisible wall, then back past the tower, and disappeared.

Darius stared, then realized that this was not disaster. She had passed into the Mode of the gray machines. There was no building or tower there, but she was anchored by the rope to this yellow machine Mode. He could see the rope above, angling down and disappearing about halfway down.

Sure enough, in a moment she reappeared. First her bent knees and feet showed, then the rest of her. She swung past him, and he put out his hand and shoved her farther in the direction she was going. She went farther toward the wall Mode, but did not disappear.

In a moment she was passing him again, the other way. He gave her knees a shove, but it wasn't straight, and it started her turning. That couldn't be helped.

He looked down. The machines had stopped advancing. Their platform was still. Their feelers seemed to be focused on the vanished woman. They didn't know what was happening. Well, he would be surprised too, if a machine came through his home region, climbed a tower, dangled from it, and started swinging in and out of existence.

Provos reappeared. He gave her another good shove. She

swung far out – and half of her disappeared. Her feet remained in view, evidently snagging on the wall.

Then she was coming back. 'I gone!' she exclaimed. She remembered what was about to happen.

Pleased, he gave her another shove back, and another forward when she reappeared. This time she lifted her legs and disappeared entirely, and the rope went slack without returning. She must have put her feet down on the ground, stopping her swing.

Then the rope swung back to him, the harness empty. He caught it and worked his way into the harness.

Now the machines resumed activity, evidently catching on that the prey was escaping. The platform rose again.

Darius shoved off from the tower. He did not swing out far enough. He swiped at the tower, trying to increase his motion, and set himself spinning.

He swung into emptiness. There a dizzying distance below him was the pit, with the gray machines waiting. Then he was back passing the tower. He shoved at it again as well as he could, slowing his spinning but not gaining much on his swinging.

Then he was back over the gray machines. One was aiming what seemed to be a metal tube at him. From the tube came a rope which narrowly missed him. They were trying to catch him in the air and haul him down to them!

He swung back into the yellow-machine Mode. The platform was almost up to the level of his feet, and a machine with big pincers was reaching up. The pincers appeared to be padded so as not to do damage; they wanted to catch him, not kill him, as he had suspected. They were coming close to succeeding, because he simply could not get himself swinging enough.

Swinging. Something clicked. The children's game with swings – they could pump themselves up higher without touching anything else.

He started pumping, extending his feet and moving his body. Why hadn't he thought of this before? He gained momentum.

A pincer reached up to catch his passing leg. He kicked it

away. That started him spinning, and he was unable to pump. Trouble! He reached out and banged a hand into the tower as he passed, trying desperately to get straightened out. He succeeded, but at the expense of momentum.

He resumed pumping – and saw the yellow pincers directly in front of him. He could not avoid them this time!

He held his breath, tucked his feet under him, then swung them out in a two-legged kick. He smashed into the pincer machine, shoving it back. The platform moved, its support tower beginning to fall.

As Darius pumped himself up, he saw the gray machines taking aim again, and the platform falling, in alternate Modes. Then he broke through and caught a glimpse of a new green world, its surface barely under him. He could not quite stop at it; he needed one more good swing. But those swings were dangerous!

Then hands caught his feet. Provos had tackled his legs, trying to hold him there. But if he dragged her back with him –

She managed to hold him long enough so that he could pitch his upper body forward and brace against the ground. He struggled out of the harness.

Provos caught the harness, quickly undid it, and let go of one rope. She pulled, and the other rope disappeared. Soon the length of it had been hauled in. They had made it, with their equipment.

Later, several more Modes away from the pit and at a suitable camping site, they talked. Provos no longer remembered the business with the tower and rope, but he told her of it, and she told him that nothing dangerous was to occur during their stay in this particular Mode.

'Provos come why?' he asked her. Now he was sure that she was an asset to his journey, and wanted to know what she was getting from it. Was she along for the duration, or would she be deserting him when she found what she wanted?

She tried to convey a confusing concept, and it seemed that she had forgotten part of it, because it was in the past. But his memory of their meeting, and her memory of what he was to tell her in the future, enabled him finally to put it together.

Her memory of future events was hazy or null, but she did have memories of him, because he was to be a constant part of her next few days.

Provos suffered from amnesia. She had been able to remember her future perfectly, in as much detail as she desired, right up until a mysterious blank. As it approached, she viewed it with increasing trepidation, until she realized that it was not necessarily the end. Perhaps it was better viewed as a great new adventure occurring after some mishap such as a blow to the head. Since she could not avoid it, she decided to approach it positively. So she had packed her things, as for a long journey, and told her friends she was going to another region. That way they were not concerned about the future absence of her presence in their lives.

Now she was in that adventure, and enjoying it. She still suffered amnesia of the future, but not as badly. She understood the reason: because she had no future experience in most of the Modes they were crossing.

She had no plans for the future. She would know the future when she remembered it, and she was content to wait for that memory. It was actually rather exciting, being unable to tell what she was doing tomorrow, in contrast to the deadly dull existence she suspected she had been having in the past. She was not concerned about Darius' convenience, as she did not remember him telling her he disliked her company. When he preferred to move on alone, she would know it before the time came, and they would part.

Indeed, Darius realized that he did not object to her company. He was not looking for any personal complications along the way, and she presented few, which were more than compensated for by her brief insights of mischief forthcoming. She was a good companion for this treacherous journey.

'But how do you feel about your own death?' he asked. 'Will you see it coming?'

She certainly hoped so! She was not at all disturbed by his question. It turned out that she feared her death no more than he feared his birth. It was merely one end of a person's existence. But that part of her life she could not remember, which was in the past, she preferred not to think about, for it was filled with unkind mystery and foreboding, as well as with hopeful speculation. Exactly as was his future for him.

'But now you have a taste of what my perspective is like,' he told her. 'Because you can not anticipate most of your future either.'

She agreed that was frightening, but she would bear up under the challenge of it, knowing that it was bound to be alleviated one way or another before too long. She put her hand on his, with pity and comfort for his misfortune to be locked always in the past.

'Thank you,' he said, moved in mixed manner. But she had already lost the dialogue, and proceeded in a businesslike manner to the settling in for the night.

9

DDWNG

There were more realities than Colene had dreamed of. Some were inhabited by what were probably human beings or the equivalent; most were not. They passed quickly through the inhabited ones, which tended to cluster, and lingered in the wilderness ones. Wild creatures, as a general class, were not as dangerous as civilized ones. Seqiro was able to stun any creature who threatened, or simply to change its mind. In fact, she discovered, he could generate a mental field around them that discouraged insects, so that mosquitoes and biting flies did not come close. The first time she had slapped at a mosquito he had inquired, and then sent out the no-insect thought. Just like that, no problem. He had been satisfied to use his tail to flick away pests, until then.

She had liked him from the start. Each new thing she learned about him enhanced the feeling.

They walked for another day and slept another night. She kept no count of the number of realities they crossed, but judged that such a day's travel should represent about five thousand of them. The calculation was simple enough: ten feet per reality, if they crossed it at right angles as they usually did. Ten miles in the day, because they walked maybe ten hours at maybe three miles an hour, taking time for eating and rest. The tens canceled out, and the number of feet in a mile – about five thousand – was the number of realities. But it didn't matter. What counted was that they were making progress toward Darius. She knew they were; she felt the strengthening rightness of the route.

Most realities were overgrown with vegetation, but they did encounter a series of them with rocky sections, and she was able to ride her bicycle through these. Otherwise she would have been dead tired, because this was a whole lot more walking than she had done in a long time. She was lucky that her camping experience had prepared her somewhat; she knew how to conserve her strength and not push her limits.

Seqiro, in contrast, seemed indefatigable. He had evidently made it a point to maintain his health and stamina, and it showed.

I could carry you, he thought. *It would not represent a burden to me, as you weigh little.*

'I just don't think of you as a riding horse,' she said. 'You're my companion.'

Granted. But a companion may walk or be carried.

She smiled briefly. 'If it comes to the point where we really need to get somewhere, and I'm really holding us back, then you carry me. Until then, I feel more equal afoot.'

Because in your home reality horses are beasts of burden.

'Never to me!' she protested.

But your mind indicates that the association is there. You are concerned with what others will think, though none are here to see.

'Never argue cases with a mind reader!' she said ruefully. 'Or with someone smarter than you.'

I am quite stupid compared to you.

'No way! Everything I tell you, you understand right away, better than I do. So you're smarter or older or both, or just plain have more experience.'

None of these. I am your age in years: fourteen. That is mature for my kind, but my experience of my reality is less than yours of yours. I depend on your mind.

'Do you, Seqiro? Maybe you needed me to fetch your supplies and load them on you, and to open your gate. But once you got out of your reality, I became superfluous. You have just remained with me out of sympathy.'

By no means. I remain with you because I need you, and because we are compatible.

199

'A girl needs a horse,' she argued. 'But does a horse need a girl? Wouldn't you be happier out grazing, if the grass would stay with you?'

I would be satisfied grazing, he agreed. *But I am also satisfied to be traveling with you. Since I can not safely graze, and can comfortably travel with you, this is the preferable course.*

'But you could travel just as well without me! I'm really holding you back.'

Not so. I would be unable to travel without you. This is the major reason I did not break out of my confinement and enter the Virtual Mode alone.

'I don't believe that!' She was feeling that self-destructive urge, trying to persuade him to do without her. She didn't want to be alone; in retrospect she found her prior travel frightening. But to be a drag on this beautiful horse – that just wasn't right. 'Give me one good reason why you can't travel without me.'

My intelligence would revert to its normal level, and I would be unable to fix on a specific distant destination. I would soon be captured by any creatures who saw me as a beast of burden.

'But you're smart! I couldn't be talking with you like this if you weren't!'

I draw on your intelligence, which is excellent. In your absence I would retain only the memory of you, not the power of your mind. If other creatures captured me, and none shared minds with me, I would remain dull. I was dull until I made contact with your mind from afar; then I became more intelligent than any of my kind.

Colene was amazed. 'You mean – it's all me? I'm really talking to myself?'

You are talking to me, and I am as intelligent as you – because you share your mind with me. If you withheld your mind, I would indeed be just a stupid horse.

'But your kind controls my kind, in your reality! I saw it, I felt it. Your minds make hash of our minds.'

Our leaders retain intelligent humans who provide them with good power of the mind, much as your leaders retain strong horses who provide them with rapid transportation. In your reality your riders control your horses despite the inferior strength of the humans. In mine, the horses control the humans despite the inferior intelligence of the horses. It is a matter of who is in charge, and how power is wielded.

She was coming to accept it, reluctantly. 'So you needed a smart companion, so you would understand where you were going and how to get there. And I'm that companion.'

Yes.

'And if I'd turned out to be a bad human man, you'd still have had to go with me, because it would have been either that or stay under stall arrest.'

Yes.

'But I turned out to be a sweet human girl, and you like that better.'

Yes.

She turned to him. 'I was joking, Seqiro.'

No.

'I mean, about being sweet. I'm not sweet, I'm suicidal.'

Yes, you were suicidal once, and sweet. Now you are only sweet.

'You believe that?' she demanded

Yes. So do you. This is why I believe it.

She stepped into him and hugged his neck as well as she could. 'I love you, Seqiro.'

Yes. I also love you.

'But would you love me if you weren't picking it up from my mind?'

No. That is not an emotion I would understand alone. But it is pleasant now.

'I think I like you even better this way. You are my ideal companion.'

Yes.

'Yes,' she echoed. 'We are ideal for each other. Seqiro, we must stay together!'

Yes.

'You keep agreeing with me, and I love it!' she exclaimed.

Yes.

'Yet how is it you know so much, when I don't know it?'

A horse has good memory. I have learned much in my life, and when I am with you I am able to apply it relevantly.

She walked on with restored attitude. Seqiro did need her,

perhaps more than she needed him, and this was an enormous comfort. She had made it possible for him to escape his fate, and he would remain with her until he found what he was looking for – which he could best find only while he was with her, sharing her mind. That might be forever. That was long enough.

They stepped across a boundary, and suddenly there was barrenness. As far as they could see, the forested slopes had been abruptly denuded. The air was cold and dry.

They retreated, and the friendly trees reappeared. 'What happened?' Colene asked, baffled.

Nothing in my reality explains this. But you have thoughts of nuclear war in yours.

'I don't think it's that,' she said with a shiver. 'No slag. No green glass. No deadly radiation – I hope.' She glanced at him. 'I don't suppose you can detect radiation with your mind?'

Focus on it, and I will try.

She concentrated on deadly rays, uncertain of their names or how they would feel, but sure that they would cut up the tender cells of her body and mess up her genetics. Invisible shafts of destruction, like X-rays only worse. Would this be enough for him to fathom? She doubted it, yet she hoped, because otherwise they were at an impasse. How could they risk that barren waste, without being sure it wouldn't kill them just because they were there? They couldn't go around it, because it was evident that it extended everywhere on that planet. There had not even been any clouds. It was just so utter and final!

I can detect such radiation, Seqiro thought. *My telepathic mind is very sensitive to intrusion, and such rays would intrude. There are none.*

'Are you sure?' she asked eagerly, but knew it was a foolish question. Seqiro knew what he knew.

Yes, I am sure. But this may be immaterial. If that waste extends across many realities, we shall not be able to cross it.

'It can't extend forever!' she exclaimed. 'My sense says that where I'm going is somewhere beyond it. Darius didn't say anything about a desert.' But she realized that Darius hadn't said anything about the intervening realities, because the first time he had simply cut through directly. Only with the Virtual Mode did every reality between them become significant.

Then we must cross.

'But suppose it *does* cross many?' she asked, flipping across to the other case, as was her fashion when in doubt. 'Do we have supplies to make it? I don't want to be stuck in Death Valley without water!'

I see the bones of horses in your vision of that valley.

'Yes! It's awful! I've never been there, but I've seen it in movies. Oh, Seqiro, what shall we do?'

You love my company, but you would not be satisfied with it indefinitely. You must rejoin your human man. Therefore we must cross, because the alternative is not suitable.

'Yes, we must cross,' she agreed. She wished she could say it with more confidence. Where was the hero-istic, die-for-her-beliefs girl she longed to be? Not here, unfortunately.

They camped for the night, so as to be able to start early in the day. They agreed that the desert might get hot in the day, and cold at night. They might do best to cross it rapidly and get back into comfortable realities. But if it turned out to be more than a one day trek, they would be better off to maintain a measured pace, resting in the heat of noon and in the cold of night, preserving their strength. They could make a three day crossing, but not if they exhausted themselves on the first day.

Colene fetched dry sticks of wood, and bunches of dry grass, and used one of her precious matches to light a fire. Seqiro had checked and ascertained that there were no high powered minds in this reality, so that the fire would be safe. She was very pleased to have it, for psychological as well as physical reasons.

While she stared into the blaze, she reviewed plans with Seqiro. He would quest ahead for minds. He could tune in to both animals and plants, but the distance depended on circumstances. A strong telepathic mind similar to his own could be contacted across a continent, while dialogue with a nontelepathic mind was limited to about half that. The Virtual Mode was similar, making the different realities seem like one;

without it he would be confined to one reality. The less similar a mind was to his own, the more limited the range. Thus plants had to be fairly close for him to receive.

'Plants have minds?' Colene asked, startled.

Indeed they do. But not similar to yours. We find the best grazing by tuning in to the healthiest grass.

'But doesn't the grass hurt when you bite it off? Why would it tell you where it is?'

It does not suffer in the way you would. It is philosophical about being eaten. It accepts what is. Since grazing promotes the growth of more grass at the expense of weeds, there is a certain compatibility between us.

Colene shook her head. 'I hope so! I'd hate to have my head chewed off every week or so!'

A plant would hate to have to eat through its head, or to pull its roots from the ground and walk about.

She considered. 'I see your point, maybe.'

Everything was normal, for a single reality. But Colene was unable to relax, let alone sleep, for a time. The barrenness ahead of them worried her.

'Can we talk, Seqiro?' she asked after a bit as the darkness closed in.

We may talk, he agreed.

'Say, I just realized: you never argue with me. Not really. You point out things, you clarify what I don't know, but you always go along with what I'm thinking about.'

It is true. I reflect your interests, as mine are not of great moment.

'How can you think that? You're the most wonderful person I've met, next to Darius!'

True. But I am not wonderful without you.

'You're a horse! A horse is wonderful by definition.'

As is a girl.

'Let me tell you what a horse is to me. I'm going to introduce you to Maresy Doats.' She summoned her mental picture of her imaginary friend.

She is a winsome mare.

'Well, I never thought of her as having sex appeal!'

I would have to smell her to determine that.

She laughed. 'So you're just like any man!'

No. Human males are always interested in reproduction. Horses are interested only when the mare is ready. We do not waste energy. We regard this as more sensible.

'Well, Maresy is sensible. She always knows what to do. The trouble is, others aren't always sensible, and they don't listen. It's all recorded in my book, *For Whom Was That Neigh?* It's based on a picture I have of Maresy Doats. Do you want an example?'

Yes.

'Now why did I know you would say that? Okay, here it is. Maresy and another mare were grazing in this pasture. It was the only pasture they had, and there was no other source of food. Just the grass. A tough variety that hung on through the winter. Now Maresy is smarter than the average horse, and she did some figuring, and realized that at the rate they were grazing, they would run out of grass before spring, and then starve in the winter. But if they slowed down their grazing, and ate less grass, they could stretch it out so that it would last until spring, when it would start growing again, and they would survive. They might be lean, but okay. So it made sense to do that.

'So she told the other mare. But the other mare just went right on grazing, paying no attention. She wasn't smart like Maresy, and didn't understand anything except eating until she was full. She ate like a horse.

'So what was Maresy to do? If she stopped grazing, then there would be enough for the other mare, but Maresy would starve now. If she didn't stop, they would both starve later. So should she give up her life so that at least one of them would survive, even though it was the undeserving one? Or should she prolong her own life for a while by continuing to graze?'

She should kill the other mare, and have enough for herself.

'But Maresy wouldn't do that!' Colene protested. 'She believes in life, not death!'

But if there is life only for one —

'Yes. So she's in trouble. I call it the pacifist's dilemma.'

'*How does the story end?*

'I don't know. We'll just have to wait and see.'

How long?

'I don't know.'

I do not see the point of this story.

'It has no solution, but it does have a point. You see, Maresy stands for me, and for people like me, who are smart enough to see that the world – I mean, in my reality – can't go on this way. It is using up all its resources, and when they are gone, it will be impossible to feed everyone, and most or all of us will die. It doesn't have to be that way, but everyone else, like the other mare, refuses to see the problem, and just goes on grazing at top speed. So we will all suffer, when we don't have to, because of the shortsightedly selfish ones. We won't know exactly what happens until it happens, and then it will be too late. I think that's part of what makes me suicidal. I mean, what's the point in hanging onto life, when it's all going to end anyway, too soon?'

But you are free of that, now, with the Virtual Mode.

'Yes. So I'm not suicidal now, maybe. But I feel guilty for bugging out on my world.'

With the situation as you present it, that is your only choice. You are freeing your world of your presence, so that someone else can survive.

'Say, yes! That's a good way to look at it.' Somewhat cheered, she relaxed, and soon was asleep.

They did start early, as soon as they could see their way. Immediately the barrens, as Colene thought of this region, were all around them, before and behind. It was as if life had never existed anywhere.

At first the land was reasonably level, but this changed with realities, and it became so ragged as to be an unkind challenge. Bare stone rose up in twisted contours, and sank into rubble. Tors gave way to pits, forcing them to wind around their edges, slowing progress. Meanwhile the sun rose in the bleak sky and the bright light beat down on them. Colene fashioned a hat from cloth to protect her face and arms, and covered Seqiro's head and neck similarly, fearing damage from the intensity of the rays. They were a strange looking pair, swathed in coverings fashioned of loose clothing, but there was no one to see.

Then the land descended. It was a great cavity, so large that it featured its own mountains and pits and convolutions, as if it were a continent in reverse. It extended ahead until the rim of the horizon cut it off.

Colene gazed at it with dismay. Then she had a revelation. 'It's a sea!' she exclaimed. 'An ocean! We've come to the end of a continent! A sea without water!'

All water is gone from these realities, Seqiro agreed.

There was nothing to do except descend into it, because her sense told her that Darius was somewhere across this region. 'I hope we don't have to cross the whole Atlantic or Pacific!' Because that would be doom; they could not walk that far.

That brought another concern. 'How will we know if it's too far? I mean, if it is, we should turn back, so at least we don't die of hunger or exposure. But if we turn back, when we could have made it across –'

If we reach what we deem to be half our ability to travel without new supplies, and I still can not detect life ahead, then we should turn back.

'You can detect life behind us?' she asked. 'I mean, you're not just thinking that to reassure me?'

It is fading, but I can feel that life behind.

'Okay. If you get so you can't feel it behind, and you still can't feel it ahead, we'd better turn back. That's not the same as giving up; it just means we'll have to find a better way.'

Agreed.

Yet privately she wondered what better way there could be. They would not be able to go around the barrens the way she had around the hostile bear, because these were entire realities, each one a universe in itself. If there were a million of them, they just had to be crossed, because there didn't seem to be any way to skip over parts of the Virtual Mode.

Well, if they had to retreat, maybe Darius would be able to find a way from the other side. She was sure that he was looking for her, too; he wouldn't have set up the Virtual Mode and then just twiddled his thumbs. They could meet in the middle. So maybe he was coming to the other side of this, now, and was thinking about how to cross, and all she had to do was go back and wait.

But she was more independent than that. She wanted to make it on her own. So she hoped they made it across.

I echo your sentiment.

'Oh, was I thinking too close to the surface? I didn't mean to bother you with this!'

I am becoming increasingly attuned to your mind, so can read more deeply with less effort. I did not mean to intrude.

'Oh, no, that's all right, Seqiro! You understand me, the way Maresy did. I don't mind you in my mind. I just didn't want to burden you with my worries.'

You are concerned about survival now, rather than death.

She laughed, somewhat self-consciously. 'For sure, I'm not being suicidal, now that I'm up against possible death! I'm reacting in a disgustingly normal way. I guess that's an improvement.'

You have reason to live, now.

'Yes. Because of Darius – and you, Seqiro.'

But if you lacked these folk, your self destructiveness would return.

'I guess it would. I'm no bargain, emotionally.'

If you had not had those bad experiences, you would not have become self destructive.

'Well, I don't know about that. Those experiences weren't necessarily bad, just different or shocking. I hadn't known how the people lived in Panama; plenty of other people do know, and they aren't suicidal. I did a lot of good at that hospital, and the doctors and nurses aren't suicidal. The rape scene – that I could have done without. But I didn't get beaten up or anything, and it sure taught me to be wary of liquor and of men! That camp episode really worked out okay, and word never got back to my folks what had really happened. It taught me not to trust anyone, not with my true secrets, and that was a good lesson.'

But you trust me.

'Now why did I know you were going to come up with that? I guess I am breaking my rule. But I also guess I meant not to trust anyone *human.* I trusted Maresy, because she's a horse, and horses can be trusted. You're a horse. Trust just sort of comes with your territory.'

I like Maresy. But there are many horses in my reality who can not be trusted. You are as foolish to trust an animal blindly as to trust a human being blindly.

Colene sighed. 'I guess I am. Okay, I won't trust any other animals either. But is it okay to trust *you*, Seqiro?'

Me alone, he agreed. *Yet do you not also trust Darius, who is human?*

That set her back. 'I don't think I do trust him, exactly. I love him, but that's another matter. When he told me of his wonderful magic land, I didn't believe it. I wish I had! So I guess there is danger in not trusting people, too. I hope he forgives me!'

He must have forgiven you, because he set up the Virtual Mode, so that he could rejoin you.

'Yes, he did that.' Then she paused in her descent of a slope. 'Seqiro! Is it possible that it wasn't Darius who set it up? But someone else? I mean, how would I know, for sure?'

If it was Darius, you will know when you meet him.

'Unless it's someone just pretending to be him, because he wanted an innocent girl or something. Lots of men want young sex-slaves. I really don't know Darius that well.'

I will be with you. I will know his mind.

'Yes! You will know his mind, Seqiro! You must let me know whether it's really him, and how he truly feels about me. I'm not going to marry him, I know that, but I'm willing to be his mistress and helper if I just know he loves me.'

I will inform you of his feeling for you, if you don't object to my intrusion into your private matters. Understand that I will be partial to his sexual sentiment as well as his emotion.

'I understand! I want him to want me, every which way from Sunday! Just so long as he loves me!'

It shall be known.

They continued into the waterless ocean, which seemed even more barren than the continent, because of what should have been there. A continent could be a natural desert, but an ocean could only be an unnatural desert.

That brought another horrible realization. 'Seqiro! Suppose we reach the next living reality – and we're at the bottom of the sea? We could drown!'

She felt a wash of panic, and knew that her thought had struck through to his natural mind. It was a horse's nature to spook and run from danger. *So it seems. But your intellect suggests that we might simply retreat through the boundary between realities and be dry again.*

'Well, at least we wouldn't be thirsty!' she exclaimed too cheerily. The notion of being suddenly under a mile or so of water terrified her. She realized increasingly that though she had been suicidal, she was quite choosy about the way she might die. Water would be too suffocating, and she didn't like that.

It would also be crushing. Suppose they were crushed to death before they could retreat? 'I think we had better be pretty careful how we cross boundaries,' she said, shaken.

I will detect the ocean life, which will give us warning.

'Not if it's a sterile sea!' For now she realized that the presence of water was no guarantee of life.

I will flick my tail across them, Seqiro suggested.

'But you would have to travel backwards! No, let me take something of ours – here, this kerchief of mine will do – and I'll flick it ahead of me, and when it gets wet, we'll know.'

Agreed.

They moved on, with Colene ahead, constantly flicking her kerchief as she approached each boundary. It became automatic: one, two, three steps, flick, step, flick and step across, and start over. It was about five of her steps between boundaries, about two feet per step, but she wanted no accident. It would have looked strange to an outsider, but it was a sensible precaution.

Now she was not sure whether she did or did not want to encounter such an ocean. If they found no water, they might have to walk thousands of miles through this dread desert, and would die of dehydration; already their water supply was diminishing at an alarming rate. But if they did find it, how would they get through?

Suddenly there was something. Colene clapped her hand to her mouth to stifle a possible scream. A light was blinking to the south!

I see it, Seqiro thought, responding to her thought. *A beacon. It seems that we are not alone.*

'But can you detect life?'

No. But life must have placed it there.

'Then maybe it's safe to check it,' she said. 'Unless it's got killer machines or something.'

What would be the point of that?

'I don't know. But whatever sterilized all these realities may intend to keep them that way. If that beacon picks up a sign of life, it may trigger another sterilization treatment.'

I suspect it can spot us as readily as we have spotted it. I am aware of no harmful radiation associated with it. Is it possible that it simply marks a path through the barrens?

'Maybe so!' she agreed, encouraged. 'There has to be a way through, so maybe someone left markers. If we have to gamble, let's gamble on the positive interpretation.'

Nevertheless, they were diffident as they approached the beacon. It disappeared when they crossed realities; it existed only in one. But it was easy to approach, because of its constant flashing.

It turned out to be a simple machine: a ball mounted on a thin metal pole stuck into a porous section of the sea floor, which blinked. At its base was an arrow painted in bright red, pointing east.

'A direction marker!' Colene exclaimed. 'Pointing the way!'

Could it be your friend Darius?

'You mean, to show where he's been? Or to find his way back?' She focused seriously on that for a moment. 'No, I don't think so. He's from the reality of magic, and this is plainly science. Super-science, I think; that ball's opaque, yet it flashes. It must be someone else. Maybe there's a regular caravan through here, with markers to steer it straight.'

I doubt it. This Virtual Mode has existed only a week in your terms.

She nodded. 'Well, one person, maybe, but not Darius. But it will do for us, certainly; this should be much faster, because now we know where we're going, sort of.'

I agree.

Heartened, they resumed travel.

211

Meanwhile the contours of the bottom of the ocean were a revelation to her. Instead of being flat and sandy, as she had somehow fancied, they were phenomenally more varied than those of the continental land. There were mountains and valleys and rifts and lattices of twisted stone. There were holes so deep they filled her with dread, and slopes so sharp that they resembled walls. One section was like a monstrous banyan tree, with thousands of pillars reaching down to lower platforms, from which more pillars extended on down. Another was like an upside-down mountain with mounds supporting its edges. Elsewhere there were what seemed to be worm holes in myriads, ranging from pinhead to handspan diameter, disappearing into darkness. And the opposite: pencil-thin towers of packed sand, their sedimentary origins showing in streaks crossing the formation. There had surely been water here once; what had happened to it?

In fact, how could this region have been rendered so dry, without disturbing these natural formations? She was able to knock over the pencil towers with her hands; they were not made for sidewise pressure. Any heat great enough to vaporize all the water should have generated savage storms. If some cosmic drain had opened in the bottom and let it all flow out, there should have been some pools remaining and some gouging as the drainage rivers formed. Instead it was as if the water had simply vanished, without even making any currents.

Then her bandanna snagged on something. She jerked it back, startled, for to her eye she was merely flicking it in air before a sea of air. She checked it.

The tip was dry, but looked as if it had recently been wet. Because the water couldn't cross the boundary.

'Oopsy, Seqiro! We've struck water!'

The horse stepped up and turned broadside. He flicked his tail. It struck something.

I felt the liquid, he agreed.

Colene put up her hands, carefully, and felt the air before her. The boundary was icy cold and slick. 'Like ice,' she announced. 'I guess we didn't have to worry about drowning; it's under such pressure we can't get into it anyway.'

212

I sense no life.

So it was lifeless water. Some realities had been dried, some frozen, or at least sterilized. The two of them could not continue crossing boundaries.

This was not exactly a relief. 'What do we do, Seqiro? Do we turn back? We can make it from here, at least.'

But if we find a way to enter the next reality, we will have water, greatly extending our range.

'I don't think so. We can't take it with us.'

'We can if we drink it carefully, saving our own water for emergency use.'

'But it must be salt water! We can't drink that!'

It is my understanding that we can. In my reality we have a technique for filtering impure water through sand to make it pure. We can do that.

'Or we can evaporate some, and condense the vapor!' she agreed, turning more positive. 'But we still have to get up to the top of it, and then what will we do – sail across it?'

Seqiro sorted through the picture in her mind, of a girl and horse standing precariously on a raft. *I prefer not.*

She laughed, humorlessly. 'I guess not! So unless there's a big change coming beyond the water-reality, we're sunk anyway, no pun.'

I fear that is the case. But we should try to explore it if we can. If we can find land, and cross more realities, I can quest farther for life.

'I guess you're right. This is about midday now; let's see if there is any rise to the level of the surface north or south.' She meant to the left or right, because their progress was generally eastward. 'Maybe an island, at least. But which direction do we go? It would be a shame if there is a perfect island north, and we go south and fail to find it and have to give up and go back.' She tried to make it sound cheery, but knew that her dark forebodings were coming through clearly to the horse.

Perhaps we could explore both directions, one going north, the other south, and double our chances. We may discover another beacon.

'Seqiro, you're a genius!' she exclaimed. 'And we can stay in mental contact, so the other will have the news first thing.'

They did it. Colene went north. She tried to suppress her belief that they were wasting time and energy, because even if they found an island and were able to cross the boundary, they would still have virtually impassable water to cross. These barren realities were an awful barrier!

She came to a rise, but it was followed by a depression. She saw a mountain in the distance, which should be an island, but it was to the northeast, in the territory of another reality, impossible to reach from here.

'How about you?' she asked, thinking at Seqiro.

I may have found an island. But I can not find an ascent.

'Keep looking!' she exclaimed. 'I have nothing here; I'll come join you.'

She hurried south, now trying to suppress unreasonable hope. 'Have you found a path up yet, Seqiro?'

No. I fear I am lost. I am caught in an endless trench.

'I'll watch out for it!' Suddenly she thought how much worse it would be if her companion got trapped, and she had to choose between staying with him or saving herself. Even if she had no choice, if something happened to him, how could she go on alone? His marvelous mind had become her main emotional support.

Thank you. But away from you I am just a horse.

'You're so much more than a horse!' she protested. 'But a horse is good enough.'

In due course she reached the mountain. It did seem to rise high enough to be an island, depending on how high the surface of the water in the other reality was. But between her and it was a deep channel, as if the mountain had sunk down in the semi-molten floor eons ago, making a depression. This must be Seqiro's endless trench.

She found a place where she could safely drop down into it, the drop not so far that she couldn't scramble back. 'I'm in the channel, Seqiro. Where are you?'

Not far from you. I shall wait.

Soon she caught up with him. He was standing, breathing

hard, the sweat rolling off his hide. 'Why Seqiro! What happened to you? You're steaming hot!'

*I'm afraid I panicked. I galloped, but found no end to the channel.
I recognized landmarks I had passed before, and realized that I was
trapped.*

'You ran all the way around the mountain!' she exclaimed.
'Oh, Seqiro, you wasted valuable energy and are losing water
in your sweat. Didn't you know better?'

I did not.

'But you're so smart!'

*No. Away from you I am not. I maintained contact with you,
but only your thoughts came through, not your underlying power
of mind.*

She realized that he had meant it literally when he warned
her about that before. So, alone, he had reverted to his underlying nature, and spooked when unable to figure out how to
escape the channel.

Then she realized something else. 'You couldn't have run
around the mountain! Half of it's in the other reality, under
the water!'

*True. I realize that now. The loop evidently is completed on
this side.*

'Well, let's get you out of this and climb that mountain,' she
said. 'Now that you're smart again, did you see a good way for
you to do that?'

Yes. There is a navigable slope to a dead-end path.

They walked back to it. Sure enough, it was possible for a
horse to climb up on the mountain side, but then the path
ended as it seemed about to cross over the top of the channel,
which was deep and narrow here. It was as if there had once
been a bridge here.

And there, in an adjacent reality beyond the trench, was
another stick-ball beacon. This was certainly the right place!

But I will do better with your help.

'Sure! What do you need from me?'

*Tell me when my front feet are about to land just before the
bridge. I am unable to see them when my head is up.*

'Okay.'

Seqiro got up speed and galloped toward the brink. 'Now!'

she cried as his front feet came down. He brought his hind feet up close to them, then heaved up his forefeet and leaped over the gap. He recovered his balance and slowed to a stop. He was out.

'I guess maybe we should stay together after this,' she said. 'I really didn't like being apart from you anyway, Seqiro. I worried –'

I understand. And of course he did, for he could read the complex of her emotions as she spoke.

They explored the mountain from outside the channel, and found a likely ascent. But it was a narrow ledge in places. 'Um, will you be able to turn around, there? I mean, if –?'

Perhaps you should explore ahead, and I will rejoin you when you come across a turning place.

'Okay. But let's just not separate any farther than we absolutely have to, okay?'

Agreed.

So she ran and hurdled the trench and mounted the twisty steep path, catching handholds on the carved stone abutments to help haul herself up. She found a kind of landing, and thought its description to Seqiro, who then followed her up. They continued similarly, by stages, their progress complicated by the wall of cold water. When the best path crossed that boundary, they had to back off and find an alternate path. Thus it was evening by the time they reached the top, and they were tired. They had seen no other beacons or signs of life.

'You know, if this doesn't give us some way to move on rapidly, we're sunk,' she said. 'It will be all we can do to get down the mountain and back to the last habitable reality.'

I shall be disappointed for you in that event. But perhaps Darius will find a way to cross from the other side, and you will still be unified.

'Gee, I hope so! It's not that I'm not satisfied with your company, Seqiro, but –'

You need a human male like Darius, just as I need a mare like Maresy, to complete your life.

'Yeah.' She led the way along the leveling summit, looking for a good place to camp for the night. But the only good one was on the east side of the mountain, beyond the boundary.

She knew exactly where that boundary was, now, after bumping into it so many times on the way up.

Then she did a mental doubletake: this was the top. They should be able to cross that boundary now – if they ever could. So she stepped gingerly into it – and passed through.

It was indeed an island. Ahead it sloped to a rocky shore just a few feet below the level she stood. The waves washed against the barren stone, making froth.

'Seqiro! We're across!'

I saw it with you. The horse appeared behind her as she looked back, seeming to materialize from nothing. *But I fear that this too is impassable.*

'Yeah.' Her elation of the moment faded quickly. The surface of the ocean extended to the horizon, featureless. Then she had another thought. 'But the beacons pointed this way, so there must be something.'

At least we can wash.

She forced her mind away from the disappointment. She really hadn't expected any more than this. 'Yes, we can both take a good dip, and I can wash my clothes.'

This time Seqiro let her remove his load and harness, and she stripped. Nakedness didn't matter with an animal, and if it did, it wouldn't have mattered with this one. He could see her naked mind.

They stepped cautiously toward the limited shore, passing through another boundary just at the verge of the water – and stopped short.

There was a pontoon wharf projecting into the sea. It cut off abruptly about ten feet out, and seemed of recent vintage, with bright paint and gleaming metal chains connecting the floats.

But what was the point of a wharf, here? Was it waiting for a ship?

It is a bridge. We can see only what is in this reality.

Suddenly it made sense. The path hadn't ended; it continued on across the water. But only part of it was in this reality, because it was on the Virtual Mode. 'So the beacons did know what they were doing,' she breathed. 'Well, let's wash, and – maybe we had better spend the night here, and eat and rest, before we start across. We don't know exactly what we may encounter out there.'

True.

They washed up, finding the water chill but refreshing. Colene felt a special freedom, being naked in the open. Somehow it seemed that if she could be naked all the time, she would never be suicidal.

She walked out along the bridge, crossing the next boundary. The pontoons continued unbroken. But the appearance was of a ten foot segment ending before and behind her. It looked far more precarious than it was. There was no doubt now: the bridge was part of the Virtual Mode. Someone from an anchor reality must have set it up. But who?

We shall discover that when we follow it to its source.

'But how do we know that source is friendly?' she asked as she toweled herself off, using a dry shirt. She would have preferred to let herself dry naturally, but she was shivering and had to get clothed before she did herself harm.

I will be able to tell, if I am let into the mind of the anchor person.

'You can't just peek?'

I can enter only a willing mind. Once I do, I can communicate freely, regardless of the language of the person, and can control that mind, and therefore the body. But I can not penetrate a hostile mind, or even an indifferent one.

'But you controlled the minds of those human servants in your reality, so we could escape.'

Not exactly. Our humans have been tamed, in the manner of your horses and other animals, so are receptive. Wild humans would not be receptive, any more than wild horses in your reality allow themselves to be ridden. They had discussed the differences between their two societies as they walked; Seqiro now understood her framework well enough. *Even so, particular humans associate with particular horses, and do not allow unfamiliar horses to govern them if their own horses forbid it. In the stress of the moment I was able to strike through, but that was a limited opportunity.*

'But you and I made immediate connection!'

Because you are highly receptive.

'Well, I'm not tame!' she said indignantly.

But you desired compatible company. You were extremely lonely and nervous. That enabled me not only to join you, but to reach you from a distance, and across realities.

She nodded, now chewing on cold bread from his supplies, because there was nothing here from which she could make a fire. He was eating a ration of mixed grains. 'I was that, for sure! I still am. I need you, Seqiro, I really do! Back when I started getting depressed I did some research, and decided I fit the profile of BPD: Borderline Personality Disorder. I mean, alienation from my parents, sexual betrayal by a date, inability to cope with what I was learning about the evils of the world, and I was sort of on a roller-coaster of mood swings with nowhere to go. I really didn't know who I was, yet I hurt something awful with rejection even when maybe it wasn't real. I would get so damn depressed, even when there didn't seem to be any good reason. I didn't dare trust anyone, especially not after that business with Mitzi, even though that worked out okay, in a way. But I couldn't stand being alone, either. Even when I was in the middle of people who seemed like friends, I knew it wasn't true, and I just kept cutting my wrists and hiding them. I kept sort of wanting to tempt men, make them get hot, make them really want my body, but I didn't want sex with them. I knew that was crazy but I couldn't stop. Little Miss Self Destructive, that was me – until I loved Darius. Then I lost him. Then came the Virtual Mode – and you.'

I understand you and need you as you do me, but I have no sexual desire for you.

'Yeah. I can parade around naked with you, and it doesn't matter. I thought I just wanted to tease men, but now I think it's something else. I just want my freedom, freedom from what's bugging me, and throwing away my clothes in public makes it seem as if I'm doing that, but it doesn't mean anything with other girls, that happens in the showers anyway, so it has to be men, and when they get hot it sort of proves I'm getting there, I mean I want to be attractive, but it's sort of dangerous too. Like – you know, once I was eating cereal, and it wasn't sweet enough, so I put sugar on it, and it still wasn't sweet enough, so I put more, but no matter how much I put it wasn't there.

Then someone said "Try salt," so I put a little salt on it, and suddenly that stuff was so sickly awful sweet I couldn't stand it. I'd been putting on the wrong stuff, not knowing, because it hadn't tasted sweet enough. So with the nakedness and me – I'm looking for salt, but sugar is all I have, so I keep trying but it keeps not quite working. Does that make sense?'

Yes.

'And then when I found the salt – Darius – everything sort of came together. But I didn't quite believe him, and –'

Suddenly she was sobbing. She leaned her forehead against his warm side and the tears flowed down.

You were afraid of intimacy, both physical and emotional.

'I guess so,' she said into his hide. 'Did I ever blow that one!'

Yet you did what any practical person would have. Magic is not believable in your reality.

'If I had loved him enough, I would have believed him!'

Love is not precisely what horses experience, but we have learned something of it from our association with humans. In our judgment, the best love is based on practical considerations. Trust should not follow love; love should follow trust. You condemn yourself because you were unable to do it backwards. You should not.

She lifted her head. 'I never thought of that!'

Because you had no compatible and objective mind to explore it with. You do need me – and with me, you are whole.

'With you I am whole,' she echoed. 'But Seqiro, are you whole with me?'

Yes. My need for you is primarily physical and mental, for I have neither hands nor intelligence alone, but I had those things in my normal existence. You provide also the emotional factor I need, the quest for new things and new meanings. In this you are my completion, as I am yours.

'Yes,' she breathed. 'Yes! We are whole!'

Then they settled down for sleep, Colene curled against his warm side with a blanket over them both.

Naturally her own thoughts interrupted it. 'Seqiro! If you have to be let into a mind, if it's a wild mind, how come you could handle those mosquitoes?'

Their minds are comparatively simple. The complex human minds

220

are another matter. Mosquitoes could bar my penetration, had they the wit. But they don't realize that, and I would not advise them of it.

'So it does make sense, after all.'

Yes. He seemed amused. She snuggled against him and drifted off.

In the morning they set out on the pontoon bridge. It was solid enough to support Seqiro's weight, though it did sink somewhat where he stood. Now it was Colene's turn to shore up his confidence. 'These things are strong. See, the platform part of it consists of long metallic planks, so even if the pontoon you're over sinks, the others take up the slack, and you'd have to weigh a lot more than you do to make them all sink. In my reality they drive trucks across these things. So it may feel insecure, and look insecure because all we can see is one little segment at a time, but believe me, you're safe.'

Now I have confidence. For he had seen her mental picture of the heavy trucks driving safely across such bridges, and her trust had become his.

However, she led the way, with a hand lightly touching his nose. This was so that her light body would encounter any possible weakening in the bridge first, and to guide him, because his eyes were not well placed to see the bridge. Her mind and hand became his guidance. Only the lack of a halter on his head would have showed an outsider that this was not a girl leading her horse. It *was* a girl leading her horse, but the relation between them was different.

The surface of the sea continued, but the color of the water shifted as they crossed realities. *Life!* Seqiro thought. *I sense faint life ahead – perhaps very primitive, in the depths of the ocean.*

'Then we're getting somewhere!'

The signs became stronger. It was as if they were stepping through a paleontological exhibit, tracing the world from its sterile inception through the first suggestions of life and to the first multi-celled organisms. Things started showing in the water, living froth, then tiny jellylike creatures, then swimming crustaceans, and then actual fish.

And another island. This one had shrubbery on it, or primitive trees. The bridge went right to it, each short segment appearing as they proceeded until one touched the island, and for the first time in hours they set foot on land.

It was a relief to have the shade of fernlike trees, but they decided not to linger, because the pontoon bridge seemed endlessly long on the Virtual Mode despite its shortness in any one reality, and they were limited to the supplies they carried. They could more readily rest after they got safely past this region.

So with regret they moved out on the bridge again, trusting it to extend itself on through the Virtual Mode, and soon found themselves back in the middle of the placid sea.

Until Colene stepped through a boundary and found herself in a wind-screaming storm. Big waves rocked the bridge so hard it seemed about to be torn away.

She ducked back, and the storm cut off abruptly. Her hair was matted across her face and her blouse and jeans were wrinkled. 'We've got a problem.'

So I saw. Seqiro had not yet crossed, but his mind had been with her. *If it is confined to one reality, we can cross quickly.*

'Maybe so. But suppose it isn't?'

We can wait for it to subside.

'We don't know how long these storms last. Maybe it's always stormy in that reality.'

They discussed it, and decided to let Colene cross to the following reality, tied with a rope to Seqiro. The rope was part of his supplies, so would remain firm across the boundaries. If she got washed off the bridge, he would back away and haul her to this calm section. If she found that the following reality was calm, he would move across and rejoin her. They would remain in constant mental touch.

She knotted the rope firmly around her middle, and passed a loop down between her legs and up around her shoulders, so that there was no way for her to slip out of it. She was afraid of that terrible storm, but knew this was the best way to tackle it.

She ventured across the boundary again, wishing there were handholds. But there was only the level planking, which she now realized was vibrating with the force of the storm beyond. That had not been evident while Seqiro was walking, but now he was still and they both saw that part of the motion was not from his hoofs.

The storm caught her again. This time a wave was washing over the bridge, making the pontoons tip at what seemed like a precarious angle. She lost her balance and fell, and the water carried her into the sea. She inhaled to scream, involuntarily, and took in a mouthful and some of a lungful of froth.

Then she was in the calm water, having been carried across the boundary by the wave. Seqiro was backing away, hauling her in. She managed to catch hold of the edge of a pontoon and cling there, choking.

Calm. Cough. Calm. Inhale. Cough.

It was Seqiro, assuming control of her breathing, getting her to clear her lungs without panicking. She let him do it; it was much easier to ride along with his procedure.

Sooner than otherwise, she was back on the bridge and on her feet. 'Thanks, Seqiro,' she gasped. 'I needed that.'

Then she gathered her strength and charged back through the boundary.

This time a wave had just passed. She forged through the knee-deep water, able to keep her footing, and by the time the next wave loomed, she plunged across.

Into bright sunlight. The storm was only one reality wide! 'Come on, Seqiro!' Then, immediately, she reconsidered. 'Wait – let me spy the waves. It's much easier to cross between them.'

She sat at the edge of the boundary, clung to a pontoon, and cautiously poked her head across. She got a faceful of salt water. She drew back, blinking the salt out of her eyes. Then she tried it again, and found a lull. 'Now!'

The bridge vibrated with extra force. Suddenly the horse appeared, almost galloping along the bridge. The water splashed up from his legs.

Colene threw herself to the side, into the water, lest she be inadvertently trampled. How big Seqiro looked from this vantage! He was a massive horse, and splendid in his motion. She had forgotten that, in her constant communion with his mind.

He entered her current reality, and she had to scramble up before he overshot her position too far and yanked her along by the rope. They were across, but she hoped they did not have to do that again soon.

The nature of the ocean changed faster than any individual reality suggested, and land came into view by jumps with each crossed boundary. Adjacent realities tended to be similar, but sometimes differed by significant stages within that similarity. Now they seemed to be headed for a reality whose far shoreline was considerably west of the one they had started with. Perhaps this world was turning slightly faster, so that it had gained on the others. No, it would be the other way: if it turned more slowly, a given spot on the globe would be west of the others. It hardly mattered; what counted was that they were getting across the ocean much faster than they might have.

By nightfall they set foot on what in her reality might have been Europe. Now she remembered how quickly they had reached what seemed to be the Atlantic Ocean; she had not walked any twelve hundred miles to the coast! So this effect must have existed all along; she just hadn't paused to realize its significance. Now she was glad they weren't traveling in the other direction!

Life had continued to progress, and now there were modern fish and animals and birds, though she did not recognize the individual species.

The pontoon bridge stopped at the shore, but here there was a well marked path leading east. Someone certainly had set this up – but who traveled it? They had encountered no one, and seen no footprints or other signs of use. It had to have been done recently – within the past week – because before then this Virtual Mode hadn't been in place. What did it mean?

We are approaching superior minds, Seqiro thought. *Not many realities away. They are closed to me; I can fathom only their power.*

'Not Darius' reality? Magic?'

No. I suspect science, like yours, because if they set up the bridge –

'High-tech,' she agreed.

224

They seem to be human. They may be friendly. However –

'Um, Seqiro,' she murmured, really not speaking at all, more or less subvocalizing so as to focus her thoughts. 'We don't know what we're headed into, but I think maybe they're expecting us. Maybe we should, you know, not let them know too much about us. Until we know more about them.'

This was my thought.

They considered, then decided to do something neither of them really liked. Colene made a loop of rope and tied it about Seqiro's nose, and held the other end like a rein. She climbed up on his back with the supplies and rode. Now it seemed that he was a plain unintelligent horse – she could not bring herself to think 'stupid' – under the control of a human. It seemed to be a necessary charade – just in case.

They advanced through more realities, the path broadening as if to signal that they were close to their destination. Other paths intersected it at acute angles to their route, evidently going the same way. Were there paths reaching as far out as theirs, in other directions? All constructed in the past week? What an effort that must have been! And why? Colene still didn't trust this.

'You know,' she subvocalized, 'if this turns out as suspicious as it seems so far, and you have to keep on acting like a dumb animal, you'll be put in a stall and I won't be able to be with you without giving you away.'

True. But a stall is no discomfort for me, and we can remain in mind contact throughout. I believe I can now reach you across a continent, so we will not truly be separated.

'I hope not! But I have an ill feeling about this. Someone has gone to an awful lot of trouble to show us in.'

We must continue as we have, until we are able to proceed through this reality and resume our journey. Obviously they know someone will be coming on the Virtual Mode, but not who or from what direction, or they would not have fashioned so many paths.

'That's what bothers me. This is obviously another anchor. Why didn't the anchor person just come on out to meet us? If he wants to escape his reality, why take all this trouble to bring us *in* to it?'

225

I think we shall find out. I doubt we can avoid the encounter which threatens, so it is better to proceed into it as if innocent.

'We *are* innocent,' she muttered bleakly.

They crossed several more realities – and were abruptly in a huge building. This was evidently the anchor place.

A man stood before them. He was in what was evidently a uniform: a princely robe of what looked like silk or fine artificial material. A metallic band circled his head at forehead level. His hair was reddish and receding, and his eyes were black and piercing. He looked to be in his fifties, running to density rather than fat.

Seqiro stopped immediately. Colene, uncertain what to do, decided to remain mounted. That way she could go with Seqiro if he bolted. 'Hello,' she said tentatively, her throat feeling somewhat constrained.

'Hello,' a ball hanging near them said, mimicking her voice and intonation precisely.

I can not get into his mind, Seqiro thought. *But I think that device is trying to communicate.*

A translator! That made sense. She faced the ball. 'Hello. I am Colene, and this is my horse Seqiro. We are from a far reality, and only passing through this one. We would like to stay the night and go on in the morning.'

'Hello. I am –' the ball said.

Colene tapped her collarbone with a thumb. 'I am Colene.' She glanced down. 'This is my horse, Seqiro.' She indicated him. 'Who are you?' She pointed to the ball, and then to the man.

'Hello. I am –' the ball said. Then the man lifted one hand and tapped himself. 'Ddwng.' The ball spoke again. 'You are Colene. This is my horse Seqiro.'

She smiled. 'My horse, not your horse. This is your palace.' She gestured around the chamber.

'Seqiro is your horse. This is my palace. You are from a far reality.'

That machine was fast! 'A far reality,' Colene agreed. 'On the Virtual Mode.' She gestured back the way they had come. Then she oriented on the man. 'You are Deedwing.'

'Ddwng,' he corrected her. There seemed to be a stutter at the beginning and no vowels in the middle.

'D-dwng,' she agreed, almost getting it. 'Who are your people?'

The translator ball took some dialogue to get that straight, but in due course answered: 'My people are the –'

'DoOon,' Ddwng finished.

'Do-Oh!-on,' she repeated, noting the three different 'o' sounds. 'Ddwng of the DoOon. I am Colene of the Americans.'

The introductions completed, Ddwng stepped forward. He smiled, offering his arm for Colene to brace against so she could dismount without tumbling. She put both hands on it, finding it very strong, and jumped down.

Other people appeared. Except that they weren't exactly people. Colene tried not to stare, sure that it would be bad form. They had the heads of sheep!

'These are nulls of the Ovine persuasion,' Ddwng said through the ball, noting her surprise. The actual words were less precise, but that was the essence. 'Palace servants. They are of human intelligence and perception.'

'Oh. Thank you.'

First the Ovines saw to her horse. Colene made clear that she wanted her mount well treated, and Ddwng led them to a chamber that would do for a stall. They were now in the anchor reality, and things did not shift every ten feet. She arranged with Ram, the male Ovine, to get good hay and grain and water for the horse, for Seqiro could eat the food of an anchor reality and retain it. Plus a block of salt! Then, with regret, she left him, for it would not do to show too great an attachment to a mere beast of burden. Seqiro advised her in this mentally, while playing the part of animal perfectly. They still did not know whether they could trust the folk of this reality. At least the DoOon seemed to have no notion of telepathy; their sophisticated ball indicated that they depended on computerized data banks for translation.

Then they saw to Colene. Ewe, the female sheep, approached bearing silken robes. Colene realized that she must look pretty ratty, after the day's hike and the soaking down in the storm.

Her clothing had dried on her and must look that way. She nodded affirmatively.

The sheep-woman led her to an elegant private chamber. Ddwng did not follow; evidently he honored basic human protocol with regard to males and females. But she still didn't trust him. She remembered how her date had behaved well enough, until he got her alone with his friends and their liquor. This could be a fancier version of something similar.

There was another hanging ball here, and it continued to respond to all her remarks. Evidently it was all part of a network, and they wanted to get as much of her language as possible, quickly. That was fine with her. She gave it all the words that came up, and instructed it in basic syntax, correcting it when it made an incorrect assumption. This was the easy way to establish communication!

Meanwhile she suffered herself to be undressed, bathed, and redressed by the quiet female. She was very good at her profession, evidently born to be a servant to nobility. For Colene was being treated like a princess, and garbed like one. Whenever she spoke to Ewe, that creature nodded her head forward in a set motion, evidently both bow and acknowledgment, and did her best as quietly and efficiently as possible.

Soon enough Colene was not only clean and clothed, her hair was flowing and lustrous, and she wore a diadem that scintillated iridescently. Her fingernails matched the diadem, and her toenails too, in comfortable yet elegant sandal-slippers. The fatigue of the day was fading; the sheer luxury of her apparel was banishing it.

She looked at herself in a mirror. She was stunning! As lovely as she had ever imagined herself to be in her most foolish flights of fancy. She showed no private flesh, yet somehow the gown made her look utterly feminine.

Then they guided her to another ornate chamber. This was evidently a dining room, and suddenly she realized how hungry she was. She and Seqiro had been so busy following the pontoon bridge that they hadn't stopped to eat since breakfast.

Seqiro: the horse was doing fine. His thoughts told her of his best meal in days, and the attention of servants who had the heads of horses, who scrubbed off his hide and brushed out tangles in his mane. He could not read their minds, but their attitude indicated that they had not seen a genuine horse before, but understood hoofed animals, so had a general notion how to treat him.

Ddwng was waiting for her. He showed her to a seat at a table for two, and sat opposite her. 'You are comfortable?' the ball of this room inquired.

'Yes, thank you,' Colene replied. Indeed she was, physically. But what was this leading up to? She tried not to show her continuing tension.

'You are beautiful,' the ball said.

'Thank you.' Then, aware that it spoke at the direction of Ddwng, she made the servant nod-bow to him.

Evidently pleased, he returned the nod. If he had had doubt about whether she was civilized, it was being resolved.

Ovines brought in platters. Each had an array of odd but interesting-smelling substances. But she hesitated to choose, not wanting to make some gauche error. 'Please – you choose,' she said to Ddwng.

He nodded again. In a moment she had a plate of things, similar to his own. She watched him lift a utensil resembling a single chopstick. When he touched it to a morsel, a bite-sized segment of that morsel adhered to it. Good enough.

They ate in silence. The food, strange as it was, was excellent; she could get used to this in a hurry. There was a beverage too, tasting like a cross between beer and chocolate milk; she hoped it wasn't alcoholic, and it didn't seem to be. Ddwng evidently wasn't trying to get her drunk. Why should he bother? She was in his power. That was the fly in this lovely ointment: soon enough Ddwng would get down to business.

They completed the meal, and the servants brought mouthwash that left her mouth feeling absolutely clean after one rinse. That was certainly easier than brushing her teeth!

Then they adjourned to a chamber containing a fountain whose fluid changed colors as it moved. Around it were exotic plants – perhaps ordinary here, but alien to her.

'Now we shall formulate our understanding,' the ball said.

'Of course,' Colene agreed, hoping that her suddenly

renewed tension did not show. 'What is your interest in me?'

'You are traveling the Virtual Mode with your animal. I have an interest in the Virtual Mode. I would like to know where its Device of origin is located.'

'I don't really know about that,' she admitted honestly enough. 'It must have been set up by Darius. I am traveling along it to reach his home reality, or to meet him along the way, I hope.'

'Darius is your promised man?' The ball was doing the talking, but the expressions were on the face of Ddwng, and soon it was as if he were talking. He evidently had some kind of ongoing translation, so that he understood what she said.

'Yes. I love him.' She wanted no misunderstandings: she was taken.

'He is a fortunate man.'

She tried to suppress her girlish delight in being flattered. 'I would like to get moving again tomorrow, with my horse. We had to cross quite a number of realities that were, well, empty. Do you know whether the ones in the other direction are okay?'

'We have not had occasion to explore far, but they seem to be similar to those through which you passed.'

'You went to a lot of effort, setting up those paths. Why did you bother?'

'When the Virtual Mode was established, we could not know its origin or mission,' the ball said. 'We knew that those on it would have difficulty with this region, and perhaps suffer harm. So we constructed paths as far as feasible, and set markers beyond them. This seems to have been effective, as you arrived on one of these paths.'

'Well, I'm sorry I can't help you. Why do you want the Chip?'

'A Virtual Mode is normally a temporary thing. With the Chip, we could establish Virtual Modes at our discretion. This would be an excellent thing for our society.'

'The Chip can do that? Can set up a Virtual Mode from anywhere, anytime?'

Ddwng smiled. 'Indeed it can, Colene,' the ball said. 'So you

230

can see that a Chip is one of the most valuable things in all the realities.'

'I sure do, now! I thought it was just some routine thing they could do in Darius's reality.'

'That may be the case. But I gather it is not routine in your reality, as it is not in mine.'

'In my reality, we don't even know there's more than one reality!'

'How did you discover that?'

He seemed interested, and nice, so she told him. In fact she was acting just a bit more naive than she was, because deep down she definitely did not trust him. Stupidity and ignorance could be significant assets for a girl, when they weren't actual. 'Darius was looking for a wife, and he didn't like the ones where he was, so he made a spot trip to my reality. Somehow he knew that I wanted out of my situation and might go with him. But I didn't quite trust it, and didn't go. Then he set up the Virtual Mode, and now I'm trying to get back to him. But it's one hell of a trip!'

'Evidently so. But have you considered that if you are traveling toward his reality, and he is traveling toward yours, you may pass each other without meeting?'

'Se –' she started, then caught herself. She didn't want him to know that the horse could pick up Darius' mind when he came within several realities. 'Seems I didn't think of that! Gee, I hope I haven't already missed him!'

Ddwng smiled again, evidently becoming satisfied about her naiveté. The ball spoke again. 'I am sure you have not, because he has not passed through this reality, which seems to be between his and yours.'

'But maybe he went through a corner of it and you didn't see him.'

'That is unlikely. The void realities are extensive, and difficult to pass. He should have intercepted one of our paths and followed it here, as you did.'

That did make sense. She now saw where Ddwng was leading, so she set it up for him. 'But how will I know which path he's coming in on? I mean, if I go out tomorrow –'

'Readily solved. You will simply wait here for him, and be

231

reunited here. This will surely be best in any event, because we have excellent facilities, and he may be tired from the struggle with the void realities.'

'Gee, that's nice of you!' she exclaimed happily. But inside she was not at all sanguine. This person had gone to an extraordinary amount of trouble to make long paths, and she doubted that he was doing it from sheer niceness. He wanted the Chip, as he said, and that meant he needed Darius to lead him to the reality where the Chip was.

But that Chip was evidently the potential source of almost unimaginable power. What would Ddwng do once he had it?

She wished she could think of a way to see that Ddwng didn't get it. But if she made any suspicious move, she was now afraid that she would proceed from the status of Guest to that of Prisoner.

She would have to wait until Darius came, and then warn him not to tell where his reality was. Maybe they could head back to hers, until they got free of Ddwng, then cross this region somewhere else. Or start toward his reality, and turn aside. There were surely ways and ways, if she could just warn him without alerting Ddwng.

'It sure is lucky that you're here, with a good reality in the middle of the bad ones,' she said brightly. 'I'm afraid we would have been in real trouble otherwise.'

'It is fortunate,' the ball agreed.

It was a disaster, she feared.

10

CAPTAIN

Suddenly they were in a barren region. There seemed to be no life at all in this Mode, though the prior Mode was lush.

Darius looked at Provos. 'Do you have any memory of this?'

'I have no memory of this,' she said, not answering so much as anticipating his coming response. 'We do not remain here long.'

'Let's move on, then,' he agreed.

They crossed into the next, and the next, but the barrenness continued. This seemed to be an entire segment of lifeless Modes, unlike any they had passed before. The ground was nothing but rock and sand; there was no water.

She could not remember their future as long as they kept crossing to new Modes. But suppose there was no resumption of living Modes within their walking range? Her memory of the future would do them no good; they would be dead.

'Provos, you may not remember the terrain,' he said carefully. 'But can you remember your association with me? Do you know me from more than a few days in the future?'

'I remember you from a fortnight in the future,' she said. 'Then it becomes confused.'

Two weeks. That suggested that it was safe to plow ahead, because they would not die in that time. Heartened, he did just that.

But the barren Modes continued for the course of half a

day's travel. The naked sun beat down, making an oven of the landscape. Darius became doubtful. Yet Provos seemed unconcerned, so he said nothing.

Then they spied a flash of a light to the side. It turned out to be a little signaler stuck in the sterile sand. Near it was an arrow pointing onward.

Evidently someone had been here before them. Since the Virtual Mode had not existed for a long time, this had to be recent. Could Colene have passed this way? No, her arrow should have been pointing back the way he had come.

They moved on. Now the sun was descending, so that they had to shield their faces from it as they proceeded westward. Several hours later they found another flashing signal, with its arrow. Then they found a path. It was just a thin layer of silvery material laid on the rock, disappearing as it crossed to the next Mode. But it wound on through the bleak crevices and dunes, going somewhere. It was dusk now, and they decided to camp, then follow the path in the morning.

Provos remembered no problems in the coming hours. With neither weather nor animals to contend with, this seemed reasonable. But there was also no shield against the chill of night. The stone had been burning hot, and it retained much of its heat, but the air was turning frigid. There was no wood from which to make a fire. His thin blanket was not enough to shield them from the intensity of the chill that was developing.

Provos looked around. Then she stooped to lift the end of the path. The material came up readily. She walked with it, bunching up a length. Of this she made a blanket. She signaled him to join her.

The path material turned out to have a good insulating property. Whether as tent or blanket, it held in the radiating heat of the stone and kept them warm.

By morning, even so, it was very cold, and the two of them were closely embraced, huddled under the path. Darius wished it could have been Colene with him, with her lovely little body and innocently seductive manner. But with the dawn came the heat of the sun, and soon the air was warming.

The reflective path remained cooler than the surrounding

stone. They walked on it and were more comfortable than they had been the day before. Now they were obviously going somewhere. But who had set this up, and why?

The path was leading in the direction of the steepest change of Modes, which meant it was going toward an anchor. But probably not the right one. Darius had found his way first to Provos' anchor Mode. Now they must be going to a third one, and they could not know what to expect of it.

Suddenly there was water. The land had been desert-dry, but now there were lakes to the sides and vapors rising from the stone. Farther along there was life: thin, tenacious lichen coloring the rocks. But as they proceeded, this became more ambitious, until there was a general covering of primitive vegetation, and the appearance of insect life.

Then there was animal life. At first it was not far removed from the lakes, and was small, but it progressed rapidly. When man-sized reptiles appeared, Darius got nervous. But it was easy to avoid a predator by stepping across a Mode boundary. They just had to be careful not to walk directly into one, as there was no way to spot them ahead. They learned to count their paces, pause, and use his mirror-tube before moving on. This slowed them, but seemed necessary.

The path became bolder, and the scenery more recent. There seemed to be no large predators in this section, so they put away the mirror tube and moved more rapidly, because night was coming again.

Suddenly they were in an enormous chamber. There was an extremely elegant young woman, obviously of high social standing. She turned and saw him.

'Darius!' she cried, and flung herself into his arms.

It was Colene! Thus suddenly they had come together.

'Beware,' she whispered into his ear before she kissed him.

But already a man was walking toward them. He had reddish hair and piercing black eyes under a metallic band resembling a crown, and wore a kingly robe.

'You must be Darius,' a voice said in Colene's language. It came not from the man but what appeared to be a hanging ball.

'I am Darius,' he agreed as Colene relaxed enough to let him speak. Her whispered warning: what did it mean? That this was a hostile figure of some sort? Yet what could he do if it was?

'And your companion?' the ball asked.

Provos did not speak Colene's language, and not a great deal of his own language. 'She is Provos,' he said.

'This is not good,' Provos murmured in his language.

What was she beginning to remember? He knew it took a while for her to clarify her memories of a new Mode. Since her warning coincided with Colene's, he knew he had to be very careful.

'I must talk with you,' the ball said. 'Come with me.'

It seemed that it was the man who was really talking, as he was gesturing.

'Go with him,' Colene said. 'I will see to your companion.'

Darius looked at Provos, but she seemed to be willing to go with Colene despite the barrier of speech. He nodded.

In a moment he was in a separate chamber with the man, evidently private. 'I am Ddwng of the DoOon,' the ball said, still in Colene's language. 'I need your Chip.'

'The Chip that set up the Virtual Mode?' Darius asked, surprised. 'It is not mine to give.'

'But you could lead me to it.'

'To my Mode, yes. But the Cyng of Pwer would not give it to you. Chips are valuable.'

'I know. If you lead me to your Mode, I will get it from your official.'

'Why do you want it?'

'We are confined to our Mode. The Chip will enable us to visit other Modes.'

Darius considered. He did not like this situation. Both Colene and Provos had expressed doubt. Why should this evidently powerful man be so eager to go to other Modes? Could he be a human version of the dragons, seeking to invade new territory to the disadvantage of the folk there?

But it might not be wise to turn him down flatly. 'I will think about the matter.'

236

Ddwng frowned. 'There are things you should know, as you think,' the ball said. 'Colene will be withheld from you during that period.'

'Withheld?' Darius asked, dismayed. 'But I entered the Virtual Mode only to fetch her!'

'Then your decision should be easy. I shall grant you ten days to decide. If you are negative, we shall sterilize Colene and make her a common concubine.'

Suddenly Darius understood how accurate the warnings were. Ddwng was holding Colene hostage to Darius' performance! Surely there was no good motive there.

'In the interim, you shall perform an assignment,' the ball continued. 'The manner in which you acquit yourself will determine your situation after your decision.'

Darius suspected that anything he could say would only complicate his situation. But there was one way he could improve his chances. 'I will need the services of Provos.'

Ddwng hesitated, then evidently concluded that a small concession was in order. What he wanted was Darius' cooperation, not his antagonism. 'She will join you.'

Then a servant appeared. His head was that of a sheep. The creature was evidently waiting for Darius, so Darius got up and accompanied him from the room. They walked to a relatively tiny chamber. 'Stand in there,' a nearby hanging ball said.

Darius stepped into the little chamber. A panel closed him in. The chamber shook. Then the panel opened.

A man stood outside, but not the same one. This one was fully human, and wore a rather handsome deep red uniform. He lifted his right hand, spreading his fingers. 'Welcome aboard, Captain,' a ball said.

Darius shook his head. 'You have mistaken me for someone else. I am here only to do an assignment for Ddwng of the DoOon.'

'This is true, sir,' the ball said, evidently speaking for the man. 'You are to complete a mission as Captain of this ship, the FTL *Flay*. I am your executive officer, Jjle.'

Darius stepped out of the little chamber. 'But I know nothing of ships! I can't even find the sail!'

Jjle smiled. 'This ship has no sail, sir,' the ball said. 'It is a destroyer-class thousand-light-year craft. I am competent to operate it, as I shall do at your command.'

'No sail?' Darius asked blankly.

'Sir, if you will permit the personal remark, I suspect you have come into this command rather suddenly. May I proffer a suggestion?'

'Yes, please, J-jlee! I have no idea what –'

'Allow me to show you to your quarters, where your nulls will acquaint you with the necessary background. When you emerge, no other member of the crew will know that this is new to you.'

This had the sound of good advice. 'Yes, thank you.'

'The appropriate term is "affirmative", sir. When we reach your quarters, tell me to "carry on".'

'Affirmative,' Darius said.

They walked down a short squared-off metal hall to another door panel. 'Your touch will key it open, sir.'

Darius touched the panel. It slid aside to reveal a chamber beyond.

'I look forward to serving with you, sir,' Jjle said.

'Uh, yes. Uh, carry on.'

The man lifted his hand again, fingers splayed. Then he turned smartly and departed.

Darius stepped into the chamber. The panel closed behind him. How he had come from the palace on the ground to this 'space' ship he did not know, but it was actually no stranger than stepping through Mode boundaries.

The chamber was opulent. Lush carpeting covered the floor, and fine murals were on the walls. Three odd statues lined one side. Near the ceiling were ornate cabinets set into the corners. There was a huge picture window overlooking a lovely placid river valley. This was definitely not where he had been! But neither was it on the water.

Then he saw a statue move. It was breathing!

He looked more closely. The bodies of the figures were human, but the heads resembled those of cats. One body was evidently male, for it was of masculine proportions and had a cod piece fitted obviously into his shorts; another was female, with full breasts and hips distending her tight dress; the one between them seemed to be neuter.

'Who are you?' he asked.

The male stepped forward marginally. 'We are your nulls, Captain Darius,' a ball he hadn't noticed before said. 'We are of the Feline persuasion. I am Tom.'

The neuter figure stepped forward. 'I am Cat.' The pitch and intonation differed, though it was still the ball speaking.

Then the female: 'I am Pussy.' This time the tone was sultry.

'Nulls?'

'Nulls are subhuman servants. We exist to serve you in any capacity you desire.'

Darius pondered that, not knowing what to make of it.

'Your attention, sir,' the ball said in a neutral voice. 'A person is beyond the panel.'

'Who?'

'The woman Provos.'

'Let her in,' he said, relieved.

The panel opened. Provos stepped through. She seemed to take this reunion for granted, evidently remembering their future association. 'I presume you interceded to bring me here,' she said.

'I interceded to bring you here,' he repeated, because that was evidently the dialogue she remembered.

She turned to the three feline nulls. 'It is pleasant to commence our association, Tom, Cat and Pussy,' she said.

She spoke in Darius' language, which the folk here did not seem to know. So he translated.

The three were startled. Darius was sympathetic. 'Provos is a woman of special ways,' he said.

'These folk are to be trusted,' Provos advised him. 'You will get to know them while I clean up and retire.' She walked across the room to a panel set in the wall, and tapped on it. It didn't open.

'Uh, obey her touch as you would mine,' Darius said to the panel. It opened, and Provos stepped inside another tiny chamber. The panel closed after her.

Darius addressed the felines. 'I would like to sit down and get to know you.'

Immediately Tom walked to another panel. It opened, and from it slid an oblong board. The board puffed out and became a chair. Tom set it down before Darius.

Darius sat in it. 'Make yourselves comfortable,' he said.

The three got down on the floor before him and curled up rather in the manner of cats, their limbs tucked under them, their heads up, watching him. This was all right for Tom and Cat, but it caused Pussy to show such a generous cleavage that it was distracting.

'Pussy, get yourself a chair,' he said. 'I will talk with you.'

She rose and produced a chair. She sat on it in the human manner, crossing her legs somewhat loosely. Her skirt was not long enough for this maneuver, so that the whole of her inner thighs were now visible for his inspection. She wore no diaper. Indeed, she seemed to wear no panties either.

He decided to try to ignore this, lest he seem too fussy. 'Pussy, please clarify for me what it is the three of you are expected to do for me.'

'We exist to serve you in any capacity you desire,' the sultry voice of the ball said. The cat-woman's thighs spread a bit more.

'Yes, so you said before. But what capacities do you expect me to desire of you?'

'Information, body attendance, sex,' she said via the ball, confirming the message her legs had been sending.

'Information is the one I desire now. How did you come to be the way you are?'

'We are androids, manufactured in the factory from recon-stituted human genetic material. We have no souls. Our heads are modified to conform to several animal patterns, though we retain the ability to perceive and communicate as humans do. As a class we are the nulls; as a subclass we are the Felines, male, neuter and female. Our only pleasure comes from being of significant service to our human masters, and we must perform at least one such service each day or suffer.'

Evidently this was a set speech for the edification of igno-rants like himself. Darius appreciated it. 'You are performing such a service to me by giving me this information?'

'Yes,' she agreed eagerly.

'What happens to a null who fails to perform such a service?'

'On the first day we suffer emotional pain. On the second, physical pain. On the third we die.'

The DoOon did not treat their servants gently! 'Suppose I just tell you that I need no services, and to relax?'

'The nature of acceptable services is listed and programmed,' the ball said in her voice. 'We can not deviate. If you wish some service which is not programmed, you must arrange it by having us reprogrammed on a temporary basis.'

'Suppose I do not need a service, but another human being does. May I have you do it, abating your need?'

'No,' she said sadly. The ball seemed to be fading out of awareness.

The neuter null lifted a hand, evidently a signal for attention. 'Speak, Cat,' Darius said.

'Pussy's answer is incomplete. We are differentiated by type as well as by sex. Tom is strong and capable of violence at your behest; he will defend you against attack, even by a human being. Pussy is sympathetic and versed in the arts of gentleness, massage, seduction and sexual peformance. I lack either nature, but am the most objective and intelligent of your Felines. I am capable of interpreting your commands and questions and verifying your actual intent when you misspeak yourself or are vague. Accordingly I advise you that while Pussy's response is technically correct, there are ways to circumvent this restriction.'

'Then I should be talking with you, rather than Pussy,' Darius said, interested.

'We would not presume to say that,' the ball said for Cat.

Darius faced Pussy. 'Should I be talking with Cat instead of you?'

'Yes.'

'Thank you, Pussy. I will talk with him, if this will not hurt your feelings.'

She looked confused. 'He means kindness, Pussy,' Cat said to her. 'He appreciates what you have done so far.'

'Oh, thank you!' she said, relieved. As always, it was the

ball that spoke, but the distinction had become meaningless; it was her voice, and her thought.

Cat faced Darius. 'This was an example. When you said "if" this would not hurt her feelings, she was not sure whether they should be hurt, which would mean she had in some way failed you. I provided the reassurance you intended. If I interpret your intent incorrectly, or if you prefer that I not do this, advise me and I will desist.'

Darius was fascinated by this information. It was apparent that these servants could indeed be useful. 'How may I circumvent the restriction against assigning a service to another person?'

'One way would be to volunteer to do a service yourself for that person, begin it, then have one of us complete it for you. You are free to make commitments in ways we are not.'

Darius nodded. 'You serve me because you serve the Captain?'

'We serve you because we have been assigned to you. An officer of the Navy normally keeps his own nulls to serve him wherever he is employed. If you wish other nulls, we can be exchanged. But for the duration we are loyal to you, not the office, and you may trust us always to serve your interest to the best of our understanding and ability.'

Provos emerged from the cleaning chamber, looking refreshed. She glanced at Darius. 'You need more sleep and rest than you get this night,' she said reprovingly in his language. 'At least have them give you a nourishment pill.'

'I will show you to a bedchamber,' Darius said, rising. He walked toward her, having no idea where it was or whether it existed. He looked back. 'Pussy, please complete this task for me, and see that Provos is as comfortable as I would make her.'

Pussy jumped up, her breasts bouncing. 'It is this way,' she said, almost purring as she led Provos to another panel and through to another chamber.

'Thank you, Darius,' Provos said, familiar with this protocol from her memory.

He settled down with the remaining two Felines. He realized that he was hungry. 'Nourishment pill?'

'Immediately,' Tom said, and rose to fetch a tablet.

Darius accepted the pill, and gazed at it. 'This will feed me?'

'Yes. You may order a conventional meal if you prefer.'

'No, I'll try this.' If Provos remembered it as satisfactory, it probably was. He popped the pill in his mouth and swallowed it with saliva.

He was no longer hungry. Evidently this was something like magic. That made it acceptable. He returned to business. 'The executive officer called me sir. Why did he do this, and why don't you?'

'"Sir" is a token of respect given by a human to one of a higher rank in the Navy,' Cat said. 'We are not human, so lack the status to show respect. One must possess sufficient status to have his token of respect be worthy.'

'Pussy has performed a service for me, and you are performing one now. If it is not convenient for me to find a service for Tom to do, how can I avoid causing him distress?'

'His distress has no force against your convenience. You may ignore it.'

'It would cause me distress to cause any of you needless distress.'

'Then I can suggest tasks which would not cause you inconvenience.'

'Yes.'

'Is there anything you desire which would be awkward or inconvenient for you to achieve at present by your own action?'

'I'd like to be with Colene!' Darius said before he thought.

'This is a human person?'

'This is the human person I came to be with. But Ddwng has separated us, pending a mission I must complete for him. I don't want to do a mission, I want to take Colene home with me. But I think this is beyond your capacity to remedy.'

'It is,' Cat agreed. 'But we can provide you with partial satisfaction with no more effort on your part than you choose to exert.'

'Then do it.'

Tom got up. He touched a section of the wall opposite

Darius, and the mural became a scene of an office so realistic that there seemed to be a window between the two chambers. A null with the head of a dog sat at a desk.

The Canine glanced at them and spoke in an incomprehensible language.

'Speak English, Bitch,' Tom snapped.

'What do you want, Tom?' she inquired. It was probably a ball speaking for her, but since the sound came through the window it made no difference.

'Information, by order of Captain Darius of the *Flay*,' Tom said curtly.

'I will give you Dog.' She touched a button. The picture changed. Now there was another office, with what appeared to be a neuter Canine. 'What information, Tom?' it asked.

'The present location and accessibility of the human Colene, visitor to this Mode.'

Dog touched buttons of his own. He studied what might have been a screen they could not see. 'The human Colene is the present consort of the Emperor Ddwng. As such she is accessible only by his leave.'

Darius was stunned. Consort?

'The Captain requests that leave,' Tom said.

'This may require some delay.'

Cat glanced at Darius. 'We'll wait,' Darius said.

'Proceed,' Cat said.

The picture changed again. Now it showed a woman with the head of a pig. 'Tom, why do you seek this contact?' she asked.

'I speak for Captain Darius, Sow. He does not answer to you.'

Darius appreciated the imperious attitude Tom was showing. That was about the way he felt. It seemed appropriate that the bureaucracy should be represented by swine.

A male pig-head appeared. 'By order of our master Ddwng, Darius will answer to the Swine,' he snorted. His tone was arrogant in the masculine fashion.

'Boar, Darius wishes contact with Colene, with whom he has had prior connection. Screen contact will do on an interim basis.'

A third Swine appeared, evidently the neuter. 'This may be granted. But there is information I must impart first.'

Tom glanced at Darius again. Darius nodded.

'Impart it, Pig.'

'Colene's present status is nominal. She is not subject to present sexual use by the Emperor, but is required to present herself and comport herself as his consort. This is a compatible existence, and her status is one to incite the envy of all women. If Darius fails to accommodate Ddwng in the required manner at the deadline, Colene's ovaries will be removed for the genetic bank and she will be given as a full-human concubine to whatever officer is selected. Should she resist, she will be lobotomized to the degree necessary to make her docile. She has not been informed of this.'

Darius felt faint. He had known that pressure would be brought to bear on him, to make him help Ddwng obtain the Chip. Sterilization of Colene had already been threatened. But he had not realized how ruthless the full course would be. Colene was hostage to his cooperation – and he seemed to have no way to fight it.

'And should Darius do the Emperor's will?' Tom inquired.

'Colene will be restored to him whole, and they will be given their freedom, either as ranking persons within the Empire or to travel to another Mode.'

What choice did he have? Yet a person who would make this kind of threat and back it up would probably also break his word. It might be pointless to agree. At least he had ten days to think about it.

'Message received,' Tom said. 'May Darius now see Colene?'

The screen changed again. Suddenly Colene was there, in her ornate gown, sparkling hair and bracelets. She was beautiful in her vibrant youth. No one would know from her appearance that she was suicidal, and she had surely kept the secret.

She saw him. 'Darius!' she exclaimed, stepping toward him.

Unable to help himself, he stepped toward her too. They met at the screen/wall between them, the images of their hands touching the cold surface. They tried to kiss, but again it was only images meeting.

'I asked to be with you,' he said.

'We're not even in the same stellar system,' she replied. 'I'm still on Earth, and you're on an FTL ship crossing the galaxy.'

'Ddwng wants me to lead him to the Chip.'

'Don't do it!' she exclaimed. 'He wants to conquer the other Modes too!'

'But if I do not –'

'We won't be allowed together,' she finished. 'I know that, Darius. But we owe something to our realities. We can't let them be despoiled. I love you, and I want to be with you, but not this way.' Her face shone with tears. 'If you find a way to escape, don't wait for me. Just get gone!'

'Colene, I love you too, and I curse the moment I failed to bring you with me. There are other ways – we don't have to marry – I found a woman who can – we can love, if –'

'Prima,' she agreed. 'I understand. It is good. It's not what I first dreamed of, but I love you so, I don't care. But not – you know. Not this way.'

'Not this way,' he agreed.

'They're not cutting us off,' she said, surprised.

'Because the more we see of each other, the more we will be willing to sacrifice for each other,' he said.

'Yes. So I guess we'd better quit, now.' Her tears were streaming down her face. 'But it's been great, Darius!'

'It is not over!' he protested. 'It can't be over! I went to the Virtual Mode only for you!'

'My life is nothing. It's complete. But you – thank you for stepping into my life, Darius, however briefly. You made it all worthwhile.'

She turned away. He did the same. What irony, to seem so close, yet be so far! To exchange vows of love, yet to have to deny the realization of them.

He became aware of the three Felines. Pussy had rejoined the group.

He stepped into her and embraced her. She was completely soft and responsive. He buried his face in her furry hair and let himself hurt.

'You may take me in your bedroom, or here, as you wish,' she murmured.

She misunderstood the nature of his emotion. 'Another time,' he said. 'I have much still to learn, here.' Then he disengaged, resumed his chair, and organized his thoughts.

He looked at Tom. 'That was a significant service,' he said. 'Now you may retire; I will not need you until morning.'

Tom walked to a niche, lay on the floor, curled up, and put his head down. In a moment he was asleep.

'You also,' he said to Pussy. She selected another nook and curled up similarly, showing firm upper thigh. Apparently it was simply her nature to display her body.

'From you I need more information,' he said to Cat. 'What does "FTL" mean?'

'It is an acronym for "Faster Than Light,"' it explained. 'This ship, for example, is the FTL *Flay*, capable of traveling a great deal faster than the velocity of light through a vacuum. It is proceeding at that rate to the site of your mission, and will arrive in approximately fifty hours travel time.'

'I am from a culture where the velocity of light does not matter. Translate that into something I can follow.'

'If you walked entirely around the globe of Earth, you would travel about twenty-five thousand miles, as this language has it. If you completed that circuit seven or eight times, you would cover the distance light travels in a single second. The spans between stars are such that we prefer to measure them in multiples of the amount light travels in a year. This ship traverses a thousand light-years each hour, so its destination is fifty thousand light-years from Earth, or about half way across the galaxy.'

Darius found that translated version was not much more intelligible than the original. 'So we are now an enormous distance from Earth, and going farther away.'

'That is correct. But we shall return as readily as we go.'

'What is the mission I am to accomplish?'

'A monster is rampaging on a colony planet, and the natives are unable to dispatch it. You will do that.'

With magic, Darius knew he could set a monster back. But

magic had not worked for him in any of the Modes beyond the region of his own.

Still, he should test it. He removed his pack and brought out his golem-figure of himself. 'To the far corner of this chamber,' he murmured, and made the figure jump.

Nothing happened. There was not even a tug in his stomach. Magic was not operative here.

Darius sighed. He was in effect a man without special power. 'I am not skilled in this.'

'It is not necessary that you be so.' The Felines seemed to have no interest in his peculiar action with the figurine; evidently his business was his business, unless he made it theirs. 'You will have merely to give the necessary directives. Nulls will assume the risk and complete the job.'

'So I'm a figurehead,' he said.

'No, nulls have no initiative in such respects,' it reassured him. 'A ranking human being must be in charge of the operation.'

'But any human could do it, even a complete ignoramus.'

'Yes.'

'So why did Ddwng bother to send me? Just to get me out of the way for a while?'

'I can not speak for the motives of the Emperor, but it seems reasonable that he has several reasons. He may wish to give you time and experience so that you can come to the conclusion that it is best to accede to his wishes. He may wish to keep you away from Colene. He may wish to prevent you from departing via your Virtual Mode. He may wish to keep you out of mischief without imprisoning you. And he may wish to discover how competent an officer you have the potential of being, in the event that you are converted to his cause. This mission accomplishes these things.'

The reasoning was formidable. 'I think I had better do as good a job as I can, until I decide what I will do.'

'That seems appropriate,' it agreed.

'What is known about this monster?'

'It seems to be a beast set on wanton destruction. It sets fire to villages, floods pastures, and fouls food supplies. No one has seen it, but its presence is manifest.'

'Why don't they lock doors and set guards?'

'They do, but the monster is extremely cunning about locks, and can stun guards.'

Darius pondered that. 'What are the natives like?'

'They are similar in outline and manner to Earthly snails, but larger. They are reasonably intelligent and capable, but slow.'

That surprised Darius. He had assumed that the natives were human, with a culture distinct from that of the colonists. Snails? This was a far land indeed!

He continued to question Cat, learning more about the various aspects of this Mode. It seemed that there were many intelligent creatures in what was called the galaxy, but that the humans had become dominant and now governed and exploited all of it they wished. They had risen to dominance thousands of years before, because of their ability to make ships that traveled faster than light, to nullify the effects of gravity, and to make weapons that could kill individual creatures or destroy entire planets.

But when they had sought to invade other Modes, the dominant cultures of those had taken action. The humans in most Modes were isolated on their home planet, causing trouble only to the creatures there; only in this Mode had they mastered the elusive secrets of super-science that enabled them to spread out and molest the larger galaxy. The creatures of other Modes had an ancient compact which prevented them from committing genocide in any single Mode. So they isolated this Mode by sterilizing the adjacent Modes and barring any contact from beyond. So it had been for a thousand years.

That explained what he and Provos had seen on the way here. 'But then how did this come to be an anchor Mode for our Virtual Mode?'

'We can only conjecture,' Cat said. 'The lives of empires are long, but the lives of individual creatures are short. Some creature must have become careless, and not been watching when your Virtual Mode was instituted. In fact, the possession of a Chip by human beings in any Mode constitutes a violation of the proscription. It seems likely that in due course this error will be corrected, and human beings will be confined again, to either their conquered Mode or their individual world in other Modes.'

'Unless Ddwng succeeds in getting his hands on the Chip in my Mode first,' Darius said. 'Then he will spread his minions across many Modes in a hurry, making it impossible to isolate them without doing enormous damage to innocent creatures.'

'This I suspect is the strategy,' Cat agreed.

'I see why he wants my Chip.' Darius was careful not to mention that it was only one of many in his Mode, evidently a forgotten hoard. 'But why is he giving me ten days to make up my mind? Surely time is of the essence.'

'Ddwng is competent, and comes from a lineage of competent Emperors. He is surely doing what is most advantageous to his purpose, considering all factors. It may be that the risks of forcing the issue rapidly are worse than those of giving you time, despite the danger of having the error discovered. Perhaps it is unlikely that the error will be noted until the Chip begins to be exploited. But it seems that the Emperor is not willing to risk too much time, as he has set the limit.'

That reminded Darius of the threat against Colene. Evidently Ddwng didn't know that she was suicidal, so that he was unlikely to get any long servitude from her if she didn't like it. But the nature of the threat was perplexing. 'Why have her ovaries cut out? There are surely more painful tortures that would not disfigure her.'

'She would not be disfigured,' it said. 'The surgery would be painless. Torture is done not by mutilation, but by infliction of harmless pain.'

'Harmless pain! How can that be?'

Cat got up and went to another panel. It opened, and from it it took a small disk. 'This is a pain control. It is attuned to you, so that it will not affect you. But it will cause discomfort in any other person, whether human or null, within its range, to whatever degree you choose. This dial sets the level.'

'Harmless pain?' Darius repeated.

'You may demonstrate it on me if you wish. However I must caution you that if you do not wish to render me unconscious, do not turn it to the highest range.'

250

'Demonstrate it on you? I have no wish to hurt you, and what would it prove? Demonstrate it on me.'

'This is a thing I may not do, for I think you do not understand what you are asking.'

'Set it at the minimum level, and show me how to turn it on. And how to detune it so that it affects me as well as you.'

'This setting will detune it,' Cat said. 'This is the minimum level.' It moved the dial. 'This activates it.'

Darius touched the detune setting. Then he turned it on.

Abruptly he experienced an ugly feeling. It was as if he were just coming down with a fever: a malaise not yet incapacitating, but a harbinger of worse to come.

He looked at Cat, who seemed unaffected. 'You feel it too?'

'Yes. But I am accustomed to it.'

Darius moved the dial. The discomfort increased. His body began to shake, and sweat appeared on his skin. His breathing became irregular. 'You feel this?'

'Yes.' The Feline did look a bit uncomfortable, but not nearly as much so as Darius felt.

He nudged it up farther. It felt as if he were walking into a furnace which was heating his bones, causing them to swell and split. Yet he was only three notches up, on a scale of ten.

He turned it off. 'It is effective,' he agreed. 'And I do seem to feel no aftereffect. I can see that this would be effective for discipline. But that leaves my question: why do surgery on Colene?'

'That is a prerequisite to demoting her to servant status,' Cat said. 'Humans, unlike nulls, are capable of reproduction. On colony planets they still do it naturally; on the more civilized worlds they do it via the birth banks. Once her valuable human eggs are safe, she can be treated in any manner. This is expected to cause you distress.'

'It does,' Darius said. 'I don't want any part of her removed, and I want to be with her myself. But surely there are many human women in this Mode; why take the eggs from Colene?'

'The human genetic pool has been highly refined and modified,' it said. 'As you can see by the manner that we nulls have

251

been crafted from the leftover parts of it. No human suffers from genetic maladies; none grow fat or weak or are stupid. All live long lives by primitive standards, and enjoy health throughout. But the genetic pool has become inbred, and the rate of population increase is declining. Fewer eggs are viable. It seems that primitive vigor has been sacrificed along with primitive liabilities. New genetic input is needed, to broaden the base and invigorate the pool. Colene represents an excellent source of that input, being young, intelligent, and healthy. It is unfortunate that the other woman, Provos, is beyond the age of similar harvest.'

Darius was horrified anew. 'So they aren't going to let her escape with her ovaries. But then why should I cooperate? Ddwng's word means nothing.'

'That is not true. The Emperor's word is always good. It would be beneath him to make any false statement. There is reason for you to cooperate: if you provide the Chip that enables Ddwng to transcend Modes, he will be able to bring in other women with their genes, and will have no need of Colene's genes. He will release you both as promised, together with Provos and the horse.'

'The what?'

'Colene has a horse. You were not aware?'

'I was not aware,' Darius said, surprised. 'I thought she came alone.'

'No, she preferred to ride, so she brought her horse. He was loaded with supplies for them both.'

Darius did not know what to make of this. Colene had had no horse! How had she gotten one? She wouldn't have stolen it. However, she was welcome to it, as far as he was concerned. A horse could be a useful animal when properly trained, and evidently this one was.

It was coming clear why Ddwng was giving Darius time to think about his decision. The more he learned, the more futile it seemed to try to oppose the Emperor. He still didn't like the notion of letting a conqueror loose among the Modes, but he feared increasingly that if he did not cooperate, Colene would suffer immediately, and then increasing pressure would be brought to bear until he capitulated. Darius did not consider himself to be a brave man; if he were put in pain from the pain dial, he would be in serious trouble. Ddwng had surely known that Darius would discover this. There was probably more to learn, which was not good news.

'I think I had better retire,' he said. 'I seem to have used up half the night already.'

'True. Do you wish for a sleep ray, or for Pussy's company?'

'Neither, thanks. Let me just clean up and turn in.'

'As you wish.' Cat settled to the floor, but did not sleep; it was alert for any other directives.

Darius stepped into the cleaning chamber he had seen Provos use. He got out of his clothes. Light flashed. That seemed to be it; he was clean. He picked up his clothes and discovered that they were clean too. Probably he had not had to remove them. But since he did not intend to sleep in them, it didn't matter. He bundled them up and stepped back out.

'My bedroom?' he inquired.

Cat jumped up. 'Here.' It indicated another panel.

Darius entered, and found a chamber with an excellent bed. He suspected that only the Captain rated such accommodations. That was all right; he was ready for this. He dumped his clothing into a shelf-niche and lay down naked.

But before he slept he remembered his screen contact with Colene. How lovely she had been! He had not chosen her for beauty, if he had chosen her at all; somehow he had just gradually discovered that she was the one he wanted to be with. She had been kind to him in her Mode, but it was more than that.

How had she come by a horse?

And – *how had she known about Prima*?

He remembered now: he had been telling her that he had found a suitable woman to marry, so that that part of his search was over. It freed him to love Colene. Colene had said she understood, and she had named Prima. But he had not mentioned that name this time, and he could not have mentioned it before, because he had not encountered Prima before embarking on the Virtual Mode. Somehow Colene had learned the name and what it signified.

253

It had not been Colene directly with whom he talked, but an image. With magic, images could be false. Surely that was true in this super-science realm. Yet Colene's ways had rung true. She had wept when she told him they must part, and she had reacted in other authentic ways. She was suicidal; she would not have told Ddwng that, because she told no one. Only Darius himself, and then only when she loved him. This time she had said that her life was complete, and he knew too well what that meant. Complete because she intended to end it. When she lost him. That had to be Colene! A false image would have tried to convince him to capitulate; she had done the opposite. Had she begged him to do it, he might have yielded; she had begged him not to. That rang true.

But the name. Colene could not know of Prima. Yet how could a false image know it either? No one should know it, not even Provos. He had not mentioned her to Provos. Or had he? He had used the mirror tube Prima had devised; perhaps he had after all mentioned its origin. Or Provos could have remembered the name from some remark he would make in the future. And Provos had been with Colene for a while.

Yes, it was possible, he realized. Provos must have told her. Colene would naturally have asked about him, and Provos would have told what she remembered of future conversations. So the little mystery was solved.

Relieved, he slept.

He must have slept longer than intended, because he had the impression that too much time had passed. But he woke refreshed.

He got up and looked for his clothes. But they were gone. 'Pussy!' he called.

Immediately she appeared, and he realized that he had in his haste spoken the wrong name. He had wanted Tom, the male. Now he was sitting naked on the bed, and the voluptuous female Feline was gazing at him expectantly. 'May I be of service now?' she asked.

'Yes. Fetch me my clothes.'

She touched a panel, and out came a glittering robe. She proffered it.

'That's not mine,' he protested.

'It is the Captain's robe,' she explained. 'It would be amiss for you to go about the ship out of uniform.'

Darius acquiesced to the inevitable. 'Very well. Carry on.'

He meant for her to depart, so he could dress. Instead she proceeded to dress him. Well, she did know what she was doing, and he did not. She had to perform her daily service, and he hoped this counted.

Did it? He realized that he had better be sure, lest he cause inadvertent mischief by assuming too much. 'Does this acquit you of your daily service, Pussy?'

'No. This is routine. I must do more for you than this.' She smiled, inhaling, and her breasts swelled, making the fabric of her dress turn translucent in that region. The signal was clear enough.

So much for that. 'I think you know that I love the human woman Colene. I do not have sexual interest in others at this time.'

'But I am not a woman!' she protested happily. 'I am a null. There is no conflict with your woman.'

'No conflict? Colene comes from a culture where men and women are supposed to be true to each other during their association. She would not appreciate my doing anything with you.'

'Then you must explain to her. It is quite normal. Married couples use their nulls all the time. It eases the stress of monogamy and provides variety. A null is much more accommodating than a spouse, because a null has no pride and no rights.'

No pride and no rights. Darius had been coming to like the nulls, but now he realized that the culture that fostered them had a brutal disregard of human pride and rights, and had to be condemned. If he cooperated with Ddwng, he would be facilitating the spread of that system to other Modes, like a loathsome disease.

But it would not be expedient to express his doubt to her. She would only take it as rejection, and therefore some defect in the quality of her service. 'Perhaps another time,' he said gently. 'I have much to learn of the ways of the DoOon, and must get to it.'

'Yes,' she said, disappointed.

Provos was in the main chamber, with a meal set up for them both. She remembered the time of his awakening, of course. 'This is an interesting society,' she remarked. 'But I am sorry you are giving them the Chip.'

'I am?' he asked, startled.

'I understand that it is what you must do to be united with your young woman, and I appreciate your desire, but I wish there had been some other way. Or is there some factor in the past which changes the effect of your action?'

'No, there is not,' he said. She remembered that he was going to agree to Ddwng's demand! He had hoped that her knowledge of the future would enable him to do the opposite. Apparently he was to discover no such device.

The meal was catered by Pussy, eager as always to be of any possible service. But how was he going to find daily services for her other than the one she expected?

Provos glanced at the buxom feline woman. 'I also fear that Colene will not understand your sexual use of this creature,' she said. 'I suspect she will be hurt, considering that you will so soon be rejoined. It would seem to be a virtue in a man to be able to wait a few days.'

He was going to do that? Provos was a good woman who spoke her mind plainly, and it was not possible to argue with her. She was not condemning him, merely voicing her disapproval. But in the light of his determination not to use Pussy in this manner, this was a distressing revelation.

Provos was speaking in Darius' language, which he thought the translator balls did not understand. But now Pussy perked up. 'Oh, thank you, Darius!' she exclaimed. Then, to Provos: 'When?'

'Before he kills the monster,' the old woman replied.

So he was going to succeed in his mission, though he knew so little about it. Actually, he would give the order and a minion would dispatch the monster, giving Darius the credit. No genuine accomplishment there!

He made no comment. He realized that the folk of this Mode,

however loyal they might seem to Darius, were all minions of Ddwng and would report to him. Darius could afford to say nothing of his true thoughts – especially since it seemed that his course was already plotted.

Darius went out to see to the operation of the ship. It was indeed traveling rapidly through the night sky; the simulation – he found it more comfortable to think of it as a magic picture – showed stars passing by at the rate of one or two close ones each minute. The executive officer Jjle with his Caprine nulls saw to the routine; in fact Buck was seeing to it, with authority delegated by his master, and Doe was keeping track of the internal operations of the ship. Goat was at the communications center, coordinating with the planet of destination and with other FTL ships in the area; it seemed that it was important that no two ships pass too close to each other, because of harmonics of hypershift. Darius made no pretense of understanding the technical details; this was obviously a smoothly functioning system.

'We shall rendezvous with Planet Yils in twenty-three hours, sir,' Jjle informed him. 'Have you any directives?'

'Carry on,' Darius replied.

The exec nodded without trace of a smile. Darius completed the tour of the ship, gradually becoming comfortable with it and his position in it. He was a figurehead, true – but it seemed that all captains were figureheads, normally.

He repaired to the ship's library, which was merely a chamber with screens in contact with a number of planets in the galaxy, and with the help of Cat and the resident Ovine neuter, Sheep, he learned as much as he could assimilate about the colony on Planet Yils. The first human mission had come there approximately a thousand years before – all times were scaled to the Earthly measurements, because this was a human empire – and settlement had proceeded. There had been a lively export of 'escargot' for wealthy cuisine, until someone had noticed that the big snails were intelligent. Technically they qualified for sapient-species recognition and protection. But the Empire had never been much for technicalities, so the export continued on a muted basis. The natives were placid folk who did not hold grudges, so there was no fuss.

Now, however, the marauding was becoming an embarrassment. The actual value of the damage was not great, but the seeming inability of the colonists to stop it reflected adversely on the Empire. There was also the suspicion that the natives might be finally developing notions of objection to human rule, and of course that had to be emphatically squelched. It was necessary not only to stop the monster, but to ascertain exactly how it had come on the scene and what had enabled it to operate so long without being stopped. The suggestion of mind-blasting was especially sensitive. The Empire had overwhelming superiority in conventional weapons of all types, but something that could stun a mind without physical contact was alarming.

Darius retired to his quarters and pondered. This just might prove to be a more difficult mission than had been suggested. Was it possible that Ddwng really was providing him with a challenge that would prove his mettle one way or the other? Mind-stunning, if done by intelligent creatures who were organized, could prove to be a threat to more than just a single colony.

Then why assign the mission to an ignorant outsider? It wasn't to get rid of him, because Ddwng wanted him to survive to show the way to his home Mode and the Chip there. Darius was not a conspirator by nature, but he had a certain notion of the ways in which people of doubtful loyalty could be tested. They could be provided with the opportunity to do some secret wrong. Believing they were unobserved, they usually revealed their basic natures.

Suppose Ddwng hesitated to trust himself to the Virtual Mode with only Darius as a guide? The Emperor would not be able to take any of his loyal minions along unless he remained in constant contact with them, which would be awkward. How well Darius knew! That meant he would have to trust Darius and his companions of the Virtual Mode. After requiring Darius' cooperation by threatening the young woman he loved. That would seem chancy indeed!

But if Darius turned out to be trustworthy, the risk became

feasible. If Darius' nature was honest, then his word, once given, was good. That might well be more important to Ddwng than the outcome of the mission on Planet Yils. That ten day deadline might be as much for Ddwng as for Darius: time to study the visitor to this Mode, to come to a conclusion about him.

Darius was a Cyng, a man of inherent power. He had never had the need to deal in anything other than the truth, and hardly cared to demean himself by doing so now. But he had never before been faced with such a difficult choice. Should he save the woman he loved by pledging to enable a conqueror to ravage other Modes? That would represent a loss of honor. But if the alternative was to lose Colene –

Well, he still had most of nine days to make the decision. Or did he? Could this span of time be another kind of test? A person who waited until the end to make the pledge surely was doing it only as a last resort. One who made it at the outset might simply be saying it as a matter of convenience, without sincerity. The sincere man would take time to study the situation and think it through, then make his decision in timely fashion.

Provos believed he would make the pledge. But she could not know what was in his heart, and neither could Ddwng. A liar and a truth-teller would say the same thing, to get his way. But in a situation of challenge and decision, the reactions of the two would probably differ. Ddwng and his minions had surely had a great deal of experience in judging how the two differed.

But a single episode was not enough. It was necessary to know a person as well as possible, and to judge whether his decision was consistent with the pattern of his personality. Even if a person made a commitment with sincerity, he could not be trusted if it was not in accord with his nature. Men did not always know their own wills.

Darius realized that he had probably been under observation throughout, waking and sleeping, and would be for the duration of this venture. It didn't matter; he had been too busy getting his bearings to act in any way atypical of himself. But now that he realized this, it did matter. He could not form a

259

pattern of action consistent with one decision, then decide the other way.

But he hadn't made his decision! How could he be consistent with an unknown?

Provos had given him the key to that. He would have to comport himself in a manner consistent with a decision to accede to Ddwng's demand. If he then did so, it would be trusted. If he did not, then the pattern would be inconsistent – but that would not matter, because an inconsistent pattern was similar to a negative one, for Ddwng's purpose. Either would mean that it was not safe to enter the Virtual Mode with him.

Was the choice truly between Colene and the welfare of the Modes? He would have to search for some compromise. But meanwhile he would assume that he was going to agree to give Ddwng the Chip. He did love Colene, and this was the only likely way to save her.

He looked up. There were the three Felines, not watching him, but alert for any required service. Cat had been of service today; the other two had not. He had to do something about that.

'Tom, try to enable me to see Colene again,' he said.

Tom jumped to manipulate the screen. This time he quickly got through to the Swine. However far the ship was from Earth, it seemed to entail no delay in communication.

But the bureaucracy would not be rushed. Tom had to go through the litany of requests and clarifications. Finally a man with the seeming head of a horse appeared on the screen. 'The Lady Colene is not accessible at the moment,' Stallion said.

'Why not?' Tom demanded.

'Because she is riding her horse.'

Darius was surprised. A horse had been mentioned, and it had slipped his mind. She was allowed to ride it? But of course they wouldn't let her ride it into the Virtual Mode. She must have ridden it all the way to this Mode, to prevent it from being lost in the intervening Modes.

'Stick with it,' Darius said. 'She won't ride forever, and when she's done she will be available.' He did want to see Colene again, but that was not all of it; he wanted to be sure that Tom had enough of a challenge even if he failed to get Colene so that it counted as a full service.

Meanwhile, what should Darius do? His research and his thinking had fatigued him more than he realized, but it was too early to go for his night's sleep. He wanted to maintain a regular sleeping schedule if he could. He wasn't hungry yet. And he hadn't figured out a service for Pussy.

'What can you do for me?' he asked her with mock exasperation. 'That requires no thought on my part?'

She inhaled.

'What else?' he asked quickly.

'I can give you a relaxing massage.'

He considered that. He liked it. 'Agreed.'

'On your bed,' she purred, guiding him to his bed chamber. He let her do it. She was probably very good at this, and his body did feel tight.

Before he knew it, she had pulled off his robe. But of course it wouldn't be good to crumple the Captain's uniform. He lay face down on the bed.

She was good at it. She kneaded his shoulders, and the tension melted away from the muscles there. She stroked his back, and it relaxed. She massaged his calves, and they felt like new. She worked on his thighs, and they were invigorated.

Then she started in on his buttocks. He had been sitting for much of the time he had been on the ship, and there was tenseness to be released here too. But as her hands reached around and inside, a new kind of tension developed. Embarrassed, he lay still and did not say anything.

Until she turned him over. 'Uh, no,' he said, resisting.

'But I have to do the other side, or my service is not complete,' she explained, sounding hurt.

He was stuck. He turned over, revealing his erection. She had surely seen similar before. He closed his eyes.

'Oh, what a beautiful member!' she exclaimed, delighted.

She did his chest muscles with similar finesse, and his stomach. Then she got on the bed, straddling him, her thighs outside his. He opened his eyes and saw that she was naked; she was evidently able to doff her tight dress in a single fluid motion. She leaned forward, her breasts

261

descending invitingly toward him. She was trying to seduce him.

All he had to do was tell her no. But if he did, what would that indicate about his impending decision to cooperate with Ddwng? And if he refused her offerings, then told Ddwng yes, and Ddwng considered his maladaption to the customs of this culture, and concluded that he could not be trusted, what then of Colene? Pussy was nice, but she was meaningless; she would be exactly as nice in exactly this way to any man she was required to serve. It was Colene who counted. He could not risk anything to imperil Colene's welfare.

The safest thing to do was nothing.

Pussy took that as assent. She lay on him full length, sliding up enough to kiss him with her feline mouth. It was a human mouth; it only looked feline. All of her cat features were more suggestive than actual, as if she had had just enough cosmetic surgery to lend the effect.

His resolve to be passive dissolved. His arms closed around her body. His hands stroked the sleekness of the small of her back, and below. Her posterior was as marvelous to touch as to see. Then they were turning over, his eagerness taking charge. She was intended for this use, and –

The wall became a window screen. Colene stood there, as if right beside the bed, staring down. Everything was visible. She blinked.

Darius froze in place. The call! How could he have forgotten the call! Tom had kept at it, finally completed it, and put it right through to Darius, where he happened to be at the moment. In the middle of a sexual act with another woman.

'I guess you're busy right now,' Colene said, turning away. The screen faded and became the wall.

Pussy looked at him, concerned. 'Have I done wrong?'

'No.' She had been true to her nature.

'She was not supposed to see?'

'I was not supposed to be doing it.' An understatement!

'I will tell her what I did!' Pussy said, tears starting down her face as she sat up. 'You did not tell me yes! I have done you a disservice, my master!'

What could he say? What was the penalty for a disservice?

He feared it was formidable. He was already in critical trouble with Colene, and no apology by a null would make that right. What would be the point in punishing Pussy?

'You were not at fault,' he said. 'I let you do what I wanted you to do. I did not know Colene would see, but if I had done it without her seeing, I would have been deceiving her. The fault was mine, either way.'

'You must not take the blame for me!' she protested. 'I have done you a disservice, and I must pay. I am so sorry to have done this to you. I wanted only –'

'Enough!' He spoke more forcefully than he had intended, startling her. 'You have done me no disservice. I have done myself the disservice. But if you feel you had any share in it, I will require two services of you tomorrow, and thereafter the matter shall be forgotten.'

She had to think about that a moment. 'You want my service tomorrow?'

'Yes, of course. Not necessarily of this type, but a service. Or two. Be ready.'

'Oh, yes, my master! I will be ready! But now –'

'Dress me. Now I shall eat.'

She hastened to oblige. They emerged to the main chamber, and she hurried to fetch food.

Provos was there. She had evidently been walking around the ship, knowing her way by memory, and the members of the crew tolerated her as a guest of the Captain. 'Something happened?' she inquired.

'So to speak.' He knew what she thought he had done, and she was not far off. He came close to her, needing the illusion of privacy. 'Provos, do you remember what the penalty is for a null who does a disservice?'

'Why of course. The null is destroyed immediately. It is unfortunate, because no null ever does such a thing intentionally, but it seems that some mistakes are not allowed. Why do you ask?'

'I had a concern that one might have made such a mistake.'

'No, not that I remember. The nulls of this ship are very competent.'

263

'I am glad to know that.' He was indeed! Pussy had been offering her death, to try to spare him embarrassment. He had managed to avoid that as much by luck as intent. His luck had been opposite with Colene. He knew it would be useless to try to call her back.

And all because he had allowed his passion to get out of control. He had indeed done himself a disservice.

The following day he had to worry about the two services from Pussy, as well as the single ones from Tom and Cat. So he did the obvious: he asked Cat.

'You do not wish to make sexual use of Pussy?' Cat inquired.

'I do and I don't. She is an attractive and innocent creature. But Colene would not understand.'

'Colene already does not understand.'

'All too true! Still, my feeling for Colene is such that I prefer not to be guilty of what disturbs her, even if it is too late for such restraint. I punish myself by denying myself that which I foolishly desired.' It was, he knew, a pointless gesture, but the hurt he had done Colene was gnawing at him, and this was the only way he could think of to ameliorate it even slightly.

'As you prefer. There is another alternative. On rare occasions, at the master's discretion, services may be postponed, pending greater service at a later time. You are about to undertake a mission with some risk. You can require Pussy to join you on that mission, as a bodyguard.'

'A bodyguard! Is she good at that?'

'No, violence is against her nature. Tom will be with you, of course; he is adapted for violence. It would be a stressful thing for her, worthy of several services.'

'I don't want to put her under stress!'

'She is already under stress.'

As with Colene, he was damned either way. 'I'll do it.'

Darius did some more thinking about the possible nature of the monster. It seemed unlikely to him that even the most intelligent snail could do the type of mischief described. That suggested that the monster was human. That in turn suggested that something more than incidental vandalism was involved. Perhaps Ddwng knew it.

He discussed it with Jjle, without speaking of his suspicion. 'What is the standard way to deal with a problem like this?' He had learned the answer from Cat, but he had a reason to clear this with the exec.

'Locate the troublemaker with a fair degree of certainty and bomb the region,' Jjle replied.

'But doesn't that kill many innocent folk along with the guilty one?'

'It does. But since the normal trouble is terrorism or incipient rebellion against the Empire, and the penalty is known, this is an effective mechanism. Few loyal creatures would seek to shield a guilty one.'

'I will do it in another manner. I will not bomb the region; I will enter it myself and try to nullify the monster. I intend to kill no innocent folk, either human or native.'

'I do not recommend this,' the exec said, alarmed.

'Neither do my Felines,' Darius said with a smile. 'They are unanimous against it. But I believe it is my authority to handle this mission as I choose.'

Jjle gazed at him with a certain wary appreciation. 'That is correct, Captain. But I must insist that you be appropriately protected.'

'I will take Tom and Pussy as bodyguards, carrying weapons.'

'A female null? This is irregular.'

'But my prerogative.'

'True, sir.' There was a slight emphasis on the 'sir', a nuance of disapproval. 'But two nulls is not sufficient protection. You will require shielding.'

'Armor?'

'It could be called that. It will shield you from both physical and environmental threats.'

'Agreed. The three of us will be so protected.'

He returned to his chambers, knowing that a message would be sent to Ddwng, and that the Emperor would confirm Darius' authority, because Ddwng wanted to learn more about him. None of the members of this ship owed allegiance to Darius, only to the Emperor. All thought him foolish and perhaps crazy, but they had to go along with him as long as Ddwng did. They feared he might only get himself killed.

But Provos had remembered him killing the monster, so the success of his mission was not in doubt, merely the manner of its accomplishment. Of course Provos had been in error about him having sex with Pussy, but only because she had made the reasonable assumption about his session in the bedroom. Provos did not know the literal future, only that part of it she was to learn. Darius had been caught in compromise. Anyone would have drawn a similar conclusion. Especially Colene. And he was in effect guilty. But however Colene now felt about him, he still loved her, and the thought of her being sterilized and lobotomized was intolerable. He *had* to save her.

So if Ddwng wanted to discover Darius' nature, this would provide a clear indication. He would accomplish this mission in his own style. But he still had not decided whether to accede to Ddwng's demand for the Chip. If he could find a way to save Colene without giving up the Chip, he would do so. Just as he hoped to find a way to nullify the monster without hurting anyone.

'Tell me about shielding,' he said to Cat.

'It is an electronic armament which prevents any fast-moving missiles from touching the wearer,' Cat replied. 'It also intercepts any radiation or sonics which would be harmful. Only officers of the Empire are allowed to utilize it.'

'Or those designated by such officers.' Darius was catching on to the rules of Empire.

'True.'

'Do you think it will intercept the mind-stunning attack of the monster?'

'It should, as there surely is some physical aspect of this. True mental transmission between minds is unknown; all claims of such have been investigated and debunked. But it seems indiscreet to expose yourself to it.'

'It seems indiscreet to me not to,' Darius said. 'Tom and Pussy and I will go after the monster protected in this manner.'

Cat was silent. That was his indication of disagreement so strong as to be a possible disservice if voiced. No null could afford to call its master a fool.

The *Flay* arrived at Planet Yils on schedule. There was no fanfare; it simply took up what Jjle described as an orbit, and Darius stepped into the transfer chamber with his two Feline bodyguards. Tom was confident; Pussy was nervous. Tom carried what was called a laser rifle, and Pussy the pain dial. She had to bear a weapon for this type of service to count, though she seemed afraid of it.

The shields they wore were invisible. They were generated by small boxes carried in pockets. Darius knew the power of magic, but distrusted the power of super science, so tested the shields by having his Felines make mock attacks against each other and himself. They could make contact with each other, but the moment any motion became swift enough to harm a person, the shields cushioned it and slowed it down to safe range. The faster the motion, the greater the cushioning effect, until it became quite un-cushionlike. When Darius, emboldened by slower maneuvers, attempted to strike Tom with a stick, the stick seemed to smack into a wall, and it broke in half. Thrown stones bounced off harmlessly. A direct charge at Pussy resulted in both of them bouncing back, cushioned by their shields so that neither was hurt.

This did seem to be about as good as magic. But would it really be effective against the monster? Darius had a nagging doubt.

They met the commandant of the colony, an old human man in an Empire robe. 'It struck again six hours ago,' he announced. His language was unfamiliar, but Darius now carried a translation ball which worked both ways. 'We have set up a cordon, and believe we have it isolated. Unfortunately a number of colonists reside in that sector.'

'We are not going to bomb the sector,' Darius said.

'You have a way to point-spot the monster?' the commandant asked, relieved.

'We are going to search for it ourselves.'

'But it can stun human minds!'

'We are shielded.'

The commandant looked doubtful. 'I would not wish to seem critical of Navy equipment, but unless your shields are more potent than ours, they will not be effective. This seems almost to be a case of – something unknown.'

So maybe it *was* direct mind contact! The commandant didn't want to name it as such, fearing ridicule for believing what was supposedly supernatural, but he was hinting. 'I have had some experience of this type,' Darius said, understating the case. Receiving and amplifying and broadcasting mental power was his specialty of magic. If by any chance the monster's power related, Darius might be uniquely equipped to handle it. He had tested sympathetic magic here and found it to be inoperative, but perhaps mental magic would work. Certainly the two were different, because even in his own Mode, few folk possessed the power of multiplying feeling, while anyone could do ordinary magic.

Could this be coincidence? Colene had arrived at this Mode before him, perhaps because of his delay when he returned Prima to his own Mode. Ddwng had surely questioned her. She could have told him what she knew of Darius' power of magic, which the Emperor well might have interpreted as supernatural mental power. By the definitions of this culture, that was what it was. Darius had not been aware of any mental interactions with the folk of this Mode, but it was possible that though most were deaf to the transfer of joy, some few might be receptive.

Ddwng was evidently no ignorant functionary. He had given Darius a mission that might exploit his particular talent, if it were operative here. Ddwng might be extremely interested in knowing the status of that talent.

Darius decided to assume that this was a good connection and that he could be effective in dealing with the monster. He let his peculiar awareness extend, seeking a mind that was in some fashion similar to his own. A mind that could transfer joy – or other emotion. Or simply the deadly absence of emotion that was unconsciousness.

In a moment he found it. To his perception it was a nucleus of malignancy. Something was hating.

Darius had not had occasion to magnify or broadcast hate. There just was no market for it. But the principle was the same as for joy. He could transfer it without affecting himself. If there were no suitable recipients, the emotion would be lost – but that was a suitable way to deal with hate.

All this happened in a moment. Meanwhile, he was answering: 'It shall be known soon enough.' Then he set forth with his Felines into the cordoned region.

Most of it was native. The Yils came out to meet them. They were indeed like snails with the body mass of men or greater, slow moving. One had positioned itself to be in the main aisle they were following. Did it want a dialogue?

Darius stopped before it. 'What is your concern?' he inquired.

The snail wiggled feelers. 'You are the Empire Captain come to abolish the menace?' the translator ball inquired.

'I am.'

'This mischief is not of our doing.'

'But is it of your toleration?' Darius inquired sharply.

'It is known that we have no power to inhibit human beings from doing what they choose.'

'Such as exporting your citizens as cuisine?'

'This is a concern.'

'I will ask the Emperor that this be stopped. But the power is his, not mine.'

'We thank you, Captain.' The snail withdrew into its shell, clearing the aisle ahead.

Pussy lifted a hand. Darius nodded, giving her leave to speak. 'Why should you do anything for the natives?'

'Because they are feeling creatures, and deserve sympathetic treatment.'

'This is an odd concept.'

'You deserve it too.'

'That is odder yet.'

Darius smiled, not arguing the case. He tuned in on the bolus of hate, walking that way. 'I suspect your weapons will not be effective,' he told them both. 'But have them ready. Should I fall unconscious, kill whatever creature is before us. It may be a human being.'

269

They nodded. They were responsive to his will.

The snails did not use houses; their shells were sufficient. They had many slick paths through their cultivated sections; the paths branched and rebranched, becoming smaller, like the structure of trees. It was evident that there was no centralized feeding system; each snail had its own patch to graze. It seemed to be a live and let live society. Unfortunately the human conquerors did not have a similar philosophy. Now they wanted to break into other Modes, so as to get new genes to revivify their stock, so they could maintain and expand their empire. His sympathy was with whatever power had decided to confine this empire to this one Mode.

But if he told Ddwng no, what then? Destruction for Colene, if torture of her did not make him yield. Then probably torture of him. And in the end, if he died without yielding, Ddwng would still be able to set out on the Virtual Mode and perhaps find Darius' Mode and the Chip. He was an anchor person; he should be able to sense the right direction the same way Darius and Provos did, and as Colene surely had. He merely wanted to avoid the serious risks of traveling alone into unknown territory. But he could take them if he chose. What would defiance accomplish, in the end?

They were coming close to the source of the hate. But there seemed only to be a snail snoozing at the end of its pathlet, having grazed its fill. It was withdrawn into its shell.

But hiding behind that shell was a human child. 'I see you,' Darius said.

The child stood, and the nucleus of hate shifted with his body. This was the monster: a boy of perhaps seven years. No wonder he had escaped detection! He was just an ordinary gamin, a neglected urchin, probably stealing food to survive. But his mind was an absolute horror.

'In the name of the Empire, I am come to bring you to justice,' Darius said, observing the ritual. 'Yield, and you will not be killed.'

Both Felines looked at Darius, evidently suspecting that he had gotten severely confused. A little human boy? Hardly a monster!

For answer, the boy unleashed his fury. It struck Darius –

270

and was rebroadcast outward. He was unaffected. But he had learned something: the boy could direct his power. He did not strike at every mind within his range. Harnessed, this could probably be useful to the Empire.

'Yield, and perhaps you will be granted a good life in return for the use of your power on behalf of the Empire,' Darius said.

He sensed the lad's understanding. But there was no trust there. The boy hated his own kind. He must have been rejected, cast out, orphaned. There was something strange and vulnerable about his mind, as if it had been weakened, not strengthened, and in its distress had channeled most of its force to this incubus of hate. So great was that destructive force that it could overwhelm even a 'deaf' mind, such as those of this Mode. But the hammer that could shatter a stone could not do the same with a sponge or a rubber ball. The boy could not prevail against Darius.

The lad seemed shaken by the failure of his attack on Darius. But his little face was set in a grimace of hate which echoed that of his mind. He had no intention of yielding to the Empire. But Darius tried again. 'I have the means to destroy you. I ask you to yield and save yourself.'

Apparently it was a lost cause. The mind-monster would not or could not be reasonable. He would have to be stunned and taken in; perhaps the empire super-scientists could do something with him, or at least confine him so that he could not do physical damage, such as torching granaries.

'Dial him, Pussy,' Darius said.

The Feline lifted the dial and turned it on. Level Three discomfort struck Darius. He had never reset the device! It was tuned to him as well as to others. The Felines expected to be affected, and were prepared to endure it in order to accomplish the mission. It would surely be far more potent against the boy than against them.

Indeed, the boy felt it. He staggered as if physically struck. Then he sent a jolt of hate directly at Pussy.

Pussy collapsed with a little meow of pain. She could not ward off the power.

The boy staggered forward and snatched the dial from her

hand. He touched the detune switch, then turned the dial up to maximum.

He had not understood the dial well enough. All he had done was to restore Darius' exemption – and hit himself with the maximum degree of pain. He collapsed.

Darius stepped forward and took the dial from the boy's flaccid hand. He turned the dial down to zero.

But it was too late. Pussy, already unconscious, was unaffected. Tom, caught by the dial, was now sprawled on the ground. And the boy was dead.

Darius had after all killed the monster. And, in his own judgment, bungled the mission.

Back on the *Flay* with his staggering minions, Darius was the object of covert stares of awe. 'The monster took out your bodyguards, sir – and you killed it alone?' Jjle inquired. 'Without a weapon?'

'Not exactly. It was the pain dial that killed him. His mind was more vulnerable to it than others. But my success was chance as much as design.'

'As you say, sir.' But the awe remained.

When he reached his chambers, the wall-screen was on. There was Colene, in her preternatural beauty. 'Oh Darius – you're all right!' she cried.

He was taken aback. 'You are speaking to me?'

'Of course I'm speaking to you! I love you!'

She couldn't have forgiven him! 'And I love you. But –'

'I know your culture's different. You can't be expected to – I understand that – and anyway, you're a man. Oh, Darius, please give Ddwng the Chip! It's the only way we can be together!'

'Colene, I want to be with you more than anything. But if I –'

'It'll be all right! Honest it will! He'll let us go, if – please, Darius!'

Why had she turned about so completely? She should be furious with him, yet she was urging him to betray their Modes so that she could be with him. He would have to think about this.

'I will consider,' he told her.

'Please,' she repeated, and faded out.

Darius sat in the chair and considered. He thought of the monster-boy, so recently dead. He thought of Provos, who had said he would kill the monster, and who had also said he would agree to commit to Ddwng. He though of Colene.

He had offered the boy the chance for a kind of amnesty: fair treatment and a chance to serve the Empire, if he turned his talent to the welfare of the Empire. He knew Ddwng would have honored that, because it made sense. Instead the boy had attacked him – and destroyed himself in the process. Utter folly.

There was no doubt that Ddwng had power over Darius and Colene. He could make them happy together, or keep them apart, or torture them or kill them or let them go. He was no fool. If Darius tried to cross him, Darius would be destroyed. But if he cooperated, he would be rewarded. He was to the Emperor as the monster/boy was to Darius himself. What was his choice?

Provos said he would accede. Colene had begged him to. He didn't like it, but it did seem to be his only practical choice.

'Get me the Emperor,' he told Cat. The two other Felines were recuperating from their ordeal.

In a moment Ddwng was on the screen. He must have been waiting for this.

'I have destroyed the monster,' Darius said to the Emperor. 'I promised the natives I would seek to end the exploitation of their kind as food. I am requesting –'

'The word of a minion of the Empire is good. That exploitation shall cease forthwith.'

That was certainly swift! Darius had promised only to ask, and here he had succeeded in changing empire policy. But that was the minor issue. He braced himself for the major one.

'Today I am in your Mode, sir, in your power,' Darius said. 'In my Mode the power will be ours. I will guide you there, but the Chip is not mine to give. I will introduce you to the Cyng of Pwer, who may elect instead to kill you. You must

273

let Colene and her horse and Provos and me into the Virtual Mode, and we shall do you no harm there. This is the deal I proffer.'

'Agreed.'

Darius stared at the man. 'No bargaining? You will risk yourself this way?'

'You are a man of honor. You will advise me of the appropriate manner to approach your official. It is enough.'

'A man of honor? How can you know that?'

'It is not only your words and actions we have watched. We know the physical and brain-wave patterns of deceit. You have at times withheld information, but you have not given false information. You are to be trusted, and after I possess the Chip you will be given a ranking position in the Empire, if you wish it.'

'You can not trust a person whose cooperation has been obtained under duress.'

'That depends on the man. Now relax, Captain Darius; your mission has been accomplished, and you will return to Earth.' Ddwng faded out.

So it was done. Darius did not feel uplifted. He had done it to save Colene.

Colene. What were her feelings toward him, now? She had seen him with Pussy, then called him back to plead his acquiescence to the demand of the Emperor. She did not know the threat against herself. What could account for the change?

Was there a threat against him, too, which she knew about? But if she was angry with him, she could simply let it happen. Instead she had said she loved him and wanted to be with him.

Maybe she really did understand. But maybe she was doing what was expedient now, and there would be a reckoning later. After they were free of the DoOon. If they got free.

11

CONSORT

Colene looked at her wrist. The scars had faded. She had not cut herself since meeting Darius. But now she was getting that feeling again.

When she had come here and realized that she and Seqiro were prisoners, she had hoped they would be able to escape soon after Darius arrived. But he had been whisked away almost immediately to a distant stellar system. That prevented her from even trying to flee. She knew she would have to wait until he returned to Earth.

Oh, Ddwng was treating her well enough. He dined with her often, and was always exceedingly polite. One might have supposed that an Emperor of a Galaxy would have better things to do, but apparently his staff was more than competent, and he seldom had crisis decisions to make. She had feared that his interest in her was that of a man for some wild primitive strange woman, but he seemed genuinely curious about her ways and feelings. What she would do if another type of interest manifested she didn't know. She didn't want to make him mad – not while Darius was far away – but she didn't want any more to do with him than absolutely necessary.

She had three nulls of the Equine persuasion to tend to her every need and want. Indeed, they were compelled to do one or more services for her each day. Had she been a man, she would have had no trouble finding something for Mare each day; she was as luscious a piece of woman-flesh as could be imagined, from the neck down. But Colene was a girl, and though Stallion would have been glad to do for her what a man did, hired sex was not her interest. So she was kept busy keeping them busy.

She was allowed information on Darius' progress, and she followed it compulsively. Unfortunately that meant being aware of the time he spent with *his* nulls, particularly Pussy. What an apt name for that juicy Feline!

He called her, to her surprise; she had assumed that direct dialogue between them would be forbidden. So she tested it farther by urging him not to agree to give Ddwng the Chip. Then she waited somewhat apprehensively for the Emperor's reaction.

There was none. She did not trust that one bit.

She was allowed access to Seqiro, too. Actually she was in constant mental contact with him, but she wanted more than that. So they played the game of riding, because both agreed that his mental powers should be hidden. The people of this reality had no awareness of telepathy, treating it as a supernatural notion. Seqiro reported that their minds seemed opaque to it, not because of being guarded but because they just did not seem to be organized that way. The animals could be touched, but Seqiro did not even send the mosquitoes away, lest an attendant notice. He was being the complete dumb animal.

She returned to the palace interior to learn from Horse that Darius had tried to call her again. 'Well call him back!' she said, her heart leaping. 'Immediately!'

It placed the call. Tom received it. 'Darius is busy at the moment,' the cat-head said.

'Oh, he'll talk to *me*!' she said confidently.

'As you wish.' The picture changed.

There was Darius, naked, in the process of having sex with Pussy. She was so surprised and dismayed that she couldn't think of any appropriate reaction. 'I guess you're busy right now,' she said lamely, and faded out. That description was appropriate: she thought she was going to faint.

'You seem surprised at his activity,' Horse said. 'I should clarify that it is normal to –'

'Oh, shut up!' she snapped. She charged to her bedroom and flung herself down among the plush pillows, sobbing.

Your mind is in turmoil, Seqiro remarked.

She let him have her feeling in an inchoate blast. Then, aware of his distress, she apologized. *I'm sorry, Seqiro! It's just that – oh, what will I do?*

The horse pondered, using her intelligence and his objectivity. *You are being polite to Ddwng, because you fear what he might otherwise do. Those watching you are under the impression that you like him. Perhaps Darius finds it similarly expedient to give others the impression that he likes his situation.*

By screwing the pussy? she demanded, her image savage.

Yes. It would suggest that he was not acclimatizing, were he to spurn her.

Colene struggled with that. She did know the nature of men; they were always interested in sex, and took it when they got the chance. That night with the boys – she had represented Opportunity. She had had no illusions after that. Darius was a man, and he had treated her decently, and he said he loved her. But how was he with other women? He had not tried to hide that from her: he expected to marry some other woman, and have sex with her if she wanted it, and in his castle he had mistresses. In fact, as Seqiro had read in Darius' mind in that brief time he was in the palace, he had found the perfect woman to marry, named Prima, who could greatly extend his ability to radiate joy to others. Prima was no love-match; she was twice Darius' age. The only thing distinguishing Colene from those other women was the fact that he loved her.

Yes.

With a woman, sex and love were aspects of the same thing. That was why the abuse of sex was so horrible; it soiled love. But with a man they were in different ball-parks. A man could love one woman and have sex with another. It was part of the basic misunderstanding between the sexes. She had learned the hard way. So Darius could love Colene and have sex with Pussy. She understood that with her mind.

Yes.

Why, then, couldn't she understand it with her emotion?

You do understand it with your emotion, Seqiro thought.

277

It merely requires time for the pain of that understanding to subside.

She did understand it. Her problem was in accepting it. When she walked carelessly and stubbed her toe and it hurt, she understood what had happened, but the pain remained. After a while the pain faded, and she made sure not to stub her toe there again.

Darius might not even want to dally with the cat-woman. But as Seqiro suggested, if he did not give the impression of going along with the system, he would not be trusted, and would never be given any real freedom.

In fact, she realized something else: if the very walls of Darius' bedroom could become video screens when he didn't want it, they must have that capacity any time. Was it possible that they were always tuning in on him, wherever he was? The four of them – Darius, the old woman Provos, Seqiro and herself – were strangers here, and there was something Ddwng wanted from them. Why wouldn't he watch them closely? If he had thrown them in dark prison cells he wouldn't have had to watch. But not only did he keep them in excellent style, he had given Darius a significant mission to perform.

Because Darius can show him where the Chip is.

Yes. In order to get that Chip, Ddwng would have to trust himself to the Virtual Mode, where Darius could dump him in a deep hole in some barren reality and let him die. If Ddwng had to trust Darius, he wanted to know him well. So it figured that Darius would be watched closely, and all his actions judged. If Darius had caught on to that, he would play the role, because the alternative might be much worse than being a ship captain.

You are forgiving him.

She was forgiving him. Or at least finding reason not to blame him, which wasn't exactly the same thing. There was a hard core of rancor that remained, but she was good at burying such things. She was capable of accepting what had to be accepted, and moving on.

Meanwhile she had a date with Ddwng for another meal. It was time for Mare to get her ready for it.

Ddwng was the root of her problem. He was the one who

kept her apart from Darius, and put him in the position of having to hold women other than Colene in his arms. If her core of anger needed a focus, that was where it should orient.

Seqiro, link with me when I'm with the Emperor. I want to know what's truly on his mind.

The horse was doubtful. *I have not been able to penetrate any mind in this reality.*

But Seqiro couldn't get into any un-tame mind in his own reality without that person's permission. This might merely be a more extreme case of that. *I will try to open his mind.*

Then she summoned Mare. 'Let's see what you can do when you go all out,' she told the Equine. 'Make me into a princess. That is your service today.'

Mare smiled. This was a challenge she was ready to tackle. She swung into a program that demonstrated more competence than Colene had realized existed.

Soon she was clean and garbed in a scintillating pale green dress which made her look twice as good as she could ever be. She had never thought of herself as voluptuous, but in this outfit she was long-legged, sleek-hipped, narrow-waisted, and with a decolletage that could have come from a classic painting. Her face and hair were angelic; special reflective pins even gave the impression of a halo.

Colene stared at herself in the mirror. She would not have believed that she could be this adorable! It was said that clothes made the man, but men were pretty dull physically, regardless. It was the woman that clothes made. She was the living proof of it.

Too bad she had to waste this on Ddwng. She would much rather have wowed Darius. But it was in her mind that the Emperor did have some reason for this frequent interaction with her, and it probably wasn't sexual, so it was suspicious. If she could manage to dazzle him just a little, to get him closely focused while Seqiro was tuning in, maybe, just maybe there would be an avenue to get Seqiro into his mind. It was certainly worth a good try.

Stallion guided her to the shuttle. Here in the palace the windows to other cities or ships or worlds weren't used;

it was more physical. Maybe because such windows represented accesses to the palace, and it was supposed to be secure from intrusion. The shuttle was nice enough; it was like an enclosed amusement park ride, gently wafting to its destination. Stallion maneuvered it to Ddwng's dining hall, let her out, and took it back; private personal nulls were not welcome in the hall itself. Only the palace nulls.

Ddwng was there, resplendent in a purple robe which complemented her dress perfectly. A little alarm sounded somewhere in her head: coincidence? No, probably he had known what she was wearing – because probably those walls had eyes here, just as on the FTL *Flay*, and he had access to those eyes. This could be confirmation of her prior suspicion that they were all being watched.

But no one here could see what was in their minds. Seqiro had ascertained that. So if she never voiced her true feelings, they could be known only through her actions – and she was pretty good at masking feelings.

She took the Emperor's elbow and walked with him to the table. The Ovine nulls were there. Ram placed Ddwng's chair, Ewe placed Colene's, and Sheep stood by for their order.

Colene hardly noticed the excellent exotic food. She was genuinely interested in Ddwng this time, but not in as flattering a way as he might suppose. She wanted to tune his mind to things which Seqiro might read. She hoped that if the subject were narrow enough, and the interest strong enough, and she were close enough, serving as a focusing point, it just might work. It *had* to work, because it just wasn't safe to be ignorant.

She started obliquely. 'You know, in my reality, things like anti-gravity and faster-than-light travel are impossible. They just can't be done. Are you sure that –?'

'The fundamental laws of physics differ from reality to reality,' Ddwng said. 'We have known that, and understand that there are realities in which our science is inoperative, but where magic is operative, or psionic powers. Darius comes from a reality with magic, and his companion Provos appears to remember the future. That, to us, is paradoxical.'

'She knows the future?' Despite herself, Colene got distracted. 'I was with her only briefly, before she was mattermitted to the ship to rejoin Darius, but it was my impression that even if we had spoken a common language, we wouldn't have gotten far. She seemed to know what we were about to do, but not what had just happened.'

'We are studying her. We find it interesting that her ability does appear to operate in this reality. That suggests that the fundamental laws may not be what they seem.'

Was there a chance that Darius could do magic here? That he could conjure them both away? That seemed too wonderful to be believed!

If she knows the future here, she knows what is to become of us, Seqiro thought.

But Colene was determined not to just let the future happen. She wanted to do whatever was in her power to make it the right future.

She smiled most innocently at Ddwng. 'Maybe you should ask her about your own future. I mean, about getting the Chip.'

'You do not want me to have it?'

'I didn't say that!'

I am getting a bit, Seqiro thought. *He knows you are trying to deceive him.*

'You do wish me to have it?' Ddwng asked, amused.

'I didn't say that either,' she said ruefully.

I am finding an avenue. It is very narrow, but I am attuning. He is fascinated by you, but not as a woman. He is intrigued by the challenge of fathoming your motives.

'Perhaps it would be best if you were open with me,' Ddwng said.

'I'm afraid you're going to rape me,' she said, her deathwish causing her to tread the brink.

He guffawed. For that the sound was direct rather than through the translation ball. 'I have no interest in taking any woman involuntarily. I have any I want, either null or human. Set aside your fear.'

'Rape can be more than physical. What do you want with my mind?'

He studied her for a long moment before responding.

There is something horrible, Seqiro thought. *Maintain the dialogue, if you can.*

'There are three things I want of you,' Ddwng said. 'I want the information you possess about the neighboring realities, so that at such time as I enter them, I am aware of their assets and their pitfalls.'

True.

'That's okay by me,' she said.

'I want you to persuade Darius to guide me to the Chip.'

True.

'I guess that's up to him,' she said guardedly. 'I don't see why I should try to influence him.'

'Perhaps you will change your mind when you know more of my rationale.'

There is something devious here.

'What's the third thing you want of me?' Trying to be nonchalant, she took a sip of her alien fizz-drink. It wasn't alcoholic; she would have gotten sick if it was. Ever since the rape scene, she had detested alcohol.

'I want you to be my consort.'

Colene choked, dribbling liquid on her gown. Immediately Ewe was there, with sponges, efficiently cleaning her up. But at least the delay gave her a chance to commune with Seqiro before replying.

This is not an evil thing. It is innocent. Something else is evil.

Innocent? That's marriage!

No, this is form only. You can agree without compromise.

You had better be right, Seqiro! Darius is the only man I – But that remained a complex emotional mess, too.

Her seizure had concluded. 'I thought you had no such interest.'

'I see you misunderstand. I have many consorts. All are attractive women. Most are mistresses. Their proximity to me gives them unique authority, for it is known that I do not like to embarrass them. I sometimes use them as emissaries. I would like to have you with me as I make a business trip this coming period, and the proper format for this is as consort.'

282

True. But there is something else. You have his attention; question him.

Colene leaned forward, evincing the appropriate amount of suspicion as well as presenting a bit more of the flesh of her bosom for inspection. 'You mean I should go traveling with you, and everyone will think I'm having sex with you, but it won't be true?'

'Correct, if that is the way you wish it.'

True.

'And maybe I'll have to do some public task for you, the way Darius is with that far flung mission?'

'Correct. You should find it interesting.'

True.

'And this is the way things are done in the Empire, so it's okay and won't sully my reputation?'

'Correct.'

True.

'And somewhere along the way I should talk Darius into giving you the Chip?'

'Correct. I believe your word will influence him.'

True.

'Though he thinks I'm having sex with you?' she asked sweetly.

He is receiving information. I think you are under constant surveillance, and he knows your heart rate and muscle tension. He knows you are hiding something, and wants to know what it is, but he can not read minds so must persuade you to cooperate. He is enjoying the challenge.

'I see that this would be disruptive,' Ddwng said. 'But there is no problem. Darius will be informed of the nature of the relationship, if you wish.'

Now Colene took a long moment, gazing at him. She was not considering her answer; she was focusing on Seqiro's thoughts.

All that he has told you is true. But there is something he knows would distress you greatly, that he hides. It ties in with Darius. That is what you must ascertain.

'Ddwng, I don't know what's going on in your mind,' she said in what she judged was a three-quarter truth. 'And you

283

don't know what's going on in mine.' Another three-quarter truth. 'You're playing these little games with me, wasting your time, when all you have to do is drug me and make me do anything. It doesn't make sense.'

'You are perceptive. But it does make sense.'

He is playing with you as a cat does with a mouse.

'I'll make you this deal, Ddwng: I'll do all those things you are asking me to do, if you will tell me exactly what your real game is.'

Ddwng smiled. 'Then the game would be over.'

Now he is thinking of it. I have it! Agree to everything. I will cover this with you later.

Colene trusted Seqiro. But she didn't like to capitulate readily, as a matter of obscure principle. 'Then maybe I'll just do none of those things. What do you say to that?'

'I would not recommend such a course.'

There is something else. He is grim.

'So what would you do about it?' she demanded, treading the brink again.

'I would have your horse vivisected.'

True.

She stared at him. 'You aren't kidding, are you!'

'I do not joke. But I would hope that such inducement would not be necessary.'

She sighed. 'Okay, you win. I agree to do the three things you say you want of me.'

'Excellent.'

He is surprised. To him your moods and decisions are strange. He can not be sure when you are telling the truth.

They finished the meal. Then Stallion came to escort her back to her suite.

Colene had Horse tune the wall-screen to an entertainment program. She did not relate well to the sort of television the Empire had, but it gave her a cover for her contact with Seqiro. That business about vivisecting him had her seething. But she knew that was only part of what was wrong. *Now tell me what gives? What's Ddwng's big secret?*

He told Darius that if he does not cooperate, you will be lobotomized and the reproductive cells of your body taken surgically for use by the people of this reality, to replenish their stock. They are too conformist, genetically; they must introduce variety, or suffer slow degeneration.

Colene was stunned. Now she knew why Darius was playing the game! *She* was the cause of it.

She tried to keep her face straight and her body relaxed, so that the hidden sensors could not read her reactions well. Whoever was watching her would know that something was bothering her, but might assume it was the stupid wall-program. Or the threat to her horse, which wasn't far wrong.

The more she dwelt on this news, the firmer her reaction became. It was utter fury. The Emperor was keeping her close to him and treating her like a great lady, while threatening her horse and herself with dire consequences. Rape? He was expert at it!

So what was she going to do about it? Ddwng seemed to hold most of the cards. He was holding them hostage against each other, and was unscrupulous enough to make good on all his threats. But if they all went along, and the Emperor got that Chip, he could ravage the other realities too. Was their welfare worth it?

If they didn't cooperate, it might not stop Ddwng. He would kill them and head into the Virtual Mode on his own, and maybe he would find the Chip anyway. His chances of getting it would be greatly reduced, and his chances of getting lost or killed increased, but he was obviously one tough nut and he well might get through. It which case they would have sacrificed themselves for nothing.

No, the only sure way was to be rid of Ddwng. To agree to do his will, get him into the Virtual Mode, away from his minions, and destroy him. Feed him to a telepathic bear or something.

But right away she saw several problems with that. First, Ddwng wouldn't fall for it; he would know not to trust them. Second, Darius wouldn't give his word unless he meant it, so Ddwng *could* trust him, and for Ddwng's purpose Darius was the only one who mattered. The rest of them were just to make sure Darius didn't change his mind; they had to keep

285

encouraging him to give Ddwng that Chip. How could Colene do anything else, when Seqiro would be hurt? There was probably some sort of threat against Provos, too, so she kept her mouth shut. She might know what was going to happen, but not be able to prevent it.

That gave her a passing notion. *Seqiro – did you tune in on Provos when she was here? Did she know our future?*

Her mind is permeable but strange. She was just beginning to know it. She takes time to remember, in a new reality. She seemed to see us being here for ten days, then going back into the Virtual Mode with Ddwng. She could not see beyond that.

Well, that's enough. So we are going to do it.

Yes, as she sees it.

Colene felt a surge of despair. It was already decided! They were locked in to the Emperor's fell plot. Whatever they did, Ddwng would win, because he was what he was and they were what they were. If only Darius weren't so honest! If he agreed, even under duress, he would carry through. Colene herself would have no such compunction; a pledge made under duress was not binding. Knowing what she now knew of Ddwng, she would have no compunction about lying to him. She would not let the DoOon exploit the other realities as they had this one! But she had no power. Darius didn't want to see her hurt, so he would agree, and that would be that. Should she condemn him because he really did love her?

Damn, damn, damn! Ddwng could tell when others were lying, because his instruments read their body signals. Colene was different; he couldn't quite keep track of her, because she was wildly mixed up inside. The DoOon were pretty much all of a kind, their genetics inbred; that was why they needed new blood, and her ovaries represented that. So Ddwng was trying to understand her, not because he cared about her but because he didn't want to introduce truly crazy blood into the DoOon strain. He was surveying her as he might a new breed of animal, making sure of the quality. Once he was sure that her mind did not represent a genetic danger to the stock –

Could she pretend she was truly crazy, and scare him off? No, because it was Darius he really needed. He could throw her away if he decided she was worthless. She would do better to satisfy him that she was actually a pretty genetically solid creature, and then do something wild in the Virtual Mode, like pushing him off a mile-high cliff into a mile-wide bed of carnivorous oysters who hadn't been fed for two years. But he would surely be well armed, and have electronic armor and an antigravity suit and other super science that would make him invulnerable to any betrayal she might attempt. In fact, he would probably have one of those little pain dials Horse had shown her, tuned to all of them, so that it would go off if anything happened to him and they'd all fry. She would have no way to do him harm, for sure.

But she absolutely refused to let him get away with it. She had faced down Biff in that bleeding contest; there must be some way she could beat Ddwng. Some nasty little plot she could hide in her nutty little mind, that he couldn't fathom. Some little poison needle he wouldn't even feel until it was too late. She had read once about a woman who put slow-acting poison in her vagina, and killed her false lover because after sex with her he just went to sleep, while she got up and quickly washed herself out before she got too bad a dose. If Colene had something like that, and Ddwng did rape her, what revenge! Yet even if she had something like that, and managed to kill him – what would his death do to the Virtual Mode? He was an anchor person. A dead anchor – that just might blow up the whole thing, like a rock in a fan, and kill them all. Could she afford to gamble on that, even if she had the poison, which she didn't? She was ready to die, but she didn't want to do it to Darius or Seqiro.

The anchor – there was the problem. It wasn't safe to touch an anchor person. Ddwng surely realized that, so he wouldn't kill any of them as long as he had any chance to travel their Virtual Mode, and he wouldn't do anything to them while they were on it. So he was muscling them into shape in other ways, taming them, bending them to his will. If only he weren't the anchor for this reality!

Then the answer flashed through her consciousness like a lovely meteor. *Seqiro! We can do it!*

Seqiro considered, using her intelligence and his objectivity. *Yes, it is possible, if he does not suspect.*

I'll lull him right to sleep! I'm good at fooling people. Trust me.

I do.

Colene had to laugh. Seqiro was the only one who had ever truly understood her. He trusted her because he knew her for exactly what she was: a conniving little wench. *Horse-face, I love you!*

True.

After Darius killed the monster in properly heroic fashion, according to the news release, she called him. 'Oh Darius,' she pleaded in distraught maidenly fashion, 'please give Ddwng the Chip! It's the only way we can be together!'

He seemed taken aback, as well he might be. But she was serious. She did want him to agree. 'It'll be all right! Honest it will! Please, Darius!' She even managed to put a quaver of earnestness into her voice, which would have been excellent acting except that it was real. She was absolutely sincere in this, and she wanted this entire reality to know it. Darius *had* to make the pledge!

He promised to consider. Evidently he did, because soon he did call Ddwng and agreed to guide him to the Chip, with certain manly honorable reservations. It was done.

Colene was the dishonorable one. She dreaded to think of the reckoning she would have with Darius when she did what she hoped to do. But it was better than the choice between lobotomy and loosing the DoOon on the realities. Sometimes deceit was the only way.

Ddwng took her to a far planet elsewhere in the galaxy. She had given up trying to wrestle with the concept of faster-than-light travel; it was contrary to the physics of her reality, but evidently just fine here. The same went for instant communication across the galaxy, antigravity, and all the rest. Super-science, another name for fantasy, in her home town.

They would attend an elegant ball in their honor at the chief city of Planet Kyvrn. Mare got Colene garbed for it in a rehearsal, and Horse drilled her on spot protocol. She was the Emperor's newest and youngest consort, and as such the object of much interest. She would be rather quiet in the Emperor's presence, and rather haughty when alone, for her status on this planet was second only to his. She would dance with him once, and thereafter with any man she chose. Stallion went through the steps with her, making sure she would not misstep.

'But what's my mission here?' she asked.

'This is a rebellious planet,' Horse explained. 'You will need to restore it to harmony with the Empire.'

Colene was aghast. 'A rebel world? And Ddwng is setting foot on it? And I'm supposed to tame it? Why doesn't he just stick his head in a running meat-grinder while he's at it, and I'll just pick up a section of the galaxy and shake some stars loose!'

All three Equines laughed. They had learned early that she made jokes, and accommodated themselves to it. She liked them very well. They were nominally subhuman, but actually they were intelligent enough, with Horse perhaps being smarter than she, and they were perfectly comfortable to be around. She wished there were some way to have such companions with her always, without the degradation of such permanent servitude. She had always liked horses, but would have thought that horse-headed human beings would be disgusting. That was not the case at all; they seemed quite natural now.

'This is not that kind of rebellion,' Horse said. 'This is a retirement colony. Most of the residents are former Empire officials. Here they are out of power, with no requirements, and discover that they are restive. They would never actually rebel, but their discomfort would be an embarrassment were it known, as this is supposedly an ideal world. It will be your task, in the course of the next three days, to make them comfortable with their situation.'

'It's still preposterous!' she exclaimed. 'Does Ddwng expect me to perform magic? I don't know anything about this! and if I did, what could I do? And if I could do anything – three days? I mean, Rome wasn't built in a day, and –'

'Rome?'

'Famous ancient city in my reality. Forget it. The point is, this is like – like – impossible!'

'Evidently the Emperor has much confidence in you,' Horse said dryly, twitching his furry ears.

Colene only wished that Seqiro were here. He might have been able to read the minds of the people, and get a notion how to satisfy them. But he was thousands of light years away, reverted to his dumb animal stage, awaiting her return. She was on her own, and she didn't like it one bit.

Or was she? If telepathy existed, and faster-than-light travel existed, and Provos could remember the future here, showing that it was her talent, not restricted to her reality – why couldn't telepathy and FTL merge, and enable her to commune with her friend regardless? Where was it written that the powers of one reality were nullified in another? Maybe some were and some weren't. Maybe Darius couldn't do magic here, but Seqiro could project his thoughts instantly across interstellar reaches. She had a receptive mind for him, for sure! If anybody could receive him here, she was the one!

She lay down, theoretically resting the hour before the ball, and closed her eyes. But she didn't relax, and she didn't care what the monitors thought; they could assume that she was all twisted up by the enormity of her mission. She opened her mind to her true friend.

Seqiro! Seqiro! Do you read me?

At first there was nothing. Then there was the faintest response. She focused on that, willing it to become stronger. It had to be him!

Seqiro! Read me! I need you!

Faintly, faintly, she felt his mind.

I have to find a way to make these folk feel better about being retired and useless. You must read their minds for me, if you can, to get a glimpse of what will do it. That's my only chance not to blow this mission out of space!

The faint reassurance came. He would do what he could.

It was a pretty planet. The terraforming had evidently made it into one big garden, with neatly laid out cities set up like parkland, so that the houses hardly showed through the trees.

Small lakes were everywhere, set between hills, with paths between them. There seemed to be no motorized vehicles; if there was mass traffic, it was out of sight. This was the sort of place she would like to retire to with Darius, if that ever came.

Of course that was just the image in the screen. She was sure there were slums and garbage and all the rest of the seamy side of civilization. She knew how it was; she remembered Panama. But the illusion was nice, even so.

Then it was time to get ready. All three Equines pitched in, without regard for modesty; Stallion was drawing something like support stockings up her legs while Horse was fitting her invisible bra for proper uplift and Mare was doing her hair. It was all right; there were no secrets from a person's nulls. In a surprisingly short time they transformed her from ordinary messed-up teenager to a vision of unbelievable loveliness. Each time they garbed her, they seemed to exceed prior records for success. Then Stallion took her to the matterport and via it to landfall.

She went in a daze through the halls of the receiving complex, feeling the slightly diminished gravity and breathing the slightly strange air. This was a foreign planet, all right; her body knew it. Ddwng was waiting for her at the entrance, resplendent in his own uniform robe of the day. He was actually rather handsome in his brute fashion. She pictured his Swine doing him as the Equines had done her: support stockings, transparent bra, and hair. She had to bite her tongue lest she let slip an indiscreet titter.

The ball was every bit as opulent as Colene had feared. In her wildest dreams of the distant past – circa one month ago – she had pictured occasions at which she would be the cynosure of all, impressing the ladies with her courtly presence and the men with her sex appeal. Now it had come true, and it wasn't nearly as delightful as her fancy.

The problem was that she had to watch her manners. She couldn't pick her nose or scratch her bottom or say an uncouth word. Maybe full grown ladies never even thought of doing such things, but she was fourteen, which was sort of on the verge. There were a number of pleasures of childhood that she wasn't sure she wanted to give up just yet, like computer games, and multi-decker ice cream cones with nuts and fudge on top, and putting whoopee cushions under the padding of seats in houses of worship. Every time she remembered that joke about the man breaking wind in church and having to sit in his own pew, she broke up. In short, she just wasn't quite ready for ladyhood.

But here she was, ready or not, on the arm of the Emperor of the Milky Way Galaxy (only they called it the DoOon Galaxy here), resplendent as only Mare could make her. Oh, she was breathtakingly lovely all right; every mirror pillar reflected this phenomenal creature virtually floating along in her glow. She wore a brown gown that exactly matched the hue of her hair, and both had been somehow enhanced to make them seem more livingly lustrous than any ordinary woman deserved. Opalescent sequins glittered as she moved. She could have done without the mirror-polished floor, however; she was afraid her dainty hard-soled slippers would slip, putting her into an inglorious spin. She also wondered just what the men were looking at when they bowed their heads to her and gazed into that reflective surface. Most of all she was afraid that the butterflies in her stomach would erupt in a grotesque burp, making her die of shame three times before her blush reached full definition. In sum, fun was not the operative term at the moment.

Be calm. You are making a good impression.

Her nerves lost their ragged edges. What would she do without Seqiro! She reminded herself that every lady faced the same problems, and most of them survived satisfactorily. Anyway, this wasn't forever. After the first dance things would start getting normal.

Ddwng brought her to the center of that stage. He made the little nod to the assemblage, and as one those hundreds returned it. Colene remained frozen, as she had been told to do; her turn was not quite yet.

'I am glad to revisit Planet Kyvrn,' the Emperor said. The miniature translation ball Colene wore at her throat, just above the nascent cleavage of her seemingly-too-low but actually-promising-more-than-could-be-delivered decolletage, murmured his words to her. She was surprised to see that many of the attending men and women wore similar balls. Apparently they could not understand Ddwng's language any more than she could. That gave her another shot of confidence. A dozen more like it, and she might even begin to think about being at ease. But it would help if someone else made a slip first.

'I am sure any questions will soon be resolved,' Ddwng continued. 'To that end I bring you my consort of the moment, Colene, who will be among you three days.' He made an eighth turn toward her, and Colene made the requisite head-nod to him, then did a slow pirouette and bowed more deeply to the audience, so that her upper gown line promised even more of her bosom than before. The material was adhesive, so there was no danger of even a tenth of an inch more exposure than Mare had decreed, which was a relief. She could stand on her head and nothing would pop out. But she might have a problem with her skirt. For a delicious instant she was tempted to do a cartwheel and really wow the audience. But that was her deathwish manifesting, and she had enough to occupy her attention already.

Then Ddwng took her in his arms and danced with her. He was smooth, evidently coached by his own null of the Porcine persuasion. Colene wondered whether he had sex with Sow. But the image wasn't as insulting as intended, because that female swine was both beautiful and sweet-natured. No Miss Piggie there!

She followed his steps, and it was exactly as Stallion had shown her. It was a set format, hardly more challenging than the box step, and she could probably do it in her sleep. The weird thing was that moving in unison with Ddwng this way, being lovely in his arms, she could almost fool herself into thinking that he was a decent character. There was just something about dressing up, and about dancing, that made everything seem better than it was. But deep down she would never be fooled. *Will you dance with me after my lobotomy, dear*? She had to stifle a wry smile; it was her kind of humor. She had been afraid of physical rape, not realizing how much worse it could be. Her reproductive organs cut out of her and put into a cold sere laboratory . . .

Suddenly the dance was done. Ddwng made the little bow to her, then spun about and walked away. She was on her own.

The tableau was frozen. They were waiting for her. She looked at the circle of men, and spied the oldest and by his clothing the most important. Old men were hardly safe, but tended to be less dangerous than young ones. She walked slowly to him.

'I will dance first with the handsomest,' she said. She heard his ball translating as she spoke.

He stepped forward. 'Governor Rrllo,' her ball said. 'I thank you for this significant privilege.'

They danced in exactly the same fashion as before; the set routine was handy this way. His hands did not stray. Around them other couples now danced also. The ball was underway.

Engage him in dialogue.

Yes, so that Seqiro could tune in on Rrllo's focused thoughts. Colene had a mission to perform, and her one in a million chance of succeeding would become even less if she didn't take advantage of every opportunity to try to understand these folk.

'I didn't really choose you for your handsomeness,' Colene said to Rrllo. 'I wanted to talk with you.'

'I am shocked to hear that,' he replied with a chuckle. Their two translation balls were close together and seemed to be talking to each other. 'You thought I would know what's going on behind the scenes?' The translations had become so facile that his idiom was rendered without hesitation into her idiom.

'Yes. I –' She brought a faintly woebegone look to her face, with little effort required. 'I have almost no chance to figure out the problem, let alone solve it, but if there's anything I can do, I'll at least try. I thought perhaps you would help get me started.'

You aren't fooling him, but he is intrigued. You have honored him by selecting him to dance, and he would like to help you. But he is wary.

'You have a better chance than most,' he said. 'You have the ear of the Emperor, for the moment.'

'But what is it that the people here want?'

He shook his head. 'That is no mystery. But the solution – that is the mystery.'

'It is all a mystery to me! This seems like a nice planet.'

'It is very nice,' he agreed.

He knows. But he doesn't want to tell.

'Please, Rrllo! After the ball – may I see you? I mean, visit your house, get to know your family, talk with you off the record?'

He seemed taken aback. 'Nothing is forbidden to a Consort. But our private lives are of little interest.'

He remains wary. You may be trying to trick him into saying something treasonous.

So it was like that. Colene felt that old familiar deathwish gamble urge coming on. It wasn't that she truly needed to solve this riddle; she expected to fail regardless. It was that when she got into something, anything, the underlying nature of her started taking over, and the decorous rules started suffering.

'Do you know what Ddwng does to those who displease him?' she inquired.

The man stiffened. 'I know.'

'Then you know that I face lobotomy if I mess up.' She wasn't sure how true this was; it probably depended more on whether Darius messed up. But it was certainly a threat against her. And perhaps against any of the residents of the planet who contributed to that failure.

'That, no,' he said. 'Surely not merely for failing an impossible mission.'

'Would you gamble on that?'

He considered, now realizing that his own hide could be on the line too. 'I will meet you after the ball. Tomorrow morning?'

She smiled bittersweetly. 'Thank you, Rrllo.' She was learning how to handle the reins of power.

After that, she came close to enjoying the dance, though she kept thinking of the Sword of Damocles. That was the case of the courtier who was given a fine meal to eat, with a heavy sword hanging by a thread over his head; distracted by that threat, he hardly enjoyed the meal. Thus the King showed him the liability of power. Colene now had an excellent notion how the poor man had felt.

Next morning, more appropriately dressed for going places, she went with Rrllo. 'Now show me Panama,' she said.

'I beg your pardon?'

The translator ball hadn't caught up with that one yet. She felt a small morsel of satisfaction. 'I would like to see how the other half lives. The folk who don't get to go to fancy balls. Who don't hobnob with the Emperor.' For it was in her mind that it would be from this class that a revolution would most likely brew.

'The servant class,' he said. 'We can't afford three nulls for each person, but there is a cadre of nulls that passes from house to house to catch up on business.'

Nulls. Her expectation deflated. There would be no revolution there. 'I changed my mind. Let's just go to your place and talk.'

'As you wish.'

His place turned out to be an elegant futuristic (to her perception) cottage on the edge of a lakelet, with pleasantly exotic trees and shrubs surrounding it. His wife was exactly the kind she expected, and the neighbors were too. Rebellion? This just didn't seem to be the place for it.

He remains intrigued by you. There is a certain naive sincerity you evince which is normally lacking in consorts. He may cooperate.

'Look,' she said forthrightly. 'You folk used to have a lot of power in the Empire, and now you've been put out to pasture. I guess that's a comedown. But why would Ddwng think there's a rebellion brewing?'

'There is no rebellion brewing!' Rrllo protested. 'We are satisfied retired citizens.'

'But he has spy-eyes to check every nuance of every reaction of every person. He has to know you're up to something. Why he figures it's anything I can do anything about is beyond me.'

296

'You are speaking with unusual candor.'

He's getting interested.

'I'm from another reality. I was on my way to meet my – the man I love, and this reality was between, so I passed through here, and he came from the other side, and now we're both in Ddwng's power and if we don't do what he wants we're in trouble. So I'm doing what he wants. He wants me to fix things here. So if there's anything I *can* do, I'm damn well going to do it, so I can get on out of this reality. Now if you'll just tell me what you want, maybe just maybe I can do you and me some good. I admit it's unlikely, but why not give it a try?'

Rrllo was amazed. 'You are from another reality? There has not been a connection between realities in a thousand years!'

'There is now. Ddwng wants to get our Chip so he can go into other realities. We'd rather not give it to him, but we don't have a lot of choice, so we'll do it. It's better than lobotomy.'

Then she realized that she had made a terrible mistake. She should never have mentioned her knowledge of the lobotomy, because now Ddwng would know she knew, and he hadn't told her. He could have the hint that she had a source of information he didn't know about, and that could expose Seqiro and ruin everything.

'You are inadvertently speaking treason,' Rrllo said.

She nodded grimly. 'Yes, I guess the news is already at Ddwng's HQ. But what does he expect when he abducts travelers and threatens them to make them do his bidding?'

He thinks you are trying to trap him into treasonous dialogue.

'There are no recorders here. It would be too expensive to mount and maintain them in an unimportant site like Kyvrn. This conversation is private. But you are mistaken if you suppose we have any animosity toward the Emperor.'

'No cameras?' she asked, hope flaring. 'You mean no one will know what I just said, if you don't tell them?'

'I would not presume to report on the private words of a Consort. Surely you have excellent reason for your utterances.'

She smiled. 'I guess you couldn't tell him anything he doesn't already know.' Apparently the man did not realize the significance of the lobotomy reference. What a relief!

'But I'm really not trying to trick you. I'm just telling you that I have a different perspective. I'm really not the Emperor's mistress; it's just a title he put on me so he has a pretext to put me here.'

'But he introduced you as –'

'Yes. But it's not real. I guess he wanted you to think you rated higher than you do. But Rrllo, I'd sure like to make good even though it's hardly possible. If you'd just help me a little bit, maybe we can both come out ahead.'

He is impressed by your directness. He is inclined to trust you.

'Let me tell you then what I assumed you knew,' Rrllo said. 'This planet is a retirement community for officers of the Empire. As such, it is elite, and we receive excellent care. There is no poverty or crime. But some of us feel that we were retired too soon, and that we could have given further years of service to the Empire, and maintained the associated perquisites. Instead we have been displaced by younger, relatively inexperienced officers. Are you surprised that we feel a certain dissatisfaction?'

Colene shook her head, perplexed. 'Why retire you if you're still doing well?'

'This is our question. We feel the policy is misguided, particularly since genetic deficiencies are appearing more frequently in following generations. In all candor, we feel that those who replace us lack, as a whole, the ability we have, even after allowing for the difference in experience.'

'And I guess it wouldn't do much good just to say that to Ddwng.'

'It has been said to him already.'

'And he responded by sending me.'

'This is the case.'

True.

Colene pondered for about forty seconds. 'Maybe it's his way of changing his mind. If I suggest something he's ready to do anyway, then he can say he's doing it for me, and no one will think he's wishy-washy.'

'Oh, he does not wish to wash anything himself!'

Colene paused, realizing that she had slipped another colloquialism past the translator. 'I mean that he's given to changing his mind readily.'

Rrllo smiled. 'He is not given to that.'

'See, I'm about as unusual a Consort as he could have, when you get right down to it. I might come up with something pretty wacky, because I'm from out of town. Rather than make it seem that he sent an unqualified Consort, he might just agree to what I suggest. So maybe what you need to do is to tell me what to suggest, and maybe it'll happen.'

Rrllo stared at her. 'You are a most unusual young woman.'

'I guess I am. But why don't we try it? Because suddenly this makes sense of things. That he knows what he's doing, and he thinks you have a case. So my chances and yours aren't nearly as remote as we figured – if we play it right.'

You have surprised him. He has decided to go along with you.

'As it happens, we do have a proposal, if the Emperor does not find it insulting.'

'I have a feeling he knows what it is, and that he's ready to do it.' She was coming to a better appreciation of Ddwng's subtlety. The man was a cunning and unscrupulous customer, but what he did made sense. She only hoped that he had underestimated her more than she had underestimated him. It was an excruciatingly dangerous game she was playing.

'It is this: we would like to bring our expertise back into play. We would like to be designated advisers in our specialities – which cover the gamut of those necessary to the operation of the Empire – and consulted when there are problems which the younger officers might have difficulty with.'

'To pull things out when they bungle.'

'I would not have put it that way.'

'You're not an alien teenage pseudo-Consort.'

He smiled. 'Indeed I am not.'

'Let's try it! Set me up with the detail and the arguments I'll need, and make sure I have it straight, and I'll tell him as if it's my own idea. If we're right, he'll choose to believe that. We have today and tomorrow. Is that enough time?'

'It should be, as our desire is straightforward.'

They got to it, with a growing conviction that this was

indeed what she had been sent here to do. Colene met a number of the other officers in person and by wall video, and rehearsed the arguments as carefully as she had done the protocol of the ball. When the time came, she would be ready.

It happened as expected. It had obviously been choreographed as precisely as the ritual of the dance. Planet Kyvrn was officially designated as an Advisory Resource, and the residents were presumably encouraged and would feel more positive henceforth.

'You did so well!' Mare said enthusiastically as she gave Colene a massage. Her hands were so gentle and proficient that the lingering tension just faded away. She could appreciate how Darius, subjected to such treatment, could – but she shoved that hastily out of mind. She understood, but there was a tight knot of emotions that would have to be picked apart at another time.

She returned to the recent exhilaration of the successful mission. So Ddwng had programmed it to succeed; so it still had been fun. He had used her in a harmless way to justify his change of policy.

But something nagged, and her morbid aspect kept trying to sniff it out. She had never been one to accept things without question, especially when they were nice. She was always alert for the worm in the apple, and she liked to fathom the whole worm. Which reminded her of two things: the question about what it was better to find in an apple one was eating; a whole worm or half a worm? Where was the other half of the worm? She had made a friend sick at lunch with that one, once. The other thing was a bit of verse her grandmother had told her once, and Colene's beady little mental eye for the grotesque had fixed on it instantly. The verse was about a college professor who tended to transpose the first letters of words when he got excited. Once he had the unpleasant task of informing a prominent woman that she had taken the wrong pew in church: 'Mardon me, Padam, but you are spitting in the wrong stew. Please let me sew you to another sheet.' But the one about the worm was what Colene was after now. The

Prof was bawling out a bad student. 'You have hissed three of my mystery lectures. In fact you have tasted the whole worm!' Well, when the worm was some subtle flaw in a person's understanding, it was indeed better to taste the whole thing.

Why had Ddwng used her for this task? Surely he could have used any beautiful, stupid Consort for this purpose. The answer was reasonably plain: he was studying Colene, because if she were crazy underneath, and it was a genetic defect, he didn't want those genes in the DoOon gene-pool. But if he were studying her, did it make sense to turn her loose unsupervised? Surely he would want to have his machines taking her stats all the time, especially when she thought she was unobserved.

So had Rrllo been lying to her when he said he wouldn't report on her indiscretion? No, because Seqiro had found the man true. But why should Rrllo report? He was just another actor in the play. There would be a monitor on Colene, maybe one Rrllo didn't know about, so Seqiro couldn't get it from his mind.

But there couldn't be a camera following her around! So how could it be done?

'Will there be anything else?' Mare inquired, having completed the rubdown. She spoke through the translation ball, as always.

'No thanks,' Colene replied automatically. 'I'll just lie here and sag for a while.'

Mare let her be. Then an almost tangible light bulb flashed. The translation ball! She had worn a special one at the planet. That was the recorder.

So Ddwng knew what she had said, including the bit about lobotomy. He would know that no one had mentioned this to her. So he would have a direct question to ask her, and if she didn't have a direct answer, she might face that lobotomy sooner than she had figured. That would ruin her plan for escape, not to mention her life.

Oh sweet Jesus! she thought. *How am I going to get out of this one?*

You will have to deceive him with a half-truth, Seqiro replied.

She realized it was true. She couldn't tell Ddwng about

301

Seqiro; that would ruin everything and get the horse destroyed. She couldn't claim it was a lucky guess; he would never buy that.

She mulled it over, and finally came to something she hoped would work.

Sure enough, on the way back to Earth Ddwng had dinner with her, and after the amenities he put it to her directly. 'You surprised me, Colene. I may have underestimated you. How did you know about the lobotomy?'

'I'm telepathic,' she replied without hesitation. That was the half-lie, flat out.

He gazed at her. 'We regard such claims as without substance.'

'Yes. That's why you had so much trouble with the monster of Yils. You just couldn't believe it was possible to stun someone by pure mental force.'

'Darius is telepathic too?'

'Not exactly. He can receive and rebroadcast emotion, without being affected. He's more like a catalyst. So the monster couldn't mindblast him. As you suspected.'

'You are evidently well matched to Darius.'

'I evidently am. His mind, my mind – I think it's going to be fun, when we finally get together and explore the interactions.'

'What am I thinking now?'

She shook her head. 'It's not that simple, Ddwng. It's not like watching a program on the wall. Your mind is all guarded and complicated. You have to be unguarded and have a very strong thought, and even then I don't necessarily get it. The lobotomy was so strong, and related to me so directly, that I picked it up. It was when we were eating, and you told me the three things you wanted of me – to be your Consort, and such. I thought it was sex, but it was lobotomy. After that I decided to agree to your three things. You didn't wonder what changed my mind?'

'I did wonder.'

He is concluding that it is true.

'Well, now you know. The only other thing I got was about

302

genetics, but that wasn't clear. What do genetics have to do with me?'

Now he believes he knows what you have been hiding from him. Your knowledge of some of his plans.

'Our gene pool is too limited. We have achieved perfect health and uniformity, but along with the liabilities of genetic diversity, we eliminated some of the strengths. You may have genes we can use.'

'So you're going to breed me like an animal –' she broke off, fixing him with a carefully rehearsed stare. 'Surgery! *You intend to take my ovaries!*'

'So you did receive that thought.'

'How could I miss it! You monster! You told me that you would let us go if we got you the Chip!'

Ddwng lifted his hands in a gesture of conciliation. 'I will do that. If we achieve the other realities, there will be many gene sources, and you will be superfluous. It is only if we fail that we shall have to take whatever offers.'

'Don't take this personally, Ddwng, but sometimes you remind me of a slimy tapeworm. You don't care whose guts you destroy, so long as you get yours.'

He smiled. 'I see we understand each other.'

And it seemed that her ploy had worked. She had shown the correct amount of perception and outrage, and he believed that she could read his mind – in sometime glimpses. He would probably stay clear of her now. But she would have to watch her step most carefully from here on, if she expected to survive and to save her friends. This was no part-time hood she was facing off; Ddwng was deadly dangerous.

They traveled back to Earth, which was a great relief. This super-science stuff was all right, but Colene felt most comfortable with Earth, even in its multiple alternate realities. The five anchors of the Virtual Mode seemed to be on Earth, so that all the anchor folk were human or familiar animal, though the underlying rules of the universe might shift. If Darius made it back, and they set foot on the Virtual Mode, and if her plan worked – but she refused even to think of that, lest she somehow give it away. She could afford to make no more mistakes.

The first thing she did on Earth was hold communion with Seqiro. Now she knew better than to vocalize or subvocalize; pure thought was the only way, and that with circumspection, so that there was no outward hint about where her mind really was. In fact, she made sure to have something doing to account for her emotional reactions, as a cover. In this case another violent entertainment program. DoOon tastes seemed to be similar to lowbrow American, which didn't say much for their improved genetics.

Seqiro! I'm so glad to be close to you again!

It is wonderful, he agreed. His thought came in far more clearly, now that they were close.

It was like a bad connection, there in the region of Kyvrn. I could barely receive you.

Receive me? There was no contact there.

She was startled. *But there was! You gave me key readings on the reactions of others. I needed those.*

We lost contact when you left Earth. I reverted to unintelligent animal level. I am restored only now, with your contact.

Something was wrong. *But I read you!*

There was no contact between us. The conviction was absolute.

All that key support from him – had been only her imagination? Then how had she picked up the attitudes of Rrllo? *You mean – I really did read a mind myself?*

This seems to have been the case. You have been learning from me during our contact, gaining some of my mental ability just as I gain some of yours.

So her half-truth had been a three-quarter truth! An awesome new horizon was opening to her.

Colene gazed at the stupid program on the wall, her mind reeling. What a development *this* was!

12

DECISION

Darius watched the constellation which included Earth's sun approach with mixed feelings. He had accomplished his mission and agreed to give the Emperor the Chip. His choice had been between Colene and the welfare of the other realities. He had chosen selfishly. He was not proud. But it was done, and now he would carry through.

It was the ninth day of their residence in this Mode. Tomorrow was Ddwng's deadline, and their probable venture back into the Virtual Mode. Darius knew the way back to his own Mode. What would happen there? He would have to see Ddwng safely there, and ask the Cyng of Pwer to give the man the Chip. Then what? Would Pwer do it?

Darius feared he would. Because Ddwng would bring a pain dial and use it on him. If that did not work in that Mode, something else would. Ddwng was a hard man.

'You are pensive,' Pussy said via the translation ball. 'How may I make you feel better?'

'I fear there is no way.'

This time she did not offer him sex or a massage. Only her unadorned sympathy. That turned out to be about as effective as anything.

All too soon they were there. The FTL *Flay* took up orbit around Earth, and made ready for the exchange of captains. 'It has been a pleasure to serve you, sir,' Jjle said formally.

'You made it easy,' Darius said. 'I hope you have pleasure

in the next mission.' Then he bid parting to his Felines, shaking hands with Tom and Cat and kissing Pussy. 'There were aspects of my mission I did not appreciate. But you were a delight. I am sorry to leave you.'

They did not respond, for he had neither questioned them nor given them a directive. He knew that they would serve the next captain as loyally as they had him, if the man did not have his own set of nulls. Sentimentality was wasted here. Nevertheless, he felt it.

Then he saw a tear in Pussy's eye. That heartened him. Her emotion was surely transient, but it was there.

He stepped into the transporter cubicle with Provos, and out again in the Emperor's palace on Earth. An Ovine neuter was there to guide them to their chamber for the night.

But when he got there, he discovered that it was occupied. There were three Equines, looking very much like his Felines but with their heads shaped to suggest those of horses. They evidently came with the suite.

Then he remembered something. Colene was served by Equines. Could it be?

'Whom do you serve?' he asked the neuter, who would be Horse.

'We serve Colene, who has directed us to make you comfortable until she returns.'

This seemed too good to be true. Ddwng was allowing them to be together? 'Where is she now?'

'Dining with the Emperor, as she normally does.'

Was Ddwng taking more of an interest in Colene than business? Darius felt a tinge of jealousy, but a larger tinge of satisfaction. Colene knew her own mind, once she made it up, and she wouldn't hesitate to use any influence she had. She would have more influence on Ddwng than the Emperor realized, if he wasn't careful, and she would use it to make him do what she wanted. She wanted to return to the Virtual Mode and travel with him, Darius. He was sure of this.

Maybe she had even used that influence to prevail on Ddwng to let the two of them be together this night. She could have hinted that she would make sure that Darius did not change his mind about giving Ddwng the Chip. Ddwng also might suppose that there would be key dialogue between them, which his sensors would pick up, which would reveal any potential treachery.

Well, there would be no treachery. Darius had given his word, and he would honor it. Maybe Colene expected him to do something foolish or deceitful, but he would not. He was betraying the realities, but not his nature. He hoped Colene would never know why.

What, then, was he to do this night? He did not want to be close to her before they could discuss things and come to some understanding, and he had no intention of discussing anything with her in this Mode.

'Please show us to our separate chambers,' Provos said to the nulls. 'We shall eat after we are established.'

There was the answer. Provos remembered what was to happen.

Mare showed Provos to one chamber, and Stallion showed Darius to another. He saw that a bed had been set up; they were ready for the guests. He used the toilet chamber, checked himself in the mirror, and returned to the main chamber.

Horse had already set up the table with the meal of the day. Provos reappeared, and they sat down opposite each other, as they had regularly while on the ship. Darius hardly noticed what he ate, being preoccupied by his thoughts.

They were, oddly, not of Colene at the moment, but of Provos. He had traveled for some time with this odd woman, and still hardly knew her. She had seldom spoken to him recently, maintaining her disapproval of his decision. He hardly faulted her for that; he did not like it himself. But would she have let Colene be destroyed?

Well, her memory of the future was surely short, now, because she could not remember across realities, and tomorrow they would resume those crossings. He could only hope that some agency other than his own prevented Ddwng from getting what he wanted.

Stallion departed. 'He is going to fetch Colene; it is time,' Horse explained. Like Cat, the neuter was the intelligent one. Darius nodded.

Colene returned. She was an absolute vision of beauty, in a

pale blue gown and diadem. Darius caught his breath, unable to speak. He had never seen her like this!

Her gaze fixed immediately on him. Of course she was not surprised; she had known he was coming. 'What, no Pussy?' she inquired with mock wonder. He noted with odd surprise that her words came from her rather than from the translation ball. 'Take Mare for the night.'

'I would be with her as I was with you,' he said with hurt dignity. 'But without the love.'

She looked at him for a moment more. Then her face crumpled. 'Oh, Darius, I'm sorry!' she cried, and flung herself at him. He barely had time to rise from his chair before she collided, bearing him back against the wall. 'I love you, I love you, I love you!' she wailed through her tears, into his shoulder, destroying the careful makeup Mare must have applied.

He wrestled her around until her head came up. Then he kissed her. 'I love you,' he said.

'I would do anything just to be with you!'

'Yes.' That was what they had done, betraying the realities.

'Please – be with me tonight.'

He tried to say no, and could not. His separate chamber would not be used.

But when they were together, he remembered how young she was. In his culture a woman was old enough when her body indicated she was ready, and by that token Colene was legitimate. But in hers there was a set age of consent, and she was below it. They were not in her Mode now, but her values were of it, and it would be wrong to presume on her innocence. What could she know of the reality of sexual indulgence, however pleasurable it might be?

Also, he knew that everything they did was being watched and recorded; the walls were eyes. He had no shame in sexual expression, but with Colene, with love, the first time, there should be privacy. He could not explain this to her, because she did not know the true ways of the DoOon.

Meanwhile she stripped naked for him. He demurred. 'Not yet,' he said. He also refused to take her as a gift from Ddwng.

When this terrible business was done, and they were safely in his Mode, then it would be all right.

'And what of Pussy?' she demanded with mercurial temper.

'I will be with you as I was with her.' He embraced her, and did nothing more, though his desire was manifest.

'Damn you!' she whispered.

'I will not say it would not have been otherwise, had you not appeared when you did,' he confessed. 'After that, I thought only of you.'

She lifted her head. 'Really? You really didn't do it? Because of me?'

'Yes.'

She paused a moment, as if listening to a distant voice. 'Yes, it really was that way, wasn't it! I am so sorry I doubted. Well, it's me now.'

'Yes. That is enough.'

'It's enough,' she agreed. 'Well, almost; you were naked with her. So get naked with me.'

Darius sighed, not annoyed, and removed his own clothing. His body was aroused, and he did not try to conceal this from her. She wanted to know whether he desired her, and this was answer enough. But his desire was matched by his discipline.

Colene gazed at him with evident satisfaction. Then she planted herself against him, her breasts and thighs pressing close.

He knew what she was doing. The little vixen was tempting him, as she had before, but more directly. Well, she could excite him, but she could not make him forget his resolve. He closed his arms around her and stroked her sleek back, and did no more. He was perversely glad she was doing this, because it was her way.

So it was that they slept, embraced, remaining chaste in their fashion, as they had when in her Mode. The odd thing was that she seemed pleased rather than rejected. Why would she offer her body to a man and be happy when he seemed to lack the gumption to use it?

* * *

Next day they gathered in the chamber of the palace where the anchor was. Colene stood beside her huge stallion, whom she had named Seqiro, her hand on his nose to guide him. Darius was becoming increasingly curious about that animal, who seemed to be more than ordinary, but he would not inquire where Ddwng could listen, which meant anywhere in this Mode. Provos was as usual impassive.

Ddwng was something else. The man was solidly garbed in an all-terrain suit with many full pockets and assorted devices whose purposes were obscure. He used a personal shield, which didn't show but made him impossible to touch with any velocity, and carried a special pain dial. 'So that we may best understand each other,' he said, 'I shall make a small demonstration.' He touched the dial, and the pain coursed through Darius, at about the second level. He saw Colene stiffen, and Provos, and even the horse twitched his skin as if flies were stinging it. It was tuned to them all.

Ddwng touched the dial again, and the pain abated. 'I believe this will operate throughout the Virtual Mode, as will my shield. I trust Darius, but I do not trust the rest of you, or the horse who is responsive to Colene. Should anything happen to me, the dial will automatically lock on maximum. It will respond only to me.'

'You made your point,' Colene said. 'You don't trust us, but you have promised to let us go once you have the Chip.'

Ddwng nodded. 'Once I have the Chip.'

Darius doubted that the pain dial would be effective across the boundaries, but that didn't matter. It was his word which bound him, not any threat to his body.

'You understand,' Darius said, 'that you and the anchor are linked. You will be able to consume only food you carry with you from the anchor Mode; other food will do you no good. You will not be able to transport any object or substance that is part of a foreign Mode across the boundaries of the Modes, and anything from your Mode that you leave behind will remain in the Mode where you set it. So you must have all the supplies you will require for a journey of several days.'

'I discovered these things when I laid out the paths,' Ddwng said. 'I used machines to facilitate my work, but I had to be in contact with those machines at all times or they would not cross the boundaries. I could not assign the work to any other person, or to a robot.'

'Robot?'

'Computerized machine,' Colene put in. 'Golem, to you.'

'Yes, I thought you understood,' Darius said to Ddwng. 'But I have undertaken to guide you safely to my Mode, and I need to be sure you understand the nature of the inherent threats to you. You must also be cautious about stepping across the boundaries in some sections; there may be rough terrain, or predators, or traps set. We shall have to proceed extremely cautiously when approaching the pit, the region of several realities that has been mined. We can not cross it safely, but we should be able to go around it. So if I tell you to do something, do not take offense; it may be an emergency.'

'I am a realist,' Ddwng said. 'You are the leader for this excursion.'

'One other thing you need to know, in case we become separated: how to tune in on the most direct path. Since anyone who gets isolated from the group will have no way but this to rejoin the group, by converging on a common destiny, we all must be able to do it.' Darius glanced at Colene, realizing something. 'The horse – he is from another anchor? He can cross boundaries without having to be in contact with you? You will nevertheless have to guide him, and not let him get lost.'

'Yes, I won't let Seqiro get lost,' Colene agreed. 'And warn me long before we step into any pit! I don't want to have to haul him out!'

Even Ddwng smiled briefly. 'I wondered whether you would raise this matter. It was evident that none of you were traveling randomly. How do I tune in? I was aware of no path before; I laid out my paths only geometrically, to intercept those who crossed the blank realities. This is not a physical thing?'

'It is a mental thing,' Darius said. 'In your Mode you do not employ magical or mental mechanisms. Magic simply does not operate; I experimented and verified this. I assumed that the same applied to the mental component, but discovered that it did not. The monster was simply a human child with a freak mental talent. It may be that your people have had this ability bred out of them, but that they can recover it with effort and training.'

'We shall try to broaden our gene pool with this in mind,' Ddwng said.

Darius knew how serious that was. Had it not been for that reproductive threat against Colene, his decision might have been different. 'So for your own security, you need to be able to use your mind this way. You need to be able to feel the route. I'm not sure how you can do this, except by trying to blank your mind to other things, until you develop a subtle awareness of direction.'

Ddwng considered. 'And if I can not?'

Darius shrugged. 'You will be dependent on the rest of us to guide you. Should I suffer an accident, Provos or Colene can continue.'

Ddwng glanced at the other two. Provos seemed uninterested; her future was blank at the moment. Colene was leaning against her horse, also seeming unconcerned, which probably meant the opposite. 'I prefer to master this now.'

'That could take forever!' Colene protested. 'Why don't you practice it on the way?'

That only set Ddwng more firmly. 'We shall wait here until I succeed.'

Colene made a face. 'Suit yourself, Emperor.'

Ddwng stood at the anchor and closed his eyes. 'Nothing,' he reported after a moment.

'You are used to making demands which others must receive,' Darius said. 'For this you need to be receptive. I am not sure how to guide you in this. Perhaps it would be better to wait –'

'I may be getting it,' Ddwng said. 'Something very faint, a distant thought – a strong thought. I –'

He looked surprised. Then the universe turned.

Not quite literally. The land seemed to tilt, yet it was level. But the palace chamber tilted, sinking down, and Ddwng with it, while the rest of them remained as they were. The Emperor looked surprised but helpless to stop it.

312

Provos lurched into Darius, bearing him back toward Colene and the horse. *Hold on!*

He grabbed on to the harness on the horse's body. The horse was a comfortingly stable object right now, while the rest of everything slowly went skew. Ddwng and his chamber sank all the way out of sight, and another floor or ground level descended. This level was a tree-filled landscape. Its trees tilted with it, seeming unaffected.

Darius stared, his eyes unfocused. The forest was passing through the plane the three of them and the horse stood on, but there was no physical contact. Above it came a setting of lesser plants and shrubs, no trees. That entire setting swung through undisturbed.

Another scene swung down. This was a barren desert similar to the one they had crossed coming to this anchor. What was happening?

Ddwng freed his anchor.

It was not a voice but a thought. It felt like Colene.

The desert swung down, gaining velocity. Another desert replaced it, and another.

He tried to speak, but somehow could not. There was no air, but he was not gasping. He seemed to be in suspended animation, though he could move. Anchor? Ddwng wouldn't do that!

Seqiro took over his mind and made him decide to free the anchor.

The horse? Darius stared at the more rapidly moving scenes, which were now sliding through at a blurring rate.

Seqiro is telepathic. He has linked us. I didn't tell you before, because we had to fool Ddwng. We caught him by surprise when he opened his mind, and before he knew it he had freed the anchor, and he's gone. Now we have to find another, so he can't connect up again.

A telepathic horse? Darius had never suspected such a thing! A thought from outside had made the Emperor do what only he could do, and release his anchor, cutting his Mode free of the Virtual Mode? Darius had honestly intended to deliver on his commitment to Ddwng, despite his detestation of the necessity. But now, astonishingly –

Yes. It was the only way. I planned it, but I couldn't tell you or anyone. Seqiro tuned in on your mind, so I know how you love me. He says you have a marvelously straightforward and honest mind, no trouble at all to relate to. It was wonderful sleeping in your love last night. But I couldn't tell you, because —

Because he would not have broken his word to Ddwng. Colene had intended all along to do this. Yet she had pleaded with him to cooperate with Ddwng!

I lied. To fool Ddwng.

She had lied — to them all.

I had to do it! It was the only way!

She had practiced deliberate deception. She had broken her given word. In the process she had rendered his pledge void.

Oh-oh.

How could he love a dishonest woman?

The chaos turning around them shifted its nature. There was sound, now, as if the Modes themselves were humming. It was music, but neither pleasant nor innocent.

The passing Modes were forming a new pattern in their larger perspective. Instead of resembling some changing Earthly landscape, with mountains lifting and sinking like ragged waves, they became geometrical. Three dimensional crystalline outlines formed, changing their configurations in odd ways. Lines and balls passed through, strung in endless spirals. Light flared in divergent colors, each color inconstant, becoming a nucleus for lesser flares, and lesser yet, and on. Well defined shapes became cloudy, dissolving into other well defined shapes; the cloudiness was only in the inability of the observer to fathom the nuances.

Fractals! It was Colene's amazed realization.

There came a shape like a hairy bug, growing rapidly larger, with fire playing about its fringe. Within that fire loomed expanding curlicues, and within them spiderweb-like structures linked to each other by smaller webs, and within those patterns forming seeming tunnels to infinity.

The change was slowing, as if the final orientation was coming into alignment. The new anchor was being set.

Then the whirling Modes abruptly firmed. They came to a sudden stop, with no physical impact. It was as if the Mode

314

on which the four of them stood had been still, and the rest of all the universes had stopped their motion.

They stood at the verge of a strange stone cliff overlooking a heaving sea. Into the face of the cliff were set two enormous red roses. Before them was a young woman in a red dress. A stiff sea breeze was blowing her thick black hair to the side. Beyond her was a green valley, and beyond that a hill on which perched a stone castle.

The weird music was stronger now, not loud but penetrating to the gray matter of their bones and the marrow of their minds.

The girl seemed as startled to see them as they were to see her. Darius knew that they had just connected with a new anchor Mode, and that she was the anchor person. But the young woman had no prior experience with Virtual Modes. To her, the three of them and the horse had just appeared from nowhere.

She is Nona, Colene's thought came. *Hello, Nona. We are friends.*

Darius hoped that was the case.

AUTHOR'S NOTE

Now don't get mad at me. This is the first novel of the Mode series, and there's no concealing the fact that there is a whole lot more to go. This is a complete episode, introducing the concept of the Virtual Mode and the major characters. The next novel, *Fractal Mode*, will follow in about a year, featuring Colene, Darius, Provos, Seqiro and Nona in a setting that is not exactly our own. Let's face it: Colene and Darius hardly know each other, and it would be unrealistic to think that they could just get together and live happily forever after. There are real problems for them to work out, and their love is really infatuation. She has a score to settle with him about his sexual attitude, and he has one to settle with her about her lack of integrity. Promising relationships have been known to founder on just such issues. This process will not be simplified by the presence of another attractive young woman as an anchor-figure. And what of those who made the Chips, and isolated the DoOon? With each novel, an anchor figure will be lost, and a new one gained, with the new Virtual Mode. If you object to this sort of complication, don't buy the sequels; the series will languish without your support, and shut down in due course. Oh, it hurts to lose your favor!

I had three fantasy series going, and a collaborative fantasy series. Two are being shut down now, and a third in another year. Only Xanth will continue, and Mode will join it, inheriting aspects of the Adept and Incarnations series. It's not that I don't like fantasy, but that each series has its natural cycle, and the cycles of some are longer than others. You may wonder about my reference to fantasy, as there was little fantasy in *Virtual Mode*. Well, this is to be an anything-goes project, and *Fractal Mode* will have a good deal more magic. It all depends on the Mode, you see. So this may be referred to as a fantasy series, though that pinches its definition. It's an imaginative series which does not shy away from realism, as you may have noticed.

It is also an Author's Note series; readers of my Incarnations series will have a notion what to expect: that slice of my life occurring during the writing of this novel, complete with discussions of social issues and unfinished thoughts. Reaction to such Notes has been fairly neatly polarized, with the critics ranging from grudging acceptance to deep disgust, and the readers ranging from interested to enthusiastic. The most common comment is that the Notes make the author real for the reader. As one reader put it, approximately: I make my characters live; the Notes make *me* live.

So what happened in the three months of this writing? A slew of things, professional, personal and in between. I started in mid Dismember and finished in Marsh – and in this period I learned that the 1990 Xanth Calendar from which these months are borrowed sold well enough to leave me with a probable 50% loss of the money I invested in it. Apparently the publisher underprinted, so that many stores never got it, and many sold out and could not get new stock. I even received a letter from a reader with a wonderful idea: why didn't I do a Xanth Calendar? So much for getting the news spread! I did the Calendar for love rather than money, and feel the artists did a fine job, and there will be similar calendars following, but an ongoing losing proposition can not endure indefinitely. Sigh.

We had an extremely mild winter – possibly the warmest Jamboree and FeBlueberry since American records began, which is a bad sign considering the question of the global warming trend. But just before Christmas Florida was hit by one of its worst cold waves. We live in the middle of a tree farm on a peninsula in Lake Tsoda Popka, and our climate is moderate compared to that of the region, which is mild enough. But our thermometer dropped to 16°F, and we had a light snow flurry – the first I've seen personally in thirty years in the state – and most of our decorative plants died. We had been given a set of poinsettias by our American publisher the year before, and we planted them and they grow very nicely and were just starting to turn their top leaves from green to red in the style of that plant, when the freeze destroyed them. Sigh.

And the mail. I answered 166 letters in Dismember, 160 in Jamboree, and 205 in FeBlueberry. I had tried using a secretary for a year and a half, but discovered that I wasn't cut out for dictating letters; I'm a lot less intelligent and literate when I speak than I am when I write, perhaps because I can revise what I write when I see it on the screen. I hated seeing the stupid words I spoke go out. So finally I returned to typing them myself, and my wife did the filing. I found that I could take two days off a week and do up to fifty letters that way, and that sufficed. The other five days I had to write my novels, trying for 3,000 words of novel text a day, in addition to perhaps 2,000 words of related and unrelated notes. I use my 'Bracket' system, you see: whenever the going gets difficult in the novel, which may be every few minutes, I go to my notes file and enter a dialogue with myself, exploring the problem and possible solutions, until I work it out. Many a week I didn't make my target, because there is more to a writer's life than text and correspondence – phone calls to/from agents, business associates, relatives and fans also take time – and sometimes I try to sneak in a little leisure with my family. I feel properly guilty when I do that, but it happens. In this period I received a package of letters from one publisher dating back as far as nine months. I answered them immediately, but some did come back for want of a current address. I hate that.

I see a parallel between Darius' situation as Cyng of Hlahtar and my own with respect to my readers: publishing my books multiplies the joy I bring to others, but fan mail depletes my resources. I can not keep answering indefinitely. One fan pointed out that I won't be able to cut down on letters as long as I keep writing Author's Notes, because the notes make me seem like a person and a person can be written to. But some-how I don't want to feel less like a person. So I struggle along, my responses getting later and briefer, knowing that this, like the Xanth Calendar, is probably doomed to extinction in due course.

There are limits, however. On FeBlueberry 26 I received three separate solicitations for fund-raising auctions. Each wanted me to contribute an autographed book of mine, or some other item they might sell to raise money for their worthy purposes. Now at first glance this seems reasonable, but I have been on the receiving end of so many such solicitations that my perception has shifted. My objection is based on two main factors. First, the cost to me, considering the value of my time expended in preparing, packaging and mailing an item, is probably substantially more than it will sell for at the other end. Thus it is a losing game, overall; if I wanted to contribute, it would be cheaper for me to send a check. Second, while stocking libraries and such is good, I feel the cost ought to be borne by the community that library serves, rather than folk like me, who will never see it. Such solicitations in their essence boil down to transferring the cost to strangers. I once received a letter from a young man who had decided to become a millionaire by soliciting money from every address he could get; the principle is the same. So a library is a more worthy cause than a greedy person; that simply suggests that the end justifies the means. I feel the means is unjustified, and I oppose it on principle. At first I did contribute to such efforts, until I had a request for copies of every one of my titles, plus manuscripts and magazines, to be shipped overseas at my expense. Thereafter I wrote letters explaining why I did not. This day I decided to stop responding to them at all. Call me ungenerous if you will. The line has to be drawn somewhere.

What kind of fan mail do I get? Mostly compliments on my novels (thanks), requests for pictures (I ran out long ago), and suggestions for future writing (but I have plenty of my own ideas). But some are different. One letter in Dismember was from a woman who had not read my books, but she informed me that I was ignorant and sarcastic. Why? Because her friend had asked me how I really felt about fan mail, and I replied that I'd rather be writing my novel. I responded to her politely, inquiring how she would feel if *she* had to answer up to 160 letters a month which squeezed out all her free time and some of her working time at her own expense, and someone asked how she felt about it, and she said candidly that she'd rather have more time to herself, and that person then called her ignorant and sarcastic? I received no response. Well, that's one way to cut down on mail. God preserve us from the self-righteous.

Another was from a woman who had read the rape scene in *Unicorn Point* and declared herself an ex-Anthony reader. I replied that I was sorry to lose her, but that when a person does something another person deems unconscionable, the latter has little choice but to withdraw support. I mentioned that I had just done something similar myself. Oh, you want to hear about that? Well hang on; this is a major discussion.

More than a year back I heard from a prisoner who had murdered his girlfriend. It was a brutal and to my mind pointless crime for which he was condemned to death. He was politically conservative and believed in the death penalty. His quarrel with the system was that his lawyer kept making appeals on his behalf which he didn't want. He had committed the crime and deserved to die for it, and he was frustrated by the continual delays.

Now I am politically liberal, and I don't like the death penalty. That does not mean I like murder. I don't like killing, whether it is done by private enterprise or the state. I don't like killing animals either, which is why I am a vegetarian. No need to belabor my philosophy here; you are welcome to read all about me in my autobiography, *Bio of an Ogre*, and if your local bookstore doesn't carry it, don't kill the proprietor, just reason sweetly with him. As Ferrovius reasoned all night with a pagan, in G. B. Shaw's *Androcles and the Lion*, and in the morning not only was the man a Christian, his hair was as white as snow. The pacifistic approach can work wonders when practiced by ogres. I'm sure your store will agree to stock the book. But I try to answer my mail without regard to the nature of the letter writer (well, junk mail gets checked and thrown away), and so I answered the murderer's letters. I made no bones about my sympathy for the victim of his crime, and agreed that he had a right to insist that he pay the penalty in his fashion. You see, I believe in the right to life, and also in the right to death, so I support legislation to allow patients to say no to heroic measures used to prolong their lives in the face of terminal maladies. Note that I do not say that all killing is wrong, just that I don't like it. Absolutes are hard to come by, for those of liberal persuasion, and truth does generally seem to be a shade of gray.

Well, the murderer wrote again, and I answered, and it continued. Sometimes I will cut off a too-persistent correspondent, because I really do have other things to do than to engage in frivolous dialogue, but this person's letters were serious and well thought out. It turned out that I was the only one who did keep up with him; his friends and family did not. He assumed it was because I cared for him. No, I was simply being true to my standard. But as long as the correspondence continued, I thought I might as well learn something useful, such as why would a man murder a woman who by his own account was true to him and wanted nothing but good for him? Men murder women every day; is it just their way of proving how macho they are, or do they do it to prevent the women from moving on to other men? If we could only fathom a common underlying motive, and discover how to debate the situation before an innocent person gets killed, we might spare the world much grief. In this case there turned out to be no simple answer.

The murderer expressed interest in science fiction and supernatural phenomena, such as flying saucers. That sparked a notion. I suggested that he write to a fanzine: that is, one of the amateur magazines of the genre where pros and fans exchange remarks in the letter columns. I gave him information on the best one I knew, considering its frequency of publication, the variety of interests of its contributors, and its open-forum philosophy. I had been writing to it for years, taking on its hard core conservatives. I had addressed the feminists: 'I am a man. I like looking at women. That does not make me a sexist.' Indeed, I support much of the feminist agenda, and I value the company and input of women. I

321

suspect I receive more fan letters from women than most writers of this genre, and I often have female protagonists who are sympathetically portrayed, as you may have seen in this novel. I also took on reviewers: I believe that a reviewer should indicate how well a book relates to the needs or desires of its readers, rather than pushing a private agenda. Gun control – I favor it, though the case is not clear-cut. Minimum wage – I favor raising it to keep pace with inflation. Affirmative action – I favor it, not as ideal, but the only practical way to redress a long-standing wrong. In fact, if you run your finger down the classic liberal agenda – or, if you are conservative, poke your finger up at it – you will find me there most of the time. One major exception is abortion; I don't like it because of my objection to killing. But I don't like the anti-abortionists either, because they seem to have little regard for the welfare of mother or baby and generally don't seem to support the obvious method of not having babies: contraception. I took on all comers in this fanzine, being one of two blatantly liberal writers to do so, and as I see it, we showed up the conservatives as ignorant and mean-spirited clods. But fairness requires that I admit that the conservatives didn't necessarily see it that way. One had a sense of humor about it: when I chided him for making sense on one issue, when I depended on him to be always wrong, he replied that it wasn't his intent to make sense. It is possible for folk to disagree and still respect each other. So I thought it would be interesting if the murderer stated his case here, and let the cynics and conservatives argue his case with him. Is the death penalty a deterrent to crime, when a murderer wants to be executed and the system won't oblige? Just why does a person commit murder? Maybe such a discussion would elicit truths which would enable society to deal more realistically with crime. Such a dialogue would also give the murderer some social interaction in a limited environment, which could be a positive thing. I'm generally interested in beating swords into plowshares, philosophically.

He was hesitant, but he did write to the fanzine. The fanzine editors were hesitant, but did publish his letter. The dialogue began. He made it a point to respond to all challenges or questions directed at him, and he made no apologies for his crime; he wanted truth, not sympathy. But once he had honestly addressed the matter, he wanted to get into other subjects of mutual interest. He wrote a positive letter – and the editors refused to run it.

They explained that they had gone to a convention, and several unnamed parties had approached them and expressed dismay at the murderer's presence in the fanzine. So they cut him out, not for anything he said, but because of essentially anonymous objections to his presence. They said they did this to be fair to those hidden folk, and that they had a right to choose who would appear in their fanzine.

Well, they did have that right. But I also had the right to withdraw my support from what I deemed to be invidious editing. I sent one letter putting my position on the line, and when they did not change their policy, I did not write again. Naturally that left me open to charges that I was a bad sport, and there were a number of insults directed at me. Another pro writer wrote in my defense, protesting the 'pre-emptive smear' and upholding the principle of free speech. In fact the 'make no sense' conservative also wrote a stirring objection to their censorship. I could almost get to like conservatives like that. But the editors were adamant about their policy and about my supposed bad nature, accusing me of attacking another contributor and of calling names. Their basis for this was my suggestion that needless cruelty to animals is an early sign of sociopathic behavior, in response to the other's seeming pride in squishing spiders. Readers may remember Jumper, the spider character in *Castle Roogna*. You don't see the Disney folk sit on their hands when someone disparages the Mouse; well . . .

I can't say I was happy to go. I had enjoyed slugging it out with those of differing opinion, and the interactions had been by no means predominantly negative. I had trouble sleeping several nights, upset about the business. But the principle of freedom of expression is fundamental, and I simply could not allow so egregious a violation to pass. It is in the extremes that our philosophies are tested, and those of us who are serious do not set aside our ethics merely because in some cases they become inconvenient or distasteful. Does a murderer have rights too? Yes, even the worst among us must be granted their right to speak. Imagine applying the editors' logic to other cases: anonymous folk approach a city councilman, saying they don't like the presence of blacks in their neighborhood, so in fairness to them he sets up apartheid. Anonymous businessmen approach a congressman, saying they don't like foreign competition, so in fairness to them he introduces a bill to ban all imports. Anonymous fundamentalists dislike certain elements of the Catholic Church, so they have the government ban Catholicism in the name of fairness. Does that seem far-fetched? There are regions where exactly such things have happened. But in America most of us disapprove of them. We believe in freedom of expression, even for those we don't like. It is part of our Constitution.

How did the murderer react to this exclusion? He apologized for causing the magazine this trouble and asked that his subscription money be used to purchase some tapes he liked, and the balance donated for useful purposes. To my mind he acquitted himself in a more honorable manner than those editors did. I continued the correspondence with him. I believe I did come to understand the rationale for what he did, though I disagree with it. Because he spoke in confidence, I shall not describe it here, except to say that I believe it vindicates the liberal case for socially responsible activity as a preventive for disaster.

So yes, I do understand the principle of withdrawing support from an endeavor one has previously valued. Since I am as adamant about maintaining my freedom to incorporate any elements I choose in my fiction as those editors were about their prerogatives, I can only tell readers who object to such elements to go their own ways. The woman who objected to the rape scene was not abusive or anonymous; she stated her case politely and gave her address. So she received a polite response. I do not vilify those who stand on principle, and I tend to value those who do stand on an opposing principle more than those who agree with me while lacking principle. But lest there be any question: I do not approve of rape. I merely defend my right to show rape onstage, as one of the evils of society.

So I departed that fanzine, disliking the smell. The editors are probably still wondering why professionals are so touchy. I had supported the publication with money, letters, and recommendations. I gave it one last item: my report on the convention where I had met Jenny, the girl paralyzed by a drunk driver, and that was it. I left not only because of what had been done, but because the editors were unwilling or unable to grasp why they were wrong. It marked the probable end of my active participation in fanzine fandom, because this had been one of the best fanzines. What are the worst like? Don't ask!

Ah yes, that brings up Jenny. She has been discussed more fully in the Xanth series, where she has become a character, and you may have met her as Jenny Elf in the graphic edition of *Isle of View*. For those who haven't, a compressed recap: in FeBlueberry of 1989 I received a letter telling me how a twelve year old girl had been struck by a drunk driver and almost killed, and had remained almost three months in a coma. I wrote to her, and my first letter did bring her out of the coma. I continued to write, though she remained paralyzed and mute and could not respond. Later I attended a convention in her area, so I could meet her. She was treated well there, and I believe she enjoyed herself, though she remained so weak that most of her time was spent lying on her back. That was the report I sent to the fanzine. The significance for this novel is that during this period we passed the anniversary of my first letter to her: one year. I have an artificial rose from her corsage beside my computer screen as I type this, a memento. It resembles the roses on the clifflike structure as the novel ends; there will be more on them in the next novel. In this period Jenny resumed going to school, but not the one she had attended before; this one is for folk like her, whose needs are special. She seems to like it.

And on to Ligeia. Ligeia is the name I gave to the first of a number of suicidal teenage girls I have heard from. All have the same name, to preserve their anonymity, because often their nature is a secret from their parents and I don't feel I have the right to betray their confidence. What have I to do with girls forty years my junior? The same as with prisoners: I answer my mail. But though I will not name them individually, I will do so collectively. This novel has considerable input from them, as you may have guessed. Colene represents a composite of these bright and tormented creatures. If you know a girl exactly like Colene, she is not any of my sources, because none is that close to her overall.

I am no expert on the subject of suicide, and I can't say I ever properly understood even my daughters when they were teenagers. In this day of the revelation of fathers who abuse their daughters, I have been hyper-conscious of the proprieties. When does a father stop playing with his little girl? Some it seems don't stop; they proceed into sexual molestation. But the other direction is not ideal either: isolation from one's children. We have been a close family, but I stopped physically touching my daughters early, and felt the gradual alienation. Would one of them tell me if she had a serious problem or felt suicidal? Maybe, and maybe not. I have always been there, and ready to help if asked, but they tend not to ask. I suffer the perhaps universal inadequacy of fathers. So I have had the nagging suspicion that the feelings expressed by the Ligeias, which they don't tell their parents, could also be felt by my daughters, and they wouldn't tell me. But mine have not been abused or neglected, and have suffered neither poverty nor family breakup. I hope that's enough. They are now going to college, and thence into the larger world. As has been said: a child is someone who passes through your life and disappears into an adult. Am I sublimating the distancing I regret in my own daughters by being more sensitive to these Ligeia girls? I don't know, but it is possible. I prefer to think that I am simply trying to do what is right, whatever the context.

The first Ligeia was deeply disturbed. She believed that there had never been love in her home, and she was isolated and hurting. Cautious, I put in an indirect query via the school system, to see whether she could be helped by private counseling there. The school counselor went straight to her parents, putting her into deeper trouble. So much for the sensitivity of the system; no wonder girls prefer to keep the secret. 'No one can be trusted,' a later Ligeia told me, and I had to agree. You see that attitude in Colene. First Ligeia One wrote to me; then she phoned me. She declared that she loved me, and was upset when I demurred. She wanted to talk for an hour or more at a time, and on subjects I balked at, such as sex. Call me conservative if you will, but I feel it is not the proper business of a man who is not a doctor or counselor to talk to a girl just about young enough to be his granddaughter about the specifics of sex. There is too much potential for abuse. When she started calling on consecutive days I had to put the brakes on, because she was sticking her family with horrendous phone bills and I was losing time from my work that was worth even more. In addition, my daughters were bothered. 'She's trying to take more of your attention than we are!' one protested with some accuracy. I set a limit: one hour cumulative per month; I would hang up on her if she overreached it. This was no easy thing, because this girl wasn't kidding about suicide; once she was cutting her wrists as she talked to me. There was more, but let me digest it down to this: in due course her folks seem to have put her in some kind of institution, and her outside contacts were abruptly cut off. I do not know whether she is alive today. In fact, I do not know whether any of them are alive, other than those now in contact with me, and I hesitate to inquire.

Perhaps my favorite was the first Ligeia Two, who was artistic and sensitive to her individuality. I think she could have made it professionally as an artist, and she wanted to pursue this career, but her folks had other plans for her. Later I saw the movie *Dead Poets' Society*, which hit home to me on several levels. I attended such a school, and later I taught English at such a school. But in this case I'm thinking of the young man portrayed there who wanted to be an actor, and could have made it, but his father refused, and he committed suicide. Parents can do terrible harm to their talented children that way. I tried to help her by putting her in touch with another person – and this went wrong, and she overdosed on pills. They caught her in time and I heard from her in the hospital, and not thereafter. I could have killed her, just by trying to help her. It is foolish to speak of such emotion in such a connection, but there was that in me that could have loved her. She was a sweet and sensitive girl. Had she been my daughter, her art would have been allowed to flourish.

Others wrote once or twice, and not thereafter. 'Why is life so unfair?' one asked. In that case I had confirmation from a relative of a deeply disturbed girl. But what I said to her was limited; I had become too conscious of the danger of doing harm myself, without meaning to. I stopped trying to keep track of them; I don't know how many there have been. Some women have written, and only later revealed their suicidal tendencies. Others have only skirted the notion, for reason: they had been abused, or raped, or otherwise devastated. There is a lot of grief out there, and only a fraction of it ever goes on record. A number told how they made it through to successful marriage and family. As a general rule, based on my observation, if they make it through their teens, they are probably all right. But it is never certain.

You may wonder whether some are just making it up, to get my attention. I don't think so. Some send me pieces they have written, or sketches they have made, and I think I am experienced enough as a writer and as an adult depressive to have a notion whether they are faking it. Some of this material horrifies me. Some is presented as fiction, but I know that a person that young would not write that kind of fiction or poetry if she didn't have a basis. The details are too real, the material rings true. They are not fooling about death. They are obsessed with it. I believe, I believe.

Why does it seem to be exclusively female? This is a matter of natural selection. There are suicidal boys, but a boy is likely to try to kill himself with a gun, while a girl is more apt to try it with pills or wrist slashing. The gun is more effective. I understand that twice as many girls try suicide as do boys, but that twice as many boys succeed as do girls. So the main reason I heard from relatively few suicidal boys may be that those who might have written were already dead. At least my own depression is mild. One might expect the author of funny fantasy to be light-hearted but professional comics may be quite otherwise privately, and my affinity may be closer to Colene and Ligeia than to the happy folk.

328

Now I have some credits for elements of this novel. All of them relate to the characterization of Colene, but to protect privacy I will not identify the actual items here. Some of the contributors may have felt suicidal at some time; some have not. Some are young; some are not. What they have in common is that they happened to mention things in letters which I asked to use. They can not in any other way be classified. I list them in alphabetical order by first name:

> Amanda Wagner
> Frances Wagner
> Kimberly Adams
> Ligeias – anonymous group
> Margaret McGinnis
> Yvonne Johnston

And a sketch titled 'Someday' sent by Oria Tripp: a young woman walking through shallow water toward distant mountains, her hair and dress blown out by the wind. She reminds me of Colene, and of the one to come in the next novel, Nona: girls with more hope than prospects. Then there's Emily Ivie, with a literary project: 'It is a waste of paper to speak of it.' Colene would have said that too. But not all the women I hear from are related to such things. Let me tell you about another kind.

Some years back I had one or two fan letters from a young woman in America, unremarkable. Then she sent me a newspaper clipping describing her work with raptors, which are birds of prey. She would take care of injured ones and nurse them back to health and set them free. Folk would bring them to her. She did not get paid for this: she just did it to help the birds. Suddenly this young woman came alive for me, and I dubbed her the Bird Maiden. I mentioned her in the Author's Note in the reprint of my Arabian Nights fantasy tale adaptation, *Hasan*. In that novel, the Bird Maiden had a feather suit which she could put on so that she could fly; Hasan captured her by hiding the feather suit. He married her and took her home. But later she recovered the suit and flew away, with her two children. After a fabulous adventure, Hasan won her back. So there's really not much connection between that bird maiden and the one who cared for raptors, but I was satisfied with the designation and so was she, indeed, she flew overseas (today it is done by airplane) and was captured by a modern-day Hasan in Germany, fulfilling the romance.

So did she live happily ever after? Well, it's too soon to tell, but she had a scary moment in this period of my writing this novel. At this time the Bird Maiden has a daughter, Alessandra, eighteen months old, cute as only that age can be. After the Christmas holiday, with her husband back at work, Maiden decided to catch up on some postponed housework. She got a bucket of water, a sponge and a squeegee and started cleaning the windows of their upstairs apartment. She squeezed out past the heavy glass door, onto the balcony, into the just-above-freezing outer air and started scrubbing from outside while Alessandra watched from the warm inside. Maiden pretended to scrub the little girl's face through the glass: fun.

Then Maiden heard a familiar thud. Alessandra was clasping her hands with pride at her accomplishment. She had managed to operate the lever that effectively sealed the door back in place from inside. She was too small to work the lever the other way. Maiden was locked out on the balcony with the temperature in the 30s with no shoes, just a sweater and sweat pants. She had not expected to stay out long. The apartment's front door was locked from the inside with the key still in the lock; no one could enter that way. What was she to do?

She watched the street below, and hailed a little old lady on her bicycle. The lady tried not to laugh as she went to ring the bell of the folk in the apartment immediately below. The downstairs lady came out and threw Maiden a coat and pair of shoes, which she donned. Alessandra noted that, so she dashed to the coat rack and brought her own jacket and boots. Maiden tried to keep her occupied, but the little girl tired of that and ran to the kitchen, out of sight. What was she getting into?

The locksmith arrived and drilled out the lock. Alessandra reappeared and put her fingers into the new giant-sized key hole. The locksmith had to coax her to the side so he could finish. The door opened, and Maiden was rescued. Oh, sweet warmth; she had been sooo cold! She hugged Alessandra – and the little girl was disappointed. She knew that the excitement was over. But what a grand adventure it had been!

The Bird Maiden wondered how many more days like this there would be before her marvelous little girl turned eighteen years. 'So, how was *your* Christmas?!' she inquired.

Meanwhile, the world continued. Panama was invaded, and the Communist Empire crumbled. The United States population reached 250 million. Robert Adams, author of the Horse-clans series and a Florida resident, died. He was just under a year older than I. TV personality Andy Rooney was suspended because someone else claimed he had made a racist remark, though he denied it and has no record of racism. Apparently the TV executives have minds like fanzine editors. Then the program he was on dropped 20% in the ratings, and suddenly the execs had a change of heart and brought him back. I think those execs should have been suspended, not Rooney.

There is worse. At this time the child of Dr Elizabeth Morgan was discovered with grandparents in New Zealand. Dr Morgan had ascertained to her satisfaction that her daughter was being sexually molested by the father, but the court had decreed that unsupervised visits be allowed. Maybe I'm no expert, but too many correspondents have told me how they were molested as children; a man who does this takes any opportunity he can get, and an unsupervised visit is folly. I feel that Dr Morgan's caution was reasonable. So she hid her child rather than accede to this – and spent two years in jail for defying the will of the court. It took, literally, an act of congress to get her out. So much for trying to protect a child: the innocent gets punished instead of the guilty.

What happens when the mother does not try to protect her child? The book *Dark Obsession*, published at this time, showed how Bobby Sessions admitted in court to having sex five hundred times with his teenage stepdaughter. She finally blew the whistle on him, and he spent six months in a luxury hospital and was released. She was shipped to a fundamentalist home for troubled children where girls were regularly beaten.

But sometimes the worm does turn: she sued her stepfather and won $10 million.

Let's return to more positive business. I had mixed news on my ongoing projects. My erotic novel *Pornucopia*, published in America only in expensive hardcover and forbidden to readers under age 21, was selling well, and there was a flurry of interest by foreign publishers. I don't object to sex, you see, just to sexual abuse. My collaboration with a teenage boy who was killed by a reckless driver before completing his novel, *Through the Ice*, was published at the same time, and reports indicate it is also doing well. My 200,000 word historical novel about the American Indians who encountered Hernando de Soto, *Tatham Mound*, was taken by Morrow/Avon. The collaboration with Robert Margroff, *Orc's Opal*, was taken by Tor. I took time off *Virtual Mode* to do a chapter in my collaborative novel with Philip José Farmer, not yet titled, and a segment of 49,000 words was put on the market. The main female character there is Tappy, a blind thirteen year old girl, a bit like Colene in her isolation and the drama of her changing situation. I had started it as a story in 1963; a complicated situation and a quarter century had brought it to this point. The galleys for my provocative mainstream novel *Firefly* arrived, and I broke to proofread them. In that novel I show voluntary underage sex, the girl being five years old. More of this happens than we care to advertise.

I placed two of the last three novels which remained unsold from the days of my blacklisting in the 1970s, and set up to rework the third with a publisher interested. I had built up a total of eight unsold novels while weathering the blacklist – you can read about that too in my autobiography, but the essence is that I got in trouble for being right, somewhat in the manner of a whistleblower – and it was good to eliminate the last tangible vestige of it. This campaign of mine to get all my novels into print is one reason I may seem more prolific than I am; I've been writing novels steadily for twenty-five years, and by the end of 1990 the number of books I have had published may come to 82. That's about three and a quarter a year, average.

I read the finalists for a story contest and decided on the

winner. I reviewed revisions for the novel *Total Recall*, necessary to bring the paperback edition into conformance with late changes in the motion picture.

The ladies of Putnam/Berkley visited and brought me a print of the cover for *Phaze Doubt*: the editors had finally taken one of my suggestions, and got a beautiful cover painting of a little girl playing hopscotch with a BEM (Bug-Eyed Monster). At last we would see whether the author's notion of a good cover works to sell copies. You see at this writing I have made the *New York Times* bestseller list with eighteen different titles, which may be the record for this genre, but all have been in paperback, none in hardcover. Other fantasy writers make the list in hardcover; why can't I? Grumble. But in this period I did crack the *Publishers Weekly* hardcover list with the final Incarnations novel, *And Eternity*. Barely. I always was a slow starter.

I wrote a letter to a parole officer on behalf of a prisoner with AIDS, urging compassionate release, as he will otherwise be dead before he gets to see his folks outside. I had corresponded with him for two years, finding him to be a pleasant and principled person; I doubt he would be a menace to society.

My laser printer broke down shortly after the warranty expired: a counter which could not be reset, evidently defective when delivered. $20 part, $560 repair bill. Par for that course. Which brings me to my present computer setup, for those who are interested: Acer 900 AT-clone, 73M hard disk, 5.25 and 3.5 inch drives, VGA monitor, laser printer; Fansi-Console for my Dvorak keyboard, Sprint for word processing, XTreeGold for file handling. I got that last program in this period, and had a time-wasting ball playing with its nice features, such as the ability to set up parallel windows, with different directories in each, or to show and work with the files of several drives simultaneously. I had changed from Dec Rainbow with reluctance, but it was the readiest way to get Sprint, which looked like the ultimate word processor for me, and now I am quite satisfied with it. I set up the Piers Anthony Interface, which is in effect my own word processor, following my rules, like no others.

333

I started exploring the literature on computer games, playing with the notion of crafting a Xanth game that would be superior to what else exists. I know nothing about such games; naturally I figure I can do a better job than the experts, just as ignorant reviewers figure they could be better writers than I am. We shall see.

A reader advised me that the main thing at issue in her divorce settlement was custody of the collection of Anthony novels. Well, that seems reasonable to me.

And my daughter's horse, Blue: at this writing she is 32 years old, and still spry though her head is turning gray. When Blue came into our lives, horses galloped into my fiction, as you may have noticed. Unlike Seqiro, Blue can not read minds – I think.

I had a sore tongue during this novel. Finally, on the last day of editing, I figured it out: there was a roughness on a tooth, and my tongue was rubbing against it as I read my text to myself – I do that to hear it as well as see it, because I relate to it with more than one sense – that chafing was awful. So my wife hauled me into see the dentist the same day. Sure enough: a gold onlay (not inlay) had worn through, and there was an edge. Maybe now my tongue will heal.

Meanwhile the problems of the world accelerate and population runs out of control and the environment degrades apace. We are headed pell-mell for end-of-the-world disaster. About the only saving grace I see is the dawning awareness of increasing numbers of people that this has to stop. My daughter Penny brought home a book titled *How to Make the World a Better Place – a Guide for Doing Good*, which tackles questions of the environment, hunger, socially responsible investment and consumerism in a realistic manner. Many other good books are appearing, and I am getting them as I do preliminary research for a major novel relating to this subject. I feel obliged to turn my resources increasingly to the service of the universe rather than merely to my own well-being, and the talent I have for writing is my chief instrument. I try not to proselytize unduly in my fiction, but this is the Author's Note where I do speak my mind.

But let me finish on more personal notes, because these

334

Notes as I see them relate not to lectures but to feeling. I'm sure my readers differ from me on many things, but I hope that we share the essence of wonder and longing for what we may never quite understand.

I have pictures in my study of my wife at age one and a half or two, phenomenally cute, with her father. I had been looking at them, and then the song 'Scarlet Ribbons' came on and I suffered a certain siege of nostalgia for a situation I had never really known, for my wife was somewhat older when I met her. Our own daughters were like that, and they too have grown up. How precious children are! It is foolish to wish that time could stand still, yet tempting.

There was another episode in this period that touched my heart for inconsequential reason. My mother visited for two days. She is in the neighborhood of eighty and travels by train, and naturally the hours are inconvenient. We had to get up early to get her to the station on time. We used the house speaker system to wake us: at 5 AM the local radio station blared on throughout the house. As I was blindly scrambling into clothing, a popular song played. It was a pretty one, with touching words, in contrast to my bleary mood. It suggested that he close his eyes and let her take his hand so that he could feel the beating of her heart. I have a mental picture of bittersweet young Colene taking Darius' hand and holding it to her bosom, longing for love. Isn't that the way we all are, in the hell of our anonymity?

Marsh 8, 1990: Harpy Reading!